# DARK
# ROOMS

Lili Anolik is a contributing editor at *Vanity Fair*. Her work has also appeared in *Harper's*, *Elle* and *The Believer*. She lives in New York City with her husband and two young sons.

# DARK ROOMS

## Lili Anolik

HARPER

*Harper*
HarperCollins*Publishers*
1 London Bridge Street
London, SE1 9GF

www.harpercollins.co.uk

A Paperback Original 2015
1

A catalogue record for this book
is available from the British Library

ISBN: 978-0-00-756334-0

Set in Sabon LT Std by Palimpsest Book Production Limited,
Falkirk, Stirlingshire

Printed and bound in Great Britain by
Clays Ltd, St Ives plc

Find out more about HarperCollins and the environment at
**www.harpercollins.co.uk/green**

*To my brother, John*

"I was terribly, terribly pretty. I looked like an angel but I was a fiend inside."

–Lee Miller

# PROLOGUE

The first time I saw Nica after she died was at Jamie Amory's Fourth of July party. I'd slipped into the study, dark and cool and strictly off-limits, was crossing the carpet to get to the liquor cabinet, when I felt someone behind me. I paused, flesh prickling. Slowly I began to turn. A set of doors, French. On the other side of the glass, a girl. I didn't run, didn't move, didn't even breathe, just stood there looking, looking, this girl so familiar: straight black hair, narrow nose, scarlet bloom of mouth, top lip nearly as fat as bottom. My skin recognized her before I did, rippling once then tightening on the bones.

My sister, Nica.

I was surprised to see her. Stunned. Yet a small part of me, the dark, secret, hidden part that didn't listen to reason, was not. I'd known she was going to be at this party all along, had known without knowing I knew, in a way that had nothing to do with my eyes or ears, with what I could sense with my body. That's why I'd crashed, wasn't it? To greet her, take her around, show her to everyone who'd lost faith, given up, bought into the lie that dead means gone? I reached out to touch her as she reached out to touch me, the tips of our fingers meeting on the pane, misting it a little. I began to fill, nearly to bursting. She seemed just as full, mouth open, stretching wide, laughter I could almost hear spilling out.

Almost but not quite.

The doors were old-fashioned: two clear rectangles framed in wrought iron. At the center was a latch, small and black. I seized it. Twisted, rattled, jerked. Unbudging, as if set in cement. I let go, tried again with a different grip. Hand slipping on slick metal, my body lurched forward, right temple smashing into glass.

I staggered back, a hurt in my head that made me throb, a jolt in my blood that shocked me mad, a ringing in my ears that turned me dizzy. I looked around for something to throw. A chair, maybe. But the only chair in the room was overstuffed leather, arms wooden and elaborately carved—too heavy even to lift.

I looked back at Nica, took a step toward her to I don't know what. Plead, I suppose, beg her to stay. And as I did, she leaned into me. Her eyes were hot, our mouths close, almost touching, our breaths intermingling if not for the pane.

Again I pulled on the latch and again the latch refused to yield. As I continued to pull and pull, hard as I could, so hard it felt like I was wrenching my fingers from their sockets, I watched her expression changing, dimming, her features going limp, listless. I'd lost her, I realized. She'd wander off, leave me alone, this time probably for good. It was already too late. Inside me something crumpled, and I let my head fall against the iron bar running down the door's middle, my whole weight slumping behind it.

Suddenly, a giving sensation followed by a tumbling one, forward and then over. At first I was frightened, no ground under my feet. But as the stationary objects rushed away—the French doors, the short balcony outside the French doors, the rail, waist-height and rounded and shining—so too did the fear. I felt exhilarated, thrilled, as if I were in one of those dreams where I have the power of flight, am amazed at how easy it is. All it takes is faith. Trust in my heart I can fly and I can fly, nothing to it. Air streaked past me, singing in my ears, whistling through my body, emptying it out, blowing it clean, purifying me, making me perfect. I was soaring, streaking, gliding, hurtling, harder and harder, faster and—

A burst of electric white. A pain like my face had exploded. Time passed. For long seconds I lay on the ground, breathing dirt, spine quivering, teeth vibrating, vision doubled and knocked out of focus. No plan was in my head, no thought. I felt broken, everything on me soft, dented, my brow already swelling, battered tissues gorging themselves on blood, skin split and streaming.

Around me a breeze stirred, picked up. I waited for a lull. Then, neck trembling, eyes loose and lolling, I dug my fingers into the soil and slowly, very slowly, raised myself onto my elbows. I turned. Directly above me, on the second story of the house, was a pair of open doors, the twin panels spread like wings, the latch at the center swinging lightly back and forth.

I looked around. Nica was nowhere in sight. Had she jumped from the little balcony? Gotten fed up, ditched me like I thought she would? Or had she fallen from the little balcony, knocked off it when I went careening through those doors? Was she lying on the ground someplace, hurt, maybe unconscious? Or, I wondered, my gaze turning to the pool, illuminated only by the moon, the lights surrounding it doused to discourage partygoers from cooling off with a swim, had she landed in the water? Panic cutting through the pain, I stuck my hands and knees beneath me and crawled over to the edge.

Sure enough, there she was, at the bottom. The most obvious damage had been done to her face, which looked smashed in and puffed up at the same time. She wasn't moving, was perhaps too stunned to, but her eyes were open and seeking mine. Now it was she who needed my help. I'd give it to her. Of course I would. Just as I was about to take the plunge, though, a drop of blood trickled down the bridge of my nose, dangling for a second at the tip, then falling. When it hit the water, Nica's face broke apart in a series of shivery concentric ripples, and that's the moment I realized.

For a long time I stayed there, crouched at the lip of the pool, peering into the black water, my own dim reflection wavering on top. I brought myself into focus as best I could: a translucent shadow, visible but invisible too, a lonely little ghost haunting itself.

Light suddenly flooded the room behind me and above me. Turning into it, I shielded my eyes.

"Grace," someone said. "Grace."

# PART ONE

# CHAPTER ONE

The last time I saw Nica before she died was on the way back from the tennis courts of Chandler Academy, the private boarding and day school in Hartford, Connecticut, where we were both students and our parents were both teachers. It was a Friday in April, a few minutes past five o'clock. Practice had just ended.

Nica was in front of me, walking fast, head down, racket bag rhythmically slapping her hip. Her skirt was pleated and short, rolled at the waist to make it shorter still. As she bent to retrieve a fallen sweatband, I glimpsed an underside of thigh, tan and smooth-muscled, a flash of cotton, too, hot pink like a lick of flame. I called her name once, then again. She didn't turn around, though, until I put my hand on her arm.

Stopping, she stared at me, eyes slow-focusing in her head. "Oh," she said, "I didn't know it was you."

"Who else would I be?"

"Good question." With a blink, she turned, started walking again. "Mr. Schaeffer said he was going to stick around, run drills for anyone who wanted to work on overheads."

"Yeah?" I said, struggling to keep pace.

"I figured you'd want to."

I was the team's number one player. Had beaten out Nica for the spot. As far as mechanics went, she was the superior. Her strokes were sharper, crisper, cleaner, landed deeper in the court and with greater penetration. But I was a little faster and a lot more willing to scrap. If the rally became extended, she'd almost always go for the kill shot, hit something with verve and ambition that sailed just past the baseline; whereas I'd push the ball back to the center of the court, wait for my opponent to make the mistake. Basically, I was better at tennis the same way I was better at school, which is to say, I wasn't. I was just a grinder and a grubber. She had too much style to do either.

"My overhead doesn't need work," I said, the breeziness of my words undercut by my strained tone.

She nodded distractedly.

I came clean. "Actually, I pulled a muscle a little bit hitting serves. Thought I'd give it a break."

This time she didn't bother to nod, and for a while we walked in silence.

Trying again, I said, "So, are you going to that party tonight with Maddie?"

"Unh-uh."

"I thought I heard you say you were."

She looked at me. "You were listening to our conversation?"

I shrugged: an admission.

When she was quiet, I snuck a sideways glance at her, scanning her expression to see if she was mad. She didn't appear to be, though, just thoughtful, eyes downcast, fixed on the moving patch of ground in front of her. Since her mind was so obviously elsewhere, I watched her more openly than I normally would have dared. She looked different lately, beautiful as always but sloppily so, uncared for—hair in a crooked ponytail, feet slip-sliding in untied sneakers, lips chapped and swollen.

At last she said, "I only told Maddie that to get her off my back."

And that's when I understood. It wasn't me Nica had been trying to avoid. "Maddie was bugging you?"

"Wouldn't take no. You know how she is."

I wanted to shake my head, say, *How?* But instead I lied, nodded. That familiar feeling of disconnectedness, the sense that people were mysterious to me in a way they weren't to each other, descended. Before it could turn into full-on depression, I shook it off. Said, "If you're going to be home tonight, I could help you with your French paper. I know it's due Monday and—"

"*Donnez-moi un* break, okay?"

"What do you mean?" I said, surprised. "Why?"

"Because I'm not going to be home tonight."

I half laughed. Of course she wasn't going to be. Of course she wasn't.

"And neither should you," she added.

"But I always go to bed early the night before a match. You know that. And tomorrow's is a big one."

We'd reached Houghton Gymnasium by this time, were standing at the rear of the building, a few feet from the entranceway to the girls' locker room. It was private here, and the late sun was mild. I tilted my head back to feel its warmth. A faint breeze was on the air, and when it blew, I could hear the clink of rope against metal flagpole. Nica turned to me. Slowly she lifted her right hand, brought it to her left

9

nipple, then shook it rapidly back and forth: titty hard-on. Titty hard-on was a favorite gesture of hers and Maddie's. It was meant to convey excitement—sexual—but, coupled as it always was with blanked-out eyes and a bored expression, was actually meant to convey the opposite of excitement—of any kind. So, basically, it was a put-down.

"What's that for?" I asked, hurt.

"You're already in college, Grace. Have been since forever."

Not since forever. Since mid-December. I'd applied early decision to Williams. Nica, a junior, would apply to colleges next year. "So?"

"So you have no excuse for being well-rested anymore. Maddie invited you to the party, too, you know."

Trying to act casual, as if my interest was low, "Maddie said that? She said I was invited?"

"She implied it. Same thing."

It wasn't. Not remotely. I flattened the corners of my mouth to show Nica I wasn't fooled, but otherwise let it go. Then I said, "If you're not going to the party with Maddie, where are you going?"

"Out."

"Hot date?"

She smirked.

"Guess you and Jamie are giving it another shot, huh?" Jamie was Jamie Amory, Nica's boyfriend of two years, her ex-boyfriend of two months.

I tried not to look relieved when she said, irritated, "How many times do I have to tell you? Jamie and I are over."

"So it's a mystery man."

That smirk again.

"Not that much of a mystery. I know he likes to brand his girls."

10

It was a shot in the dark, but it hit. Nica's jaw dropped. "How?"

"X-ray vision," I said. And when she just looked at me, "I was brushing my teeth this morning. You came out of the shower in a towel. You reached up to open the medicine cabinet. I saw your armpit." The tattoo inside her armpit, specifically. An arrow, bloody-tipped.

Groaning, she said, "I'm going to have to throw out every bathing suit, tank top, and sleeveless dress I own now, aren't I?"

"Or stop shaving under your arms."

"Gross."

I wanted to ask her who the guy was, but I didn't want her to tell me only because I'd asked. I looked at her. She was staring off into the distance, worrying a shred of dry skin on her lip with her front tooth, like she was making up her mind about something. There was a shard of gold in her left iris, which, in certain lights and at certain angles, turned the eye from dark hazel to pure green. That was happening now.

Finally, her gaze came back to me. "I probably won't be in till late tonight. Can you cover for me with Mom and Dad? Tell them I'm staying over at Maddie's?"

"That depends. Will you answer my questions when you get home?"

She held up her hand, three fingers raised: Scout's honor.

I pretended to think it over. "Fine," I said, with a sigh.

She nodded her thanks, then opened the side pocket of her racket bag, pulled out her cigarettes, her zebra-striped Bic.

"Come on, Nica, we're still at school," I said, peering around anxiously as she lit up.

She exhaled. "Relax. We're alone. Want one?"

I made a scoffing noise, a show of waving away her minuscule smoke cloud. "Those things are going to kill you, you know."

She considered what I'd said, then shrugged. "Like I want to live forever."

She started laughing. And a second later, to my surprise, I did, too.

I woke up the next morning from a bad dream I couldn't remember—there and gone, too fast to be pinned down—drenched in sweat, heart pounding. Immediately I was struck by the conviction that something was wrong.

Nica.

I threw off my blanket and ran across the hall, opening her door without knocking. The room was in its usual state of full-scale squalor: unclosed drawers, unclean laundry, undusted surfaces, uncapped pens, lip-gloss tubes, soda and nail-polish bottles. The comforter was pulled down on the bed, and I could see the ghost of Nica's body imprinted on the sheets, the pillows flat and dented. The fleece I'd borrowed from her earlier in the week, returned yesterday, though, was still at the foot, neatly folded, label facing up, which meant she'd slept someplace else. Looking at it, I told myself what I was feeling was anger. If she got caught by Mom and Dad, she'd not only get herself in trouble, she'd get me in it, too, since I'd lied to cover for her.

I stood there for a minute, absently rotating my shoulder, limber after a night's rest and pain-free, trying to think what to do next. My cell vibrated in my pocket. I whipped it out, hoping it was her. It wasn't. Just the weather update I had sent to my phone hourly on game days. No missed calls either, so I called her. Voice mail picked up. At the beep I said, "Thanks a lot, Nica," in a tone that was angrier than

I felt, the anger from before, if anger was ever really what it was, having already dissipated, replaced by unease. But why, I wondered, unease? There wasn't anything weird or out of character about Nica spending the night in a bed that wasn't hers. She sneaked out all the time. Maybe then it wasn't her I was uneasy about. Maybe I was uneasy because I was supposed to play an important match in a couple hours. Telling myself that must have been it—prematch jitters—I slipped a sweater on over my pajamas, headed downstairs.

The house was quiet, and my footfalls seemed to echo on the stairs. I could hear an appliance in the kitchen—the microwave, bleating plaintively because someone stuck something in it, forgot to take the something out. And then another sound—a tapping, faint. Not Dad. He'd be at Chandler, supervising morning detention. Not Mom, either. She'd be in her darkroom, working. Had already been there for hours, no doubt. Besides, this wasn't her kind of noise. Too furtive, too cautious. There it was again. I stood, rigid, ears aching with the effort of listening. And then, suddenly, I realized: Nica, trying to attract my attention without attracting Mom's. She wanted me to let her in. I flew down the last step and into the kitchen.

It was empty, no one behind the back door. On the other side of the window above the sink, though, was a slender rhododendron branch, knocking against the pane with the breeze. I stared at it, trying to remember if I'd seen Nica take her keys with her yesterday, until the microwave sounded again, and I reached for its handle. Sitting on the rotating glass tray was the bowl of Grape-Nuts and soy milk Mom ate most mornings. I started for the darkroom, about to duck my head in, tell her breakfast was ready. Then, anticipating the way her face would go hard and flat, the snap of her voice, if I interrupted her, broke her concentration, I stopped. I turned instead to the back door, thinking Nica might be outside, waiting until Mom went upstairs to shower.

But the backyard was as empty as the kitchen, not a soul. It was a beautiful morning, though, the sky a deep blue streaked with wispy white, the sun a rich, buttery yellow. I stood there, the rays gently pressing down on my skin, seeping into it, warming it, and breathed in the daffodil-scented air. Through an open window, the sounds of the Wheelers, our next-door neighbors, eating breakfast floated lazily toward me: the murmur of their voices, Mrs. Wheeler, pregnant, asking Mr. Wheeler to bring her her calcium supplements and a glass of orange juice; the soft scrape of a chair leg against tile; the suctiony pop of a refrigerator door; and then the jounce and slosh of a juice carton being shaken. I could hear the delicate wing beats of the sparrows, fighting for space on the perch of the bird feeder dangling from the yard's lone tree. Somewhere far away, a car engine revved to life, and, beyond that, the dim drone of a lawn mower.

I started walking through the grass, its sweet-smelling wetness sticking to my ankles and feet, over to the fence at the far edge of the property. Our house was owned by the school, and though not quite on campus, very close to it, separated only by a graveyard and a line of trees. When the trees weren't full, you could see clear across the graveyard to Endicott House, Jamie's dorm. They were full now, though, so the view was obscured.

I slid between two posts and entered the tiny woods. As soon as I did, the sunlight and warmth and snatches of family dialogue fell behind me. Inside, everything was green and black and cool and dank, dark with the stench of dampness and shadow, of ferns and fungus. The scrub pines surrounding

14

me had branches growing every which way, tangling together in a sooty snarl that blocked out the sky. Their bark looked mean, rotten, and when I touched it, it crumbled under my fingertips, dry as a scab. Something caught in my throat and I shivered. Wiping my hands on my pajama bottoms, I quickly began walking the thousand or so feet to the other side.

When I reached it, was standing at the edge of the graveyard, I made a scan of the horizon for Nica's fast-moving form. Many a dawn would she slip out of Endicott in one of Jamie's sweatshirts, the drawn hood concealing her hair and most of her face. Cutting through the rows of tombstones and markers, she'd steal in our back door, undetected, except by me, watching from my bedroom window. She and Jamie weren't a couple anymore, but there was a better-than-even chance that the new guy, with whom she'd obviously spent the night, was also in Endicott. That or Minot, the other guys' dorm.

I didn't see Nica as I was hoping to, though. Instead, out of the corner of my eye, I saw a flash of movement or color. Only when I turned around, no one was there. Suddenly I noticed how quiet everything had become. Motionless, too, the leaves and trees perfectly still, not so much as a whisper of a breeze on the air. I closed my eyes. My ears filled with the beating of my heart, the in-outs of my breaths, the contraction of my throat muscles—sounds, I realized, that were always there but hidden, tucked away under every other sound—each shift, throb, flutter magnified, made significant, by the deep silence around me. And then a branch snapped and my eyes flew open. Pulling the old cardigan tight around my chest, I turned, started back to the fence.

That's when I heard the police siren in the distance. It ripped into the morning, tearing it in two. For a moment I

15

froze, transfixed. Then I began to run, but heavily, the way you do in nightmares, my limbs clumsy and strange, my feet sinking into the spongy earth, catching there, everything ground down and in slow-motion, and all at once I understood that I *was* in a nightmare: last night's, the one I couldn't remember but now, suddenly, in flashes, could. Still, I hauled my body along, through the trees, over the fence, toward what I knew—knew because it was there, all of it, in that piercing mechanical wail, knew because it was prophesied in my dream, as elusive as a scent, a shadow, a ghost, knew because it was written in the very blood flowing through my veins—would be as bad as it gets.

As I reached the sidewalk in front of my house, I spotted the cruiser with the siren. It was whipping around the corner of Upham, wide into the right lane of Fiske, rear tire bouncing off the median strip. An unmarked sedan followed seconds later. No swirling cherry lights, but I could tell it was a cop car nonetheless. No mistaking it for anything else. And watching the two vehicles cut sharp rights onto Schofield, the street the graveyard entrance was on, I felt my legs buckling, collapsing beneath me. I dropped first to my knees, then to all fours, the shock of certainty hitting me: Nica was dead.

My sister was dead.

# CHAPTER TWO

Nica's body had been found by Graydon Tullis, a sophomore in Endicott House who'd snuck into the graveyard
with a couple of guys from food services to get high before
morning detention, the very session my dad was overseeing.
Afterward, the food services guys had headed down campus
to start their shifts at Stokes Dining Hall, and Graydon
had headed east to main campus. He was applying Visine
as he walked, chin tilted back, lower lid thumbed down,
when he tripped on something, went sprawling into a face-
plant. He turned around to investigate, thinking it was a
tree root, or one of those baby tombstones your eye can
sometimes skip over.

But it wasn't.

It was a pair of feet in frayed-lace Converse. Slowly
Graydon's gaze traveled upward, all the while the old camp
song "Dem Bones"—*with the toe bone connected to the foot
bone, and the foot bone connected to the ankle bone, and
the ankle bone connected to the leg bone* . . .—running
through his mind. (A dazed-sounding, pouchy-eyed Graydon

told me all this a couple weeks later. Not that I asked. He cornered me as I was ducking out of Stokes, apple in hand, looking for a deserted classroom to eat it in.) And then his gaze arrived at the hipbone connected to the backbone. His first thought was how teeny-tiny the hole was and yet the crazy amount of blood that had leaked from it. His second thought was how the other colors that came out of the body—the greenish beige of snot, the watered-down yellow of pee, the milky off-white of semen—were dull, muted, earth tones. Blood, though, was so vivid. So vivid it looked fake! Like the stuff you squeezed out of a tube on Halloween.

His gaze kept going, up and up and up—*with the back-bone connected to the shoulder bone, and the shoulder bone connected to the neck bone, and the neck connected to the head bone . . .*—at last reaching the face. The moment he realized who it belonged to was the same moment he realized he could smell the blood as well as see it. All of a sudden, a wave of nausea washed over him, made him vomit (a weak, indefinite brown) where he knelt.

Stumblingly, he ran to my house. He was hysterical, babbling and breathless, but Mom understood him well enough to let him lead her by the hand to the graveyard. She was the one who called 911.

An ambulance arrived only minutes after the police cars. But it was too late. Nica was already gone, a bullet from a .22 lodged deep in her left kidney. Time of death was established as between 6:45 and 7:30 A.M., though she'd likely been shot earlier. The knowledge that it took a while for her to bleed out—hours, possibly—was almost more than I could bear, and I knew if I thought about it, really thought

18

about it, I couldn't. So I didn't think about it. Wouldn't let myself.

It was surprisingly easy not to listen once I set my mind to it. When the details of the murder were told to me, I just sort of let them wash over my brain and out my ears. Which is why I'm not exactly clear on how the police deduced that whoever killed Nica probably wasn't a stranger to her. But deduce it they did. And when it was discovered that I was the last known person to have seen her alive, they were very eager to talk to me.

Oh, those endless, bleached-out hours going over my story with Detective Ortiz. The stale air of that box of a room at the back of the station, the hard plastic of the chair, the can of Coke gone warm and flat from sitting out too long, me saying the same words in the same order again and again, telling Detective Ortiz everything Nica told me the day before, skipping only the part about the new guy— an omission for Jamie's sake, it would hurt him to know she'd moved on so fast—just wanting to go to sleep, that total exhaustion, where even my face was numb, and none of the talk mattering anyway because she was already dead dead dead.

Her sophomore year, Nica was named homecoming queen. The victory was a fluke. Not that she wasn't one of the prettiest girls in school. In fact, she was probably the prettiest. Which should've all but killed her chances. A word about Chandler: Chandler, as a school, thought it was too cool for school, too cool for a lot of things. The only way it would deign to participate in any of the traditional rah-rah teen rites of passage was ironically. And Nica, as it so happens, lost the vote. She came in a distant second to Quentin Graham, a Mississippi boy who showed up to class several days a month in a Chanel suit and pillbox hat. But the administration refused to recognize a male, no matter how chicly turned out, as a legitimate contender. (Refused, basically, to recognize the other meaning of the word *queen*.) And Nica won by default.

It was an utterly forgettable event in her life. She sat next to Mr. McFarlan, the assistant headmaster, wearing a crown—a Burger King one, borrowed for the occasion from Maddie's boyfriend, Ruben Samuelson—for five minutes at morning chapel the day before alumni weekend. That was it. The only reason the title rates a mention is because it was a detail so seized upon by the media after she died. It put, I think, the Good Housekeeping Seal of Approval on her loveliness, made it official. Officially poignant, too. And pretty soon it started to seem as if her full name actually was *Homecoming Queen Nica Baker*.

Edgar Allan Poe, in his essay "The Philosophy of Composition" (Studies in American Literature: The Rise of the Supernatural, Ms. Laine, sophomore year), stated that, "the death of a beautiful woman is, unquestionably, the most poetical topic in the world." And Nica was not just dead, she was murdered. Raped, too. Her story thus offered up the most potent narrative combination known to man, everybody's favorite set of lurid extremes: sex and death, Eros and Thanatos, kiss kiss and bang bang. The public couldn't get enough.

Once Nica's identity was released, our house was besieged. TV news crews, journalists, and photographers were all camped out on our lawn, waiting for a whimper, a tear, a twisted feature—some scrap they could wolf down, some tasty little bite that would tide them over until the real meat came: a break in the case. Trespassing on private property was illegal, so the police set up a barricade, pushing the motley crew back, forcing it onto the sidewalk and street, which made its presence feel no less oppressive, and getting in and out of our driveway near impossible. I'd say the experience was surreal except I hate that word. It was surreal, though, the merciless intensity of those people calling out my name, my mom and dad's names, the flash cameras constantly going off, giving the scene the queasy, too-bright, side-tilted quality of a hallucination.

Mom, Dad, and I fought back the only way we knew how. By withholding. After that first day, the police pretty much left us alone. They were very polite, deferential almost, less because of who we were, I think, than because of what Chandler was, the influence it wielded in Hartford. And once they were done probing us, our stories and our alibis, we returned to the house, retreated to our rooms to cry. Well, Mom and I to cry, Dad to I don't know what. His eyes were bone-dry, as if they were unable to weep or didn't see the point. But mostly we retreated to our rooms to wait. Eventually, we reasoned, boredom would set in or another sensational crime would be committed—a murder victim who was even younger than Nica, who was actually rich, not just by-association rich, who got violated more egregiously, more bloodily, more kinkily—and the restless pack would move on, leave us to grieve in peace.

Five days passed. Six days. A week. Then two weeks. And, still, the case was no closer to being solved. All the statistically likely guys—Dad, Jamie, Ruben, the two or three male students with a documented history of aggression toward female students, even several of the male teachers who were on campus that weekend—had been ruled out as suspects. Plus, my family was staying mum, giving up absolutely nothing. Sections of the crowd, I noticed, were starting to break off; there were fewer news vans parked along the curb. The strategy seemed, finally, to be working.

And then, Dad got careless.

It was three o'clock in the morning. The street was quiet, almost staged-looking, the houses that lined it resembling props on a movie set, all lit by a moon that was high and round and bright as a lamp, casting a soft golden glow. And Dad, convincing himself that all was as harmless as it appeared, decided to take the garbage out for Tuesday morning pickup.

From a window in Nica's room I watched him as he carried the bags to the curb, one over each shoulder, seeming to stagger under their weight, three or four pounds at the most. He'd just finished stuffing them into the blue plastic can, was standing under the streetlight, lid still in hand, eyes turned to the ground as if he were trying to remember where he was and how he got there, when a woman emerged from behind the Wheelers' hedges. She was older than any of the media people I'd seen so far, and sadder, her soft brown eyes baggy, tired-looking, her camera-ready makeup smudged and starting to fade, ending abruptly at her jawline. Heavier, too, her bosomy flesh making her appear almost maternal.

"Mr. Baker! Mr. Baker!" she said. "Do you have time to speak with us?" She was out of breath from running the ten or so yards across our lawn. It put funny spaces between her words. And her skirt had hiked up. I could see the control-top portion of her pantyhose, her chubby thighs. I felt sorry for her.

22

Dad turned wearily, gave his back to her and the denim-shirted man with a camera trailing in her wake.

"It's been two weeks and the police still have no suspects," she said. "Care to comment?"

Slowly he started making the trek to the front door.

"Do you think they're doing everything they can to find your daughter's killer?"

He kept walking, maintained his plodding pace, like he didn't even hear her. He was almost at the porch steps.

A little desperate now, "You want to know what I think? I don't think they are. I think they're too scared to conduct a real investigation. I think they're afraid to go after any of the kids at this school—your school, Mr. Baker, the school you and your wife have devoted your lives to—because they believe that if they do, the kids' fathers will come at them with a team of high-priced defense attorneys, make sure that the only jobs in law enforcement they'll be able to get after this case are at the mall."

This time he heard her, and what she said stopped him cold. My dad's always been a gentle guy—mild, slow to anger, unconfrontational in the extreme, rarely yells and never swears. So it was something of a shock when I saw him do a sharp one-eighty, march back to where the reporter was standing. He was still holding the garbage lid, and now had it thrust out in front of him like it was a shield and he was charging into battle. When he reached her, he shoved his face in hers. Said, "You want to know if I think one of these rich kids is getting away with murder?" She craned her neck to give herself room but managed to get the microphone in front of his mouth. "The answer is, yes, I do. Jamie Amory. My daughter dumped him months ago and he couldn't handle it, couldn't handle being said no to, so he decided to make her pay."

"But Jamie Amory has an alibi," she pointed out.

"His alibi's shit! He's shit! A rapist and a murderer!"

Hearing these words, the reporter's sympathetic cow-eyed expression vanished and she smiled. When she did, I saw her teeth, and my heart sank. They were small and sharp and inward-sloping: the teeth of a predator. The smile didn't last long, though. Was wiped off her face when Dad threw down the garbage lid, wrapped his fingers around her wrist.

"Shit!" he said, squeezing. "Do you hear me? Shit, shit, shit!"

She began to arch backward, a panicky look in her eye.

"Hey, pal," the cameraman said, "hands to yourself, okay?"

Dad spun around. "Who are you calling *pal*, asshole?" And, letting go of the reporter's wrist, he swung out.

Unbelievably, he connected with the cameraman's jaw. There wasn't much force behind the punch. It probably didn't feel too nice, though, and, once the cameraman shook it off, he carefully placed his equipment on the ground and threw a punch of his own. He was a middle-aged guy and out of shape. Still, he had a good three inches and thirty pounds on Dad. But as he pitched forward his suede boot slipped on the grass, so that his punch ended up being even weaker and more off-target than Dad's. Until that moment, I'd thought all violence was agile and sure-footed, almost balletic-looking, as it was in the movies. I was surprised to see how awkward it really was, how clunky and no-rhythm. The two men, panting and grunting, taking time out from combat to bend at the waist, wheeze and suck air, exchanged graceless blow after graceless blow until, finally, Dad fell on the sidewalk with a thud, not because the cameraman landed a KO, but because Dad took a wild overhand right that missed everything and lost his balance.

For a while he lay there on the asphalt, either resting or passed out with his eyes open. Whichever it was, he looked strangely at peace, his chest rising and falling gently. Then the cameramen leaned over to touch him, make sure he was okay, and he let loose with a howl, a gross moan so dense with pain and rage and sorrow that it just stopped time.

I yanked the window curtain from inside my cheek, belatedly aware that I'd been chewing the fabric. I ran downstairs and out the door, pulled Dad away from the cameraman in whose arms he was now sobbing, and took him into the house.

Dad cried for five hours straight. Cried until his eyes dried out and he wasn't crying tears anymore. Cried until Mom turned on the TV to cover up the ragged, torn-off sounds he was making, after which he was too shocked to cry. There he was on the local morning news, cheeks clogged with blood, mouth frothy with saliva, eyeballs like the kind you buy in a gag shop, calling Jamie Amory a rapist and murderer. Mom and I exchanged sleepless, dread-filled glances. I flashed on a T-shirt that Ruben once wore to class, was ordered to go back to his dorm room and change. Scrawled across the chest in sky-blue letters was the phrase SHIT, MEET FAN.

Only for Dad it never got the chance to because later that morning Manny Flores was discovered in his room by a dorm monitor after he'd missed his first and second period classes. He was hanging from a beam, a ripped-up bedsheet cinched around his neck. Not quite hanging, actually. His room was in the attic, and the ceiling was sloped, making it impossible for his feet not to touch the ground. So he improvised, thrusting his body forward, cutting off his air supply. At any point he could have stopped the strangulation by simply standing up. It was an agonizing—and agonizingly slow—way to die, which means he must have wanted to very badly. Lividity indicated that his death occurred between nine and eleven P.M., several hours before Dad's run-in with the reporter.

Manny was a day student who'd been living in Endicott House since Christmas when his mother ran off with her boyfriend, basically dumping him on the school's doorstep. I didn't know him. Not many people at Chandler did. He kept to himself, didn't play sports or participate in any extracurricular activities. No gun was found in his room, but, as I said, he was a day student, a local, from the kind of neighborhood where getting your hands on a .22 wasn't a big deal. And since Chandler was less than half a mile from the Connecticut River, getting a .22 off your hands wasn't a big deal either.

The papers didn't print his suicide note, but the police showed it to my family as a courtesy. Here's what it boiled down to: he loved Nica, Nica didn't love him. Unrequited affection, the oldest one in the book. As an explanation it was both lucid and murky, coherent and incomprehensible, profound and banal. I wished he hadn't said anything at all.

The whole thing went to a fast fade from there. The publicity had already hurt Chandler. Several parents, feeling the environment unsafe, had insisted on yanking their kids out, midsemester or not. Something like twenty percent of incoming freshmen had rescinded their acceptances. The school wanted the case closed as quickly as possible. The police couldn't have been more cooperative. And just like that, it was all over. "Justice was served" when "confessed murderer"

26

of "homecoming queen Nica Baker" acted as his own "judge, jury, and executioner."

Sound of two hands slapping dust off each other. Done and done.

# CHAPTER THREE

When I returned to Chandler, everyone was nice to me: students and teachers, administrators and maintenance workers. And all day long I sat in class, in the dining hall, in the library, hunched under that niceness, cramped and stiff. I expected things to be easier, or at least more natural, with Jamie, Maddie, and Ruben, but they weren't. The three of them rallied behind me, made a point almost of claiming me, of showing everybody at school that nothing had changed, that we were still best friends, though we'd only ever been sort-of friends, me never quite able to fit in or keep up. They loyally sat with me at lunch, walked with me to class, saved me a seat in the snack bar. Yet when we were alone, there was a tension, a hostility even—all of us trying to sound polite, but with an edge, my edge just as sharp as theirs—and it surprised me because I didn't know what it was or where it was coming from.

Until, all of a sudden, I did. My dad, what he said to the reporter about Jamie—that was the source of tension between them and me. Actually, not what Dad said, but what I didn't say in response to it: that I never believed it. Which I never did, not for a second. (Jamie rape and murder Nica? Not in a million years!) And in the conversation we were having under every other conversation we were having, the one that was conducted in tones of voice and pauses and breaths rather than spoken language, they were asking me to say it. Not publicly. There was no need to embarrass my dad further. Not even out loud. A nod or a look at the right moment would have been enough. It was fair and valid and entirely within reason that they wanted me to say it. I didn't want to, though. I don't know why I didn't want to, but I didn't want to and, what's more, I wasn't going to. And no matter what words I was saying to them on top, underneath I was only saying one word, *No,* and they heard me loud and clear.

A week or so into my return to Chandler, I was sitting on the quad with Maddie during a free period. The school newspaper was between us, opened to the horoscope page, and we were splitting a kiwi-strawberry Italian ice. Our sunglasses were on and we were talking. She was talking anyway, telling me about a trip she was planning to take to Glastonbury to pick up a pair of pants for Ruben for his birthday, or maybe a pair of pants for herself to wear to Ruben's birthday. One or the other.

Maddie was a pale girl, angular and beaky-faced, but she had a body that was blade thin and a gaze that was cool and contemptuous, which was better than pretty somehow, and in her presence I usually felt self-conscious to the degree that eye contact was difficult. Usually but not that day. That day, I guess, I couldn't be bothered. I looked down. Saw ants marching out of a crack in the pavement in an orderly black line. I poked at them with the wooden spoon from my Italian ice. They began to swarm.

Maddie, I suddenly realized, was no longer speaking, was looking at me in an expectant way, and I understood that she must have asked me something. I looked back at her, hoping her face would offer a clue as to what the question was. She was wearing pearls and a T-shirt that said LOVE SLAVE. Her long blond hair was heavily gelled. "Sorry," I said, giving up, "what did you say?"

"I said, do you want to go with me?"

A beat, then, "To Glastonbury?"

"Jamie told me I could borrow his car. Or we could take your shit heap."

I threw down the spoon, wiped my sticky hands on the patch of grass in front of me. "Yeah, all right."

"How about after school since there's no practice today? We could get dinner while we're there. Check-in at Archibald isn't till nine."

Another beat passed. Maddie lowered her sunglasses. I could tell she was waiting for me to do the same, but I didn't want to look at her without the dulling amber tint.

"What do you say?" she said.

"I'd like to go. I would. It's just, today's a little tough."

"What about tomorrow then?"

"Yeah, tomorrow's no good either."

"Oh really? And why's that?"

"Well, see, because—"

We talked in this way for a while, and then suddenly we weren't talking anymore. I don't know who turned away from who, but I do know I didn't care.

That moment marked my official break from Jamie, Maddie, and Ruben, after which I was pretty much on my own. But then, apart from Nica, I'd always been on my own as far

30

as that crowd went. I had friends who weren't Nica's, of course. A group of girls I talked to after class, met up with on weekends, took my yearbook picture with. Margret, Lydie, and Francine. But the sad truth was, the connection between them and me wasn't real. I hung out with them because I had to hang out with someone and, on the surface, we had things in common—quiet natures, serious about school, neither popular nor unpopular. ("Wow," Maddie once said when she walked in on us sprawled out on the family room floor, doing our homework, "it, like, boggles the mind how nondescript you all are." She was wasted at the time. Stoned, too, I think. Still, though.) Basically it was a relationship of convenience. We offered each other warmth and comfort, the protection of safety in numbers. Law of the jungle: stay part of a pack and you're more likely to live to see another day.

Sometimes there'd be a house party that was in the vicinity of local, a party Nica, Jamie, Maddie, and Ruben would regard as hopeless if they bothered regarding it at all, and Margret, Lydie, Francine, and I would go together. But as often as not I'd leave early, bored after a couple hours of wandering in and out of other people's rooms, looking at the photos on mantels, the books on shelves, pretending not to notice the uncool debauchery going on around me. I'd either call my dad, ask him to pick me up, or, when I was old enough to have my license, simply drive off. Occasionally my cell would ring later with questions about where I'd disappeared to. Mostly not, though. Even at a second-rate gathering, my presence—or lack of—didn't really register. I was included. I just wasn't necessary.

After I came back to school, Margret, Lydie, and Francine made an effort to be supportive too. Let me know they were there for me. The thing is, I didn't want them there for me. I wanted them away from me. They got the message pretty quick. There'd be the odd hurt or wondering look cast in my direction. But mostly they respected my wish for space and kept their distance.

And there were other people, too, people I didn't know except to nod hello to in the hall, and they'd come up to me out of goodwill or kindness or curiosity, and that was fine. Usually they'd try to start a conversation, but their words would quickly turn into blah blah blah, and I'd lose the thread, stare into space until they'd get uncomfortable and leave. Soon no one came up to me and that was also fine.

One new person, however, did enter my life during this period: Dr. Karnani, the psychiatrist I'd asked my parents to find. Asked because I thought I was having a nervous breakdown, and if I wasn't, I could be, should be. An anxiety disorder of some sort was, I figured, my best bet for getting shipped off to a mental institution. Not a *One-Flew-Over-the-Cuckoo's-Nest* nuthouse-type deal, state-run for hardcore crazies—I didn't want that, no straitjackets or horse tranquilizers for me—but something low-key, gentle. A sanatorium maybe, the kind of place that catered to people with quote sensitive natures unquote who needed quote rest unquote. I'd sleep in a room with white walls, look out the window for hours at a time, be guided to meals by nurses with soft hands and voices, nothing expected of me, every decision made by somebody else.

Though most days I felt numb and in a fog, I would, every so often, experience these attacks that would just completely undo me. Something would happen, some small thing—a T-shirt of Nica's would turn up under my bed, or a movie she liked would play on TV—and, before I knew it, the door to the cell I kept my memories locked behind would burst open, and the vicious little thugs would swarm me, push me to the ground, hit me, kick me, violate me in any way they could think of. And for hours afterward, I'd be weak and shaky and without defenses, jumping at every noise, ready to cry at the drop of a hat. What I wanted was to be protected from these attacks. What I wanted was to feel numb and in a fog not most of the time, but all of it.

And I got what I was asking for from my sessions with Dr. Karnani. Or at least from the prescriptions she wrote me at the end of them. Benzodiazepine derivatives, the most miraculous of the miracles of modern medicine, as far as I was concerned: Xanax, Valium, Klonopin. On these drugs, I didn't just feel numb and in a fog, I felt sealed off, like I was behind a pane of glass and no one and nothing could touch me.

But the day came when I could no longer stomach Dr. Karnani's wrinkly neck and breath that stank of garlic and constant questions about my feelings and my feelings about my feelings, and I stopped showing up for our appointments.

So what, then, did I do for drugs?

Well, I wasn't being totally honest before when I said I broke with Jamie, Maddie, and Ruben because I did still see quite a bit of Ruben. Our relationship now, though, was less personal than professional. Ruben dealt—mainly prescription drugs, but a little ecstasy and ketamine, too, the occasional popper—out of his room on Friday evenings between five and seven thirty, dining hall hours. I started swinging by.

Each exchange followed essentially the same script.

As I walked up to his door, I'd pull out my cash, a portion of the over-thousand dollars I'd saved from my summers teaching tennis at the rec center, have it ready in my hand. I'd knock twice. He'd make me wait a little, but then he'd open the door. More often than not he'd be dressed in a filthy kimono, the one his dad bought him on a business trip to Tokyo, and a pair of high-top sneakers with no laces. He'd be stuffing his face with potato chips or cookies or SpaghettiOs or one those microwavable pizza things shaped like a fat stick with the crust on the outside. When he'd see me, he'd smile wide, say, "Gracie," drawing out both syllables of my name. "Nice of you to stop by."

"Hi, Ruben," I'd say.

He'd hold up an *uno momento* finger, making me wait again as he swallowed, ran his tongue along the line of his teeth, top and bottom. Then he'd say, "You look a little under the weather today. How're you feeling?"

"Okay. Having trouble sleeping, though."

"Huh. Bummer."

"Bummer," I'd agree.

"Not sleeping's becoming a regular thing with you. I've got to say, that surprises me. You don't seem like the kind of girl who would develop that sort of problem."

"Yeah, well, just goes to show you."

"Is it better this week or worse?"

"Worse."

"Oh my my. Worse again? You're turning into quite the little raging insomniac. You know, I have trouble sleeping, too, but I keep it under control. Don't have trouble sleeping every single night." When I wouldn't say anything back, "Not sleeping, you pay a high price for that."

"Tell me about it."

"Can you afford it?"

My voice tight, "I've managed so far, haven't I?"

34

He'd shrug, say, "Just trying to look out for you." Then he'd reach inside the pocket of the school blazer hanging next to the door. As he'd start to hand over the pocket's contents, though, he'd slap a palm to his forehead and squeeze his eyes shut, like an idea lightbulb had switched on in his skull and he was blinded by the brilliance of it. "Hey," he'd say, "have you ever given yoga a shot?"

At this point in the exchange, I'd be getting impatient but would be doing my best to hide it. If he saw it, he'd drag things out even longer. "I haven't," I'd say.

"It's supposed to work wonders on you high-strung types. Keeps you from sweating the small stuff."

"Then I'll have to look into it."

"It's good for your body, too. Gets you nice and skinny. Not so skinny, though, that you lose your breasts. Man, there's something about a thin girl with big tits."

"Yeah," I'd say.

"There is one thing that definitely won't work for you, Grace. Know what that is?"

I'd shake my head, but inside I'd be perking up because I knew he was about to say the magic word, the word that meant I was getting what I came for.

"Drugs." He'd wag a stern finger at me. "I want it on record that I'm anti-narcotics, pro-family values."

"Noted," I'd say.

He'd nod, satisfied, then place in my hand several pamphlets, the ones with titles like *So Help Me God: Substance Abuse, Religion and Spirituality* and *Understanding the Agonies of Ecstasy* that fill guidance counselors' offices, and in each of which was folded a clear plastic baggie containing ten pills— Xanax, Valium, or Klonopin, depending on what he had in stock—as I placed in his hand twenty-dollar bills, a twenty per pamphlet. He'd always hold on to the pamphlets for an extra couple seconds, make me really pull before he'd release them.

I'd press my palms together, bow my head, say, "*Namaste.*" I'd try to say it sarcastically, but usually I'd be so grateful to have my supply for the week that I'd wind up sounding embarrassingly sincere. Then I'd slip the pamphlets into my bag, scurry off, as he called out, "Sweet dreams," to my retreating back.

A brand-new life was settling around me. It was ugly and it was empty, but I was okay with it because, thanks to the drugs, I wasn't really in it. Not really being in it, however, had its consequences. I quit tennis team and lit mag. Actually, not so much quit as stopped showing up. Also, I failed all my classes, every single one. In a short six-week period I managed to completely torpedo my GPA. It dropped a grand total of 2.1 points, making it a not very grand 1.8.

So I was surprised but not too when one morning my guidance counselor, Mr. Howell—Shep to the students he advised or was dorm parent to—found me in the hall, told me that Williams had pulled its acceptance offer. He handed me the number of the dean of admissions, urged me to give a call, explain my situation. That afternoon, I went to him, said I couldn't get through to the dean. But the truth was, I didn't even try. I lacked the energy: pick up the phone, press the correct buttons in the correct order, wait while a secretary put me on hold, plead my case to a tweedy academic type with a tight mouth, use my sad story to make that tight mouth go loose and blubbery. I felt exhausted just thinking about it, bone tired before I'd done a single thing. I sensed dimly, though, that I might want the option of college in the future; so, right there in Shep's office, sitting under a home-made poster of a dove with the word *peace* in its beak, I let the tears come to my eyes, keep on coming.

He fell for the act, reaching for the receiver with one hand, there-thereing me with the other. By the end of the day, Williams had rescinded its rescission.

# CHAPTER FOUR

If I was so done with Chandler and Chandler people, why then did I show up at Jamie's Fourth of July bash a month after graduation?

A simple chance encounter the day before.

I was standing at the foot of my driveway, opening the mailbox, pulling out the bottle of generic Xanax I'd ordered from some online Canadian pharmacy at a rip-offy price and had been waiting on for almost a week. (The Internet had become my dealer since summer break started and Ruben went home to New York, taking his pamphlets with him.) I turned around and there was Jamie, walking toward me in madras shorts and an inside-out T-shirt, his racket bag swinging loosely from his shoulder. His hands were in his pockets and his head was down.

I was trying to decide how best to avoid him, taking an inventory of my options: shove my head all the way inside the mouth of the mailbox, duck behind my dad's car or the Wheelers' hedges, run back into the house. Just then, though,

Jamie looked up and our eyes met. *Oh, shit,* I thought. *Oh, who cares?* I thought.

I waited for him to reach me. At last he did.

"Hey," he said.

"Hey," I said. "How are you?"

"Good. You?"

"Good."

It was his turn to speak, only he couldn't seem to think of anything to say. I watched him struggle. He was nice to watch, tall and fair and slender with the kind of delicate, crystalline beauty teenage boys almost invariably grow out of, lose by the time they become men: high cheekbones, flower-petal skin, full lips, intensely red, the borders blurry and undefined. It was funny; it used to be the sheer privilege of talking to him made talking nearly impossible, left me tongue-tied and breathless with nerves, terrified that I wouldn't be able to hold his interest, while he looked on with those eyes that always seemed on the verge of sleep. Now he was the one who was anxious, and I was the one who didn't give a shit.

Finally, to help him out, I said, "So, are you on your way to the courts?"

He nodded, grateful. "Well, first I'm on my way to the track to do some foot speed drills, then I'm on my way to the courts."

"Lesson?"

"Lesson, then a practice match. I've been training a lot lately."

I wasn't surprised to hear it. As a student Jamie was solid, nothing special, but his squash had been good enough to get him into Cornell and Middlebury. Not quite good enough, though, to get him into Princeton, his dad's alma mater. When he received his rejection letter in early spring, he decided to do a postgraduate year at Chandler, spend the next six months concentrating on upping his ranking, then reapply in the fall.

"Is the lesson with Mr. Loring or Oscar?" I asked. Mr. Loring was the coach of the Chandler squash team. Oscar was Jamie's private coach.

"Oscar," he said. And then, softly, "Geez, can't someone get that kid to mellow out?"

I noticed, for the first time, that a baby was crying. Guess Mrs. Wheeler had had her little boy. "I thought Oscar taught out of that club in Canton?" I said.

"He does."

"Then how come the lesson's not there?"

"Because they're repainting the courts this week. Actually, just one of the courts. But reserving the other is, like, this major hassle, so—"

I tuned out, letting him pull the weight of the conversation for a bit. It was hard for me to believe how close we'd once been. When Nica dumped Jamie back in February and nobody knew why, not even him, he'd started calling me, nearly every night on my cell. These conversations weren't a secret, not exactly. I hadn't mentioned them to Nica, though. And if he ever had, she would've reacted, I knew, with wounded surprise. *"What's up with not telling me?"* she'd have asked, to which I'd have said—I'd scripted my reply, rehearsed it in my head many times, the casualness of my delivery, the tone of my voice jaunty and absentminded by turns—*"I didn't? Really? Huh. I thought I did."* Technically I hadn't been doing anything wrong. Nothing remotely romantic or flirtatious was going on in those dialogues. Mostly I'd listened as Jamie went on about how confused he was by the way my sister had ended the relationship, how wrecked that she'd left him, how much he loved her still. But if the interactions truly had been so innocent, I wouldn't have kept them from her. And I remembered that during that period, when she and I were talking or hanging out, there'd sometimes be a pause and I'd feel a tickling sensation—of guilt or excitement, possibly both—at the back of my throat.

I tuned back in. Jamie had finally loosened up, was going on about tomorrow night's Fourth party becoming an annual thing (his parents spent every July in a villa outside Florence, and, as of last summer, no longer insisted on taking him with them, good squash courts, coaches, and hitting partners being tough to reliably find in rural Italy), how many kegs he had on order, who was bringing what weed from which county in Northern California. While I waited for him to stop talking, I touched my lips experimentally with the tips of my fingers, the flesh there so dehydrated it felt like dried sponge. I began to think about how I hadn't slept much in the past few days because I'd run out of pills, and how nice it would be to place a couple under my tongue, let them dissolve, drip slowly down my throat, then curl up in bed, burrow deep into those sheets I hadn't changed in weeks and just drift off.

"So, anyway, you should stop by," he said, caught up in his enthusiasm, and then, remembering who he was speaking to, got a look on his face like he wished he could snatch his words out of the air, shove them back in his mouth.

He visibly relaxed, though, when I said, "I definitely will," which we both knew meant I definitely wouldn't.

"Cool," he said. "Cool, cool, cool."

And then we fell into a silence, this time agitated on my end. Thinking about the pills had made me want the pills. I was almost desperate now to be alone with them. And because he showed no signs of moving on, was, in fact, zoned out, tapping the beat to some song playing in his head against his collarbones, I knew that I'd have to prompt him.

"So," I said, "you should probably get going, right?" Then, realizing how that sounded, "I mean, I wouldn't want to make you late or anything."

Jamie, getting the message, nodded. We said our good-byes, went our separate ways: him to fresh air and sunshine, me to my musty bedroom and drawn shades. And that, I thought, was that.

Except it wasn't.

I had no interest in going to the party. I had no intention of going to the party. And yet I went to the party. Why? When I say I don't have a clue, I'm being literal, not flip. The drugs I loved so much, the ones I was now frankly and unambiguously abusing, didn't just cut me off from other people, but from myself, as well. My mind and body were totally disconnected. Even physical sensations felt distant and not quite real. Sometimes I'd be smearing gloss on my lips, and the information coming from my fingertips would directly contradict the information coming from my brain, insisting that the warm, smooth skin and the hard ridges of teeth underneath belonged to a person other than me.

All of which is to say my motives were a mystery. I can't fathom why I did something so inexplicable and ugly as showing up at a party where I wasn't wanted. And that wasn't even the most inexplicable and ugly thing I did that night. No, the most inexplicable and ugly thing I did that night was dressing head to toe in my dead sister's clothes, the very ones she'd worn the year before.

It was as if I was sleepwalking. I entered Nica's room, walked over to her closet, pulled out the items I was looking for one by one. I changed into them, then tucked my blond hair under a dark wig I had from an old costume. (The Halloween before last, Nica, Maddie, and I had gone as the original *Charlie's Angels*, Nica as Farrah Fawcett, Maddie as Kate Jackson, me as Jaclyn Smith.) Stepping into the bathroom that Nica and I had shared, I opened the medicine cabinet door, removed the bottle of perfume Mom had mixed for her at a fragrance shop in Martha's Vineyard. After dabbing a bit of the liquid—a blend of blood orange oil and vanilla bouquet oil, an unexpected scent, both sharp and sweet, rough and tender—on my neck, behind my ears, I shut the medicine cabinet door.

Looking back at me in the toothpaste-flecked mirror was a reflection so like Nica's it shocked my heart, stopped it cold for a second or two. The resemblance between us had always been strong, closer to that of twins than sisters. Only our coloring was different. But no, not only our coloring, something deeper, something under the skin, something in our spirits or our souls was different, as well; so that, finally, even though we looked exactly alike, we looked nothing alike. She was beautiful and I wasn't. Or maybe I was but nobody, me included, could see it.

The differences, though, whatever they were, were disappearing right before my eyes. I tried to focus on my image, hold it steady, but it kept slipping, Nica's falling into its place. And then behind Nica's image came something else, a memory. I shut my eyes to ward it off, only shutting my eyes didn't work. It simply played out on the inside of my skull:

There we were, the two of us, Nica and I, getting ready for this party one year ago. My jeans were in the dryer so I was in a T-shirt and shorts, lying in the bathtub, a cushion from the downstairs couch behind my back, keeping Nica

43

company. She was moisturizing her legs, chain-smoking, and talking to me all at the same time. When she finished massaging lotion into her calves, she looked for a towel, couldn't find one, pushed up my shirt, wiped the excess on my stomach. Then she tossed her cigarette out the window, flipped her hair upside down. Through the dipping V-neck of her thin cotton sweater I could see her bouncing breasts in a black lace bra, and I wondered where she got it, when exactly she'd switched from the plain beige ones with the tiny pink flowers in the middle to the kind I thought only adult women wore.

It was a fledgling memory, not fully formed—a fragment. Still, it made me want to bash my head against the medicine cabinet until it fell out. Instead, I washed down a couple generic Xanaxs with tap water, then a couple more. After removing the chalky white pill residue from the corners of my lips, I grabbed my bag. I made certain not to look in the mirror again before walking out the door.

Over the years, I'd been to the houses of a number of class-mates and some, though not many, were bigger than Jamie's. But his was, to me, the most beautiful by far, the way its physical splendor was touched, just slightly, by decay—the gables and turrets faded and weather-eaten, the brick of the chimney worn to a dull brown, the wood of the boxed gutters starting to splinter—giving it a kind of grandeur, a majesty. It was set back from the rest of the street, nestled into the side of a hill.

The driveway was long and serpentine and sharply graded, and I knew if I parked in it, a fast exit would be impossible, so I left my car at the end of the block. I found the gravel path at the edge of the property. I began to follow it. The gravel was slippery, and each time I looked down to see where I was stepping, I'd get a small shock, the sight of my legs and feet in the high-heeled shoes I'd never worn before striking me as altogether alien, as if I were sharing my body with another person.

At last I came to the end of the gravel path. Instead of heading to the front door as everybody else was, though, I continued on a different path, this one running along the side of the house, and still ascending if not as steeply. I passed the garage where the Amorys' cars slept, the toolshed, the box hedge, the garden with the jonquils and the daylilies, the sundial at the center, pausing at a door. I pressed down on the latch, expecting resistance but finding none.

As soon as I was inside, I moved away from the party sounds, the voices and the music and the laughter, slipping through the line of chairs meant to serve as an informal barrier to the back of the house, down the hall, beyond the dining room with the Queen Anne drop-leaf table, the billiards room with the odd-shaped alcoves, the library with the shelves that went all the way up to the ceiling, the conservatory, a room I used to think only existed in the game Clue. Finally I reached the maid's stairs. At the top was Mr. Amory's study: lots of dark wood and leather furniture, a well-stocked liquor cabinet and a stuffed elk's head, a set of glass-paneled doors that looked more like a set of glass-paneled windows and gazed out onto the pool that had been installed over Mrs. Amory's objections. The rest of the rooms on the second floor—bedrooms, mostly—would be in high demand later tonight, but not now; it wasn't late enough for coupling off. And I didn't see a single person as I crossed from the rear of the house to the front.

I arrived at the main staircase, grand and twisting and ornately carved. For a long time I stood there, surveying the scene below. The lights in the front hall and living room were dim, the furniture pushed to the side to make way for three aluminum kegs and a massive pair of speakers, pumping out an old Rolling Stones song. Chandler liked to say its students hailed from around the globe, and they did. Mostly, though, they hailed from Boston and New York. Jamie's hometown of Avon was exactly two hours from both cities—a nothing drive. And the place was already packed, people dancing and talking, drinking beer from translucent cups, taking jerky hits off sloppily wrapped joints.

I began fumbling along the wall with my hand. At last I found the light switch. My heart fluttered in my chest, a giggle slipped from my mouth, and thinking to myself, *What fun,* I flipped it. Immediately all activity stopped. Everyone looked up, dazed and blinking. I waited for the laughter that would follow as soon as their vision adjusted. But nobody laughed. Nobody even moved. They stared up at me, eyes all the way open, as if someone had put a cold fingertip to the backs of their necks. And then Maddie uttered a small cry, brought her hand to her mouth. I placed my palm on the banister, started down the stairs.

"Happy Independence Day, Slim Jim," I sang out. Nica called Jamie Slim Jim, Nica and no one else.

Jamie stood there, plastic beer cup in his hand, his face pale under its tan and covered in sweat. He swallowed, or tried to, the muscles knotting in his throat. I watched Ruben go up to him, say something, but he pushed Ruben aside, moved swiftly to the stairs, his eyes never leaving mine. "What the fuck do you think you're doing?" His voice was harsh, strange. I could see the whites on all four sides of his eyes. Sexy, sleepy, stoned Jamie—mad.

I was unable to speak, only to look.

He dropped his cup, grabbed my arm. I could feel the pressure of each individual finger digging into my flesh. "I said, what do you think you're doing?"

I was frightened, but I knew instinctively that I couldn't show it. I had to bluff, make him back off. I blinked several times in rapid succession, jammed down the corners of my mouth. And then, in the coolest tone I could manage, I said, "You're breaking my arm. Let go."

To my surprise he did. To my even greater surprise I saw that beneath his anger was fear. And in that instant I understood how disturbed what I'd done really was, how sick, how fucked up. Jamie was scared of me, *me*. I brushed past him, walked over to the kegs, drew myself a cup. I drank it down as everybody watched. I drew myself another. Drank that one down, too.

After a bit, someone hit the light switch, plunging the downstairs back into darkness. Then a different someone turned up the volume on the stereo. And, slowly, the party started up again.

I should have left at that point. I'd gone to make a scene, I'd made a scene. Mission accomplished. I stayed, though. I'm not sure why. Maybe to punish myself. Sticking around certainly caused me misery. I'd been banished in spirit if not fact from the party, and wandering through it I felt beyond isolated, near wild with loneliness. It was almost as if I was wearing Nica's magnetism the same way I was wearing her clothes, only I'd put it on inside out: I repelled people. I'd take one step toward them, they'd take two back from me. Or maybe I stayed in the hopes I could make Jamie forgive me.

The self-consciousness I was feeling was unbearable. What I needed to do was get away from myself, and the beer wouldn't let me. Not fast enough, anyway. I found a bottle with a couple inches of vodka in it sitting, abandoned, on the piano stool. I gagged as I tipped its contents down my throat, swallowing as quickly as the suction allowed. It was like drinking gasoline. But I did it, again and again, until the bottle was empty. And soon it was as if the different parts and functions of my brain were scrambled and mashed together so that hearing was jumbled up with seeing and seeing with tasting and tasting with smelling and my thoughts were mixed up with all this, too, so that I couldn't tell what went where.

My cheeks and neck and lips were hot, burning up. I considered losing the wig. I didn't, though. Remembering Mr. Amory's liquor cabinet, I decided to cool down with another drink instead. I was having a tough time walking, so I made my way to the back of the house by holding on to the furniture, one hand over the other. But even being careful, I tripped—on a curled edge of carpet, I think, or maybe my own feet—and went crashing into the row of chairs. Distantly I observed the blood from the gash in my knee pooling in my shoe, the funny angle my wrist was bent at. Finally I picked myself up, climbed the stairs, reached the study. That's when I passed the French doors and saw Nica.

A few minutes later I was bleeding all over my reflection in the pool, gauzy with pain and confusion.

A light came on.

A voice called my name.

Who did the voice belong to? I don't know. The scene ends there in my memory. A movie stopped mid-reel.

I woke up the next morning. It wasn't quite dawn yet, the air suffused with the dull glow that comes just before first light. I reached groggily for my swivel-neck lamp, grasping at empty space until I realized that my lamp wasn't there because I wasn't home. Bolting upright, I flung my gaze around the room that wasn't mine. Nothing offered the barest hint as to where I was. And for a few bug-eyed seconds I wondered if I was dead. Then I remembered. I was at Jamie's. I remembered other things, too.

Slowly I eased myself back down onto the pillow, became very still. To move even a muscle was to stir up another hideous memory from the night before. They arrived anyway, though, in wave after scalding wave. Finally, all the waves had broken over me, and I lay there cringing in shame.

But I couldn't cringe for long because something was tugging at my attention, impatient and demanding a response: pain. I was in a lot of it. My hand, in particular, the one I'd used to break my spill over the chairs. I held it up to my eyes. It looked like a rubber glove filled with water, not a knuckle in sight. I touched my face. It felt soft, shapeless, pummeled. There was a ridged scab above my eyebrow, and a lump as big as a walnut above that, and my upper lip was twice its normal size. The shoulder that had hit the ground first ached. So did the hipbone. So did the knee.

Was all this damage the result of my drugged-out, boozed-up attempt to pass through a door without opening it first, falling seven or eight feet (the way the Amorys' house was built into the hill, the second story at the back was only half a story high), or had something happened after, something during the period my memory went so disturbingly blank? At the same time I posed this question, it dawned on me where exactly I was: the spare bedroom, directly down the hall from Jamie's. It was one of last year's hookup rooms. This year's, too, judging from the stiffness of the sheets beneath me. Suddenly I felt a fear so big it filled my head, the room, the entire house. Had I lost my virginity? And then I felt a fear so big it filled everything, had no bounds at all. Or had my virginity been taken from me? All at once I was sick, barely having time to turn my face to the trash can next to the bed before an acid liquid was spewing out my mouth, my nose, dripping down my chin.

When I was emptied out, I reached for the unopened bottle of Evian on the nightstand. I drank, desperately thirsty. The water calmed me down. Someone, I realized, had left it for me. The trash can, too. A sexual predator worrying about his victim waking up dehydrated or making a mess on the rug? I hadn't been raped. And everything I was wearing the night before I was still wearing now except for the wig. I hadn't had sex either.

That I'd put myself in the position where such things were possible, though, was appalling, borderline grotesque. No more prescription drugs mixed with alcohol for me. No more prescription drugs period. This time I'd escaped with a few cuts and bruises, a minor sprain. Nasty injuries, to be sure, and painful, but nothing that wouldn't heal. I'd gotten lucky.

Two months later I found out just how lucky. I'd already been at Williams for a week. Not for classes, which hadn't begun yet, but for preseason, to try out for the tennis team. I'd won three out of five of my challenge matches and the coach had pulled me aside, told me she'd be taking me on as an alternate. She couldn't, she'd said, allow me to officially join up, though, until I underwent a full physical. School policy.

Making the Williams tennis team as a walk-on was the first sign that the dark days were behind me, that quitting the benzos cold turkey had been worth the pain and trauma, the shakes and cramps and nights without sleep. My life, it seemed, was turning around, was going back, at least a little bit, to the way it was before Nica died. I'd wanted to tell Dad the good news in person. I'd also wanted to visit the Chandler Health Center, open year-round, though at reduced hours during summer break, which it still was for a another week, to see Dr. Simons, my doctor since I was a kid. So I'd jumped in my car and headed down to Hartford for the day.

That afternoon, Dr. Simons informed me I was pregnant. Eight weeks was his rough estimation.

# PART TWO

PART TWO

# CHAPTER FIVE

I'm vomiting before I'm awake, my eyes still closed when my stomach seizes and acid floods my throat. I jackknife, lurching forward to open the door of my car but don't quite make it in time, and a pale brown mixture of Diet Coke and low-sodium Saltines splatters out of me in a series of long convulsions. After the last one, I wipe my mouth with the back of my hand, sit all the way up.

I hadn't intended to fall asleep. The house I'd been watching had gone dark just after eleven, which meant I was free to go. My lids, though, were heavy, getting heavier, so I put away my mom's old camera, the one with the telephoto lens, doubling for me at the moment as a pair of binoculars, and crawled in the back. As I stretched out, my hand brushed the sleeve of a jacket: Nica's, thin, dark blue denim, button-flap pockets. Immediately I recoiled. She'd left it there the day before she died. The way she'd tossed it, it still seemed to retain her shape. And I didn't want to touch it, make it flat, or jostle it so that the scent of her, caught in its folds, escaped. As I moved back to the front of the car, reclined the passenger seat, I told myself I'd just close my eyes for fifteen minutes then drive home. That's the last thought I remember having.

I lower the windows and get out of the car. The street I'm on is crowded with single-story houses set back among scraggly shrubs, the plaster statues of Our Lady in the front yards chipped and faded: a run-down neighborhood in a borderline part of town. The day's going to be a hot one. I reach through the window for the Diet Coke can in the cup holder, swish the liquid around my mouth before swallowing, slowly and carefully, in distinct shifts, hoping my stomach won't notice. Then I walk to the rear of the car, pop the trunk. The pack of paper towels is under a tennis hopper.

I use nearly an entire roll cleaning the passenger-side door.

It's too early for traffic and I make it home in under ten minutes. I haven't even stepped all the way inside the front door when the smell hits me: a kind of stale fustiness, a combination of dust and old furniture, of meals cooked and eaten, of frayed carpeting. If sadness has a scent, this is it. Dad would've gotten back from work just a couple hours ago, is probably in bed now, asleep. I move quietly as I go upstairs, shower and change, slip a book in my bag so I'll have something to read later.

Before heading out the door again, I walk into the kitchen, as dark as the rest of the house. I open the refrigerator, the sudden bright light making me blink. On the bottom shelf, in front of a carton of milk, its use-by date several days past, is an aluminum container with a clear plastic top: linguine in red clam sauce. Dad must've swung by that all-night Italian place near the Amtrak station on his way home. My stomach begins to churn again, and I have to close my eyes, keep myself from imagining the smell of the congealed Parmesan, the glistening noodles, the gynecological-looking bits of gray shellfish coated in pureed tomato.

Blindly, I reach for the milk. Next, I take the box of Raisin Bran out of the cabinet. I pour a few flakes into a bowl, wet them with a splash of expired milk, then drop the bowl inside the sink. Dad's pretty checked out these days. I doubt it would register with him that I've stopped eating breakfast, and if it did register with him, I doubt even more that it would register why. Still, it never hurts to be careful.

I'm about to get back in my car. Then I think better of it. If I smell vomit, I probably will. While I'm standing there, hand on the latch, I catch sight of the dashboard clock. It's already past eight. Immediately I let go of the latch, start walking. If I don't hurry, I'll be late to my first day of work.

# CHAPTER SIX

Chandler Academy of Hartford, Connecticut, was established in 1886 when an Episcopal clergyman, Reverend Peabody Chandler of the Boston Chandlers, converted the ancestral summer home in the Sheldon/Charter Oak section of the city into an academy whose mission was to "take the wayward sons of distinguished New England families and mold the disposition of their minds and morals so that they might become good Christian gentlemen." In 1971 the minds and morals of the daughters of distinguished families became eligible for molding, as well. The wayward part stayed the same, though. And for a school that's primarily boarding, Chandler, with its two-strikes policy, is tolerant of rule-breakers. Consequently, each fall it winds up with a high number of students who've either been rejected from or given the boot by its stricter rivals.

If Chandler's reputation is only a cut above so-so, its campus, which looks more like that of a college or a small university than a high school, is anything but. The central building, aptly named Great House, is red brick, impossibly old, and covered in ivy. Great House is set among a trio of shorter and only slightly less grand buildings: Noyes, de Forest, and Perkins. To their left is Burroughs Library, pillared, marbled, silent as dust; and to its right, Amory Chapel, its bell plundered from some bombed-out church in Europe by an enterprising alum at the end of World War I; and, a little farther on, Francis Abbot Science Center and Caroline Knox Abbot Theater. Stokes Dining Hall is south. The hockey rink and tennis courts and various athletic fields are east. So is Houghton Gymnasium and the Health and Counseling Center. And way east, so far east you can't quite see it from campus, is Chandler's boathouse, the Gordon T. Pierpoint, a stone's throw from Trinity College's boathouse, Bliss, on the banks of the Connecticut River. The dormitories—there are four of them, two for the boys, Endicott and Minot, two for the girls, Archibald and Amory—are west. They're separated from the main campus by the graveyard, controversial real estate at Chandler even before Nica's body was found there. The graveyard belongs to the City of Hartford, and technically school rules don't apply to it, making it a sort of gray zone for boarders, a moral no-man's-land. It's the hub of what the administration refers to as "narcotics-related activity." Is also the hub of alcohol-related activity. Sexual-related activity, too.

I start toward the quad, the air sharp with the smell of cut grass and lawn fertilizer, fresh paint. Campus is empty, all the students in chapel, extra-long this morning because it's the first day of the new school year. Empty except for a lone figure, a hundred yards or so ahead. And though this person has her back to me, I recognize her instantly. It's the walk, tight and clipped and harried: Mrs. Amory, Jamie's mother. She's looking primly chic in a tailored gray suit, the skirt, meant to be fitted, puckering slightly on her no-ass frame, her sheer-stockinged calves tensed and shadowed by high heels, black and wickedly pointed. She changes paths and I can see her in profile now. Her face, behind its dark glasses, is as hard and brittle as an eggshell. As plain as an eggshell, too.

I slow down, not wanting her to spot me, though there's little danger of that, so intently is her gaze focused on the doors of Great House. It's no surprise finding her on campus. She's been in charge of the Parent Giving Association for as long as I can remember and does a fair amount of volunteer work at the school besides. Plus, she's constantly ferrying Jamie to and from his squash lessons. Or at least was until the administration agreed to let him keep a car in the student parking lot for that purpose.

It wasn't always from afar, though, that I saw Mrs. Amory. Once upon a time I saw her up close on a regular basis—in the days when Nica and Jamie were together, and the three of us would spend whole afternoons and evenings hanging out in his house. She made it perfectly clear that she wasn't wild about having my sister and me around. Whenever she happened to open the door and we were on the other side, she'd draw back her thin lips in an even thinner smile, say, "Welcome," in a tone intended to convey the opposite.

Sometimes Jamie would use his mom's ice-cold mannerliness against her, maneuver her into asking us to stay for dinner. These meals were always weird and uncomfortable and never-ending. Mr. Amory, a handsome man, pretty, in fact, prettier by far than his not-so-pretty wife though not quite as pretty as his very pretty son, would pay excessive attention to Nica. From behind a pair of round, black-rimmed glasses, which somehow emphasized his good looks rather than obscured them, he'd watch her, stare openly. Then the questions would begin, too many of them with him hanging too eagerly on her replies. He'd invite her to borrow his cue if she and Jamie and I were going to play billiards, his desk if we were planning to study, his raft if it was warm enough for us to swim. Once he even invited her on a trip he and Jamie were taking to Maine the following weekend to hunt bobwhite quail. Mrs. Amory would observe these exchanges from the other end of the table with eyes that were coolly detached or coolly amused—coolly something. Then she'd start in on Nica with questions of her own, mostly falsely sympathetic ones about our mom, asking how she was doing, saying how difficult her job as a high school teacher must be, how difficult both my parents' jobs were, putting up with ungrateful adolescents all day, what noble work it was and yet so unappreciated, and how she could never do it herself.

Though she barely noticed me—I don't even think she knew my name, referred to me only as "dear"—I was the one she upset with these interrogations. They'd leave me shaking with anger and hurt. Nica, on the other hand, was totally unfazed. Would always answer politely, without sarcasm or hostility, never responding to the queries' spiky subtext, staying right on the placid surface. Actually seemed to feel sorry for Mrs. Amory more than anything else. "It can't be fun being her, Gracie," Nica would say to me in the car afterward as she lit a cigarette, "uptight, everybody around her wanting to be someplace else, her husband especially." Then Nica would do an impression of Faye Dunaway in *Mommie Dearest* that was very bad but made me laugh anyway. Usually she'd talk me into stopping at the McDonald's on Albany Ave. on the ride home. We'd split a McFlurry or a hot fudge sundae. The eggnog shake, if it was near Christmas.

I watch Mrs. Amory's straight-backed form until it's out of sight, disappearing inside Great House. The dull thud of the closing doors releases me from my stupor, and I continue on my way. As the concrete path turns into marble in front of Burroughs Library, I stop, dig an elastic out of my bag. When I've finger-combed my hair into a ponytail, I pull open the glass doors, step through them.

I step through them again two minutes later, only from the opposite direction. A crisis has arisen—burst pipe, bungling maintenance man, leak above the rare books section—and when Ms. Sedgwick, the head librarian, has dealt with it, she'll deal with me, she said. She said, too, that in the meantime I ought to go see Mary Ellen Lefcourt in Payroll, get started on my paperwork.

So I'm going.

I'm sitting in the Business Development Office on the second floor of Perkins, my I-9 and Direct Deposit Authorization forms neatly filled out and on the coffee table in front of me. Mrs. Lefcourt is still in her office with her nine o'clock, even though it's nearly ten now. To kill time, I'm browsing through a copy of the *Staff Handbook,* learning all about the proper protocol for reporting falsification of expense vouchers, when I hear voices rise up in anger—one voice, actually, male, young-sounding—rise up and die down almost immediately.

I crane my neck to see where it came from and notice a door at the end of the short, offshoot-type hallway. The sign outside it reads GLEN FLYNN, DIRECTOR OF FACILITIES. A second later, Mr. Flynn himself appears, a nervous-looking guy with fidgety hands, a red bow tie. He closes the door behind him, but not all the way, hurries over to Mrs. Waugh, the office secretary, whispers something in her ear. She shakes her head disapprovingly, either at what he just told her or at him. With an anxious backward glance, he exits. I re-immerse myself in the *Handbook,* wait for Mrs. Waugh's fingers to start tapping on the computer keyboard again. When they do, I close the *Handbook,* stand, begin walking toward the door like I'm in search of better light. Then, casually, I prop myself against the wall opposite.

The crack in the door is narrow. I can't see much through it, and what I can see tells me what I already know: that the room is an office, and that the angry-voiced person is indeed male and young. He's pacing back and forth, his gait lurching, wobbly. It takes me a second to put together that he's drunk, and I wonder if when Mr. Flynn scurried off, it was to get campus security. A slice of his body is visible, but none of his head. I'm starting to think I'll never get a good look at him when he pauses to bend over, peel the thick fabric of his jeans from the backs of his knees. And for a brief moment, I have an unobstructed view of his face. Damon Cruz.

Damon Cruz is a day student—at least, was. He graduated in June, same as me. The term "day student" at Chandler is a tricky one to get a handle on because it doesn't mean what it sounds like it means, that is, a student who spends his days at Chandler, his nights elsewhere. Not only, anyway. It also means a student who is on scholarship. When Reverend Chandler was writing the school's constitution, he included a clause stating that ten percent of the student body "must come from the community's deserving poor." At Chandler's inception, "the community's deserving poor" were, for the most part, the Polish immigrants or the children of the Polish immigrants who settled in droves in Sheldon/Charter Oak in the late nineteenth century to take jobs at the local factories, manufacturers of firearms and horseshoe nails principally. But demographics have shifted radically in the last couple of decades. Hartford is now a predominantly black city with the second-fastest-growing Puerto Rican population in the nation. Another thing it comes second in: poverty. The area's gone from working class—those factories shut their doors a long time ago—to under the underclass. So what was once a gap between the day students and the boarders is a gap no longer, it's a chasm.

There are day students, however, who manage to cross it. These students usually fit a certain profile—male, excel at a sport, come off as dangerous but not outright scary. Sex appeal doesn't hurt either. Damon could have been a crossover if he wanted. He was a star baseball player, a little standoffish, known to have a temper. His sophomore year, he punched a rival player in the face during a game, earning himself the nickname Demon and a two-week suspension from the team. (The incident received a fair amount of coverage, not just in the school paper but in the *Hartford Courant* as well. The suspension was originally for the rest of the season, then got dropped down, and there were people who felt the reduction was sending a bad message, was practically condoning hooliganism, according to one editorial.) He was good at school, too, which I knew because we were in AP calculus together for a week before a scheduling conflict forced me to switch to another section.

Apparently Damon didn't want to cross over, though. Any time I saw him on campus he was hanging out with other day students or with guys on the baseball team, a team pretty much entirely composed of day students. I remember he was going to college, UConn, the Honors Program, a popular option with smart day students since it offered a first-rate education on the comparative cheap. Was awarded an athletic scholarship, too, I think. So what's he doing back at his old high school, wasted before noon, picking a fight with some pencil-neck administrator?

I take a step toward the door, bring my eye flush against the crack. Damon's no longer pacing, is standing in front of the window now. He's placed his hands on the sill so that his weight's resting on his spread fingers. When he leans forward to look out, the muscles in his arms jump. It's tough for me to believe this guy's my age. He seems so much older—a cold, confident, hard-nosed man: thick, jet-black hair combed straight back, features that are handsome in a crude way, body that's more broad than tall, bulky through the shoulders and chest, narrow at the waist and hips.

The room's warm, and his clothes are soaked through, his wife-beater forming a second skin. Looking at it, I have a sudden memory. A girl on the tennis team, Sass Van Doren, saying something I couldn't hear to Nica when Damon walked by the courts in his fitted baseball pants one afternoon during practice, her low tone and sly grin making me understand that her words were lewd and complimentary. Nica turned her eyes to him, then said, "Rough trade, too rough for me," and went back to hitting serves. At the time, I was more focused on her remark, this cool deadpan sexual appraisal of a guy she didn't even know, the style and swagger of it, the offhandedness of its delivery, the weight of experience behind it, than I was the object of it. Watching him now, though, it's easy for me to see what she meant.

"Is there something I can help you with?"

I turn, blink into the sharp-eyed stare of Mrs. Waugh. I shake my head and start walking away. Behind me I hear her clicking her tongue reproachfully, then the sound of Mr. Flynn's door being whammed shut.

I return to my seat at the coffee table, bury my face back in the *Handbook*. A few minutes later, Mrs. Lefcourt calls my name.

The audiovisual department that I'll be running is less a department, as it turns out, than it is a room, is less a room than it is a cavern, dusty and windowless, in the far corner of Burroughs's basement. As Ms. Sedgwick shows me around, wrinkling her nose at the dank subterranean air, the clusters of mouse—fingers crossed mouse—droppings on the floor, the shelves stacked with DVDs and VHS tapes, she instructs me on my duties, which are pretty basic: a teacher or student requests a movie or documentary or television series, I deliver it along with the equipment necessary to play it. We spend some time pretending there's more to the job than that. We can only pretend for so long, though. And finally, she leaves me on my own.

I wait until I hear her footsteps fade, then I start whatever DVD's already in the machine so it'll sound like I'm doing something, curl up on a cleanish patch of floor, the phone within easy reach in case any orders come in. Before the FBI warning about piracy has cleared the screen, I'm asleep.

At two thirty I'm awoken by the tolling of the bell in Amory Chapel, signaling the end of the academic day. I stand up and stretch, turn off the TV, the screen glowing blackly, the DVD having played out long ago, and begin gathering together my stuff. I'd meant to stop by Shep Howell's office on my lunch hour, which I'd obviously slept through. No big deal, I tell myself. I'll stop by on my lunch hour tomorrow. Speaking of lunch, I notice that I'm hungry for the first time since last night. I'm thinking I'll just grab something from the kitchen when I go back home, pick up my car. Then I remember the linguine with clam sauce on the bottom shelf of the fridge, and my stomach does a slow roll. I decide to swing by the Student Center instead.

The snack bar's packed, the line snaking practically out the door. I step to the end of it and look around, surprised at how few of the faces are familiar. I shouldn't be surprised, I suppose, because, apart from Nica and Maddie, I never paid much attention to anybody younger. There is one person, though, I do recognize right away: Jamie. He's standing by the far wall, long-boned and slouchy, hip cocked against the foosball table, eating an ice cream sandwich and talking to Mr. Tierney.

Mr. Tierney runs the ceramics and woodworking studio and is resident faculty in Minot. He's a good-looking guy, young, only a couple years out of Oberlin. Is popular with his students, particularly the girls, and every term he seems to strike up a special friendship with one of them. Nica was a recent enthusiasm. The spring she died she was spending most of her free periods hanging out in the basement of Knox, working on her 3-D Studio Art project—a giant pinwheel with neon plastic curls and a bugged-out eyeball at the center.

When Nica broke up with Jamie and was cagey as to why, Jamie got it in his head that Mr. Tierney was the reason. He talked about it obsessively during our late-night telephone conversations. I saw the logic of his thinking: Nica, who was never close-mouthed, was close-mouthed; close-mouthed then not for herself, for another, another whose job was possibly on the line. Still, though, I doubted Nica and Mr. Tierney actually were involved. There was something about Mr. Tierney that rubbed me the wrong way—an insincerity, acting as if he didn't know how cute he was, how excited the girls would get when he'd sit behind them at the pottery wheel, cover their hands with his. Nica had better taste than that. Jamie began watching Mr. Tierney, spying on him, basically, which is how Jamie found out that Mr. Tierney *was* having an illicit affair, just not with Nica. With Mrs. Bowles-Mills, wife of Mr. Mills, Chandler's CFO and general counsel. One night Jamie followed Mr. Tierney out of the dorm, spotted him sneaking in the back door of the Millses' house when Mr. Mills was out of town on a fund-raising trip. After that, Jamie's suspicions subsided, at least as far as Mr. Tierney was concerned.

And it sure looks like Jamie and Mr. Tierney are on okay terms now. Jamie is laughing at something Mr. Tierney's saying. And when Mr. Tierney's name is called by Mr. Wallace—the only teacher at Chandler younger than he is, as of last year not even a teacher, a teaching assistant in the English Department—to let him know his toasted bagel's ready, he squeezes Jamie's shoulder before strolling up to the counter.

Jamie stays by the foosball table. A television monitor is above his head, scrolling the intramural sports schedule across its screen, and he aims his delicate, red-rimmed eyes at it as he licks melted ice cream off his knuckles. He's wearing a yellow polo shirt, the one with the rip in the underarm, faded jeans. This is the first time I've seen him since I weaned myself off drugs. And as I watch him, I get that old familiar feeling—the quickening of my senses, the shifting of my weight to my toes, the dizzy rush I associate with going from sitting to standing too fast—and realize that the medication functioned for me like a string of garlic. It protected me from his beauty, warded it off. Now I'm once again defenseless before it.

It's not that Jamie's all I ever think about. Or that I'm never interested in other guys, never get crushes. I do get crushes. Geoff Holzheimer, sophomore year. Caleb Knapp and Tony Chen, junior year. Corey Worman, senior year. Sometimes my crushes even get crushes back, and I wind up pressed up against one of them in the darkened corner of a party, or stretched out beneath one of them on the cramped seat of a car. These encounters, though, always end up feeling—not wrong, that's an overstatement, but not totally right, either. As if I'm settling or compromising. And before things can go too far, I slip away, pretend not to notice the baffled looks on their faces, the hurt sound in their voices as they call after me. With Jamie, though, there's nothing I don't like, no part of him I have to second-guess or make excuses for. He's the ideal, the supreme paragon, the one to whom I'm comparing everybody else.

Without making a conscious decision to do so, I step out of line, start walking toward him.

I'm halfway across the room when my stride falters. I missed her before because the foosball table was blocking my view, but there she is—Maddie—sitting at a computer in the row of computers. Buds are in her ears, and she's watching what appears to be a music video. Her eyes are on it, not me, but from the way she's smiling—lips curving up in a sort of smirk-snarl—I'd say that I've already been spotted. No turning back now.

I reach Jamie, am standing directly in front of him. He doesn't notice me, though, his gaze still stuck to the screen, now displaying the fall arts calendar. I touch him lightly on the wrist. He turns, looks down at me, lips parted, eyes glazed. Blink. Blink. Blink.

"Hi, Jamie," I say.

A single hard blink. Then, "Grace, whoa, hey. You're not at Williams."

"No, I left," I say. And when he doesn't say anything back, "Not ready to do my own laundry yet, I guess," and smile weakly.

He nods to himself a couple times, absorbing this information. "You left. Wow. Okay. That's a little, uh, drastic."

"Yeah."

"So you're back at Chandler. Not as a student, though, right?"

I explain to him my new position.

"What, like tapes and DVDs and stuff?" he says, when I'm done. "Nice, nice." He leans over, and with a supple twist, plucks a bud from Maddie's ear. Through the hole in his shirt, I see a flash of blond underarm hair, a shade darker than the hair on his head. "Hey, did you hear about Grace?"

Maddie turns to me with an expression I recognize, dread: taunting time. I feel her eyes running over my face and body with gleeful dislike, looking for something to find fault with, make fun of. "Did I hear what about Grace?" she says.

He tells her what I told him.

She releases a snort of air, letting him know what she thinks of the job, of the A/V department, of me in general. Then she says, "So you dropped out of the liberal arts college ranked number one by *U.S. News & World Report*?"

"For now," I say.

70

"To come back here?"

"For now," I say again.

A beat. And then Maddie says, "Are you retarded?"

"You should be nice to her, Maddie," Jamie warns. "She's the one you'll be renting your porn from this year."

"Nobody rents porn anymore," she says, then reinserts the bud, turns back to the computer screen.

Jamie looks at me, shrugs. "Some people still do."

"So," I say, relaxing now that Maddie's attention's off me, "where's Ruben? Detention already?" Last spring Ruben didn't get into a single school he applied to, so he decided to do a PG year like Jamie.

"You didn't hear? He's at Trinity. Got in off the wait list."

"His dad promise to buy a wing for the library or something?"

Jamie laughs. "It was for the science center. And not a dinky little wing either, a whole new building." He lifts his backpack off the floor, balances it on the flat of an upraised thigh as he unzips the front pocket. A zebra-striped Bic—he and Nica bought them together—falls out. Seeing it gives me a pang. It was an object I'd always coveted: cheaply cool, mysteriously cool, cool but in a way not everyone would pick up on, and thus ultracool. I'd looked everywhere for hers. So far, though, no luck.

Jamie scoops up his, continues rifling through the pocket, pushing aside a ballpoint pen, a folded-up class schedule, the Altoids tin he stores his joints in, finally coming to a bottle of Flintstones vitamins. "I'm trying to improve my eating habits," he says, as he unscrews the cap. "You want?"

I hold out my hand. He pours a couple onto it.

"Who'd you get?" he asks.

"A Fred and two Wilmas."

He leans over my palm, squints. "Those are Bettys, not Wilmas. Wilma's got the bun."

"Oh."

For a minute or so we just chew, grinding the human- and dinosaur-shaped pellets into a sweet, gritty paste that coats our molars and tongues. This is the most relaxed conversation I've had with him since before Nica died, remarkable for being so totally unremarkable, both of us keeping it light, staying on the surface. And I'm reluctant to ruin it by dredging up something dark and heavy and out of the past. But I feel I need to speak while I have the chance, will regret it if I don't. Checking first to make sure that Maddie's ears are still blocked, I place my hand on his arm and say, "Listen, I've been meaning to apologize to you."

I can feel him pulling away from me even though he doesn't move. "For what?"

"For how I acted at your party this summer."

"Yeah, you seemed a little . . ." His eyes shift, flick off into the distance.

I drop my hand. "Yeah, I was and more than a little. I'm sorry for what I put you through. I know how creepy what I did was."

He sighs. "It was creepy, but, no, you don't have to apologize for it or explain it or anything."

"But I'd like to try because—"

"No, really, Grace, don't. It was a rough time. No one knows how rough better than me."

"For me, it's still rough," I say, my voice small.

He kicks the leg of the foosball table with the toe of his sneaker. "Yeah, for me, too," he says, his voice just as small. Then he looks back at me. Our eyes hook into each other, and for a long moment neither one of us speaks.

And then the spell's broken by the sharpness of Maddie's tone: "Jamie, field hockey tryouts are about to start. I'm captain. I'm supposed to oversee. We need to get going." On the word *we,* she touches his arm, the bare part of the bicep just below his shirt sleeve, with the short nail of her index finger.

I wonder suddenly if she's interested in him. Ruben isn't in the picture anymore, and neither, obviously, is Nica. And she and Jamie are already close, have probably grown even closer since Nica's death. I feel a swift spike of jealousy.

"Already?" he says to her.

"You said you'd walk me. Are you going to or not?" Without waiting for a response, she about-faces, begins striding across the room.

He nods at the space she just vacated, says, "All right, okay, sure. Let's roll." Then he picks up his backpack, turns to me. "Well, Grace, it was, yeah, nice running into you."

And before I can say, "You, too," he's gone, has followed Maddie through the door. I stand there, staring at nothing until a kid taps me on the shoulder, asks me if I'm going to be using the foosball table much longer. I step aside.

The line at the snack bar's still long. Instead of joining it, I walk into the hall, head for the vending machines at the far end, rooting around in my bag for loose change as I go.

The pack of Wheat Thins has just been released from its coil when I hear my name called. I turn. Standing behind me is a tall man of thirty-five or so. He's wearing bib overalls, and his blond hair, parted in the middle and so long it touches his shoulders, is held back by a pair of mirrored sunglasses. His smile is sweet and broad, from ear to ear: Shep Howell.

Shep's official position at Chandler might be guidance counselor, but fairy godmother is a more accurate job title for him where I'm concerned. Not only did he talk Williams out of axing me in the spring, he also convinced Ms. Sedgwick to hire me for the A/V department last week. So he's rescued me twice in the past six months, has gone out of his way to lend a hand. And yet, the truth is, I've never liked being around him.

He makes me uncomfortable. At least, he used to. Shep's one of those adults who seems never to have grown up, has kept the clear eye and pure heart of a child. Which, of course, is great. Only not to me for some reason. I guess I feel, felt, rather, developmentally stunted enough myself—a virgin at eighteen, for God's sake, didn't smoke or drink or do drugs!— to be put off by the quality in another. Not that I thought childlike was all there was to Shep. I knew I was missing something. Had to be. Otherwise Nica, Jamie, Maddie, and Ruben wouldn't have given him the time of day. They did, though. And this in spite of the fact that he was a hippie, a subset of humanity they normally had no patience with, tie-dyed shirts and soybeans and the word *groovy* all being things they could do without. Which made me understand that he must be cool in the same way the zebra-striped Bics were cool, as in, he shouldn't have been, but was, deeply so, only his manner of coolness wasn't visible to me no matter how hard I looked. So, as far as I was concerned, he was just yet another thing I didn't get, and I tried to be in his presence as little as possible to keep from having to pretend I did.

As I said, uncomfortable is how I used to feel around him. Well, still do feel, actually, though in a completely different way. When I got Shep to call the Williams dean on my behalf back in May, I was strung out on pills. I knew I was acting in bad faith—exploiting his pity for me, his affection for my sister, the guilt he felt at having been in Lewiston, Maine, at Bates College's Jumpstart for Juniors program the weekend she died—and that seemed like a perfectly okay thing to do. When I got him to call Mrs. Sedgwick on my behalf last week, I was stone-cold sober. I knew I was again acting in bad faith, and it didn't seem like an okay thing to do, but I was able to do it anyway because I was doing it over e-mail, no eye contact or even voice contact required. After I slept through lunch today, missed the chance to stop by his office, I'd told myself I'd get to it tomorrow. Seeing him now, though, feeling the floodgates of guilt and shame opening inside my chest, I realize that I was never going to get to it. Not tomorrow or the next day or the day after that. Not voluntarily.

We stand there, facing each other. I've been smiling back at him for so long now that the air has dried my teeth and my lips are sticking to them.

At last he says, "Miss lunch?", pointing his chin at the Wheat Thins pack in my hand.

My "Yes" back is absurdly eager.

"On purpose or by accident?"

"The second thing. No windows in the A/V Department. Easy to lose track of time."

"That's right. The A/V Department's not on the main floor. You don't mind that you're spending most of your day in a basement, do you?"

"I like being underground. It suits my mood," I say, realizing a second after I say it that this could be interpreted as a complaint rather than a joke—a complaint disguised as a joke, even worse.

He nods at me seriously. "The link between emotional health and social setting has been well documented."

I hesitate, then risk it. "Or antisocial setting, in my case."

There's a long silence in which he stares at me and blinks. I begin to panic: another joke he doesn't get. He's going to think I'm an ingrate, not to mention a bitcher and moaner. I'm about to mumble an apology, explain that I haven't been sleeping much and it's making me weird, not fit for human company, when a burst of laughter blows out his mouth. Then a second burst. Soon his head is thrown all the way back and he's laughing and laughing. Finally he wipes his eyes and claps me on the shoulder. "Wow, Grace, I can't tell you how nice it is to have another Baker on staff at Chandler."

Pleased, I say, "Oh, well, thanks."

"It wouldn't feel right starting a school year without one, you know?"

I hear these words and, all of a sudden, I can't hear anything else. A sweat breaks out under my arms, behind my knees, on the palm that holds the strap of my bag. Within seconds I'm in the middle of a full-blown flashback.

After Nica's murder was solved and the stench of scandal grew less pronounced, the Chandler administration discovered it had another smelly problem on its hands: us, me and my parents. We drifted around campus, faces pinched and sallow, clothes billowy since we scarcely remembered to eat; and not eating enough meant we gave off an odor, the bad-breath putrid stink of bodies consuming themselves. People at school pitied us, but the pity was soon mixed with revulsion, so they looked down on us, as well. Anger was in there also, because their sense of duty obligated them to at least try to do right by us, wouldn't let them just abandon us as they surely wanted to. I think, at bottom, they found us morbid. I can understand why. We *were* morbid. We were beyond morbid. We were ghouls, going about our daily routines, alive yet lifeless—sordid, unwholesome, obscene, crimes against nature.

And Chandler was stuck with us. Well, not with me. I was headed off to college. With Mom and Dad, though. Between them they'd racked up nearly forty years of service, would have to give the administration one seriously good excuse to get rid of them.

So they went ahead and did.

Mom held it together at first, arriving at the art studio on time, keeping up with her teaching responsibilities, but then she began calling in sick two, three days a week, and when she did appear, she would dismiss her classes halfway through the period. And Dad started to develop a reputation for serious weirdness. Stuff he normally did, like pounding the back of a student struggling for an answer, as if the number or equation were caught in the kid's throat like a fishbone, would go on for too long or, worse, would turn into a hug that also went on for too long, until the kid said, "At least buy me dinner first, Mr. Baker," or "Hey, Mr. Baker, I can't breathe!"—something to snap him out of it. A couple of complaints were lodged and—voilà—the administration had all the ammunition it needed.

Chandler was generous in triumph, though, I'll give the school that. Mom and Dad were each offered a severance package that included a full year's pay, excellent references, and assistance in searching for a new position. The catch was, both had to accept or neither could. And if either did decline, both would be forced to take a one-year unpaid leave of absence. "A grief sabbatical," it was called.

That my parents would acquiesce to Chandler's wishes seemed a foregone conclusion. No way could they afford not to generate income for that long. Besides, a clean slate was probably just the thing for them, and for the school. It was in everybody's best interest that they say yes.

Which, apparently, was not a compelling enough reason for my mom to do so. The fight between her and Dad over her answer was an epic battle that lasted from the day the offer was presented in mid-May to the day their response was due on the first of June, the final day of the school year. I should say, in the interest of full disclosure, that I was well into my drug phase at this point, and I more felt the quivering mouths and hostile glances, the barbed words and tense silences, than saw or heard them. I was on my dad's side, of course. Not that I was much of an asset in my narcotized state. Not that I would have been much of an asset in any state. Not against my mom. She was too determined to get her own way. And I certainly wasn't surprised when I found out that she'd won and that the severance packages had been turned down. The only surprise was that Dad had managed to hold out as long as he did.

Two days after Mom declared victory, she was gone, off to some artists' commune. A fellowship she'd applied for at the beginning of the year had come through. Six months of room and board, plus a living stipend. It was just so typical of her. She'd made her point, her grand gesture, happy to fuck herself if she could fuck Chandler, too—who cared if she was also fucking my dad?—then ducked the consequences, left that part, the no-fun drudgery part, to him.

Shep must sense the movement of my thoughts because

78

he suddenly turns pale. "Oh, Grace," he says, raising a hand to his mouth. "I'm so sorry."

"That's okay," I say quickly.

"I didn't mean to upset you."

"No, I know you didn't." And I do know he didn't, but he did, and I feel angry at him for it, then angry at myself for feeling angry at him. "It's my own fault," I say. "I have to learn to be less sensitive. It's just"—and here my voice falters, tears sting my eyes—"the thought of my parents, of my mom, really, gets me riled up and weird."

He starts to say something, then just nods his understanding.

"I'm not kidding," I say. "All I have to do is think of her, and I go cross-eyed, basically."

Softly, "Yeah, I'm sure you do. I mean, I get it, Grace."

I drag my sleeve across my eyes, try to smile. "Of course you do. You're a guidance counselor. You know how it is between mothers and daughters. All those petty jealousies and pent-up resentments, arguments about missed curfews and wire hangers."

"Is that how it is between you and your mom?" he says.

I feel another kick of anger at him for not allowing me to make fun of my situation, lighten the mood, for insisting on speaking the language of the inner self at all times.

He watches me pick at a loose thread on my shirt. Then he says, "Does she know you deferred admission at Williams for a year?"

"If she knows, it's not from me. The reason I gave the school was family emergency so maybe someone in the admissions office contacted her."

"You haven't heard from her then?"

My no is hard, sharp, short.

"Has your dad?"

A sullen shrug. "You'd have to ask him. We don't really talk about her. I'm sure she's fine, though."

"I'm sure she is."

Shep and I stand silent for a while, long enough for my guilt to reawaken. Why do I keep directing my anger at him? He hasn't done anything wrong, is just trying to help. I take a deep breath, let it out slowly. "Anyway," I say, once more attempting a smile, "what you said before isn't true. I won't be the only Baker on staff at Chandler this year. My dad's bartending at the downtown Holiday Inn nights, but he's SAT tutoring here in the afternoons."

"Speaking of afternoons, what are you going to be doing with yours? The A/V room closes before three. You want me to put my feelers out, see if any of the coaches are looking for an assistant? I'm sure you could use the extra cash."

"I appreciate the offer. I really do. I think I'm all right, though."

"Okay," he says, but I see the look of worry in his eyes.

"Honestly, I am."

"You know best, Grace, obviously. I just feel like it might not be good for you to have too much free time on your hands, time to brood, think about things."

"No, I mean, all right as in I've got a lead on a second job. Like you said, I could use the extra cash."

That ear-to-ear smile again. "Well done, you! Jobs are tough to come by these days. Especially in Hartford."

"I don't have the job yet. I'm heading over there this afternoon for an interview. In fact"—I twist my neck to read the face of his watch—"if I don't get going, I'll be late."

"Then I guess you better get going."

I nod, grateful to have a legitimate, non-trumped-up excuse to end the conversation.

"Good luck," he says, as I start off down the hall. He says something else, too, but it doesn't make it across the growing gap between us.

I throw a wave over my shoulder. Then, pushing the bar on the door, I step outside.

# CHAPTER SEVEN

Fargas Bonds is located in Blue Hills, the worst neighborhood in a town full of bad ones. The building it's housed in, which also contains a liquor store and a Check N' Go, looks like the kind that's only standing because it's too much trouble to tear down—moldy blue-green paint peeling from the cracked concrete, bars on all the windows, fast-food wrappers trapped in the knobby branches of the bushes out front. Above the door is a neon sign that says OPEN 24 HOURS, next to it a handwritten one that says HELP WANTED.

I get out of the car. On my way to the curb, I step over a shattered pint bottle and a used condom, floating bloated and corpse-like in a puddle of drain run-off. I start to wonder if maybe this isn't such a hot idea. The inside of the office, though, immediately puts my mind at ease. It's nothing like the sleazy outside. In fact, it's sort of homey, like walking into someone's living room. Behind the receptionist's desk is a shelf lined with knickknacks: a box of dominoes, a shot glass filled with toothpicks that are also Puerto Rican flags, a photo of a grinning kid in a Little League uniform. In the far corner is a minifridge, a Mr. Coffee machine, a potted fern not doing too badly.

I think that I'm alone, that the receptionist must have ducked out, gone to the bathroom or something, but then I hear, coming from behind a closed door, the faint, stutter-step sound of hunt-and-peck typing. "Hello?" I say. "Mr. Fargas?"

"In here!" a voice calls out.

I don't know what I'm expecting to see when I open the door, what image of a bail bondsman I'm carrying around in my head, but whatever it is, the person sitting at the desk doesn't match it. He's a neat, quiet-looking Latin guy in his late forties or early fifties. Clean-shaven, dark suit, no tie, reading glasses. A little heavy in the gut, maybe, but heavy in the shoulders, too. He's poking at the keyboard of a computer with two index fingers.

"I'm just finishing filling out a Power of Attorney form," he says, eyes on the keyboard. "Have a seat. I'll be right with you."

I lower myself into a chair. Eyes still on the keyboard, the man nudges a bowl of Hershey's Miniatures toward me. I take a couple to be polite, slip them in my bag. Slip, too, one of the business cards stacked on a metal tray at the desk's edge. BONDS, FARGAS BONDS, it says, followed by a phone number and an e-mail address.

Finally, the man hits the Return button, looks up. "Thanks for waiting," he says. "Let me tell you how we work. We accept collateral in the form of—"

"Actually, Mr. Fargas—"

"Max."

"Max," I say, "I'm here about a job. I saw your advertisement."

"You mean, on the door?"

"No, on Craigslist. I called yesterday, talked to a woman, she said to come by at three. Actually, she said to come by any time after three."

"That must have been my assistant, Renee. So, I have an advertisement on Craigslist?"

I nod.

"Huh," he says, his voice taking on a thoughtful tone. "What does it say?"

"Not much. Just that you need someone from three P.M. on. And that a driver's license is necessary, but experience isn't."

"Oh." He takes off his reading glasses, folds them, tucks them in his breast pocket. "Are you available after three?"

"Yes."

"Do you have a driver's license?"

"Yes."

"Then congratulations. The job's yours." When I ignore the hand he's holding out to me, "What, you don't want it?"

"It's not that I don't want it. It's just, I still don't know what it is."

"And I'd pay you a dollar over minimum wage, under the table."

"Pay me for doing what, though, exactly?"

"Nothing for me. What you'd be doing, you'd be doing for my nephew."

"Okay."

"My nephew works for me, as a runner mostly. Usually he's a smart guy, very responsible. But a couple months back, he got tanked, decided it would be a good idea to go for a spin. He smashed up his car, smashed up his leg, lost his license for six months. Renee's been taking him around all summer, but starting next week she's got to pick up her kid after school, so she can only take him around till three."

"So, what," I say, "I'd be like his afternoon chauffer?"

"And sometimes evening."

"When would you want me to start?"

"Today. Now."

This time when he holds out his hand, I shake it. As I do, a sound comes from the front room: a door opening, and two voices talking—one male, one female.

"That's him," Max says, his face lighting up. "Renee, too." He calls out, "Hey, come in here, both of you. I want to introduce you to the newest member of our team."

The woman, Renee, is through the door first. She's fortyish, blond, a little chubby, in black jeans as tight as leggings. She's smiling at me nicely, though. And right behind her is Damon Cruz. He's peeling the lid off a cup of coffee, head down. By the time he raises it, he's almost walked into me. He stops short, freezes, his face only inches from my own. Up close I notice all sorts of things I missed earlier: the grit of beard, a day or two's worth, on his cheeks and jaw, the faint smattering of acne scars near his hairline, the bridge of his nose, slightly crooked, like the bone had been broken and then inexpertly set. It's a tough face, a face that matches up with the wife-beater and the muscles, the morning drinking and the pulpy mouth. There's one thing on the face that doesn't match up, though. The eyes. They aren't hooded, and they aren't hard and black, the kind that give back nothing when you look into them. They're bare and a soft liquid brown.

He's staring at me, his gaze intense but not quite focused. Then he lowers his lids in a long cutoff blink. When he lifts them again, they barely come up halfway, and I realize that his eyes normally are hooded, were wide only temporarily, with surprise. The softness in them, too, is gone, if it was ever even there in the first place, if it wasn't just some trick of light.

"Damon," Max says, "this is your driver. Her name is—" He turns to me. "What's your name?"

Damon takes a casual step back. "Hi, Grace."

"Hi," I say, surprised he knows my name, though classes are small enough at Chandler that it's hard not to know everybody's.

Max's eyebrows climb his forehead. "She a friend of yours?"

"Chandler," Damon says.

"Then I can save my breath, skip the introductions." Max holds out a stack of slips. "I just approved these bonds."

"Max, I told you, I don't need a driver. Frankie doesn't start at U Bridgeport until the second week in September. He said he'd take me around."

"The second week of September is in a few days. Forget Frankie."

"Then I'll find somebody else."

"You ready to go out again?"

"But I—"

"Or do you want to ice the knee first?"

I glance down at Damon's knees, see a brace on the left one, black so that it blends in with the dark blue of his jeans, my brain going click, click, click: he wasn't lurching around Glen Flynn's office this morning because he was drunk, he was lurching around because he was hurt.

Damon shakes his head, an angry muscle twitching in his cheek, and snatches the slips from Max's hand. Without a

86

word, he turns, exits the office. For a couple beats I just stare at the coffee cup he left on Max's desk. Then I snap to, grab my bag from the back of the chair. I have to run to catch up. For a guy in a brace, he moves fast.

# CHAPTER EIGHT

That puke smell sure isn't fading in a hurry. For the rest of the afternoon I sit in my car, windows down, breathing through my mouth while Damon goes in and out of the courthouse, consults with his uncle via cell. He barely looks in my direction, doesn't say a word to me other than *left, right, stop,* and *wait*. We finish at six. He tells me to take him to the YMCA downtown.

"Okay," I say, "sure. But the equipment in Houghton's nicer."

He glares at me. "You think I don't know that?"

"So why don't you go there?"

He's silent for so long I assume he's ignoring me. But then he says, "Because the fob in my Chandler ID expired today."

"Oh yeah, I forgot. First day of the new school year. Maybe, though, an exception can be made. I mean, it's to do your rehab exercises and you were, like, the best guy on the baseball team, right?"

Another lengthy silence. And then he says, "I met with some asshole administrator who's supposed to be in charge of maintaining Chandler's buildings or operating them—some fucking thing."

Glen Flynn, Director of Facilities. So that's what Damon was doing in the Business Development Office this morning. "What did this asshole say?"

"Current students only. I told him Coach Morrissey would vouch for me, to talk to him."

"So did he?"

Damon snorts. "Said he did, left the room for twenty minutes, but I doubt it. Probably hid out in the faculty lounge."

"I can let you in with my ID. Employees are allowed to use the gym too."

"Forget it. They don't want me, they don't have to have me."

I shrug, start the car.

After dropping off Damon at the Y, I drop off myself at home. I close the door behind me, toss my keys in the bowl on the end table.

The house is quiet, the only sound the laundry tumbling around in the dryer in the basement, a button or a zipper pinging the sides of the machine every few seconds. I feel a thump of tiredness, sit down on the bottom step of the staircase. Then I feel a thump of hunger, start foraging around in my bag. Find the package of Wheat Thins and two of the Hershey's Miniatures. I begin to eat. The rhythmic motion of my jaw soothes me, puts me in a trance, and I stare straight ahead, eyes unfocused, munching, munching.

Dad's voice comes down from upstairs. "Hello?"

"It's me, Dad."

"Gracie?"

"Uh-huh." I alternate bites of chocolate with bites of cracker: sweet, salty, sweet, salty.

"Good timing, sweetheart. Dinner's just about ready."

"Do you need me to set the table?"

"Already done. Just go wash your hands. I'll be right down."

I put the last bite in my mouth but my appetite's vanished as suddenly as it appeared, and it seems like too much energy to chew or swallow. So I wait for enough spit to build, then let the lump slide down my throat. Slowly I get to my feet, walk to the kitchen.

I must have seen it a hundred times, so you'd think by now it would have lost its power, fail to affect me. But it always does. *Nica's Dream,* the black-and-white photograph of my sister hanging above the table, taking up almost the entire wall length-wise and half of it height-wise. In it, Nica, eleven, is lying in the grass in the backyard of our house, head turned away from the camera. The cutoffs she's wearing have ridden up so high you can see the pale linty lining of her pockets, the dim hollow of her groin. Her halter top's twisted around her torso, revealing her stomach, smooth and concave, stretched between the twin knobs of her hip-bones. A Band-Aid hangs off her right heel and the paint on the nail of her big toe is chipped. In spite of the fact that she's slender to the point of scrawny, totally undeveloped, her body gives off a glow, a heat that's as undeniable as it is unsettling. Maybe it's the way her mouth, greedy and carnal, is nuzzling her bare shoulder. Or the way one of her hands is tucked between her thighs, like she's in the throws of a sex dream, dreaming but somehow also dead, climaxed in death, eyes closed, neck limp, skin waxy. Her other hand loosely clutches a peach, round and dimpled and fuzzed, glossed to sinister perfection. The poisoned fruit from a fairy tale.

I remember the day the picture was taken. It was in the spring, a Sunday. Mom woke up that morning hungry for peaches. She sent dad to the farmers' market at Billings Forge. Wouldn't even let him shower first. I liked to look at the arts and crafts stands—jewelry made out of sea glass, woodcut magnets in the shapes of states and vegetables, hand-knit hats with animal faces—so I went with him. In front of a sign for eggs from free-range chickens we ran into Dr. Brewster, Chandler's headmaster, tall and elegant and silver-haired; he carried a black cane like Mr. Peanut. He and Dad started talking, a conversation full of too-long pauses and downward looks, smiles that came at the wrong time. Hoping to bring it to an end, Dad asked Dr. Brewster to stop by the house for lunch. Dr. Brewster was known to be reclusive, hardly ever socialized with faculty, so Dad wasn't expecting him to say yes. He did, though.

When Dad told Mom, his eyes wet and blinky as he unhooked the canvas tote bag from his shoulder, she put down the proof she'd been examining. Silently she watched while he and I unloaded the papayas and mangos and strawberries and apricots onto the counter. Then she turned, exited the kitchen. Mom had recently taken the job of weekend high school sports photographer for the *Farmington Valley Post* because she needed extra cash to rebuild her darkroom. Her Saturdays were now spent hopping all over Hartford County, from baseball diamond to lacrosse field to tennis court. So Sunday was her one free day, and she liked to devote it to her own work, her real work, she called it.

As she mounted the stairs, she shucked her T-shirt, no bra underneath, flung it at Dad, who was trailing her, me trailing him. He paused at the threshold of their bedroom to peel it off his face, then followed her inside. She was already ransacking the closet, small high breasts bobbing as she pushed the hangers brutally apart, kicked at the shoes in her way, knowing her half-nakedness embarrassed him, not caring, taking angry pleasure in his discomfort.

He looked at her, then at his feet, blinking rapidly, as if his eyes hurt. "I could"—hesitating, trying to figure out what he could say that would calm her, that would fix this—"call Dr. Brewster. The Chandler Directory's right in the desk drawer."

"And tell him what, Hank?" she said, eyes sharp, full of scorn. "That you just remembered the kitchen burned down? It's too late."

As she yanked something silky out of a dry-cleaning bag, she glanced up at the doorway from which I was peering behind. Now those sharp, scorn-filled eyes were on me.

Dad turned, saw me standing there, unmoving, transfixed, so vulnerable to attack I might as well have had a target painted on my face. He took two quick steps to his right so that, once again, he was at the other end of her gaze, and shielding me. "Let's go make lunch while Mom finishes getting dressed, sweetheart," he said, talking to me but looking at her. And then, hand in hand, we backed slowly into the hall.

Dad barely ate or spoke the entire meal. Just sat there, gripping his fork, blinking like a nervous dog. He was waiting for Mom to act up—to pout or sneer or give monosyllabic answers, signal in some way to his boss and hers that the invitation had been extended against her wishes. I knew she wouldn't do any of those things, though. Not for reasons of self-preservation, which, as far as she was concerned, weren't reasons at all, but for reasons of pride: she'd never let an outsider see her anger. And while she hated to be social, she was extremely good at it when she wanted to be, and that day, as it so happened, she did.

Early afternoon turned into late afternoon turned into later afternoon and, when Dr. Brewster finally left, bending deeply over Mom's hand to press his lips to it, saying something to her in French in a low tone, the smile died on her face and she sagged against the back of the door. "The day's almost gone," she wailed. And as she brushed past me I could feel her frustration, hot and urgent, surging through her body, coming off her skin, scorching mine.

She grabbed her Leica and rushed outside to the daffodils blooming at the base of the tree in the backyard, the ones she'd been photographing since they'd appeared three weeks before. The pictures were failures so far, she'd said, and had torn them all up, though I loved them—the extreme close-ups of the flowers' eyes, beady and jaundiced, the whorls in their petals as distinctive as fingerprints, and, in the corner of the frame, the roots of the tree, gnarled and big-knuckled and scarred-looking, rising up out of the earth like a zombie hand.

Mom went through her usual routine: adjusting a leaf, straightening a stalk, coaxing one blossom forward, pushing another back, then appraising the composition as a whole, waiting for the light to get the way she wanted it, bringing her lens in tight. But, after twenty or so manic clicks of the shutter, she stopped. Stumbling over to the porch, she sank onto the top step.

I'd followed her outside, was reading on a blanket a few yards away. From behind my book I watched her. She didn't move. For five minutes. Ten minutes. A quarter of an hour. Finally I slid on my flip-flops, crossed the grass so that I was standing in front of her. Her eyes were shut and her face was less like a face than a mask: beautiful and sculpted and cold. I put my hand on her arm, knowing she disliked to be touched but needing reassurance, proof that she only looked lifeless. She twitched under my fingertips. Relieved, I held out my book to her. "I only have fifty pages left and I started last night. See?"

"Why don't you show your father, Grace," she said, her voice coming out a raspy whisper. "I have a headache."

"Should I get you an aspirin?"

"No thank you."

She was answering me, politely even. And I knew I shouldn't push my luck, should leave her alone. I couldn't, though. She was unhappy and I felt her emotions too keenly to do nothing. "What about a cold facecloth for your forehead?" I said. "I could go inside and get you one."

This time she didn't answer. Just shook my hand off her arm.

Dad appeared behind the screen door, a dishtowel tucked in the waist of his pants. "Everything all right?"

"Mom doesn't feel well."

He exchanged an uneasy glance with me, then stepped out onto the porch. "Claire, honey, why don't you lie down? You can take pictures next weekend." When there was no response, "You didn't eat a bite at lunch. I could make you something. Anything." After a pause, he said, "Or you could just have some of the fruit I bought. I washed all of it. I know you wanted peaches but I spoke with one of the farmers and apparently there was a frost at the beginning of the month, which means that peach season will be delayed a few weeks." His laugh came out a stutter. "There was nothing I could do."

Again no response.

I said to Dad, "I don't think she cares about peaches anymore. I think she just wants to be by herself."

He nodded, but didn't move. I could tell he had the same need I did, to touch her, make sure. He didn't dare, though. The sight of him standing there, doing that blinking-dog thing, hands dangling uselessly at his sides, made me so mad I had to look away.

And then Nica came bounding out of the kitchen, the screen door banging shut three times behind her. "Who doesn't care about peaches anymore?" she said.

She'd changed out of the cotton sundress she'd worn at lunch into a halter top and cutoffs, her feet bare, an old Band-Aid stuck to her heel, chaffed from a pair of too-tight soccer cleats. An iPod knockoff was in one hand, a can of the pineapple chunks she liked to drink the juice from in the other. She looked at the three of us. I watched her as understanding dawned, the fun going out of her eyes, the smile disappearing back into her face. She placed the iPod knockoff on the flat part of the porch railing, the pineapple can, also. Then, biting her thumb joint, she retracted her head, a small roll of baby fat swelling under her chin as she decided something. Mind made up, she threw herself down on the bottom step, inserted herself roughly between Mom's legs and slumped backward. "Scratch my frog's belly," she demanded, thrusting out her arm, twisting it so that its pale underside was exposed.

I waited for Mom to grimace in pain or push Nica away. But she did neither. Instead she opened her eyes, and, lips turning up at the corners, began running her nails lightly across Nica's skin.

After a bit, Dad withdrew. I did, too, went back to my

blanket. Why stay? I wasn't needed. Nica was there. She was taking care of the situation, rescuing Mom from despair. It seemed like she already had.

As it turned out, though, rescuing Mom wasn't so easy. Not that day. Not even for Nica.

I watched the two of them, the book in my hand nothing but a prop. Nica had moved to a patch of grass in front of Mom. Was trying, with increasing desperation, to entertain her, hold her attention. She began turning cartwheels and somersaults and handsprings, doing her best to avoid the croquet wicket sticking up out of the ground, rusted over and warped from being left outside all winter. Kept telling Mom to *look! look!* and Mom would look but only for a second, then her eyes would close again. And pretty soon, she stopped opening them altogether. I stopped looking, too. Became absorbed in my book for real.

And then I heard the same plea I'd been hearing for the better part of twenty minutes. The same plea but sounding different, like it was coming from farther away. Or higher up. I raised my head from my book, and, sure enough, there was Nica in the tree, technically peach, though we'd never fertilized it or irrigated it or pruned or thinned it, done any of the things you're supposed to do if you want it to actually yield fruit, so that the most it ever produced was a few wizened-looking nuggets that birds and insects got to before we did. Nica was balancing on a branch that was about a quarter of the way up, a bird feeder hanging from it. When she saw I was looking, she waved and began to climb.

At first I didn't understand what she was doing. And then my gaze traveled higher, beyond her. That's when I saw it: on the outermost limb of the uppermost branch a single peach, round and fat and a creamy pinkish gold. Nica, I realized, was going to pick it for Mom.

I opened my mouth to yell at her, order her to come down, but no words emerged, no sounds at all. She continued to ascend, her pace not slackening even though she was nearing the top of the tree and the adrenaline fizz she'd had when she'd started must've worn off, at least a little. Finally she reached the desired branch. And there she stood, some thirty feet in the sky. Again I tried to call out to her and again I couldn't. So I ran over to Mom, shook her arm.

It took Mom a while to crack her eyes, and when she did, they were bleary and unfocused. I pointed and she reluctantly followed the line of my finger over to Nica. Instantly, the dullness fell from her face.

Behind me I heard the creak of the screen door, then Dad's footsteps. I felt his hands resting on my shoulders. The three of us watched as Nica pushed herself away from the trunk, stepped out to the middle of the branch. There was nothing for her to hold on to now. She might as well have been a tightrope walker. As the branch thinned, it began to curve under her weight, curve and curve, ready to snap at any moment, the peach still beyond her grasp. Her movements became smaller, more cautious, like the danger of what she was trying to do had finally dawned on her. At last they stopped altogether. And for a minute, maybe more, she just stood there, looking so young, limbs clumsily long, feet pigeon-toed. *Keep going*, I commanded her silently, even though I didn't see how she could without getting herself crippled or killed. *Don't stop. Don't you dare stop.* I knew from the way Dad's fingers were digging into my shoulders that he was telling her the same thing in his head. Nica's gaze dipped to the ground and, at that moment, I thought it was over, that she was going to fall to her hands and knees, cling to the branch, crawl back to the safety of the trunk.

But I was wrong. Suddenly she was in motion again, all hesitancy gone, all uncertainty. Bending neatly at the waist, she lifted one foot high in the air, and, graceful as a dancer, separated the fruit from the twig with a deft twist of her wrist. Straightening, she held the peach aloft.

I turned to Mom. Seeing the glow in her eyes, the twin spots of color burning in her cheeks, I realized that Nica had done it, had rescued her, had single-handedly pulled her out from under the despair that had descended like dirt on a coffin. Mom began to clap and cheer. At the sound, Nica, clambering down the tree, glanced over her shoulder. Her face split into a pre-braces grin—lopsided, homely, totally irresistible. All at once I felt a jealousy so raw and sharp it was almost hatred. I could hardly bear to look at her.

And it was as I was turning my eyes away, just as she'd dropped to the lowest branch, her safe passage now all but assured, that her footing faltered and she tumbled to the ground. The distance was short, not more than five or six feet, and she stood quickly, started jogging toward us, waving the peach to show that it was as undamaged as she was. Only she was damaged. She must've knocked her head against the trunk on the way down because she paused suddenly. Raising a tentative hand, she touched her crown, like she was testing to see if her hair was wet. She gazed curiously at the tips of her fingers, then held them out to us. Red, as bright and gleaming as fresh paint.

A second later, she collapsed.

At the sight Dad and I turned to stone. Mom, though, immediately leaped to her feet and began to run. I looked

98

on, completely engrossed in the scene unfolding before me, but feeling strangely apart from it, too. Everything about it—the emotional states of the players, the dramatic poses they'd struck, the chorus of cicadas, making the dying day pulsate at its edges—so high intensity and hypervivid that it seemed unreal. Like a fragment of a dream. No, like a fragment of a movie. The way Mom was holding Nica, an arm under her neck, another under her knees, Mom's downturned face inches from Nica's upturned, exquisite profile to exquisite profile, all against the backdrop of a sky stained orange-pink by the setting sun was, I realized, just like that poster of *Gone with the Wind,* the one in the lobby of the art theater in New Haven that Mom took us to when she wanted to see something old or with subtitles.

Dad reached for my hand, pulled me out of my trance. By the time we got to Mom and Nica, Nica's eyes had already opened and Mom was laying her tenderly down on the grass, parting her hair to look at the wound.

"What happened?" Nica said, her voice dazed-sounding.

"You hit your head, baby."

"I did?"

"You're going to have a big bump."

"Am I bleeding?"

"No, baby. No blood."

"But I'm dizzy."

"I'll bet you are. Now, I want you to stay still. Just lie there."

Nica started to protest, raising herself up on one arm. Mom leaned over and pressed Nica's mouth with her own, as though to stop its movement. The kiss was soft and brief, but it pushed Nica back to the ground.

Mom stood, began walking rapidly toward the house. She

turned around to shout, "I mean it, do not move. I'll be right back."

When the screen door shut, Nica again stuck out an arm, tried to raise herself. Dad crouched down, gently put his hand to her shoulder. "You heard your mother, sweetheart. No moving."

"But there's a pebble digging into my back."

"Ignore it. You lost consciousness for a few seconds. We just want to make sure you're all right."

Nica sighed, but she was enjoying being fussed over. I could tell.

"And no more peach picking for you," Dad said. "You could have broken your neck."

Nica's eyes, suddenly bright with worry, scanned his face. "That's what she wanted, though, isn't it? A peach?"

Something shifted in Dad's mouth. He nodded, looked away.

I dropped beside her. "Does it hurt?"

"No," she said, but I knew she was lying by her tone—too cool. Her hair was spread out around her head like a dark halo, framing her face, so pale I could see the thin blue veins running under her chin, up to her ears. Shame at my earlier envy welled up inside me, jammed in my throat, making it difficult to breathe.

Nica tugged on the cuff of Dad's pant leg until he looked down at her again. "Where'd Mom go?"

"Into the house to get you an ice pack."

But when Mom came out of the house a minute later, it wasn't an ice pack she was carrying. It was a roll of film.

Dad watched her as she switched the old film out of her camera, replaced it with the new. "What are you doing, Claire?" he said.

"I'm just going to take a few shots."

"Pictures? Now? She could really be hurt."

Mom, busy working the rewind crank, didn't say anything back.

"At the very least she has a concussion."

"Oh, Jesus, Hank," Mom said, yanking on the film, pulling it taut. "Don't be such a drama queen. She doesn't have a concussion. She just banged her head a little. It's a bruise, nothing more."

"She needs to go to the emergency room."

"And I'll take her to the emergency room. Afterward. All I need is ten minutes."

"I think we should take her now. Leaving her lying on the damp ground like this makes me"—he paused, blinked—"anxious."

Mom released the shutter, then cocked it, her movements jerky with impatience. "*Anxious*. What a finky shitty little word. *Anxious*. If you mean scared, say scared."

"All right. It scares me."

"What difference is ten minutes going to make? They never let you in to see a doctor right away. It usually takes hours."

"Claire," he said softly, pleading.

"What?" Her eyes were flat, hard, showing no mercy.

"I'm fine, Dad," Nica said. Her voice sounded different than it did a minute ago. Wearier. Older, too.

Dad straightened, stepped back from her so that he was standing next to me. "Are you sure?"

"Yeah. Let Mom take the pictures."

"Five minutes, that's it."

Dad reached for my hand again and we returned to the house. While he finished washing the dishes from lunch, I ate the tomato soup he heated up for me and did my homework

101

at the kitchen table, watching Mom and Nica from the window. Mom wanted Nica to look the way she did when she first collapsed. At least I assume that's what Mom wanted because she dropped to her knees to reposition the peach in Nica's palm, to lower Nica's eyelids with the tips of her fingers. Then she began to shoot. The sight of her crouched over Nica's small crumpled form, the camera jutting out of her head like a horn, caused a tightening in my chest that I could ease only by opening my mouth and looking away. Which is exactly what I did until Mom started calling Dad's name. Nica, it seemed, had slipped back into unconsciousness during the session, lasting not five minutes, as Mom had promised, but three times that—four times—and probably would have gone on even longer if the final drops of light hadn't drained from the day.

Nica came to quickly. After that, though, Mom was as eager as Dad to get her to the emergency room. It was what Dad thought: a concussion. Minor, the doctor said. But it didn't seem too minor when Nica, in the months following, suffered from migraines so severe they made her throw up and was often unable to sleep through the night. Still, the headaches stopped eventually. So did the sleeplessness. And besides, cranial trauma was a small price to pay. *Nica's Dream* was taken during that twilight shoot, and it turned out to be Mom's first real photograph.

For a long time, though—years, in fact—Mom did nothing with *Nica's Dream*. Then last summer, on a whim, she sent it in to *B&W Magazine*. It won the Silver Award in the Single Image Contest and received a full page in the fall issue. Soon after that New York took notice. A woman with a gallery on West Twentieth, not quite an established gallery but more than up-and-coming, called and asked to see other samples of her work, then called again and offered her a solo exhibition; it was set to open in November.

I'm not sure why Mom sat on the picture for so long. Was scared of how good it was maybe. Thought it was a fluke. Nica, though, she knew was no fluke. In her youngest daughter Mom had found what she'd been searching for since the day she picked up her mom's Brownie Instamatic at age eleven: her muse and one true subject, the thing she was put on this earth to photograph.

And photograph Nica she did. Constantly. Compulsively. And Nica, selfish, imperious, didn't-give-two-shits Nica, let her. Nica would pose for Mom anytime. No matter what she was doing—Super-Glueing captions to a posterboard for her Ice Mummies of the Inca World project in her bedroom, watching a slasher movie with me (me through the chinks in my fingers) in the family room, baking chocolate chip cookies from scratch with Dad in the kitchen—she'd drop it as soon as Mom reached for the camera. Even when she turned into a teenager and her social life became more absorbing, she wouldn't think twice about telling Jamie he'd have to smoke that bag of Quebec Gold all by himself or sending Maddie off alone to some dive bar with a lax ID policy if Mom said she felt like working. Mom and Mom's needs came first, always.

This isn't to say that it was all smooth sailing between the two of them, that they never fought. They did fight, loudly and often. But fighting for them didn't necessarily mean conflict. It was just how they related. Was part of their ritual, something they'd do before almost every session. They fought, I think, for the same reasons other people meditated: because it relaxed them, helped them relieve tension so they could better focus.

There were only two times I remember the relationship becoming truly contentious. The first was when Mom decided to start taking candid shots of Nica in addition to posed. I should rephrase: the first was when Mom decided to start taking candid shots of Nica in addition to posed and didn't bother to tell Nica, never mind ask for her consent.

I was there the moment Nica found out.

I was fifteen, so she would've been fourteen, a freshman. Mom and Dad were out for the night. I was making a peanut-butter sandwich in the kitchen during the commercial break before the final round of *Jeopardy!* A scream came up from the darkroom in the basement. Nica followed it seconds later, holding a print with the clothespin still attached, and not delicately by the edges, the way she was supposed to; holding it like it was a slice of pizza, folding it in half so it was creased down the middle.

"Mom's going to kill you for going in the darkroom without her permission," I said, retying the plastic bread bag, returning it to the fridge.

"Look," Nica said, thrusting the print at me.

Dancing away from her, laughing, "No way. I'm not getting my fingerprints on that thing."

She thrust it at me again.

Surprised at her vehemence, I looked at her. She held my eye, hard and defiant, but there was something under the defiance, embarrassment maybe, or shame. Puzzled, I licked a smear of peanut butter off the web of my thumb, took the print from her. After smoothing it out, I glanced down, almost afraid of what I was going to see.

It was of her. She was in bed, asleep, a Dora the Explorer sheet thrown carelessly over her hip. Her bare back was to the camera. The side of her face was showing, the swell of a cheekbone and the dip of an eye socket, the eye in it closed. The side of a breast, too.

Irritated, relieved, I said, "So?"

"So?" Nica repeated incredulous.

"So you're not wearing any clothes. So big deal."

She stared at me in disbelief.

"Honestly, Nic, I don't see what you're so upset about."

Shaking her head, laughing softly, she took the print back. "I don't know why I expected you would."

Stung, I said, "You can't even see any nipple. And you've let Mom take plenty of nude shots before. You think I like knowing what your labia looks like?" After a beat, "That was a joke. You're supposed to laugh."

But she didn't even smile. "Yeah," she said, "Mom took this one without asking, though. Really took it, like stole it. I had no idea she was there."

"Of course you didn't. You were asleep."

Nica, gaze distant, tapped her front tooth with the edge of the photo.

"Look," I said, after a long pause, "if it bothers you this much, you should tell her."

"Tell her what? A bunch of stuff she should know without being told? To stop thinking it's okay to spy on me, not give me any privacy? To stop treating my life like it's her material?"

"Well, yeah."

"Would you back me if I did?"

Smiling, I said, "I think you've got it mixed up. I need your help when it comes to dealing with Mom, not the other way around."

For a time Nica was quiet, head bowed. I could see the corner of her mouth, though, and it was twitching. And I waited for her to come up with something funny-snotty to say back. But when she finally lifted her head, her eyes were shiny and wet-looking, and I realized that she'd been fighting off tears. "Mom's too much for me. I pose for her anytime she wants. All she has to do is ask. But that's still not enough for her. She wants the moments I'm alone—think I'm alone—too. She wants everything."

I was taken aback at the emotion in Nica's voice. And all at once it hit me: she really was asking me to go up against Mom with her. The idea of fighting with Mom, Nica at my side or not, filled me with a panic so total I could barely stand to feel it. I knew I should speak, tell Nica she could count on me, even though I didn't want to say any such thing, very badly didn't want to. I'd make myself, though, because, well, because she was my sister and I loved her and she needed me and because what else could I decently do? But a beat passed. And then another. And then another after that until the silence became terrible, and still I didn't break it. Finally, I cobbled a few words together in my head, opened my mouth to push them out, when her voice, small and whimpery, said, "All that'll be left of me will be teeth, fingernails, and, like, one eyeball. The victim of Peeping Mom."

I laughed, less out of amusement than relief. She was telling me with the jutted-out lower lip that her emotions weren't so dark or complicated they couldn't be expressed with a pout, telling me with the jokey pun of a nickname that Mom was a cartoon villain instead of a real one, telling me, basically, that this whole thing was a fit of pique, not a cry for help, and that I wasn't required to take any of it seriously. "Then we'd better fatten you up," I said, wrapping half my sandwich in a paper towel, passing it to her. "You know how mean Mom gets when she's hungry."

Nica placed the sandwich on the counter, said, "Thanks,"

then leaned forward and stared off into space, chin cupped in palm.

Looking at her face, at its shuttered-tight expression, I felt another surge of panic. Had I got it wrong? Blown it somehow? "You'll be okay, right?" I said.

She turned to me blankly. "Me? Yeah."

"Are you sure? Because I'm worried."

"You're *worried*?" She pulled back, looked at me almost with disgust.

Scrambling, "I know how difficult Mom can be. How she just takes over and—"

Nica cut me off. Her voice clipped and hard, she said, "Mom's a pain in the ass but she's nothing I can't handle. And, besides, since when have I ever said no to attention?" Her lips curled in a smile that never got anywhere near her eyes. "I'll have a talk with her."

"That's good," I said. "Talking's good."

"Yep."

"It's just . . ." I trailed off.

"It's just what?"

I looked at her standing there in front of me, eyes narrowed, arms folded across her chest, bristling with irritation and impatience. And I couldn't for the life of me think of a way of completing the sentence that might bridge the divide between us, make her receptive to me again. I tried, though. Said, "It's just, you talk tough but you're not. Well, you are, but you shouldn't have to be. Not around your own family, in your own house. And I was wrong to act like what Mom's doing with her camera is nothing. I do understand the difference between someone taking a naked picture of you with your okay and someone taking a naked picture of you without."

For a second Nica didn't move and I thought maybe I hadn't spoken out loud, only in my head, and then I saw something shift within her. Her face grew soft, opened up. She raised her arms, put them around me. "It's all right," she said. "I freaked a little, but Mom and I will work it out." Her face was buried in my neck as she spoke so that I felt her words at the same time I heard them.

"Yeah?" I said.

"Yeah. Everything's going to be fine. I promise."

"Okay, good. And, Nica, I'm here if you need me."

"I know that. I know you are," she said, but we were already separating.

She picked up her half sandwich and walked into the family room. And, after grabbing the bent photo, shoving it to the bottom of the trash can, I followed her.

Just as Nica predicted, she and Mom were able to work out the issue of the candids. She ended up agreeing to them, and in return Mom promised to show her any and all photos taken the moment they were developed, destroy whichever ones Nica found objectionable. The arrangement seemed to suit them both well enough. And never again was privacy violation a problem between them. In fact, as far as their artist-model relationship went, that was the last problem between them full stop.

Until the end, that is. In the weeks before Nica's death, she and Mom were fighting, and not in their usual style—open-mouthed, wet-eyed screaming fits that died down almost as soon as they flared up. These fights—this fight, rather, singular—was tight-lipped and dry-eyed, and went on and on. I steered clear, got nowhere near it, so I didn't know for certain what it was about. I could make a pretty good guess, though: the exhibition in November. Nica must have been having regrets, was wishing she'd used her veto power more freely. I could understand why. It was one thing for pictures to be taken of you acting up, showing off—smoking, drinking, screwing around—showing off body parts, too, when no one but you and the photographer who also happened to be your mother were looking. Quite another when the audience was a gallery full of cool-eyed strangers, city people in all black.

Mom seemed to me like the conciliatory party, which would make sense. I'm sure she felt bad that Nica felt bad. I'm equally sure, though, that she wouldn't allow feeling bad to interfere with her ambitions, and that she had absolutely no intention of letting Nica renege on their deal.

I'm so absorbed in *Nica's Dream* I don't hear Dad come in the kitchen. Don't realize I'm not alone, in fact, until the oven door opens and a blast of fiery air hits me. I glance over. There he is, moving toward me, a casserole dish between two oven-mitted hands, eyes blinking from the steam. I take a step to meet him, give him a kiss, noticing as I lean in how frail he looks, his bones seeming to grow thinner, his skin more translucent, by the day. Like he's getting ready to disappear. Or turn into something dead. Closing my eyes, I bring my lips to his cheek. As soon as his head's safely bent, I wipe the soft, too-loose sensation of his flesh from my mouth.

He places the dish on the table and we sit down across from each other, Nica stretched out above our heads. It feels a little like she's eating with us and I wonder if that's why he brought the photograph, which in his quiet way he'd disapproved of so strongly when she was alive, up from

Mom's darkroom—as an attempt to include her, keep her part of the family.

The meal goes pretty much the way every meal we have together goes. It starts out fine. We both act cheerful, chat pleasantly and animatedly about a variety of upbeat topics. Throughout the day, I actually collect funny stories, harmless bits of gossip to bring to the table, and I suspect he does the same. No matter how thorough our preparation, how good our intentions, though, at a certain point the conversation runs out. And in the absence of dialogue, we both become anxious, need to have some kind of talk going, so then it's please-pass-the-this and thank-you-for-passing-the-that. Once we've done that routine to death, another lull hits and it gets so quiet I don't want to swallow because I'm afraid of how loud it will sound, and I have to wait for a glass to clang against a dish or a spoon to scrape a bowl—*some*thing, some noise. Finally I manage to choke the bite down, and when I do I realize it's the last one I'll be able to take. After that it's just maneuvering forkfuls of food around my plate until it's okay to push my chair back, walk over to the sink.

As I turn on the tap, watch the stream of water go from opaque to clear, I wonder how it is that Dad and I have lost each other when it's only Nica and Mom who are gone.

# CHAPTER NINE

I end the day exactly the way I began it: parked in the same spot, on the same street, drinking from the same can of (now flat) Diet Coke, eating from the same sleeve of (now stale) Saltines. The house I'm watching is quiet, all the rooms dark except for one at the front, lit by the murky glow of a television set.

I reach into my bag for my copy of *Clarissa*, the book I'd grabbed from my room that morning, the one I'd be reading if I hadn't deferred admission to Williams, had taken ENGL 379 The Novel of Manners, which I'd registered for back in July. As soon as I haul the one-thousand-five-hundred-page tome onto my lap, though, I realize I might as well have left it on the table next to the bed I never sleep in. It isn't pitch-black in the car, but it's pretty close. And I can't turn on the overhead light without making myself conspicuous. Guess I'll just play Candy Crush Saga on my cell until the juice runs out or I pass out like every other night this week. And then I remember: I have a flashlight stored in the car for emergencies. I pop open the glove compartment.

A flashlight doesn't tumble out. Something else does, though. Chandler's student literary magazine of which I was at one time editor in chief, *The Rag and Bone Shop Quarterly,* known on campus as *The Rag.* (And if you were a staffer, you were on *The Rag,* tee hee.) It's the December/January issue, one of the four I was responsible for putting out. Stamped on the upper right-hand corner, in smudged black ink I have to squint through the dimness to read, are the words:

PROPERTY OF CHANDLER HEALTH AND COUNSELING CENTER
DO NOT REMOVE

Which makes perfect sense because the Chandler Health and Counseling Center is where I picked it up, one week ago today.

I'd just driven down from Williams for my surprise celebratory visit to Dad, hadn't even dropped off my overnight bag at the house yet. My appointment with Dr. Simons was for three o'clock and I was twenty minutes early, so I was camped out in the waiting area, sitting in a straight-backed wooden chair somebody must have dragged in from a classroom, looking for a way to kill time. There were no regular magazines in the rack, only a couple course catalogs from last spring, a back issue of *The Rag,* a pamphlet on irritable bowel syndrome. I picked up *The Rag.* Smirky, ready to have a good time, I opened it, knowing exactly how I was going to react, not just to the pieces inside but to the me of ten months ago who did her utter earnest best to edit—and occasionally churn out—those pieces: with affectionate disbelief. Imagine taking any of this crap seriously?

The magazine didn't disappoint. There was more than enough to inspire lighthearted contempt: a short story in which nothing happened except a girl watched the sky and thought about her life, and as her thoughts grew darker, so too did the sky; a travel essay that read like an upmarket version of "What I Did on My Summer Vacation"; and, my personal favorite, the first chapter of an as-yet-to-be-completed novel about a couple of buddies on a hunting trip, the buddies making ample use of the words *nice* and *good,* signaling that the writer thought Hemingway was pretty terrific. I flashbacked to Mom's response to my news that the graduating board of *The Rag* had just voted me editor: "Teenagers should stick to sports and bands." I was hurt at the time, of course, but now I saw she couldn't have been more right, and I started to laugh, in on the joke at last.

The laugh stuck in my throat, though, when I flipped to the next page, the poetry section. A word about *The Rag* and poetry. The poems that were submitted to the magazine generally fell into one of three categories: self-loathing (eating disorders, substance abuse problems, cutting, etc.), alienation (writer feels insufficiently loved/understood/appreciated), and sexual ambivalence (self-explanatory). The poem I was looking at now fit squarely into category number three.

A Flower's Lament

By Anonymous

I am a flower,
The kind of flower that cannot survive in the Garden
    of Eden.

113

Its soil will not nurture my roots,
Its sun will not shine on my buds.

I lie to myself about lying with him,
Tell myself that I am not feeling what I am feeling
But it is too strong,
Too strong to be denied.

He is Chaos and Desire.
I am Contradiction and Confusion.
His skin, cool and milky white,
Slides against mine, warm and Coca-Cola brown.

His body stretches up and out,
Extends with feline elegance,
His fingers in my hair,
Drawing me to him.

I bow before his Beauty,
Kneeling to receive his liquid grace.
On my tongue I swallow,
Like the wafer from my First Communion.

Jesus, He died for my Sins,
But this one's on me.
The Cross around my neck,
A chain or a noose?

And now a word about *The Rag* and anonymous submissions. There's no such thing. Not anymore. My freshman year, someone turned in an unsigned short story that had been copied off *Seventeen*'s website. It was accepted by the editorial board and the plagiarism wasn't identified until the issue had already been printed and sent out to parents and alumni. Embarrassing for the school. Even more embarrassing for *The Rag*. To be caught stealing was bad enough, but from a teeny-bopper magazine? Never mind that it was the liveliest, most entertaining piece of fiction ever to grace our pages. Because the perpetrator was nameless, he/she remained at large. Since that day *The Rag* has instituted a strict policy: student-writers are allowed to publish anonymously, but not submit.

I remember the day "A Flower's Lament" came up for discussion. The *Rag*'s board was sitting around the office, a cramped room on the top floor of Noyes, the winter issue deadline looming. The radiators were on at full blast, making the air hot and dry. At the beginning of the meeting, I'd ripped open a giant bag of off-season candy corn, thrown it on the table. Now everyone was dull-eyed and cranky, having crashed from the sugar high.

"I think it's powerful," Benny Quintana said. Benny, who one day last year had up and quit the Catholic Student Fellowship Club, pierced his right ear—his queer ear, as he called it—adopted a bored, lockjawy way of talking, and started wearing T-shirts with slogans like SIZE QUEEN and POWER BOTTOMS FOR JESUS, was our literary editor. He'd campaigned hard for the editor in chief position. Unsuccessfully, obviously. (I'd won less because people liked me, I think, than because people really didn't like him.) At present he was sprawled across the ratty velour couch a former staff member had rescued from a Dumpster, languidly fanning himself with a copy of the meeting agenda I'd printed out. "I want to publish it."

"Veto," Ethan MacLellan, our managing editor, said.

Benny let out a theatrical sigh. "Reason? Other than that you're pussy-whipped?"

Ethan claimed to object to the poem on the grounds that its religious imagery was heavy-handed, but, as we all knew and as Benny already alluded to, he was really objecting to it on the grounds that earlier Benny had shot down Ethan's girlfriend's piece about her struggles with bulimia, Benny saying that he did not need to read another first-person account of a girl finger-fucking her own throat because she didn't get enough hugs from daddy and neither did anyone else at this school, thank you very much.

"You've missed the point, as usual," Benny said, when Ethan was finished talking. "The strength of this poem isn't in its imagery. It's in the way it shows what it's like for a young male to realize he has feelings that don't fit into the heteronormative paradigm."

"A young homosexual male, you mean," Ethan said. He was wearing Buddy Holly glasses and a gas station attendant jumpsuit, the name BUCK stitched in script across the breast pocket.

"No, a young male. The experiences and emotions the poet's writing about are universal and don't deserve to be ghettoized."

Ethan shook his head. "You gay guys, always thinking that there's no such thing as an actual heterosexual. Just repressed homosexuals."

"You straight guys," Benny snapped back, "always pissing the shit out of me."

The two traded insults for a while. Finally, I stepped in, came down on the side of Benny since I had to come down on the side of somebody, and since, I guess, I didn't think anyone at school needed to read another first-person account of a girl finger-fucking her own throat because she didn't get enough hugs from daddy, either.

"Benny," I said, "will you just verify that Anonymous is actually a Chandler student? Then we can accept the poem, move on."

"Moi?" Benny said.

"You have the submission sheet."

"I do?" He started rifling through the papers scattered across the armrest of the couch. Picked one up, scanned it. "Ah, I do." His laugh came out high-pitched and explosive. "Oh my God. You've got to be kidding me."

"What?" I said.

"I did not see this one coming."

"See what one coming?"

"The kind of flower that doesn't survive in gardens but apparently just *thrives* in crappers."

"Benny, what are you talking about?"

Addressing the submission sheet rather than me, "So that's what you've been doing in Burroughs. I should've guessed. You little imp." He smiled, shook his head. "Oh, wow. Wow, wow, wow."

"Wait," I said, confused, "is it bathrooms this guy hangs out in or libraries?"

"A Flower's Lament. Sammy Jay would not approve."

Sammy *who*? Benny was being deliberately cryptic here, clearly wanted me to keep asking questions he wasn't going to provide answers to. Unwilling to give him the satisfaction, I said, impatient, "You do know the poet then? He does attend this school? That's, like, confirmed?"

"I've known him since we were in diapers. Didn't know him as well as I thought I did, though, obviously."

"Great." I turned to the other end of the table. "Ethan, where are we on layout?"

\* \* \*

117

Slowly I closed *The Rag*, the words, "A Flower's Lament," reverberating in my head. What if the poem's title was actually a pun, the lowest form of humor, according to Dr. Samuel Johnson, the eighteenth-century English essayist and critic (Imagination in the Romantic Age, Mr. Dudley, seminar, junior fall)? What if "A Flower's" was, in fact, A. Flowers, A. as in Armando, which Manny was short for, and Flowers as in Flores?

I stood, a tunnel forming before my eyes, my ears filling with a dull roar. The magazine tumbled from my lap to the floor. Leaving it there, my bag, too, with my wallet in it, my keys, my phone, I walked straight out of the Health and Counseling Center, across campus, and into Burroughs Library. The boys' bathroom was in the exact same spot as the girls', one floor above. Without knocking, I opened the door, not knowing what it was I was hoping to find, only that this was where I would find it, my heart going so hard and fast and heavy I could feel it beating in my fingertips, all over my skin.

The bathroom was empty. Immaculate, too, every inch of it bright and fresh and gleaming. The walls had been repainted. The stalls, also, that or replaced. No *so-and-so was here*s, no *for a good time call*s, no dick markers or swear words. Just blankness. Naturally, I thought, it was the start of a new school year. All traces of last year would be gone—scrubbed away, scraped off, painted over, or junked altogether—like it had never even happened. I swallowed my disappointment, moved to the sink to splash water on my face. A. Flowers was a reach, anyway, I told myself, twisting the spigot. A stupid, made-up clue, like how a crime got solved in an Agatha Christie novel, not a crime in actual life. I must've been out of my mind to think it meant anything, had any sort of significance to be uncovered or decoded, or that if it did I'd be the one to do it.

Raising my head, I caught sight of my reflection in the mirror, thin-cheeked and big-eyed, scarred from the other dumb shit that I'd done, younger and more useless-looking than I'd even imagined. Dripping wet, too. And it was as I was turning toward the paper towel dispenser that I saw it, saw them rather, the two words: *MANNY* and *FLORES,* the FLORES only partial, up to the O, the RES blocked out by the newly installed dispenser. They were scratched into the tile wall that separated the urinal section from the washing up. Just the name, nothing else. No phone number followed or inflammatory remark. One or both of those things had likely been attached originally, but it or they were now covered by the dispenser along with the second half of FLORES.

For several seconds I stared at the writing without quite knowing what it was. Then, blinking, I reached up, pressed the dug-out letters, spindly and crooked, with the tips of my fingers, needing to feel them, make sure they were real.

My thoughts were simple and definite in my head: it was Manny's name that I was touching; which meant that Manny was A. Flowers; which meant that Manny wrote poetry about swallowing another guy's liquid grace; which meant that Manny was gay; which meant that Manny was not in love with my sister; which meant that Manny did not kill my sister; which meant that someone else did.

It was just as I'd connected the final shocking dot that the door flew open, and a maintenance man, walkie-talkie squawking in his belt, entered, fumbling with the fly on his heavy khaki work pants. Seeing me, he froze. And we stood there, staring at each other, both of us caught in a place we weren't supposed to be: me in a bathroom for guys, he in a bathroom for students. I moved first, snatching three or four sheets of paper towel, hurriedly wiping off my face, then rushing past him.

I wanted to ditch the physical, go directly home, hole up in my room with what I'd just found out. I'd left my bag in the waiting area, though, right outside the doctor's office. And when I attempted to sneak in and grab it, I nearly collided with the nurse. She was looking at me, mad-faced.

"I've been calling your name for the past fifteen minutes," she said. "You better hurry up. Dr. Simons doesn't have all day."

I tried to respond, come up with a reason as to why I couldn't do what she was asking, but my mind had gone fiercely, hopelessly blank, and her mad face was getting madder and madder. So finally I just gave a resigned nod. Followed her into the office.

Thirty minutes later I was listening to the door of the Chandler Health and Counseling Center click shut behind me. I stood there, blinking into the strange, half-dazed emptiness of a school during summer break, the dirty-penny taste that follows a sudden blow to the skull coating my lips and teeth and tongue. I was in shock. I knew I was in shock even if I didn't feel like I was in shock, didn't feel like anything at all. In the space of a single afternoon I'd discovered that Nica's killer was out in the world somewhere, walking around, eating, talking, laughing at jokes, and that not only was I no longer a virgin, I was an expectant mother, as well.

I took a step toward the parking lot and started to sink to the ground. Not a faint or a full-on collapse, more a forgetting how to walk. And it was as I was sitting on that stoop, my teeth chattering even though the sun, metal-bright and fiercely hot, was beating down on my head, the prenatal instruction booklet Dr. Simons had thrust at me as I left his office in my hand, *The Rag* spilled from my bag and spread open at my feet, that I suddenly understood, made the connection between my sister and my pregnancy, between the mystery of her death and the mystery of the new life inside me.

I'd known from the beginning that something about the murder wasn't right, that it had been solved too easily, that the explanation was too pat, senseless in a makes-perfect-sense kind of way: fringey weirdo with no friends or family kills the beautiful popular girl, kills himself. None of us close to her was even slightly implicated, bore so much as the faintest hint of responsibility. We were all off the hook. And I spent the entire miserable, lonely spring trying to pretend I didn't know what I knew. That's what the anti-anxiety drugs were about. Easier to lie to yourself when the link between your brain and your feelings has been chemically severed.

But the truth couldn't be denied. Not anymore. Not with this baby growing in my stomach. It was a reminder that the past wasn't done with me yet, that *Nica* wasn't done with me yet. I thought I'd escaped both, left them behind when I moved on to college. Here they were, though, pulling me back. And the only way I could ever truly be free of them was by setting things right. What I needed to do now was find Nica's killer, and fast. Get him behind bars or under dirt before the end of the first trimester, after which, according to Dr. Simons, termination became a lot less safe and a lot more expensive. That gave me twelve weeks since July fourth, so thirty days. If I failed to complete the task at the close of that period then I would have to forfeit my life as I knew it, keep the baby. That was my vow: make someone pay for Nica's death or pay for it myself. No justice for her, no abortion for me.

Tick tock, tick tock.

My first break didn't come till four days later. It was hot and sticky when I awoke that morning, and it had been tough to get out of bed. I was fighting the growing desire to give up, to accept that I was in over my head, didn't know where to begin or what to do. Losing the fight, I reached for my cell to tell Ms. Sedgwick I couldn't take the job after all, the one I'd applied for so I could be close to Chandler, to the scene of the crime and many of its key players. Only I was unable to get through to Burroughs even after trying for more than an hour. A voice mail that hadn't been set up yet answered every time. Realizing the conversation would have to be in person, I groaned.

Not bothering to run a brush through my hair or across my teeth, I walked over to campus. Burroughs was open, but Ms. Sedgwick wasn't at her desk. While I waited, I decided to stop by the boys' bathroom, press my fingers against the name etched in the tile wall. Bask in the presence, basically, of my one piece of tangible proof. Assure myself that this whole thing was real, not a figment of my imagination. Touching MANNY FLO might, I thought, make me change my mind about quitting.

It didn't.

I returned to the library's main floor. Still no Ms. Sedgwick. I left a note asking her to call me, then began the trek home.

At the fountain outside Houghton Gymnasium I paused to take a drink, only I couldn't stop, drinking and drinking the ice-cold water until brain freeze set in.

As I straightened, dragging the cuff of my sleeve across my mouth, I looked. There, right smack in front of me, was Damon Cruz. He was on his back, doing bench presses, so close that if there hadn't been a plate of glass between us, I could have reached out and wiped the sweat off his face. My eye went directly to it, the tattoo tucked away in the hollow of his arm, peeking through a blear of fine, dark hairs: a bright red heart spilling drops of even brighter red blood.

Suddenly, there's movement inside the house I'm watching. Someone's standing by the window in the front room. Damon. He's raising his arm to pull down the shade. And even though there's no need to check a thing I've already double-checked, triple-checked, quadruple-checked, I pick up the camera with the telephoto lens. Bringing it to my eye, I zoom in on that bleeding heart, the perfect complement to Nica's dripping arrow.

# PART THREE

PART THREE

# CHAPTER TEN

It's late. I'm on my way over to Damon's grandmother's house. Not to spy on him, though, as usual. He'd texted me the address while I was still at Chandler, told me to pick him up there at midnight. No explanation, just the order.

Fourteen days have passed since I discovered Damon was Nica's mystery man, but I'm still no closer to knowing if he's my mystery man, i.e. her killer. I do know a little more about him, though. His situation, anyway. The reason he isn't at UConn now, playing beer pong in some frat house basement, feeling up a girl from his sociology class under a poster of *Starry Night* or *Breakfast at Tiffany's,* Albert Einstein making a funny face, is because the baseball scholarship he was awarded is only partial, and with partial scholarships the amount of money given varies from year to year. So if he were to, say, ride the bench as a freshman—pretty much a definite since the average recovery period for ACL surgery is six to nine months—he'd be lucky to see a dime as a sophomore. Which is why he's decided to sit this year out, wait until he's fully healed before enrolling.

Not that he's told me any of this himself. All my gleaning's been from Renee, the chatty type, fortunately. Damon still barely talks to me. Looks at me even less. I sure look at him, though. Every night through the windows of his grandmother's house. I don't know what it is I'm hoping to see—him torturing small animals, building a shrine to Nica in his closet, pouring his heart out into a diary I can later steal, find a full confession in. Whatever it is, I don't see it. His routine is the same, never changes. He and his grandmother eat dinner, move into the den after cleaning the kitchen. He does strength-training exercises as the two of them watch TV. At ten thirty, he kisses her on the cheek, goes upstairs, brushes his teeth, and it's lights out. His grandmother seems to be the only person he spends time with besides Max and Renee. At first I think this is odd, but then I realize it couldn't make more sense. All his friends are in college now, even U Bridgeport-bound Frankie. Apart from discovering that he prefers steak to chicken, courtroom dramas to police procedurals, Colgate to Crest, though, I've learned nothing.

There have, however, been two notable developments in the last week and a half: I'm feeling a faint tenderness in my breasts and a slight tightness at my waist, which, according to the website laboroflove.com, means the baby's entering its fetal period. The tail's disappeared, and the toes and upper lip are starting to form. Twelve more days and the external genitalia will be starting to form, too, bringing the first trimester to its official close.

As I turn onto Damon's street, I glance at the seat beside me and spot the stun gun—internal rechargeable battery, lifetime warranty, guaranteed to bring down a three-hundred-pound attacker in under two seconds, and, best of all, designed to look like a tube of lipstick, a bargain at $34.99 plus shipping from Amazon—peeking out of my bag. I'd ordered it so I'd feel safe when I was alone with Damon. A smart move. The purchase of a competent, responsible, savvy person. Yet as I stare at the gun's ridiculous dainty canister, a shade of pink usually only seen on boxes of feminine hygiene products, I'm struck by a depressing thought: I'm not up to the task I've set myself. Not even close. To solve a mystery, you have to have powers of penetration, be able to get to the heart of things, and I'm the perpetual outsider who understands nothing. I'll never find out what happened to Nica, who's to blame. Instead I'll blow through the handful of days I have left following the same ass-backwards pattern I've followed my entire life: me, the older sister, chasing after Nica, the younger, without ever quite catching up. I'll continue to stalk a guy who'll turn out to have nothing to do with anything; work a pair of jobs, equally crappy; eat bad, sleep worse. And this whole dropping-out-of-Williams-and-moving-back-home gambit will morph into some sort of grotesque last hurrah before I become a single mother with no college education and zero career prospects, living in the house I grew up in with my screw-loose dad.

I pull up to the curb in front of Damon's grandmother's house. I'm so used to sneaking into this neighborhood, trying to play its angles, melt into its shadows, I find it strange to be here on invitation and in the open. I feel exposed. Blatant, somehow. Like I'm asking to get caught, thrown out. Taking a deep breath, I tell myself to relax, calm down, remind myself that I'm not doing anything wrong.

I'm about to exit the car. Before I can open my door, though, Damon shoots out his. He's stiff-legged but still speedy in jeans and a navy sweatshirt, heavy clothes for such a warm night. He swings his body in the car, so fast I barely have time to toss my bag in the back. Without looking at me, he says, "Let's go."

I've lived in Hartford my whole life, but the route Damon's taking me on is all side streets and back roads, and I lose my bearings quickly. The effect, though, of relinquishing control, passively following his orders, is oddly soothing, almost hypnotic. The vibrations from the engine spread up my calves and thighs, into the bones of my lower back, as the concrete ribbon unfurls before me.

I turn on the radio. The song playing was a big hit last summer. The lyrics are about doomed love, about loss and suffering and anguish. The girl singer's voice, though, is so light and sweet and caressing that the words are transformed, become light and sweet and caressing too. Nica had been crazy about the song, listening to it over and over. I remember the two of us going to the outlet mall in Clinton for back-to-school clothes. The ride was over an hour with traffic, and Nica, who'd just gotten her license but still preferred to be driven, didn't talk to me practically at all. Spent the entire trip hunting for the song on the radio, roaming from station to station, finding it, then, before the final chord had even been struck, lunging forward, beginning the hunt again. "It's like torture," she'd said, twirling the dial manically, "because you know it's playing *somewhere*, but if you don't get to it in time, you'll miss it."

Usually when a shard of memory like this one presents itself to me, I just swallow it down. Let it cut my tongue, the roof of my mouth, my throat, inflicting the pain solely on myself. I'm about to do that now. But then, I do something different. Turning to Damon, I say, "This song."

"Yeah?" he says, impatient.

"My sister loved it. My sister, Nica." The pleasure it gives me to say her name in front of him is powerful, all the more so for being unexpected. It's like a pressure I wasn't aware of had been building inside me, building and building, and the release valve just got turned. I want to say the name to him again, get some more of that good feeling. I don't get the chance to, though, because at that moment he orders me to pull over.

"Where are we?" I say, killing the engine.

"Clay/Arsenal."

Looking around, I realize I was wrong about Blue Hills being the shittiest neighborhood in Hartford. The street we're on—I don't know the name because the sign's missing—is deserted. On it are a gas station, a corner store, a vacant lot, and several mutilated billboards. The sidewalk is trash-strewn. Half the traffic lights have been knocked out. And above our heads a pair of laced-together sneakers dangles like a bunch of grapes from a telephone wire.

"I'll be back in five," Damon says. "Lock all the doors." As he reaches for the handle, I hit the Lock button on my fob. He tugs on the handle uselessly a couple times. "Lock them after I get out, I meant."

"Tell me what's going on," I say.

"I'll tell you later."

When I don't move, he exhales heavily, releases the handle. "Luis Ramos was FTA yesterday." Off my blank look: "FTA, Failure to Appear."

"Which one's Luis?"

"Buy-and-bust. Second offense. The judge issued a bench warrant for his arrest this morning."

"And you're supposed to, what, recover him? How do you know where he is?"

"See that." Damon points to the corner store, Save-A-Lot Xpress. "It belongs to his mom. She's the one who came to Max. Put up her mortgage as collateral. If Luis skips bail, she loses too. Could wind up losing her house."

"I thought he already skipped?"

"Yeah, but Max said if I bring him in quick and without too much trouble, he'll issue a Resumption of Liability, help secure a new court date."

"Why would he do that?"

Damon shrugs. "Liked the mom, I guess. Feels bad for her. Plus, she's helping him out, making his job easier. She called the office earlier today. Told him Luis would be in the store after it closed at midnight. Said she'd leave the back door unlocked. Speaking of unlocked doors." He reaches for the handle again.

I ignore him. "So you're just going to walk through the unlocked door? Then what?"

"Then I'm going to ask Luis nicely to turn himself in."

"And if he says no?"

"Then I'll ask him not nicely."

"What does that mean?"

Damon sighs, lifts his sweatshirt. Tucked in the waistband of his jeans is an object that's small and compact and so black it's almost blue: a gun.

"See," he says, "you can relax. Everything's under control."

I don't respond. Don't stop staring, either. The gun transfixes me, the cold, hard, steel fact of it. And as I stare, I notice the muscles in Damon's abdomen, their rectangular shape, the way they're neatly cubed and stacked; it makes his body seem machinelike, too, an extension of his weapon. A thin seam of black hair snakes between the muscles, disappears into the elastic of his boxers.

"Can I?" I say, my hand hovering an inch or so from the butt.

I'm surprised when he nods.

I take out the gun and weigh it in my palm, bounce it gently up and down. "A .22?" I say, in as casual a tone as I can muster.

"A .45."

The feeling of relief I experience at hearing this is cut short by a thought: *It doesn't mean he didn't shoot Nica, just that he didn't shoot her with this gun.* I clench up again.

"Am I allowed to go now?" Damon says, snatching back the gun, returning it to his waistband. "Do I have permission?"

I unlock his door. As I listen to him struggle with his brace, I think about how scary this situation is, and how if Nica were here, she wouldn't be scared, or, if she were scared, she wouldn't let it stop her. Pushing past my reluctance, I open my door.

"What are you doing?" he says, when he sees me walking around to the front of the car.

"I won't come inside the store with you. I'll just wait outside. That way, if something goes wrong, I'll be the first to know. I can call your uncle or 911."

"Nothing's going to go wrong."

"I'll just wait then. Look, if you make me get back in the car, I'm driving away in it. You'll have to find another ride home."

For ten seconds or so we stand there, tight, facing each other. Then his eyelid twitches and he turns around, starts walking toward Save-A-Lot Xpress.

After hitting the Lock button on my fob for a second time, I follow.

\* \* \*

133

The alley behind the store is empty except for a Dumpster, a couple of cardboard boxes with the words *Del Monte Quality* stamped on the side. The pavement is damp and smells like urine. The wall is a scorched-looking brick, in it a door. Damon stands in front of this door, looking at me, his eyes huge and inky black. His hand lightly touches the gun in his waistband. My hand does the same with the stun gun in my bag. He nods at me. I nod back, glad that I don't have to speak.

Damon reaches for the knob. It won't turn, though. He grips it tighter, shaking the whole door as he twists and pulls.

"Locked," I say, trying to keep the relief out of my voice.

He lets his head fall forward, rest against the sooty brick. "Shit. She screwed us."

"Is there another back door?"

Glaring at me, "Do you see another back door?"

"No, but maybe—" I feel the cell in my pocket vibrate. I pull it out, glance at the caller ID. Dad. Wondering where the hell I am at one in the morning, no doubt. "I should take this," I say.

"Fine. I'm going to check the windows."

I nod. Wanting privacy, I hold off until he rounds the corner, then quickly run through the excuse I prepared earlier: I was hanging out with Maddie in her room, it got late, we fell asleep. An old standby of Nica's. Bringing the phone to my face, I press the Answer button. The call's already gone to voice mail, though. I start to hit Return, then pause. It occurs to me that Dad might not be calling to find out where I am at all, has no idea I'm not at the house. He might be calling to let me know why *he's* not at the house. Could be he's stuck at work doing inventory or is having car troubles (he's had that station wagon for ten years now and it was secondhand to begin with) and is worried that I'm worried—if, on the off chance, I'm even awake to worry. In fact, this strikes me as the likelier scenario. I'll bet he was expecting to leave a message. And if he wasn't, well, he'll just have to wait until I get home to be lied to.

I close the phone and slip it into my pocket, a weight lifted from my shoulders now that I no longer have to talk to him. I'm about to join Damon when I hear a noise. I turn and look. The knob. Too shocked to run, too shocked to even move, I just stand there and watch as it rotates slowly counterclockwise, listen as its tongue slips out of the groove with a soft metallic click. Suddenly the door swings open, light pouring out so that my eyes are dazed and I can't see who or what is in front of me.

And then my eyes adjust.

He's propped against the doorframe, arms folded, legs crossed at the ankle. His jeans hang low on his hipbones, and he's wearing a shirt that's completely unbuttoned, exposing a flat stomach, a boyishly smooth chest. His face, though, is not boyish at all. It's dark and craggy and pitted with scars and forty at least. When he sees me staring, his lips peel back in a smile. One of his teeth is gold.

"Was you the little mouse scratching at my door?" he says.

I feel his eyes moving over me, and all at once I'm conscious of my arms and legs, practically bare in a short skirt and T-shirt. I open my mouth to speak, but nothing comes out.

He laughs softly. "What's the matter, mouse? Cat got your tongue?"

Again I open my mouth and nothing comes out. I shrug my helplessness at him.

More of that soft laughter. "My name is Luis," he says. Without thinking, I hold out my hand to him, like we've

135

been formally introduced, like he's a friend's parent I'm meeting for the first time, a college interviewer. He closes his hand around mine and tugs, tipping me off balance, so I have no choice but to step toward him. We look at each other. A heat starts to gather between our skins, and I can feel the rough calluses on the pads of his fingers. I try to take back my hand, but he doesn't let me, tightens his grip instead, tightens and tightens until I wince. He smiles at me when I do, and I return the smile even though I'm in pain now, and terrified, mesmerized by the menace of him and that gold tooth.

Finally, he releases me. "You got a name, mouse?"

A beat passes. My hand's throbbing, and my heart's going so fast it's making me dizzy.

"That's okay," he says, "you don't have to tell me. Pleased to make your acquaintance, whoever you are." He brings his hand up to my face, rests it lightly on my cheek. He's not holding on to me now, is only barely touching me, and I want to run, but I can't. Want to reach for the stun gun in my bag, but I can't do that, either. Can't even call out. The bulk and heat and pressure of him, the beating of my heart, the glint of that tooth make me stand there limply. The smell on his fingers is strong and complicated: the sweet, rotten scent of marijuana on top; underneath, the fainter scents of fried food and ketchup and something like sweat yet not sweat, tarter than sweat, and ranker.

Tears well up in my eyes as he drags his hand across my mouth, wrenching my lips apart. I grit my teeth. I need to breathe through my nose so that his fingers can't get into my mouth. But the hot reek of him is thickening the air, clogging it, and taking it in through anything as narrow as nostrils becomes impossible; I don't even try. Seconds pass.

136

My lungs start to burn. And I realize that I'm not going to be able to go without oxygen much longer, that I'm going to have to open up, let him inside me. The only sound I can hear is the pounding of the blood in my ears.

And then I can hear other sounds, too: Damon's voice shouting from inside the store, and footsteps, draggy but fast-moving. Moments later, he flies through the door, tackles Luis. I almost go down with them but manage to grab hold of the edge of the Dumpster and stay upright. As I gulp air, they roll around on the pavement. Damon comes out on top, straddling Luis and pinning him. When he cocks back his arm, I close my eyes. My ears aren't closed, though, so what I'm not watching, I'm listening to: a fist doing its work. After a while, the quality of the blows changes. At first it's like something hard and with bones in it is being struck. Then it's like something soft and heavy and wetly fleshy is being struck.

And after that, nothing.

Reluctantly, I open my eyes. The first thing I see is Luis's face. It's pulp, basically, and gore, his nose a smear of spongy tissue spread across his cheek, his mouth so caved in and bloody the gold tooth's no longer visible. Maybe he swallowed it. He is breathing, though, a fine mist tinting the air red whenever he exhales.

I start to scream, scream and scream, and then Damon's arms are around me. They're pulling me to him roughly, my cheek slamming against his chest. I hear his heart; it's beating inside his rib cage so loud and so hard it seems to throb right through his body and into mine.

"It was the front door," he says. "It was the front door that she left unlocked."

\* \* \*

137

Damon and I are sitting on the curb in front of Save-A-Lot Xpress when a black-and-white pulls up. Two officers get out. Damon flashes something at them—his bail bond investigator badge, I think, I assume—tells them Luis is handcuffed to a drainpipe inside. Says he'll be right back.

"What about his mom's house?" I say, as he walks me to my car. "Won't she lose it now?"

The night air is close, but I'm shivering. Before I understand what's happening, Damon's unlocked the car with my fob, taken Nica's jacket out of the backseat and wrapped it around my shoulders. The smell hits my stomach before my nose: Nica's smell, her perfume—the stinging citrus, the cloying vanilla—cigarette smoke on top. Does Damon recognize it? I wonder. If not her smell then the jacket? I look over at him but his head is bent so I can't see his expression.

"Tough," he says.

"And Luis's face?"

"What about Luis's face?"

"How are you going to explain it to the police?"

He raises his head. "I was apprehending a jumper," he says, eyes hard, like black marbles. "He resisted. Nothing to explain."

"Oh."

Damon plots out the quickest route home, then makes me repeat it twice. It's obvious he wishes he could go with me, but he has to stick around for the official surrender. As I turn the key in the ignition, he says, "And Grace?"

I look at him.

"Drive safely."

I don't, though. I drive recklessly. I drive fast. I drive like I'm the victim of a crime fleeing the scene, too scared to stop or think or do anything but run. Yet no crime was committed. Not against me, at least. Luis didn't hurt me or threaten me. All he did was put his fingers on my mouth. And, besides, it's not the recollection of his behavior that I find so upsetting, it's the recollection of my own: tongue-tied and smiley-faced, blushing in a manner that mimed flirtation and pleasure. If Damon hadn't burst through that door when he did, I can't even imagine what would have happened. Not true, I can imagine, the outcome if not the particulars: me, bruised and raw and violated, definitely; damaged beyond repair, probably; diseased, possibly. Nica would never, not in a million years, have acted that way.

And as my tires hum, rolling rapidly over the asphalt, they seem to speak to me, say the same phrase over and over again: *Nica would never, Nica would never, Nica would never.*

# CHAPTER ELEVEN

I return to Damon's grandmother's. Holding vigil from my car, which has proven to be a pointless exercise, is especially pointless tonight—watching a house he's not even in!—but I don't know where else to go or what else to do.

I park in my customary spot, hunker down in my seat. My sense is that it'll be a while before a squad car drops him off, so after fast-forwarding through a pair of unlistened-to voice mails from Shep, one left several days ago, one left this morning—him wanting to take my emotional temperature, no doubt, to, barf, "check in"—I play Dad's.

"Sweetheart, where are you?" he asks in a mild tone, mildly curious, mildly confused, mildly concerned.

The message goes on, but I've heard enough. I delete it. After tossing my phone in my bag, I pull out my computer, the ancient laptop Nica and I used to share. If I hold it up to the windshield at a certain angle, I can pick up a faint Wi-Fi signal. And, though it takes forever, I'm finally able to get onto the *Hartford Courant*'s website. I enter Nica's name into the paper's search engine and begin to read the articles covering her death, articles I've read before—many, many times before in the last couple weeks—but, hey, another look can't hurt, and at least it's a constructive use of my time.

A half hour goes by, an hour, an hour and a half, the clock in the dash glowing a dreamy, pallid green. I stare out the window into unbroken darkness, a darkness so dense it seems to pulse against my eyeballs. I'm awake but barely. The computer is in my lap where I dropped it a long time ago. I'm thinking that maybe I'd better call it a night, am reaching for my keys. Just then, though, a vehicle passes, a set of headlights sweeping the interior of my car, and, for an instant, Nica's face emerges from the black with startling clarity. And then the instant is over. The vehicle continues on its course, hurtling forward, and everything slides back into dimness and shadow.

For a few seconds I'm too stunned to move or to think or even to breathe. Then I come to my senses, slap the dome light in the ceiling. There she is, cat-curled on the passenger seat, one slim leg tucked underneath her, back slumped softly against the door. Except for the neat little hole with the charred edges on the left side of her abdomen, she looks exactly the way she looked when she was alive. She's dressed in the cutoffs and halter top she was wearing in *Nica's Dream,* only she's bursting out of them since she's no longer eleven. A cigarette burns low between her lips.

I know that what I'm looking at is a figment, a mirage, an illusion, the product of my imagination dipping into my exhaustion—a dream, basically—but I also know that it's real, too.

For a long time we sit in silence. I don't want to speak first, am waiting for her to begin. At last, though, unable to take it anymore, I say, "Hi."

"Hi," she says back.

"How are you?"

"I'm okay. How are you?"

"I'm good," I say. "I'm great." And then, "Thanks for asking."

"Sure," she says, amused. "Any time."

I know how stilted my tone is, how inexpressive and life-less my words, but I can't help myself. It's as if there's so much emotion coursing through my body, there's none left for my voice; so many things I want to say, I can hardly say anything at all. I'm trying, though. I'm trying.

"It's good to see you," I say.

"It's good to see you, too, Gracie."

"I've missed you. Really."

She regards me through weighted-down lids, then languor-ously transfers her cigarette from her right hand to her left, holds the hand up to her nipple, shakes it: titty hard-on. The gesture hurts my feelings but it also soothes them because what could be more normal than her making fun of me? And when another silence descends, it's a purer, less strained version. Nica smokes and drops cigarette ash into the mouth of the empty Diet Coke can she fished from the backseat, gazes out the window, closed and made into a mirror by the blackness of night. I listen to our breaths, joining and dividing, joining and dividing, one after the other; watch her feet, propped up on the dashboard now, bare and dirty-soled, the polish on the toes chipped, the grubby Band-Aid peeling off her heel, just like in the photograph. I feel myself growing calmer, more peaceful.

A second car passes, its headlights hitting Nica full in the face, illuminating that shard of gold in her iris, changing the brownish hazel to a clear, brimming green.

142

"I'm pregnant," I say, and then inhale sharply, shocked that I blurted it out like that, that I blurted it out at all; it was supposed to be something unspoken between us. In a panic, I look over at her.

Her expression doesn't tell me what she's feeling, is a cool blank. Slowly, she brings her cigarette up to her mouth. "Pregnant?" she says, expelling a silvery stream of smoke, watching it twist and writhe in the warm still air.

I nod, anxious.

"You do realize that you have to have sex to get pregnant."

"Yeah," I say, "that's what I thought, too."

We're still laughing as the dome light above our heads flickers, burns out.

I'm in the dark again but the quality of the darkness has changed, is a medium gray rather than a heavy black, the streetlamp a dozen yards ahead making things glow dimly. I hear a noise—the click of the passenger-side door handle. Nica must be getting out. I need to stop her. We've haven't had a chance to talk yet, not really, have only cleared the air so real talk is possible. I whirl around and look. With relief I see a body entering the car, not exiting it. And then the head does a half rotation, coming around to face me. Damon. My disappointment is so sharp I feel as if I've been struck.

"You're awake," he says.

I say "What?" in a way that makes the word rhyme with *Huh*.

"I kept calling your name. You didn't move."

I'm slumped way down in my seat. Dried drool cracks on my chin when I say, "I didn't hear anything."

"Yeah, I sort of figured. I knocked on the window too."

Jesus, all that yelling and banging. No wonder Nica took off. I'm so angry, I can hardly bear to look at him. "Well, I'm up now." I push myself away from the seat with the backs of my elbows. I feel slightly dizzy, and there's a weird kind of high-pitched wailing in my ears.

"You mind?" he says, reaching for the box of Saltines in the back.

I shake my head.

He opens the cellophane sleeve with a combination of fingers and teeth. Pops a few crackers in his mouth. And for three minutes, according to the dash clock, we sit there in silence except for the sound of his chewing and the wailing in my head, like a teakettle at full boil.

"So are you going to tell me what this is about?" he says, and smiles at me. It's the first unguarded smile I've seen from him, the first smile period practically, and I'm surprised I'm the cause of it. And then it dawns on me that I'm not, that any pleasure he's experiencing is likely due to tonight's professional success, and that the feeling's just spilling over onto me.

"What what's about?"

"You, parked outside my grandmother's house at three in the morning." And when I don't respond: "Are you waiting up for me, making sure I get home safe?"

He's kidding, of course. He's not saying what he actually thinks I'm doing. At the same time, though, he is saying what he actually thinks I'm doing, his light tone and relaxed manner telling me he doesn't believe it's anything he need worry about, anything potentially threatening or harmful to him. He probably imagines I'm still jittery from the encounter with Luis, and that I'm coming to him without even knowing why, am acting purely on instinct, reduced by fear to the lowest, most primitive level—a little animal scuttling around on all fours looking for protection, understanding that its survival is in danger and nothing else.

He keeps talking, teasing me. And I realize that I'm not going to be able to hold back much longer, am not going to be able to approach him with subtlety or a strategy in mind like I'd planned. My emotions are too raw for nuance. Or safety. If he did kill Nica and he thinks I know about it, what's he going to do to me, alone with him in a car in the middle of the night? Work my face over with his fists until it looks like a sponge dunked in blood? Whip out his .45, ventilate my stomach? How would I stop him? With what? That rinky-dink stun gun, not even in my hands, in my bag in the back?

The wailing is getting louder and louder, crazier and crazier, drowning out every other sound. A wave of nausea hits me and for a second I'm certain I'm about to be sick. And then I say, "I know," the words bursting out of my face in a near scream. They stop Damon cold, midsentence. For a long moment there's dead quiet in the car. No wailing, no breathing even. "I know," I say again, calmly this time, and I look at him. His eyes are closed. "About you and Nica. I know."

Slowly his eyes open. He shakes his head, smiling to himself a little ruefully, like he's just heard a funny joke only he's the butt of it. "Oh," he says, and turns away.

I watch him as he stares out the window at the empty street. His reaction is a lack of one, and I have no idea how to proceed from it. My resolve, the anger that's carried me this far, is gone, vanished without a trace. Worse, I have the nagging sense that I've got it wrong somehow, that I'm missing something, some crucial piece of information. So when I say to him, "Will you tell me about it?", my voice is shy, almost timid.

"About what?"

"The relationship."

"Nica made me swear I wouldn't say anything to anybody about it."

My heart sinks.

And then he shifts in his seat, starts rubbing his eyes tiredly with the heels of his hands. "I suppose, though, the promise doesn't hold anymore. And you have a right to know."

"I do?" I say, scarcely daring to believe.

"I don't know. Maybe," he says, but he doesn't say anything after that. Just rolls up the Saltines sleeve on his lap and carefully fits it back into the box, wipes his fingers on the leg of his jeans.

"Damon," I say, after a bit.

He looks up at me, nervous or embarrassed, and laughs. "Sorry. I just don't know where to begin."

"At the beginning."

He laughs again. Says, "Right," but nothing more.

"Don't think about it, just talk. Forget that I'm her sister."

"Okay," he says, nodding. "Okay."


He was in his car, on his way home from a date that had gone badly. He'd been seeing a girl, a day student a year below him, Vanessa Medina. Vanessa was pretty and smart and great and he liked her a lot, but it was a casual thing. He was graduating in a couple of months and had no interest in getting involved in anything serious, as he'd said from the start. She'd said she wasn't interested in anything serious either. He sensed lately, though, that that was no longer true for her, if it ever had been. He'd tried to tell himself that he'd never been less than straight with her, and that her emotional well-being was her responsibility not his. But when the night was over he'd wind up feeling guilty just the same— like a user and a sleaze. It wasn't worth it. So he'd been attempting to subtly cool it, keep the relationship from ending in bitterness and tears.

He'd just taken Vanessa to a movie, though. Had driven her directly home afterward, and when she'd joked about her parents' nine o'clock bedtime, he'd pretended not to notice the implied invitation, then said he was working for his uncle in the morning so planned on turning in early that night too. She'd slammed the door behind her, her movements angry but her eyes hurt. And now he realized that bitterness and tears were inevitable, that he'd been kidding himself to think otherwise.

Damon's headlights arced across the landscape as he turned onto Farmington, and out of the darkness reared a figure, pale and perched on the hood of a car. A girl, he saw as he got closer. Nica Baker.

Damon knew Nica from school. Knew who she was, anyway. She was too good-looking for him not to. Her dad worked at Chandler. Her mom, also, that sexy art teacher. And she had a sister, older but younger acting, and quiet. Without quite meaning to he'd been keeping tabs on Nica, watching her in Stokes and the snack bar. She was usually at the center of a group—laughing, talking, holding court. There was a solitary quality to her, too, though. He'd some-times see her wandering the halls in the middle of the day, one hand clutching a bathroom pass, the other trailing along the wall, her expression distracted, dreamy, and when she happened to look at him, his heart would start to beat wildly, wilder with every second she held his gaze. But there was never so much as a flicker of recognition in her face, and he didn't think she even saw him. He was just a place to rest her eyes.

He pulled up in front of her, got out of his car. As he walked toward her, he saw she was wearing a jean jacket, unlined, way too skimpy for the weather, over a thin shirt. The rims of her nostrils were pink with cold. A cigarette dangled between her fingers. "Did you break down?" he asked.

"A flat." Her eyes were on him, but their expression was that blurred one from the Chandler hallways, and he was pretty sure she didn't know who he was. It was past midnight on the side of a deserted road, and here he was, some strange guy approaching her, and she wasn't in the least bit scared and, weirdly, that made him scared of her.

"We go to school together," he said. "I'm in the class ahead of you." When she didn't respond, react in any way, "Can you change a tire?"

She shook her head.

"Do you have a spare?"

"I don't know."

"Where are the keys?"

She looked at him blankly. "The . . .?"

He found them in the ignition, pulled them out, and walked around to the back of the car. It annoyed him that she was just sitting there, waiting for someone to come along and help her, not even asking for help, automatically assuming it would be given. It annoyed him even more that he was proving her right.

Thirty seconds later, he walked back around to the front. "You have a spare but it's on the car. Do you belong to AAA?"

148

She shrugged.

"Have you called someone yet? Your parents?"

"No."

"What about your boyfriend?" he said, allowing himself to sneer a little. He knew she was with that Jamie guy, the one who had the face that was pretty like a girl's face was pretty and the lazy, stoner, rich-kid way of talking.

"I don't have a boyfriend," she said.

He pretended not to notice the way his heart went fast and kicky at this information. "Look, maybe you should just have your dad take care of the car in the morning. Why don't I give you a ride home? It's dangerous for you to be out here by yourself."

Now she was looking directly at him, her gaze clear, focus having at last burned through the fog. "I'm not by myself, Damon. I'm with you."

So she did know who he was. He wondered if she knew he sometimes watched her, too. Feeling his face go hot, he said, "Make sure you lock the doors," and tossed her back her keys, returned to his car to wait.

They were on the road. He was going to tell her that she couldn't smoke in his car, but she'd stubbed out her cigarette before she got in. She'd retreated back into vagueness and distance, staring out the window at the passing utility poles, picking at her chapped lips. The silence began to work on him, turning him nervous, edgy. He decided to break it. "So, what are you doing out so late?"

"Just driving around."

"You like to drive around at night?"

"It clears my head."

"Of what?"

She might have shrugged. He wasn't sure.

Silence fell again. It was about to turn into another long one when she said, "I don't want to go home."

Startled, "Where do you want to go?"

No answer.

"We're not far from Talcott Park. Should we check out the old water tower?" It was only as he spoke that he remembered the water tower was a popular make-out spot, at least among public school kids. Embarrassed, he looked at Nica, expecting to see a knowing smirk on her face. But she seemed barely to have heard him. Irritated now, and determined to get a response, he repeated the question.

She turned up a palm, meaning, he guessed, he could do what he liked. Not wanting to but feeling obligated, he changed direction.

Fifteen minutes later he was pulling onto a patch of gravelly dirt—empty, thank God—at the foot of a small hill, atop which sat the antique water tower. He looked at it through the windshield. It was one of the first steel water towers built in the United States, and over eighty feet tall. Nica didn't seem to notice it, though. Didn't seem to notice anything.

Damon's edginess was increasing by the second, and he was about to flip the car into reverse, get the hell out of there. Who cared if she didn't want to go home? That's where he was taking her. And the sooner he did, the sooner he could start trying to forget this weird shitty night ever happened. He was just reaching for the gearshift when she turned to him and said, gesturing to the tower, "Want to climb it?"

She was kidding. Had to be. Only the thing was, he knew she wasn't. Half hopefully, though, he kidded back. "Why do you think I brought you here?"

150

Without another word, she opened her door, started up the hill. He watched for a couple seconds, blinking, then followed. Moments later they were at the base of the tower, standing in front of a ladder, narrow and rickety, that went all the way up to the top, seemingly all the way up to the stars. He glanced over at her, his eyes already dry and burning from the wind. Her hair, pure black and alive looking, whipped around her face and throat. He could see the outline of her breasts, the sharp little nipples in her tight-fitting shirt. She was grinning at him. And with a sick-sinking sensation, he realized they were actually going to do this.

"Me first, okay?" she said.

When he offered no objection, she began to climb. She was as quick as a spider. And if she felt fear, she didn't take it seriously. Or could be she didn't have that emotion, was born without it, like people born without a sense of smell or all ten fingers or a conscience. He was barely able to keep up. And as he moved higher, each rung brittle-feeling in his palms, gritty with rust, he thought more and more about what a single false step would mean: a snapped neck or, worse, a snapped leg, and the end of his baseball scholarship.

At about fifty feet up, a bar broke off when Nica grasped it. Damon heard the break first, then saw it, then saw it again, the same thing happening with the bar above. He felt his knees sag for a second in relief: they could go down now and without any loss of honor. But Nica, to his amazement, to his horror, to his utter, utter disbelief, wasn't going down; she was going sideways, away from the ladder over to the bare face of the tower, which was grooved and crosshatched. He realized that she meant to use these indentations as handholds and footholds. As she hung there, positioning herself, he called out to her, but either his voice got torn to pieces by the wind and didn't reach her, or it did reach her and she was ignoring it.

He descended slowly, cautiously, no longer caring that he'd been out-toughed and out-cooled by a girl. So grateful was he to feel solid earth under his feet he almost dropped to his knees and kissed it. Instead he looked up. Nica had started climbing again. She wasn't moving as fast as before, but she was moving, was only twenty-five feet from the top now.

Then twenty.

Then fifteen.

As she made her painstaking way up those final ten, he was willing her ascension, never taking his eyes off her, not for a second, because to do so would have meant there was nothing between her and certain death but her nerve and grip. He could feel his face contorting, his teeth actually heating up from grinding together so hard. At last she was straightening her forearms, swinging her leg over the steel edge, as casually as if she were hopping the short fence behind the Gordon T. Pierpoint boathouse. She turned around and waved to him.

Watching her come down was tense, but nowhere near as tense as watching her go up had been. When she was almost to the ground, she said, "Catch." He'd no sooner stuck out his arms than she'd fallen into them, not even looking behind her as she released her hold on the ladder.

He pulled her tight to his chest. Now that she was safe, anger came at him as hard and hot as an inside fastball. He couldn't tell what he wanted to do to her more: kiss her or hit her. And she seemed to know just what he was thinking, those slanting eyes moving over his face in a lazy, insinuating way, that full mouth twisting into a smirk, mocking his fear.

She let him do both. Or, rather, she did both to him, stretching her neck suddenly, giving him a kiss that was like a punch to the face, bending his head back till it hurt. As he returned the kiss, shaking from it or the wind, he felt, for the first time in his life, that he'd come up against someone whose will was stronger than his own, someone he couldn't break, who could break him, and probably would. And the crazy thing was, the prospect didn't frighten him, it thrilled him. Actually, it frightened him, too, but even that was part of the thrill. Bring it on, he thought. Whatever it was, he wanted it, all of it. He could hardly wait.

Damon's face is pale and drawn-looking, as if the work of memory has drained the life right out of him. Drained it out of him, but breathed it back into Nica. With the story he's just told, he's performed a miracle, a resurrection. And listening to him I feel something beyond exhilaration, exultation almost.

"Anyway," he says, and sighs, letting his head drop.

I start talking quickly, excitedly. "I actually have this vague recollection of Dad leaving the house early one morning to deal with tow truck guys. It was before Nica died, only I'm not sure how much before. A month? A couple of months? Dad was back by breakfast so—" I stop, interrupted by the sound of air sucked through teeth and a muttered, "Jesus." Glancing down, I see my hand uncurling in my lap, revealing my palm, bloody and flayed. I must've done it with my nails when Nica was on the side of that water tower and I was willing her to the top the same way Damon was. I look at the crescent-shaped divots. I know rather than feel that they hurt.

Damon picks up my palm. Brow furrowed, he runs the

153

tip of his index finger lightly across its surface. The pain comes alive at his touch—a sharp, stinging sensation. Something else comes alive at his touch, too, though, something like pain in its urgency and clamorousness, yet not pain. It's rolling powerfully through my body. I don't understand what it is and then I do: *desire,* a word used in those books they sell at the checkout counters in supermarkets; a word that pants and heaves and throbs; a ridiculous word, hysterical and overblown; a word having nothing whatever to do with me, except that apparently it does. Afraid he'll register the racing of my pulse, put together what it means, I snatch back my hand.

He starts, his jaw dropping in surprise.

"You were tickling me," I say, turning my face away.

"Sorry."

I close my eyes. Draw oxygen, nice and slow until the feeling passes. "So," I say, when I trust my voice to hold steady, "that's how you and Nica got together."

"Yep, that's how."

"Why did she want to keep the relationship a secret?"

"She said it was because of Jamie. If he knew she was with someone else, it would hurt him. She wanted to wait till more time had passed, give him a chance to get over her before we, you know, went public."

"But you didn't believe her?"

"No, I did. But he was only part of the reason."

"What was the other part?"

He hesitates.

"What?" I say.

"Your mom."

I wasn't expecting this answer, and a weird kind of panicky dread flares up inside me when I hear it. Trying to sound loose, casual, I say, "What makes you think that? Did Nica say something?"

"Not directly, no. But she was obsessed with the idea that your mom was watching her."

So relieved I start to laugh, "Yeah, well, that's because she was. My mom's a photographer. Nica was her subject."

He nods, but the nod is noncommittal.

"What? You don't think that was it?"

"I do," he says, "but it went beyond that. Nica was convinced she was being watched when we were alone. I mean, really alone, parked in my car in some faraway spot, or in my room late at night. She'd be nervous, jumping up, wrapping herself in her jacket, the jean one, the one you're wearing now, and looking out the window every few minutes. 'She's out there. I can feel her. I can feel her eyes on me.' That's what she'd say."

So Damon did recognize the jacket. "That sounds extreme," I say, "but Nica's situation was extreme. If she felt like Mom was constantly following her around with a camera, that's because Mom was. She was practically the only thing Mom ever photographed."

"Yeah, she told me. Pretty messed up."

I'm a little offended, which surprises me. "It wasn't so bad," I say.

"Having no privacy?"

"Nica wasn't powerless, Damon. They had an arrangement. Any picture Mom took, she had to show Nica, and if Nica wanted it trashed, Mom had to trash it. That was the deal. And, God, it wasn't as if Nica was shy about showing her body. She liked the attention."

"Good thing since she was going to get it, like it or not."

"It wasn't so bad," I say again.

155

He just shakes his head.

Eager to drop the subject because it's obvious to me now that there's no way that he—that any outsider—can understand how it was in our family, I say, "I'm just trying to explain why Nica was freaked out about Mom watching her."

"I didn't say she was freaked out. I said she was obsessed."

"Spare me, okay? Tomato, tomahto."

"No, not tomato, tomahto. They're two different terms and they mean two different things. If you're freaked out by something you don't want anything to do with it, just want to get away from it. If you're obsessed with something, your reaction is more"—he looks at me, then looks away—"complicated."

The panicky dread is flaring inside me again, and I know that he's going to tell me something I don't want to hear if I keep pushing. I do, anyway. "What are you trying to say?"

He turns to me and I'm startled by the ferocity in his eyes. "I'm saying that Nica hated the thought of your mom always watching her, but loved it, too. I'm saying that when she pressed her face against the window of my car or my bedroom, she was relieved to see that your mom wasn't out there, but she was disappointed, too. Maybe more disappointed than relieved." He's silent for a moment, then says softly, "I think we should stop talking about this."

"I don't want to stop."

"Grace, what I've told you has obviously upset you."

"What? No it hasn't."

"You should see your face."

I glance into the rearview mirror. I look more than upset. I look crazed—eyes bulging, mouth twitching, skin splotched with pink and red. Taking a second to smooth out my expression, breathe, I say in an even voice, "I just want to understand why you think what you think. You're telling me you're positive Nica wanted to be spied on by my mom, took some kind of sick pleasure in it or whatever—why? Because she looked out the window a couple times? That seems like pretty thin evidence to me."

He sighs. "I have other reasons."

"Such as?"

"Such as the wildness that was nonstop, never-ending, twenty-four seven. It's like she was always trying to show off for somebody, some invisible person she was terrified of boring. Who if not your mom?"

"How do you know it wasn't you she was showing off for?"

He makes a dismissive snorting noise. "I just know, okay?"

His tone annoys me—so sure of itself. I make a dismissive snorting noise of my own. The look he gives me is a hot one. I give it right back.

And then, spreading his hands, the knuckles already swollen to the size of gumballs, he says, "I know because I didn't like all the wildness. I was always trying to get her to calm down, not act up. And, besides, I wasn't someone she cared about impressing. I don't think she even knew who I was. Not really. She just had some idea about me in her head."

"What does that mean?"

"Your mom thought Jamie was perfect, the perfect guy, the perfect boyfriend. And then I come along, his exact opposite. If Jamie was everything your mom loved, then I must be everything your mom hated, so Nica made up her mind then and there that she was going to love me. I think that's why she started calling me Demon. You know about nickname, right? It's not news to you?"

I nod without meeting his eye.

"You know how I got it?"

"For punching some guy's lights out during a baseball game, right?"

His mouth twitches in irritation. "There was a little more to it than that. I didn't punch him for fun. I punched him because he kept calling me wetback, the other guys on the team wetbacks. Finally I lost it. The dumb asshole didn't even know that a wetback's a Mexican."

"I never heard that part of the story."

"Yeah, well, Chandler wanted it hushed up. Thought it was embarrassing—racism in the supposedly ultraliberal Independent School Conference. That's why I only got suspended from the team for two weeks. My point is, Nica liked the nickname because she liked to think of me as violent and thuggish. It's how she saw me. Really"—his voice turning bitter—"it's the reason she was with me."

I start to protest, and then I flash back to the Chandler tennis courts, Damon walking by, Nica giving him that assessing look, then pronouncing him *rough trade*. The words die in my throat.

Damon resumes after a pause, still bitter-sounding: "Sometimes I think she was just one of those spoiled little girls with a nice, safe life that she tangles up with craziness because she's bored. That would be fine except she tangles up your life, too, and you're fighting for safe and boring. Safe and boring sounds great to you. But she doesn't give a shit. Climb up the side of a water tower in the middle of the night? Sure. Why not? Jump on the tiger's back. Throw your body on the grenade. Anything for a kick, right? Well, I was

158

the kick of the moment. But my moment was passing. I didn't want to go to the edge with her. Worse, I wanted to pull her back. So I was really no fun and—"

That teakettle wailing sound is back in my ears. The way he's talking about Nica—I can't listen to it. I won't listen to it. I fumble for the door handle, get out of the car, start walking.

A few seconds later, the passenger-side door opens, and Damon calls my name. But I keep going, my eyes on my feet moving along the cracked, uneven sidewalk. Soon I hear his step behind me, right on my heels. And then his breath is on my neck, and one of his hands is closing roughly around my wrist. He jerks me back.

Eyes dark, blazing queerly, he says, "You're the one who wanted to talk about this. Not me. *You.*"

I wrench free of his grasp, tears burning my eyes. The house we're standing in front of has one of those inflatable kids' swimming pools on its patchy front lawn, the inevitable Our Lady statue. I can see a television light glowing bluely in a downstairs window.

When Damon speaks again, his tone is softer, gentler. "Grace, it's not like I thought the wildness was all there was to your sister. I knew it was just what she was choosing to show me. And, you have to remember, I was in love, so not exactly levelheaded and reasonable."

"But you said—"

"I know what I said. None of that mattered, though. I loved her so much I felt like I was out of my mind. Why do you think I let her talk me into those stupid his and her tattoos? I was a basket case when she broke up with me. Fucking beside myself."

"She broke up with you?" I say the words slowly, wanting to make sure I'm hearing them right.

"Yeah."

"When?"

The note of excitement in my voice must catch his attention because he gives me a funny look. "The night she died."

"Damon, why?"

"Can we sit? My leg's killing me."

We move to the edge of the lawn, drop down on the grass. He stretches his leg out in front of him, massaging his knee through the hole in the brace. I try to curb my impatience, wait until he's ready to start talking. I'm about to burst when, at last, he says, "The answer to your question is, I don't know. I picked her up at school that night. We drove to Talcott Park, like we'd done a dozen times before. It was warm out. I brought a blanket. And we were, you know, together. Everything was good, I thought. Then she got a call."

A call. Yes, yes, I'd known there'd been a call only I'd forgotten I'd known. The police had learned about it from Nica's phone records—learned, at least, that it was made if not who made it. They'd told my mom and dad and me a Chandler pay phone was the source, which didn't narrow things down a whole lot since Chandler was basically Nica's entire world. A nonclue. Though maybe not.

"From who?" I ask, trying to downplay my eagerness.

Damon lifts his hands, turns them over, the palms empty, no answers in them.

Disappointed, I say, "Well, what did they talk about?"

"There was no talk. Not on her end, anyway. She said, 'Hello,' then listened, then said, 'Okay,' once, maybe twice, then hung up."

"And then?"

"And then she dumped me, told me to take her back to school, which I did."

160

"I wonder who called her."

"What does it matter who called her? The important question is, who killed her? And we know the answer to that one."

"Not," I say, "exactly."

He stares at me, totally lost. Finally he says, "What?"

I lay it out for him. Except for me being pregnant, which isn't relevant to Nica's murder, I tell him everything: about Manny Flores and the poem in *The Rag;* about the tattoo I spotted in Nica's armpit, the answering one I spotted in his; about using my staff password to log onto Chandler's online directory and seeing Max's name in his emergency contact information, googling Fargas Bonds and finding the ad in Craigslist.

When I'm finished, Damon's silent for a long time. Then he says, "So that's why you took the job? To learn about me? Because I might have been the one who"—pausing, then skipping the verb altogether—"Nica?"

"I needed the money too, but pretty much. I knew you were heading off to college. Still, I figured I could learn about you from your uncle, get close to you through him. I had no idea you were actually working at Fargas Bonds. God"—I start to laugh—"it must have been so weird for you, Nica's sister showing up at the office out of the blue. I can't imagine what was running through your mind when you saw me."

"No, you can't," he says, and laughs back, a sharp staccato sound that ends almost as quickly as it begins.

"That you'd taken deferred admission was just a lucky break for me. I mean, there's only so much I could've found out from Max."

"What would you have done if I hadn't?"

"Spent a lot of time staking out your dorm at UConn, I guess."

161

Again we lapse into silence, and again he's the one who breaks it. "If you're telling me all this, it means you don't believe I did it."

It's not until he says it that I realize it's true. "No, I don't."

"But I just gave you motive and opportunity. And you saw I had means earlier."

I brush a blade of grass off my knee. "I know."

"So why?"

"Because I think you're delicate." And when he laughs, shakes his head, I say, "Not delicate as in effeminate. Delicate as in, like, sensitive."

We're looking at each other, and then we're not looking at each other, as if we're suddenly shy of what we might see in the other's face. A minute or so later, he says, "So, who else is on the suspect list?"

"Nobody."

"Short list."

"Yeah, well, the police were pretty convinced it was someone she knew. And I know everyone she knew, except for you."

"Why were they so convinced it was someone she knew?"

"There was something about the entrance wound, the shape of it or something. There was other stuff, too. I just don't remember any of it."

Damon chews on his lip, thinks. "And maybe because she wasn't shot in the back, so she wasn't running away."

"Maybe," I say. "I mean, probably, yeah. Makes sense."

"Were there defensive wounds?"

"I don't think so."

"She didn't fight her killer then." Damon chews his lip some more. "So what's the plan here, Grace? You're going to keep trying to figure this out all on your own, something even the professionals couldn't do, nobody in your corner, not your parents, not your friends? If you actually find the guilty person, what then? Go to the cops?"

I shrug, too dispirited to reply. He's not saying anything to me that I haven't said to myself, but hearing the words out loud for the first time makes me hear them differently. The whole thing—what I'm attempting to do—just sounds so implausible, so ridiculous, a joke, basically. Imagine going to Detective Ortiz with a page of unsigned homoerotic verse torn out of a student magazine, a bit of graffiti on a urinal wall, and demanding that he reopen the case. I'd get laughed out of the station. I realize suddenly what I'd been hoping for when I confessed the truth to Damon: that he'd offer to help. Now, though, I can't fathom him offering. Who'd voluntarily get mixed up in something as harebrained and half-assed as what I've got going on? Sitting there, I feel the way I did that day in the boys' bathroom in Burroughs, just as low, just as useless.

"Why isn't Jamie on the list?" Damon says.

I look up, surprised we're still having this conversation. "Jamie?"

"Nica definitely knew him, right?"

"Technically he is on the list," I say, careful of my tone, not wanting to sound emotional or like I have my back up. "He has to be. He's the ex. But by the time Nica was killed they'd already been over for a while. Why would he go berserk two months after the breakup?"

"He could have found out about me. Knowing Nica was with another guy would've set him off, wouldn't it?"

Thinking about how upset Jamie was when he thought Nica was seeing Mr. Tierney, I nod. "Okay, but how would've he found out? Nobody knew about the relationship besides you and Nica."

"I didn't tell anyone," Damon says.

"Did she?"

"She said she didn't. But that's not the only way he could have found out. Someone might have seen us together, at Talcott Park maybe, and said something to him. I mean, right?"

"Right."

"Well?"

A long beat. "Yes, it's possible he killed her," I finally concede. And it *is* possible. Of course it's possible. What it isn't, however, is imaginable. I just can't see Jamie ever intentionally hurting Nica.

A memory edges its way into my brain.

A year ago. Nica, Jamie, and I went to a party at Trinity thrown by Owen Fitz, a friend of Jamie's who'd graduated from Chandler the previous spring. Nica and Jamie had picked me up in the little alley behind Burroughs. As soon as I'd opened the car door, I could tell they'd been fighting by the stiff-jointed way they were sitting, their pointed straight-ahead eyes. And the ride passed in tense silence. At last we arrived at the address in South Green, an off-campus town house. It seemed so quiet and still, almost asleep—windows shut, shades drawn, lights out—that I wondered if we'd gotten the night wrong, or if somehow the party had been canceled and no one'd told us.

Jamie parked at the end of the street. Nica was out of the car before it fully stopped. She started for the town house, walking fast, not waiting for me and Jamie to catch up. I watched her climb the steps to the door, throw it open. Smoke and stink and heat and noise all tangled together tumbled through. In front of her was a scene broken up hellishly into slices and flashes: a dim room, a band, guys and girls jumping up and down, mashing into each other, a giant strobe light illuminating their sweaty faces one moment, banishing them to darkness the next. Without hesitating or looking back, Nica crossed the threshold, disappeared into the lurching mob.

I glanced over at Jamie, expecting him to chase after her or maybe to turn around, walk back to his car, leave us stranded, too disgusted to stay another minute. But he just gave me a sleepy-eyed shrug, like, let her go.

He and I ended up sitting on the moldy couch someone had dragged out onto the back porch—the only semiquiet spot in the house—talking, mostly about him and Nica. It sounded like he'd had it with her. She was too selfish, he said, too moody, too this, too that. As he continued to tick off the *too*s, I stopped paying attention to his words, started paying attention to the mouth the words were coming out of: the sensitive well-shaped lips, the even white teeth, and, behind them, the tongue, soft and supple and cotton-candy pink.

And then all of a sudden he wasn't talking anymore. I started to panic as I realized that he'd reached the bottom of his list, was expecting a response from me. "Oh," he said, "and I skipped one. Wild. She's also too wild."

Seizing on the remark, I said, "Is too wild a bad thing?"

"No, not always. There's a good kind of too wild. It's—" He leaned into me, then pulled back again. "Wow, I almost forgot who I was talking to," he said, laughing and shaking his head. "You do not need to hear that."

I gave him a curt smile. "Okay, then you do not need to tell me."

165

"No, I really don't. I will tell you, though, that your sister is that kind of too wild. Is definitely that kind of too wild."

*All right,* I thought, *I get it. She's good at sex.* "So what's the bad kind of too wild?"

"That's a tough one," he said. "I guess, I'd say a girl who's the bad kind of too wild doesn't think the rules apply to her. She likes to have her fun. More than likes to have her fun, has to have fun. And she can sometimes cross the line from wild to out of control. All that definitely describes Nica, too." He sighed and drained the rest of his beer.

Trying to match his seriousness, I said, "Well, if you're going to get the good kind of too wild, I suppose you have to be prepared to accept the bad kind of too wild along with it."

"You've got to take the good with the bad?" He grinned. "Whoa, Grace, that's pretty profound." He reached over, curving an arm around my shoulder, and flicked my opposite earlobe with his index finger. "No, honestly, I'm a little blown away right now by how deep you are."

"Quit it," I said, and slapped at his finger. But really, of course, I was thrilled to have him touch me. And when I didn't shake off his arm, he pulled on me, just slightly, drawing me into him. Our bodies fit together so perfectly. Or maybe he just knew how to make them fit because Nica's and mine were so similar. Feeling the rise and fall of his chest against my side, I was almost too breathless to speak. But I forced myself to. "And anyway," I said, "you're the one going out with her, not me. I'm just trying to make sense of it for you."

"Actually, technically we're not going out at the moment."

"What do you mean?"

"She said she wants to go on a break. Told me right before

166

we came to get you. She thinks I'm too possessive. Wants to see other people. Whatever. Believe it or not, I'm actually sort of okay with it this time."

I felt lightheaded, like I'd stood up too quickly, though I was still sitting down. "Or not," I said. "I'm going to go with, or not."

"What?"

"Oh, come on, Jamie. You two are always going on a break. They never last for more than a day or two. Sometimes not even that."

"It's different this time. I mean, I accept the fact that I'm more into her than she is to me."

"That's not true," I said, though I wasn't sure if it was or wasn't. It was true that Nica treated Jamie in a casual, offhand way, very different from the way he treated her. But I didn't know if that was because she cared less, or because she had to act like that to balance him out. After all, the relationship couldn't work—not even some of the time—if they were both hung up and jealous.

"It is true, and, like I said, I accept it. But she keeps pushing me and pushing me. And you've got to draw the line somewhere, right? If you want to have any self-respect whatsoever?" He took a deep breath, then let it out. "Next time, Grace, I'm going for a nice girl, I swear."

"Like a nice girl would ever interest you."

"She might," he said defensively. "It would depend on the girl."

"I'm not blaming you. It's not as if it's your fault. People don't get to pick who they're attracted to."

"Maybe not, but they can change."

When I heard this, my heart started beating faster. I looked at his hand dangling casually off my shoulder: if he flexed

167

his fingers, they'd be touching my breast. He looked at his hand, too. Suddenly, everything got quiet.

"God," I said, "I feel weird. I must be drunk." Lie. I hadn't so much as sipped the beer he'd given me. I closed my eyes. I could feel him watching me, though, through my lids. It seemed at that moment that he might kiss me, and whether he would or not depended on my meeting his gaze. I delayed opening my eyes, tried to make up my mind, decide if I was willing to risk it—risk being right about his intentions, risk being wrong about his intentions, risk taking a guy who belonged to Nica, on a break or not on a break—when a beery voice yelled out, "Amory!"

Immediately Jamie and I moved apart.

A guy in a lemon sorbet-coloured polo, untucked and flopping down over dirty khakis, flew through the sliding back door. He jumped on the couch, inserting himself between me and Jamie, and started humping Jamie's leg. "Dude, you made it!" Owen Fitz, the host.

Ten seconds later, Owen had dragged Jamie off to play Quarters and I was left alone. Not knowing what else to do, I went back inside the house. The scene didn't strike me as hell-like anymore, just weirdly lit and extremely loud. I stood on the outskirts of the crowd, clutching my beer, trying to appear bored and indifferent rather than awkward and at loose ends. Occasionally I'd scan the room for Nica and Jamie, not because I was really looking for them but to have something to do.

Then I heard the sound of my name. I turned. Coming toward me was Ellie Rocca, a former tennis teammate at Chandler, now a freshman at Trinity. Ellie was a nice girl, quiet, on the mousy side, and looking totally out of place among the shriekers and grinders. Seeing me, she acted happy

168

out of all proportion to what she could possibly have been feeling. Her outsized happiness was probably at seeing a familiar face. I know that's what mine was at. We hugged, and she introduced me to her friends, also nice, quiet, mousy, and out-of-place-looking. My people, I realized, with a depressing thud. The Margrets and Lydies and Francines, even though their names were Lindsay and Allie and Ashley. The ones I belonged with, and the ones I'd certainly find myself with and only with at Williams next year without Nica around to mooch off socially.

The night passed.

When the party began to die down at around two, I went off in search of Nica and Jamie. I had this idea in the back of my head: I'd run into Jamie first, and together we'd go looking for my sister. It would take a while but eventually we'd find her. She'd be sitting on some college guy's lap, tipsy, sure, though by no stretch a drunken wreck, her speech a little slurry but her decision-making abilities more or less intact, more or less A-OK. Initially Jamie would be livid, ready to storm off, let her fend for herself. Then I'd talk softly to him, remind him that abandoning her wouldn't be right, and that they were, after all, on a break and thus free to sit on whomever's lap they chose. At last I'd bring him around, and we'd try to convince Nica to come home with us. She'd refuse, tell us to mind our own business, to get lost, basically. Finally Jamie and I would walk to his car, knowing we'd done everything we could, and that you couldn't live people's lives for them. Then we'd drive off, just the two of us.

This fantasy fell apart pretty much right away, though, because I couldn't find Jamie. Nica either. Not in the living room, which was almost completely cleared out now, the

169

shades up, the strobe still going. Not in the kitchen where Owen and a girl in police boots and black leather hot pants were arguing over how long to zap an ecstasy-soaked joint in the microwave. Not on the back porch where a bunch of guys were using a Big Mac container as a hacky sack. Finally, I wandered over to the front door, opened it, stepping outside to check for Jamie's car.

And then, all of a sudden, there they were. Nica was standing next to a barbecue pit and Jamie was in front of her, kneeling on the ground. Her face was blocked from view by the curtain of her hair, but I could tell from the angle of her neck that she was looking down at him. One hand was holding a cigarette, the other was being held by his. He was pressing the palm of it to his cheek. They were entirely dressed, weren't even doing PG stuff, and were in plain sight, not only of me but of the whole street. Still, I understood that I was seeing something I shouldn't be. I didn't stop watching, though. I couldn't. Jamie's face, flashingly illuminated by the strobe in the window, transfixed me. In the sleazy light it looked otherworldly in its beauty, near angelic, the expression on it rapt and so, so tender—astonishingly tender, meltingly tender—as if he wanted to dissolve right then and there, be absorbed into Nica's body. I wished her face was visible to me, too. If I could see its expression, something would be revealed to me, I just knew it, some always-hidden thing: her feelings about him, how deep they ran. As deep as his for her?

And then she turned.

Our sight lines locked and we froze, not so much as blinking. Then, slowly, Nica brought her cigarette hand from her hip, to her mouth. Parting her lips, she released from deep inside her throat a perfect smoke ring. The ring floated dreamily upward, and just as it was about to drift into shapelessness, she thrust her finger through its center, popping it. This gesture—playful and childish but, at the same time, not playful or childish at all, a dig at both my virginity and my presumption, a put-down and a warning in one—was more wounding than any smirk or mean remark. And after she made it, she turned away from me.

I stood there for another second or two before creeping back into the house.

The ride home was uncomfortable. Not because of Nica. She was totally at ease, calling Jamie Slim Jim, resting her feet in his lap as he drove; and, now that I'd been bested so completely, she was even able to be nice to me, passing me her Mounds bar after she'd picked all the chocolate off it—an old ritual of ours. And, oddly, it wasn't because of me, either. I, too, was totally at ease. I'd stepped out of line, gotten above myself, and had been justly slapped down. It was Jamie who was uncomfortable. He kept asking me questions, scanning my face anxiously in the rearview mirror. I think he was afraid I was disgusted with him, judged him a hypocrite for getting back together with Nica after he swore he was through. But I wasn't disgusted. Far from it. I was impressed. The image of him on his knees at her feet would be with me, I knew, till the day I died. It would be what I'd picture every time I heard the words *romance* or *passion,* that phrase of purest corn, *true love,* believing in it like believing in Santa Claus or the Tooth Fairy, though secretly I did believe in it, believed in it with all my heart.

Long story short: I can't see Jamie feeling about Nica the way he did and then turning around, firing a bullet into her gut, leaving her body splayed in the dirt for birds to shit on, worms to eat.

\* \* \*

Damon's looking at me in a way that lets me know he's said something and is waiting for my reaction. Shaking off my reverie, I say, "I'm sorry. What was that?"

"I said, you *guess* it's possible that Jamie killed Nica?"

"Damon, I'm agreeing with you. What are you getting so hot under the collar for?"

"Because you're agreeing but not really. I don't know why you need so much convincing. Your dad thought he did it."

"My dad wasn't thinking straight when he talked to that reporter—obviously. Because Jamie has an alibi."

"That your dad called shit."

"My dad was wrong. It's not shit. Jamie was at a squash tournament in Westerly, Rhode Island. He checked into the tournament. He checked into the hotel. There are records and everything—police-verified."

"So what? Just because you check into a hotel doesn't mean you can't leave your room. And Westerly's only a couple hours away. He could've easily driven back to Hartford."

"You think he left Hartford after school, drove to Westerly, played a match, drove back to Hartford that night, shot Nica, and then drove back to Westerly again to play his second-round match in the morning?"

"Sure. Why not?"

Getting hot under the collar myself, "Look, I already said it was possible. Let's move on. Or if you don't want to move on, if you really want to talk about dads, why don't we talk about Jamie's?"

Damon blinks at me, taken aback by what I've just said. Not as taken aback, though, as I am. "You mean that? You think Jamie's dad could have done it?"

"I don't know," I say truthfully. "He said he was at home with Mrs. Amory. It's a weak alibi. Your wife's going to lie for you." I sigh. "I have no reason to think it except that he wanted Nica."

"Wanted her wanted her? His son's girlfriend? That's fucked up."

"I thought it was. Nica thought it was funny, though. Maybe it was funny. Maybe I'm reading too much into it." I shut my eyes, rub them hard. Then I say, "You mentioned it was cold that night at the water tower. That means you and Nica started up sometime during the winter, right?"

"No, mid-March. Just one of those cold early spring nights."

"So after Nica and Jamie broke up," I say, thinking out loud.

"You were expecting her to have cheated on him?"

"No, it's just I still don't know why she ended it with him. And if she fell for someone else, that would explain it. Did she ever tell you?"

"She refused to discuss him, which was fine by me. The two of them were done, she said. That was all I needed to know." A pause. "You and Jamie are friends. Can't you just ask? Or won't he talk to you about it?"

"The breakup? Before Nica died, that's all he talked to me about. Hours and hours and hours, every night on the phone."

I feel Damon's eyes fix me sharply.

"What?" I say, not looking at him, self-conscious because I know I've just given something away. "Like you said, he and I are friends. Friends talk."

"Then that's the first thing we should try to find out."

I stare at him. That the *we* was on purpose, not a slip of the tongue seems too much even to hope for.

"You think I'm going to let you run around by yourself, chasing after a psycho who's killed two people and—"

I interrupt. "Two? How did you come up with that number?"

"Nica plus Manny. Am I forgetting someone?"

"No," I say. "Jesus, I was. I was so focused on Manny not having killed Nica that I didn't, like, take the logical next step. Of course. Someone must have killed Manny, too."

"And made it look like a suicide."

"Wow, yeah."

We're both quiet, lost in thought.

It's Damon who finally speaks. "Get up."

"What? Why?"

"So you can help me get up. My leg's stiff. All right," he says, once I've pulled him to his feet, "I'll see you tomorrow at the office. Sleep tight." He starts off down the street toward his grandmother's.

The abrupt end to the conversation has taken me by surprise, and for a while I just stand there, watching him. When at last he's absorbed by the darkness, I snap out of it. Begin walking myself.

I've just about reached my car, when, suddenly chilly, I slip my hands into the pockets of Nica's jacket. My fingers collide with something. I pull it out. A torn-off piece of blank paper, folded in half. I unfold it.

Nica,
    Jeanne's been acting skittish lately. I'm FREAKING out. Does Bill know about us? I thought we'd been so careful, but maybe not careful enough. Could he have said something to her??? I need to talk to you. Same place? Same time?
    T

As I drive home, I keep looking at the scrap of paper on the seat beside me, rubbing my eyes over the words on it, trying to interpret them, understand how they might connect to Nica's death. Jeanne is Mrs. Bowles-Mills's first name; Bill, Mr. Mills's; making *T*, obviously, Mr. Tierney. So Mr. Tierney *was* romantically involved with Nica, just as Jamie had thought before he spotted Mr. Tierney skulking outside the Millses' house all those months ago.

The anger I feel toward myself is so overwhelming it makes it hard to breathe. Had I been a little sharper, a little slicker, not quite as wide-eyed, I would have put this together much sooner. Wouldn't have made the naive assumption that because Mr. Tierney was sleeping with Mrs. Bowles-Mills he wasn't sleeping with Nica too. Would have understood that an affair with a middle-aged woman in an unhappy marriage made an affair with a teenage girl with a reckless spirit more likely, not less.

But if *T*'s identity is clear, not much else in the note is. It sounds as if Mr. Tierney had ended things with Mrs. Bowles-Mills and she wasn't happy about it, that Mr. Mills might have seen or heard something that led him to believe Mr. Tierney and Nica were a couple, and that Mr. Tierney was afraid he'd voiced these suspicions to his wife. Why was Mr. Tierney afraid, though? Or, rather, of what was Mr. Tierney afraid? That Mrs. Bowles-Mills would rat him out to the school? To the police? That she'd turn violent? That she'd make Mr. Bowles-Mills turn violent? Toward him? Toward Nica? Or was he the one who turned violent? He sure sounded desperate in his writing, practically beside himself. Could the vector of his desperation have changed? Become directed at Nica?

The only way I'm going to get answers to any of these

questions is by asking. Confronting Mr. Tierney's a definite. What isn't, though, is whether to take Damon with me when I do. I'm torn. He's just agreed to help me find Nica's killer, which means he's entitled to be informed of any new developments. But he's also just finished telling me that Nica was the love of his life. Does he really need to hear about the other guy she'd been fucking while she was with him?

I decide to pursue the lead on my own. If it goes somewhere, then I'll tell him. But only then.

# CHAPTER TWELVE

I crawl into bed at a quarter past five, crawl out again at a quarter to eight. Queasy with morning sickness and lack of sleep, I shower and dress for work. Head downstairs to slosh milk and cereal around in a bowl, leave the bowl in the sink or on the countertop—some conspicuous location where it will have to then be moved by Dad to the dishwasher. Once I enter the kitchen, though, I take two steps toward the refrigerator and stop short. The room is filled with stink: cheap alcohol combined with openmouthed breathing. I turn. There's Dad at the table, under *Nica's Dream,* body slumped sideways in the chair, lips mashed against a plastic mat with different types of citrus fruit on it, hand curled around an empty bottle with the familiar yellow label.

This isn't the first time I've found him like this. It isn't the second time either. He hardly ever used to touch liquor. A beer occasionally or a glass of wine with dinner, but that was it. Since Nica died, though, drinking Jim Beam until he passes out is a regular thing with him. I know I should probably say something, ask him if he needs to see a counselor or join one of those programs with the steps, especially now that his doctor's prescribing him trazodone. (Not that he's exhibited much interest in the drug. He picked up his refill at the pharmacy weeks ago. The bottle's still sitting in its crinkly white bag on the end table by the front door.) And it's not as if I don't understand the impulse, using a chemical substance to allay a pain that isn't physical.

Which is why I turn around, tiptoe out of the room. After all, Dad isn't raising his blood alcohol level during the day, on the job, or posing a threat to anybody's safety. It's only at night, after he's met his obligations—obligations primarily to me, providing food and shelter, the steady presence of a parent who won't leave no matter how bad it gets—and only when he thinks he's alone, no one around to witness the gruesome and heartrending sight of a man falling to pieces. If I wake him to help him upstairs to bed, he'll realize I know about his drinking, and once he knows I know, he'll feel compelled to stop. And, the truth of the matter is, I don't want him to stop. I believe that he's been pushed past the point of endurance, that Nica's death has broken him, and that alcohol is what's keeping him going, allowing him to function; it's what's allowing him not to function, too, to shut off, lose consciousness for a couple hours. And God knows he deserves whatever peace he can get.

I decide to close the A/V department a period early, just cross my fingers and hope no late-day requests come in. As soon as seventh is over, I lock up and head to Knox Theater. Slipping in through a side entrance, I take the staircase down a level and walk along the corridor, passing the office of Mr. Savvides, the drama teacher, the storage room that contains old stage sets, some from as far back as the forties and fifties, then pause in the doorway of the ceramics and woodworking studio.

Mr. Tierney's at the wheel. He's wearing a linen shirt, shorts, tennis shoes with no socks, his thick, wavy hair mussed just so. As he works, his hand moving up and down inside an expanding clay wall, he talks to a pretty junior, Leigh Cullen. I can't hear what they're saying over the hum of the wheel, but the soft cadences of their voices let me know it's flirtatious. Leigh drops her head as she responds to something he's said. When she does, I see him look past her to catch his reflection in one of the dark wall tiles opposite.

At last he notices me standing there. He stops the wheel and jogs over to me, hand outstretched. When I don't take it, he looks down, sees it's covered in clay up to the elbow. He shakes his head and laughs as if he's done something foolish but charming. "Gracie, I heard you'd become one of us. I've been meaning to stop by the library, say welcome to the dark side. So"—laughing again—"welcome to the dark side."

Not laughing, I say, "I need to talk to you."

"Sure. What's up?"

"Privately."

"Okay," he says. "But can you give me a minute? I'm just wrapping up with Leigh here. She wants to switch into my adviser group." He raises a hand vertically beside his mouth. "I'm trying to talk her out of it without letting her know I'm trying to talk her out of it. She's a nice kid. Kind of a pain in the ass, though." Then he grins, the grin meant to show that he knows he shouldn't be calling a student a pain in the ass, is doing it anyway—a real little rascal. It unleashes a burst of rage in me.

"Take your time," I say casually. And then, when he's turned away from me, "Is this slutty schoolgirl or hot for teacher?"

I watch the color rise up the back of his neck. "What?" he says in a near whisper.

"I just wondered whose fantasy I've wandered into—yours or hers. I'd have thought your experience with Nica would have cured you of the schoolgirl fantasy. But, hey, maybe not."

"Leigh," he says in a normal voice, "we're going to have to finish this discussion another time."

Leigh makes a pouty face. "But, Mr. T, you said before that—"

"It doesn't matter what I said before. I'm saying now that this isn't a good time." Then, easing up on his tone, "We'll talk tomorrow, okay? In fact, just bring the paperwork by. I'd be happy to be your adviser."

When the door closes, Mr. Tierney turns back to me, his smile for Leigh quickly fading. "Grace, are you insinuating that—"

"That you were having sex with my sister? No, I'm not insinuating that at all." I wait until I see relief loosening his features before continuing, "I'm saying it straight out."

His only response is to stare at me. And then he says, "That's ridiculous."

"You two were hitting on each other every chance you got."

"Flirting is different than—" He breaks off.

"Than?"

After a long pause, he says, "Haven't you ever heard the old Victor Hugo line? God created the flirt as soon as he made the fool." The playful-teasing note has returned to his voice, and from it I understand that he's decided to treat my accusation as a joke. Has decided to try to anyway.

"Haven't you ever heard the old Jimmy Buffett line?" I say back. "Fifteen will get you twenty." Nica was sixteen. Still underage, though.

Another long pause. "Listen, Grace, I don't know where you got the idea that Nica and I were involved, but it's not true." All traces of jocularity are gone from his tone, and his eyes are holding mine. He wants to show me that he isn't laying a line, that he couldn't be more sincere. I'm not fooled. It's just another pose.

"I got it from you," I say, and drop the note on the table in front of him. He looks at it, then at me, then at it again. Wiping his hands on the tail of his shirt, he picks it up. As he reads, I keep my eyes on his face, watch it fly apart, go wide and flat and stretched, before snapping back together. The reaction only lasts for a second—a spasm—but I catch it. If I'd had any doubts about the affair going in, I don't now. "So the question, Mr. *T,* isn't whether or not you were fucking Nica, it's whether or not Mrs. Bowles-Mills or Mr. Mills knew you were fucking Nica."

He starts to speak, but the words stick in his throat. Trying again, he says, "Where did you get this?"

"No, that's not how this works. You don't ask the questions. You answer them."

He gazes blankly at me, the note dangling limply from his fingers. Then all of a sudden, he steps forward. The room shrinks as he leans his body into mine, seizes my shoulders, shakes me. "I said, where did you get this?"

Now I'm the one who can't speak. All I can do is stare at the two white balls of spit that have formed at the corners of his mouth.

"The answer to your question, Grace, is that I have no idea what the Millses knew or didn't know—about anything.

Now, for the last time, where did you get this?" He shakes me again, this time so hard my teeth rattle.

"The pocket of Nica's jacket," I say, almost shouting. Immediately his grip slackens. Angry with myself for getting scared, for giving in to him, I jerk my shoulders back. "Why were you so jacked up about Mrs. Bowles-Mills finding out you and Nica were together? Was she jealous? Angry that you'd dumped her? Was her temper bad? Was Mr. Mills's?"

Mr. Tierney is silent, his head bent so that I can't see his face. Sensing that the time to press my advantage is now, I say, "If you don't start talking, I'll go to the Millses. Get my information from them. Is that what you want?"

Seconds pass. He brings his hands to his face, presses his fingers to his eyes. His shoulders begin to heave. My heart starts to beat fast with excitement. I've got him. He's going to tell me what I want to know.

And then he lifts his head, his smile so big it looks like his face is breaking in two. And that's when it hits me: he was shaking with laughter, not sobs. I've overplayed my hand, I realize, have pushed him too far, made it so he's past caring.

"Go ahead," he says, blotting his eyes with the cuff of his shirt.

"This isn't a bluff. I'll go over to their house right now. I'm not kidding."

"So who's stopping you?"

I hesitate, frantically trying to think of another move. I can't. Snatching the note from his hand, I exit the studio.

Ten minutes later I'm standing on the Millses' porch, lifting their heavy brass knocker. No answer. I let thirty seconds pass, lift the knocker again. Still no answer. I cup my hands around my eyes, bring them to the glass panel beside the

182

door. The houses owned by Chandler aren't quite identical but almost: narrow, ramshackle, poorly ventilated, historic plaques from the Hartford Preservation Society in the first-floor windows. And the front hall I'm peering into could be ours. I see a side table with a Suzuki Method piano book on it—the Millses have a kid, a little girl, four or five years old, whose name I'm blanking on at the moment—a framed print on the wall, a Miró, I think, a pair of galoshes by the stairs. No people, though.

I don't know the Millses very well. They've only been at Chandler a few years and are part of the administration rather than the faculty. And, as the CFO, Mr. Mills, an intense balding guy in his midforties, travels a lot, putting the financial squeeze on the school's far-flung alumni. When he is home, he seems to spend most of his time in the garage, working on his model railroad. It's more often that I see Mrs. Bowles-Mills, a Canadian woman about a decade younger than her husband, pretty in a wan, no-makeup sort of way, wears her hair in a braid wrapped around her head. She's always with her daughter—Beatrice, I just remembered, the daughter's name is Beatrice—taking the little girl to swim in the pool in Houghton or to feed the family of ducks that live behind the Science Center. When we run into each other, we smile or wave or nod, but that's about it.

I send Damon a text, letting him know he's going to have to get himself to and from the courthouse today. Then I drop down on the porch's top step, settle in to wait for one or both of the Millses to come home. I hope it won't be long. Informing a husband of his wife's infidelity isn't exactly my idea of fun. It's necessary, though, a point of honor almost: I told Mr. Tierney I wasn't bluffing, now I've got to prove it, not just to him but to myself. Still, I'm in a state of dread, sweat sliming the back of my neck and the underside of my arms, nausea souring the pit of my stomach.

Yet as I continue to sit there, picking at the bracelet of dried clay on my wrist, I realize that the expectation of an ugly scene isn't what's troubling me so. At least, it's not the only thing. There's something else—a feeling I'm getting. I close my eyes, concentrate on this feeling. After a while I determine it's not a feeling so much as a hunch, a gut twinge, and the gut twinge is telling me that Mr. Tierney wasn't lying when he said he didn't have sex with Nica. It was his attitude toward the accusation—incredulous rather than defensive— that gave his denial the ring of truth. And once he read the note, the charge of carnal knowledge of a minor didn't seem to interest him anymore, his focus shifting entirely to the Millses. Now I'm sitting on their doorstep, a bomb ready to go off, blow their lives to smithereens, and I can't shake the sense that I've been planted here by Mr. Tierney, that he's working me in some way I don't understand for reasons that are beyond me.

But how, I wonder, could *he* be working *me*? I'm about to turn his greatest fear into a reality. It's possible, though, that he wants his greatest fear turned into a reality, is on a weird self-destructive trip. Who knows? Not me, that's for sure. I've been pretending I know, careening from conviction to conviction like a human pinball, setting off every light and spark and bell, absolutely positive about one thing, then absolutely positive about another. But, the truth is, the only thing I'm absolutely positive about is that I don't know anything at all.

No, that's a lie. I do know one thing. I know that I don't want to go on that self-destructive trip with Mr. Tierney. Yes, it's disconcerting that he was slipping Nica cryptic personal notes, evidence that there was something improper about their relationship, insufficient boundaries at the very least. Not evidence, though, that he killed her, which is all I care about at present. This isn't to say I'm done with him, or the Millses, but I need more information before I proceed.

I'm just getting to my feet when I hear the grinding of garage gears, smell a whiff of glue. I cock my head, see a pair of men's work boots sticking out the bottom of the rising door. Mr. Mills. He must've been in there the whole time. I grab my bag, book it down the front path. By the time the door's all the way up, I'm nearly across the street. Unable to resist, I turn around. Mr. Mills is standing at the top of the driveway in safety goggles and a paper mask. He looks like a monster in a creature-feature movie: half man, half insect.

I turn back around, keep walking.

I wake up the next morning depressed. Disgusted, too. The encounter with Mr. Tierney had yielded nothing but an ugly scene. No new suspects, no new leads. I half wish I'd gone ahead as planned yesterday, said to the Millses what I'd come to say. So what if I was being manipulated by Mr. Tierney, blundering into a situation I knew little about? Even if my actions were stupid, reckless, ill-informed and even iller-advised, at least they were that—actions. I'd be making something happen. Instead I'm back to where I was at the end of the conversation with Damon: trying to find out why Nica broke up with Jamie, not a clue as to how to go about it.

The A/V department is busy that day for the first time. I get a last-minute request for a screening from the Asian Culture Appreciation Society, which is meeting that afternoon. I'd set up for them during eighth only Mr. Krueger wants to show the "always be closing" speech from *Glengarry Glen Ross* to his Introduction to Behavioral Economics class during eighth, and it isn't until the period's three-quarters over that he gives me the cue to hit play.

I'm run-walking back to the A/V room to pick up another DVD player (Krueger asked me to leave the one I brought behind so he could show the speech to his Advanced Behavioral Economics class tomorrow) and a copy of *Eat Drink Man Woman*, trying to beat the chapel bell, tolling any minute now, when I realize I'm going to be late to Fargas no matter how much I hurry. I stop, pull my cell out of my bag to call Damon, tell him to cover for me. Right away, though, I get self-conscious. Cells are such a big time no-no at Chandler. Boarders are forbidden to have them; day students are forbidden to use them. If a day student is caught making or receiving a call during school hours, his or her phone isn't just confiscated for the day, it's confiscated for the semester. I'm staff now and the rules no longer apply to me, but I still feel like I'm doing something wrong. I kill the call before it goes through.

As I'm tucking my phone back into my bag somebody yells my name. I turn, see Shep. He's jogging toward me from the opposite side of the quad, blond hair bouncing, flip-flops making flat slapping sounds against the concrete. Watching him, I feel, in addition to the expected impatience, unexpected if not unfamiliar guilt. It takes me a second to trace its source: voice mails, the two he'd left that I'd never listened to.

When he reaches me, he says, slightly out of breath, "Did you get my messages?"

"I did, yeah. My cell, though, Shep"—my eyes wavering from his, dropping to the sunglasses dangling crookedly from the collar of his shirt—"it's kind of messed up. It cuts out a lot."

"Luckily, I don't put much trust in modern technology, which is why I also had a bunch of these printed." He reaches into the pocket of his overalls, extracts a sheaf of bright yellow papers, holds them out to me like a bouquet of flowers.

I pluck one. It reads:

ATTENTION MEMBERS AND PROSPECTIVE
MEMBERS OF THE OUTDOOR CLUB!
The 7th annual meeting will be held
THIS FRIDAY.
Refreshments followed by a screening of
surfer classic *The Endless Summer*.
8 P.M. at Endicott House Cottage.
Gnarly, dude!!!

The Outdoor Club, of which Shep is founder and faculty sponsor, is exactly what it sounds like: a club for people who are into the outdoors. One Sunday a month club members travel by van to some picturesque New England spot and engage in an at-one-with-nature activity, biking or kayaking or, in the winter, skiing or snowshoeing. It used to be the only kids who belonged to it also belonged to FUCCU! (Friends of Urban Connecticut Conservation Unite!), Chandler's environmental group, and Cheesed Off, Chandler's vegetarian society; they wore hiking boots with every outfit, carried around tattered copies of *The Prophet*, and cared deeply about the fate of the Sumatran tiger. But in the last couple years, the club's really caught on with the cool boarder crowd. Jamie and Ruben had both joined, Nica and Maddie along with them, and I'd never understood why. And then a breeze stirs, coming from behind Shep, sending a waft of patchouli-scented air my way, and suddenly I do. It wasn't the natural world that attracted them, it was the natural high.

Marijuana.

I can't know this for sure since when I was a student at Chandler I avoided situations in which Shep was likely to be present, and that certainly included any organization he might be head of. And since I also avoided situations in which Nica, Jamie, Maddie, and Ruben did drugs—well, not drugs drugs, pot mostly, a tab of acid every once in a while—because, though I always kept my face a careful blank whenever Jamie opened his Altoids tin or Ruben whipped out those small squares of what looked like origami paper wrapped in aluminum foil, Maddie claimed she could still feel my "narc eyes" on her, and they ruined her experience. I think I'm right, though. It's not that tough to get loaded on campus, but it's definitely easier off. And Shep's the type who'd ask what the funny smell is, believe it when he's told incense, preferring to imagine it's his senses that are lying to him rather than his students. God, that explains Nica and the others' weirdly indulgent attitude toward him, why they put up with his touchy-feely cluelessness. He's a sucker. His touchy-feely cluelessness is the best part.

Shep taps the flyer with his index finger. "I'm thinking of taking the club to Narragansett Bay the last weekend in September. Teach those landlubbers how to surf. I figured this movie would put them in the right frame of mind."

"Yeah, it should," I say, eager for him to get to the point so we can wrap up this conversation and I can be on my way. "I've never seen it. I've heard good things, though."

"Well, you'll see it on Friday at the club meeting, won't you?"

Putting it together, "Oh! You want me to run the movie for you? Like for work? For the A/V department? That's why you called?"

"No, I want you to watch the movie, for you. And not for work. For, like, fun. I called to invite you. And, rewinding, you heard good things about the movie because it is good."

"Oh, it's, um, really nice of you to think of me, Shep, but—"

"Maddie's going to be there. Jamie, too, probably. They'd like to see you."

My laugh doesn't sound like my natural one. "I wouldn't be so sure about that."

"Of course they would. They're your friends."

"They're Nica's friends."

"They're yours, too, even if you don't realize it. And they're hurting the same way you are."

I feel a twitch of annoyance. I'm not one of his charges anymore, and my emotional well-being is no longer his responsibility or concern. Instead of reminding him of this fact, though, I let loose with another unnatural laugh. "Hurting?" I say. "I think Maddie's more into inflicting pain than feeling it."

He doesn't laugh with me. "I know it seems like that. But sometimes the harder a person pushes you away, the more the person actually wants to pull you close."

"Then Maddie must really want to pull me close. Like really really want to."

"Could be."

I snort. "Yeah, to put me in a choke hold maybe."

Shep gives me a pained look, shakes his head.

Switching my tone to serious since that's how he's taking

189

everything, I say anyway, "The problem is, though, I've already sort of got plans that night."

"Got or sort of got."

"Got," I say definitely.

"So bring whoever you have plans with along."

"But don't you already have a lot of people coming?" I say, trying not to sound as desperate as I feel. "Your place isn't that big, is it?"

"It's big enough. And the more the merrier." When I don't respond, "Just tell me you'll think about it."

I'm mad at myself. Had I listened to his messages, I'd have had an excuse polished and at the ready, wouldn't be getting backed into a corner the way I am now. "Fine," I say with a sigh. "I'll think about it."

"Whew! Now don't go getting all gung-ho on me."

He's smiling widely and I give him a small one back, a small one that gets bigger, then turns into a laugh. And maybe it's because I've finally figured him out, solved the mystery of his appeal for Nica and the rest, and so have the luxury of feeling sorry for him, but, for the first time I can remember, I feel genuine liking for him, too. "I'll think about," I say again.

"Beautiful. That's all I ask."

The chapel bell tolls and the two of us say our good-byes. Instead of continuing on my way to Burroughs, though, I reverse direction, head to the dorms. The Asian Culture Appreciation Society will have to wait till next week to watch its movie. As Shep and I were talking it had hit me: the option I've avoided so much as thinking about is, in fact, my only one. Maddie. After all, she was Nica's closest friend, and if Nica had told anybody the reason for the breakup with Jamie, it would have been her. The trick will be in getting her to tell me. She'll make me beg, really grovel, and

190

once I've degraded myself will probably still withhold. But I have to try.

Field hockey practice begins almost immediately after school. Maddie, though, I know, doesn't like to change with the team in the locker, prefers the privacy of her dorm room. That gives me a twenty-minute window.

Archibald House is set back from the street by a circular driveway and a cluster of yellow birch trees, and is grand-gracious in the manner of a southern plantation: white and sprawling with tall columns and windows, fluted pilasters, carved pediments, a portico you have to climb three steps to reach. I climb them and pull open the heavy mahogany doors, pausing on the threshold as my eyes adjust to the interior. It's dim. Shabby, too, this building, like most of the others on campus, far more impressive on the outside.

I cross the foyer to the common room, smelling it before I'm in it: Murphy Oil Soap and burnt popcorn and the beeswax used in lip gloss, all mixed with the musky, hothouse scent of girls ripening into women in close quarters. It's empty. A Ouija board has been left out on the coffee table along with a York Peppermint Pattie wrapper, a leaky pen, a pack of tarot cards. I turn to the corkboard. In between a sign announcing the disappearance of a graphing calculator ("Whoever took it, please give it back. My financial aid package does not include help with supplies. Beth Gustowski") and another announcing the launch of a David Foster Wallace fan club ("We're calling ourselves The Mad Storks. If you need to ask, don't bother showing up, you poseur") is the room assignments sheet. Maddie's in 107. A double.

I start walking, eyes down in the unlikely event that I run into somebody I know. I don't see a soul, though, until I turn onto Maddie's hall. At the far end of it is Ruben. He's sitting on the floor across from her door, twisting the knobs on a pocket-sized Etch-A-Sketch. Guess the two of them didn't break up when he moved on to college after all. So much for her being interested in Jamie.

Ruben's eyes are glued to the screen of his toy, and I think I can escape without being spotted. I've just turned, taken my first tiptoey step, when his voice booms out, "Gracie!"

I turn back. "Hey, Ruben," I say, trying not to sound sheepish, like I've been busted.

He lets the Etch-A-Sketch fall to his lap. "You got to pee or something?"

"No."

"You sure?" Crossing his legs at the ankles, having fun, "Because you were moving like you had to pee, like you were going potty."

"Nope. Not going anywhere."

He pats the floor beside him. "Then take a load off. I could use the company."

After a moment's hesitation, I drop down, though across from him rather than next to. He's in the middle of a meal, I see. Chicken wings, the kind that sit under a heat lamp in the Hot Foods section of a convenience store, a bottle of chocolate Yoo-hoo propped against his thigh. Over the summer he's grown himself a set of sideburns. Also, a potbelly, which hangs over the waistband of his sweatpants, as white and dimply as cottage cheese.

"I heard you were back in town," he says, picking up a wing dripping in buffalo sauce, inserting it in his mouth. When he takes it out again, it's glistening bone. "You here to see Maddie?"

My impulse is to lie, say it's someone else I'm here to see, but I know he'll ask who and at the moment I can't think of a single person other than Maddie living in Archibald. "I am," I say.

He leers at me. "I bet you are. Want to get her all to yourself, huh?"

"I guess."

"Looking for a little alone time, are you? A little alone time with Maddie and her field hockey stick, her great big long hard field hockey stick?"

I yawn into my fist, letting him know that his leer, more or less automatic, bores me; his sex trash talk, too, also automatic. And for a while we sit there, the silence broken only by the sound of chewing and swallowing, the occasional belch.

There's a note on the dry erase board on the back of Maddie's door. The handwriting belongs to Maddie.

LB,
    If my mom calls I'm out and you don't know where I am or when I'll be back. Try not to take a message either.

It takes me a second to figure out that *LB* is Charlotte Bontemps, Lottie to her friends, Maddie's roommate, who spent the previous year studying in Barcelona because she couldn't, she said, deal with America anymore. I wonder if Maddie still has that Robert Mapplethorpe photo of Susan Sontag hanging above her bed, the one Nica bought her, or if she trashed it when she moved out of her dorm room last spring.

Ruben interrupts my reverie, saying, "So, Grace, long time no. Why haven't you been by to see me? I'm only at Trinity. Practically just down the street. Don't tell me you kicked that sleeping problem of yours."

"As a matter of fact, I did."

"Did you try yoga like I suggested?"

"Uh-huh."

"And it worked?"

"Like a charm."

"No shit."

"Who knew, right? And here I thought I'd never—hey, Ruben, would you mind not staring at my breasts?"

He looks up at me, takes the finger he was sucking the grease off out of his mouth. In a hurt tone, "I was just trying to read your T-shirt."

My shirt's not a T. It's a button-down, plain white.

Wiping his hands on the front of his sweat suit, he says, "Really, I think it's great you overcame your problem. Beat the odds and all that."

"Lucky for me I did. I was going broke."

"Sleeplessness is expensive. For future reference, though, cash isn't the only form of payment I accept."

I shake my head, less in disgust than wonder. "Jesus, you really are a creep."

"Hey, I'm a stud muffin, baby, take a bite," he says, singsong. And then in a normal voice a few seconds later, "And for the record, I don't make that offer to just anyone."

"Yeah, right."

"I don't. You used to rub me hard the wrong way. Always sneaking looks at people to see what they thought of you. Did they like you? Did they think you were okay? Oh, boo hoo, boo hoo." He shudders. "You haven't been rubbing me the wrong way lately, though. Not in the last couple months. Want to know the two words I think when I look at you now? *Not* and *bad*. Ever since you started seeming kind of"—he pauses to take a swig of Yoo-hoo, work his tongue thoughtfully around his mouth—"defiled. Yeah, defiled." Warming to his subject, "These days you slink around, too skinny and too pale, never smiling, like you're hungover or crashing all the time. And you've got this look on your face—tight, but kind of loose, too—that girls get when they're overfucked."

"Stop," I say, deadpan. "I can't take all the violin music."

"I'm not saying you *are* defiled and overfucked. I'm saying you *seem* defiled and overfucked. Anyway, I think it's sweet that you're here, taking care of your sister's unfinished business. A sense of familial responsibility is so sadly lacking in people these days, don't you find?"

I look at him, confused. Why is he bringing up Nica? What unfinished business? A sense of familial responsibility on whose behalf? And then confusion gives way to fear. Could he be referring to her murder, solved but not solved right? Did he know I was investigating it? The thought that he might pushes me to my feet. I'm not ready to explain myself to him. "I've got to go," I mumble, afraid that he'll try to stop me or say something else upsetting.

"Oh, no. Don't leave."

"I'll catch Maddie another time."

"But she'll be back any minute. She has to be. Can't run up and down the field in designer ankle boots. If you don't want to wait, I'll let you go first. Just promise me you won't let her stick a piece of gum over the keyhole. She used to do that when Nica came by."

I stand there, staring at him, my mind struggling to construct a scenario, other than the obvious one, in which Nica and Maddie would engage in an activity behind closed doors that he would wish to observe but would not be allowed to. My mind fails. Still, I want it spelled out for me: "Are you telling me that Nica and Maddie were—" leaving a blank for him to fill.

"Fucking. Well, not fucking fucking. Probably just using their fingers," he says, idly sniffing his. "Or their tongues, maybe. No big thing. All women are lesbians. It's true. Studies have been done. Oh, wow." He turns his face up to the ceiling. "Boy, are we a couple of dodos. A pair of real shit-for-brains."

"What? Why?"

"It's Wednesday. Game day. Maddie's not coming back to her room to change. She's probably on a bus, halfway to some hayseed town in New Hampshire where . . ."

As he continues to talk, I feel my eyes blink, my ears close off, my brain tunnel back six months to tennis preseason.

Mr. Schaeffer was giving us a demonstration in Houghton Gymnasium on proper bicep curl technique when Nica and Maddie showed up late for the third day in a row, hips bumping, faces flushed from running. He dropped his barbell to the floor, ordered the two them into his office, sent the rest of us out to the courts to do groundstroke drills. I stayed behind, though, lingering over an untied sneaker, and watched through the door, which he'd left open. Nica and Maddie were standing in front of his desk, gazes lowered penitently, while he ranted and raved. And then his phone rang. He turned around to get it, and as he did I saw Nica lean over, reach up under Maddie's shirt, place her index finger squarely on Maddie's sternum. As Mr. Schaeffer barked single-word answers into the receiver, she dragged the finger slowly down, circling Maddie's belly button not once but twice before slipping inside. He hung up, and she smoothly took back her hand. He resumed his harangue.

I didn't know then that Nica and Maddie were lovers. The possibility never even occurred to me. Why should it have? Maddie had been with Ruben since her sophomore year, and

Nica was so boy crazy. And, besides, Nica's gesture—touching Maddie's stomach—was hardly sexual. Except, of course, that it was. There was intimacy in it, possession, too. There was also Maddie's pleasured shiver in response to it. And I must have noticed these things, registered their implications, if only unconsciously, otherwise why would this nonevent have lodged itself in my memory?

Ruben, I realize, is no longer speaking. I look at him.

"So you have nothing to say back?" he says. "Deafening silence? That's all I'm going to get for my juicy revelation?" He laughs. "Same old kooky Grace."

"Same old kooky Grace," I echo shakily.

He takes a final messy sip of Yoo-hoo, screws the cap back on the empty bottle. "Okay, I'm out of here. Unless, of course, you want to give it another shot?"

I shake my head, not knowing what he's talking about, but knowing I don't want to give him another anything.

"Sigh," he says, "oh well." And then he rolls to his feet, takes a pen from behind his ear. "You got a piece of paper on you?"

"Sorry."

"A napkin? A tissue? A Kotex pad?"

When I say sorry again, he looks a little exasperated. After scratching thoughtfully at a sideburn, he tears off a swatch of the brown paper bag his food came in. Scribbling on it, he says, "My address at Trinity. In case, you know, the insomnia comes back. My office hours are the same."

He tries to hand the scrap to me but I won't take it, so he balls it up, drops it in my bag. "Smell you later, Gracie," he says, starting off down the hall, leaving the chicken bones and Yoo-hoo bottle behind. His miniature Etch-A-Sketch falls out of his sweatshirt pocket. He bends over, cat-quick, to

197

retrieve it, his wide-hipped body weirdly limber and graceful. And then, without so much as a look back, he disappears around the corner.

A minute later I'm walking out of Archibald House. My cell rings. Damon. Too excited now to be self-conscious, I answer right away. "I'm sorry I'm missing work again, and I know I should've called, but—"

"Grace?" he says. Something's wrong. I can hear it in his voice.

My stomach plunges. "What happened? Are you okay?"

"It's Max. He just had a heart attack."

# CHAPTER THIRTEEN

I'm nervous. It's Friday, early evening. I'm on my way to pick up Damon. It'll be the first time I've laid eyes on him in three days. The first time I've spoken to him, other than through text or e-mail, in nearly as many. Fargas Bonds has been closed until further notice. Not closed as in shut down. Max has almost half a million dollars' worth of paper out there. No new paper is being written, though. And Damon and a colleague of Max's, an older guy named Carmichael, are handling the outstanding cases. Otherwise, Damon's spending every waking moment at Max's side. I'd offered to swing by the hospital, pick him up there, but he'd told me no, that he wanted to go to his grandmother's first. Understandable, I think, as I turn onto his street. He's probably seen about as much of her lately as he has of me, is eager to check in, make sure she's okay.

He's sitting on the curb in front of the house, looking at his cell when I pull up. He puts the phone away and gets in the car. As I drive, I watch him out of the corner of my eye. He seems, not surprisingly, preoccupied. And we pass most of the trip in silence, sympathetic on my end, but still, silence.

About a mile from Chandler, I say, "How's Max?" And then, quickly, "If you don't want to talk about him, you don't have to."

"No, I can talk about him. He's all right. Hanging in there, I guess. They did an echocardiogram on him yesterday and it showed a clot in his left ventricle."

"Is that bad?"

"Well, it's not good. The clot could break off at any time, cause a stroke."

"Are they doing anything to make that not happen?"

"Sure, yeah. Lots of things," Damon says.

And I listen to him as he goes on to talk about beta-blockers and anticoagulants, statin therapy versus ACE inhibitors. His voice is calm and matter-of-fact, but I can hear the fear underneath, fear that's turning all his thoughts into questions: What if Max doesn't get better? What will happen to the business? To his grandmother? To him?

I want to say something, audition several sentences in my head, but they all sound stupid and stilted and trite—useless. And, before I know it, another silence has formed over us, like ice over water, thickening by the second.

Damon is the one to break it: "What is it we're going to tonight? If you told me, I forgot."

"No, I didn't tell you. I figured if I did, you might not come."

A tired smile. "Smart thinking."

"It's the Outdoor Club meeting. It's at Shep's place."

"Shep? You mean Mr. Howell?"

"Yeah, Mr. Howell. And we're going because he asked me to go and I owe him one, but also because I've been wanting to sort of bump into Maddie and I'm pretty sure she'll be there."

Puzzled, Damon says, "Maddie lives on campus. How hard can it be to bump into her?"

"Harder than you might think. And time's running out."

"On what? Nica's already dead, Grace."

"I know that," I say, flustered. "I know she's dead. I just—I don't want this to drag on forever. I want resolution." Forcing out a laugh, "Predictably selfish, I know."

He sighs. "That's not selfish. That's normal. Okay, so what do you want to bump into Maddie for?"

"If anyone knows the story behind Nica and Jamie's breakup, it would be her."

"That's right. She and Nica were close, weren't they?"

"Um, yeah," I say, taking a left into Chandler's employee parking lot. "Yeah, they were."

I find a space at the back. After switching off the engine, I tell Damon about my visit to Archibald House. It doesn't take long, and when I finish, I glance over at him. He's staring out the window. He touches the side of his face with his hand and I can see emotion there, intense yet unreadable. It occurs to me that he might be upset, feel I was holding out on him. Quickly I add, "I wasn't sitting on this. It's just, we've had a tough time connecting and this isn't exactly the kind of thing you can leave in a voice mail."

He's silent for several seconds. Then he nods, vaguely at first then emphatically. "No, no, of course not," he says.

It's not just his words that tell me I'm wrong about why he's emotional, it's his manner—distracted, like his attention's fixed on a conversation he's having with himself rather than the one he's having with me—as well. Is he emotional then because he regards what Nica did as cheating? "For what it's worth," I say, "I don't think Maddie and Nica were together when you and Nica were. At least not the whole time."

"Why?" he says, and this time it's his tone—curious, but not burningly so—that tells me I'm wrong.

"Because I was with Nica on her last day, and she was trying to duck Maddie."

"You don't think she's the one who hurt Nica, do you?"

"Maddie? Like physically hurt her? Like killed her? Definitely not." I start to laugh. "If she had killed my sister she'd be nicer to me, don't you think? Out of guilt if nothing else. Instead she's meaner than ever. Besides, she was at a house party that night. A sophomore from Simsbury—Davy Something—was throwing it. People saw her there. She got hammered, crashed on the couch. The police took statements and everything. In fact, she didn't make it back to Chandler till after breakfast. She'd have gotten busted except who was going to notice that morning?" After a pause. "I have done *some* investigating on my own, you know." After another pause. "And, anyway, how would someone like Maddie get her hands on a gun?"

"What about Ruben?"

Surprised, I say, "What reason would Ruben have for wanting Nica dead?"

Damon, just as surprised, "Jealousy. What else? She'd moved in on his girl. And he's a dealer. Dealers are known to carry."

I shake my head.

"Why not?"

"First of all, Ruben's not a dealer, not a real one."

"What is he then? A fake one?"

"No, he's not a fake one. Of course he's not a fake one. What I mean is that he's not a professional one. He doesn't deal because he needs the money. He deals so he has easy access to drugs. It's more of, like, a hobby for him. And no way is he going after people who are late on payments, threatening to blow their brains out. He just doesn't care enough. Plus, he's lazy. Second of all, he was in New York when it happened, at a nephew's bar mitzvah. He was on an Amtrak as soon as school ended on Friday."

"Did you see him on the train?"

"Personally? No?" I'm getting annoyed because Damon seems to be misunderstanding everything I say on purpose.

"Did a camera catch him boarding the train or getting off the train?"

"What? I don't know. I do know that the police checked him out and that he came back clean, which is good enough for me. And, besides, he wasn't jealous of Nica. The impression I got was that he was into what she and Maddie were doing. Like super into it. If he had negative feelings toward anyone, it was toward Maddie for not being more, you know, inclusive."

When Damon doesn't say anything back, I look at him. I can't see his eyes because his gaze is aimed at his lap, but I can see the way every muscle in his face is drawing tight. And when he finally speaks, he has to clear his throat first, like it's closing up with feeling. "Okay, fine," he says. "Ruben didn't do it. Just do me a favor and stay away from him. If you have to talk to him again, tell me and I'll go with you."

"You think I need protection from Ruben?" I start to laugh again. "You obviously don't know him."

"I know him. Know him enough. Know he's a dealer and a scumbag."

"Yeah, he is, both those things. But he's harmless, basically. A bark that's worse than his bite."

"You think his sleaziness is all on the outside. You think because he acts like a clown he's not dangerous."

"I can handle him."

Damon snorts. "Right. Until you can't."

Damon's behavior—so hostile, so aggressive—is confusing me, angering me, too. What makes him think he knows my friends better than I do? That he can tell me who to associate with? Give me orders? And all of a sudden we're both breathing loud enough to hear and are glaring at each other.

He looks away first, dropping his head in his hands, rubbing his thumbs against his closed lids so hard his eyeballs squeak in their sockets. When he raises his head, his face has lost its tautness, is drained and pale. "You look different," he says.

"I shouldn't. I haven't changed anything." My voice is stiff, inflectionless: mad.

"It's your hair, how you're wearing it."

"It's in a ponytail. It's in a ponytail most of the time."

"Oh," he says softly.

Relenting a bit, "I took a shower right before I came to get you. I put my hair back when it was still wet. It probably looks a little darker than normal, is all."

"Well, I like it."

"You look good, too," I say, and only as I'm saying it do I realize I'm being truthful, not just polite. He isn't dressed in his usual style. Is wearing a light blue Oxford shirt, sleeves rolled to the elbow, pants that aren't jeans. A shirt and pants that he put on to go out with me, I think. And suddenly I understand: he stopped at his grandmother's not to check in on her but to clean up for me.

Our eyes meet, and something private passes between us, too private maybe because our eyes immediately bounce apart, and we both laugh nervously.

"Well," I say, reaching down, unlatching my door, "we should probably get going. It's already quarter past eight."

"Yeah," he says. "Let's do it."

The Outdoor Club meeting is being held at the Endicott House Cottage, where Shep, the dorm's head, lives. As Damon and I near it, the nerves I buried at the start of the evening begin to surface. What if Maddie's a no-show? Or shows but refuses to talk to me? Then I'll have hit a dead end, the final one as far I can see. There are no other avenues left to try, and I don't know how I'll move forward. When Damon reaches for the door, I put my hand over his, stilling it. He looks at me for a long moment, then nods, telling me with his eyes that I can do this. I nod back.

He turns the knob and we enter.

I've never been inside the cottage before but have always been curious. The setup is basic: a large room with a small kitchen in it. At the far end is a hallway, and on the right, a door, behind which is, I assume, the bedroom and bathroom. Furniture and decoration is minimal—a picnic table, an India-print tapestry covering one wall, potted plants lining the windowsills, a couple hanging from the ceiling. A lot of earth tones. A lot of beanbag.

The atmosphere is partylike in a wholesome, low-key, no-alcohol kind of way. On the table part of the picnic table is one platter of sliced vegetables, another of chocolate chip cookies. On the bench part of the picnic table is a tub filled with ice and soda cans, plates and napkins beside it. In the background some sort of music is playing—tribal-sounding, vaguely percussive, like two sticks being knocked together.

Shep is behind the kitchen counter spreading hummus on toasted pita wedges. He must've been in a hurry when he pulled his hair into a ponytail because it's not tugged all the way through the rubber band, is half in a bun. He raises his head to reach for the sesame oil, catches me looking at him. Smiling broadly, he waves his knife, sending drops of mashed chickpea flying. I hold up my hand, breaking eye contact as I do so he doesn't take it as an invitation to come over, start talking.

My gaze resumes its scan of the room. The crowd, comprised of twenty-five or so students, is skewed to male, though only slightly; skewed to cool, more than slightly; and skewed to boarder, overwhelmingly. I home in on it, looking for Maddie. See Jamie first. No surprise since whenever I'm in a room, I seem to know instinctively where he is, a prickly warmth spreading along whichever portion of my body is turned his way. He's collapsed in one of the beanbag chairs, soda in hand, long limbs elegantly splayed. Maddie is standing above him, Ruben beside her.

Jamie must feel me looking at him because his head rotates. Our eyes touch. He blinks, waves me over. As he does, Damon whispers, "I'll see you later."

Maddie tracks my progress, her gaze first going flat, then brightening with glittery dislike. She's wearing her long hair in a painful-looking ballerina bun, the coil wound so tight her eyes are pulled up at the corners, bobby pins securing any stray wisps, tamping them down. Her lipstick, a fuchsia-tinged pink several shades too vivid for her complexion, washes her out; her cardigan, a pearly pink several shades too muted for her complexion, does the same. When I get close, she makes a big show of turning away. And I'm looking at her in profile, all nose and chin, as she slips her hand into Ruben's.

"Let's go, you," she says to him, her voice girlish, kittenish. Weird coming out of her.

He shakes her off. "Go where?"

"To the bathroom."

"You're a big girl. You can use the toilet by yourself."

"There's no lock on the door. I want you to make sure no one walks in."

"Hey, Grace," Ruben says, "Maddie's looking for someone to watch the door while she goes peeps." Turning to her: "It is just peeps, right?" Turning back to me: "Can we borrow your bodyguard?"

Dropping the baby-doll act, Maddie says, "Ruben, come *on*." She tugs his belt buckle.

"You are one spun-out little honey, honey," he tells her. But he lets her drag him across the room. As he passes the kitchen area, he looks back, brings a pinched-together thumb and index finger to his lips: a toking gesture. Mouths the word, *Later,* to Jamie.

Jamie gives a lazy smile back. Watching him, I think how his entire body has the attitude of that smile.

He turns the smile my way. "There's room for two," he says, patting the spot next to him on the beanbag chair.

There isn't, really, and when I drop down, I end up more on him than the chair. Not that I mind. I mind even less when he doesn't seem to. And for fifteen minutes at least we sit there, mashed together from hip to shoulder, my right leg twined through his left, tranquilly watching the activity swirling around us, the cliques forming and dissolving, the conversations and flirtations flaring up, abruptly dying down, only to flare up again in a different corner. It's just a few weeks into the school year, and people are still checking out the new clothes, the new haircuts, the new attitudes and poses and vibes, interested in each other now in a way they won't be in a month or two.

Ruben and Maddie return from the bathroom, though not to me and Jamie, settling by the wall with the India-print tapestry on it, fighting every so often but mostly hostile to one another in silence. Ruben eyes the girls, does lip-licky things with his mouth; Maddie eyes him, appears restless and unhappy. A few feet away, Mr. Tierney, besides Shep the only nonstudent present, looking tousled and handsome in jeans and a knit tie, is addressing a trio of sophomores, female, naturally, telling them about a trip he's planning to take to Nicaragua over Thanksgiving break. Mr. Wallace enters a minute later. Shy-faced, gangly-limbed, his glasses fogged up from the walk over, he approaches the little throng. Mr. Tierney gives no sign of seeing Mr. Wallace but he must because he shifts the angle of his shoulders a degree or two, subtly barring his friend's entry. Mr. Wallace, unaware that he's being snubbed, hangs back, politely waiting for acknowledgment. Waiting and waiting. It starts to become awkward for Mr. Tierney to ignore Mr. Wallace yet he continues to do so. One of the girls, Sophie Plunket, the prettiest of the bunch, turned off by the weirdness or bored by it, drifts away. Mr. Wallace moves into the voided space. Still Mr. Tierney says nothing to him. Finally Mr. Wallace retreats to the kitchen, shaking his head in hurt puzzlement.

I'm puzzled, too. Mr. Tierney pretending Mr. Wallace—sweet, bumbling, funny-looking Mr. Wallace—is invisible? Why, so he doesn't have to share the attention? God, what a jerk. I'm about to make this observation to Jamie, but then remember that Jamie seems to be getting along with Mr. Tierney these days.

I make this observation instead: "Wild party."

Jamie looks at me, eyes diffuse in that watery way of

someone fighting off a cold, then laughs. "Yeah, really hopping. I can't even get a sugar high."

"That's not soda you're drinking?"

"Seltzer water. Pomegranate flavored." He wipes his nose with his sleeve before handing me the can.

I hesitate, worried about catching whatever he has, but only for a second. The imprint of his lips is on the rim. I place my lips over it in a kind of kiss.

"I'm not even supposed to be here," he says, as I pass him back the can. "There's a tournament in Stamford this weekend."

"Decided you didn't feel like making the trek?"

"No, I made it. Left right after sixth period. Seeded one, out in round one."

"Anybody can have an off day."

He sighs. "Yeah, that's true. The tournament was Bronze level—kind of bush-league. There weren't that many points at stake. Still, though, I'm doing a PG year to get my ranking up, not tank it. And it's my second first-round loss in the last six months. I've already dropped from number 3 in Connecticut to number 5. I haven't even looked at my national ranking. Too scared to."

"The U.S. Junior Open isn't for a few months, right?"

"Beginning of December."

"So you've still got time to get in match-tough shape."

He groans. "Just thinking about all the training I need to do makes me tired. Like too tired even to hold my head up."

"Give it a break then," I say, sliding my hand into his hair, dampish with sweat and warm at the roots. He smells clean, though, piney, like the Lightfoot's soap he uses. He leans his head back so that I'm cradling it with my palm. I start moving my fingers in small concentric circles.

"That feels good," he says.

As I massage his scalp, I gaze down at his face, at the skin on his cheek, stretched tight across the long, curved bone, at the spit glistening on his lower lip, as pillowy as any actress in Hollywood's. And then, out of the corner of my eye, I see Shep flash two upraised thumbs at him. I jerk my head around. By the time I do, though, Shep's already back in conversation with Thad Nichols, repeating his junior year because he got mono last fall and missed most of the semester. "Oh, God," I say. "I saw that."

Jamie lifts his head from my hand. "Saw what?"

"The sign Shep just gave you." I start to laugh, laughing but embarrassed.

Careful not to look at me, Jamie says, "I didn't see a sign."

"He just thanked you for talking to me. Don't bother to deny it. Pretty soon he's going to be paying people to be my friends. That's the next step, right? Actual money changing hands?"

Jamie grins feebly. "Think I can get anything out of him now? Snack bar's open till nine and they're selling these chocolate chip cookies this year that are, like, out of this world."

Glad to change the subject, I say, "You're hungry?"

"Vaguely." He rubs his eye. "By the time I got back from Stamford, Stokes was closed."

"There are cookies here. Chocolate chip ones, too."

"No, not chocolate chip. Carob chip. Big difference. Shep made them for me."

"Why?"

"He's trying to reduce the amount of caffeine I consume. Thinks it'll boost my immune system or some shit."

"That's thoughtful of him."

"Yeah, well, I wish he'd be less thoughtful and just make me regular chocolate chip cookies. I mean, if he's going to make me cookies." Jamie heaves himself up out of the beanbag chair. "I'm going to get another seltzer. You want?"

"That'd be great. Thanks."

He nods and walks over to the picnic table, hovering above the two platters. I hope he'll take a cookie, stash it in a napkin or his pocket, just to be polite, but he doesn't. Even though I'm annoyed at Shep for humiliating me a minute ago, I feel sorry for him now. Then I feel annoyed again. How can he be so dumb? Doesn't he understand that Jamie and Ruben and Maddie—Nica, too, when she was alive—don't respond well to kindness? That they see it as weakness, something to be made fun of or exploited? It took me a while but I finally learned that lesson. Why hasn't he? He's around them enough. They like it best if you treat them the way they treat each other: dryly, derisively, cuttingly. That's how they know you're one of them.

I watch Jamie throw away the old seltzer can, pop the top on a fresh one. A bit of spray gets on his hand and he wipes it on the seat of his pants. Then, to my surprise, he turns to his right and strikes up a conversation with Polly Abbot, a senior with a rabbity face. To her surprise, too, it looks like. And delight. It's to her even greater surprise and delight when, moments later, he grabs her by the wrist, leads her to the closed door off the hallway—Shep's bedroom. Almost before I've registered what's happening, Jamie's opening the door, hustling Polly inside, shutting it again.

I stare for a long time at the blank-faced plank of wood, blinking in shock. Finally, I look away, and, as I do, I see Shep. His eyes are turned toward the same plank, his expression one of confusion. Of anger, as well, if I'm not mistaken.

211

And why shouldn't he be angry? Jamie's screwing around at a school function, not even being subtle about it, and on Shep's personal sheets? How incredibly disrespectful. For a second I wonder if there'll be a scene, if Shep will march into his bedroom, toss Jamie and Polly out. But then Thad says his name a couple of times, and when he smiles at Thad, shaking his head at his rudeness, I realize, with a little stirring of disappointment, that he's letting it go. Mr. Nice Guy.

After a minute, I haul myself out of the chair, head to the kitchen. That can of pomegranate seltzer water's not going to get itself.

Fifteen minutes later, Shep's made his pitch for the Outdoor Club, wheeled the TV and DVD player on loan from the A/V department, delivered by me that very afternoon, to the center of the room, dimmed the lights. I'm standing at the rear with Damon. Maddie's at the front, sitting to Ruben's left, the space to his right conspicuously vacant. As the strains of the movie's acoustic theme song begin to swell, I watch her lean her head into his, whisper. He looks annoyed. She whispers again. This time he nods, though not happily, and she detaches herself from his side. Threading through the bodies on the floor, she slips out the door at the back, leaving her bag behind. I count silently to thirty, then follow.

I step into Shep's backyard. Empty. I quickly walk around front. Maddie's not on the little porch, or on the path leading to Endicott either. For a minute, I stand perfectly still, resisting looking to my left. Then, slowly, I turn. Shep's cottage borders the graveyard, haunted grounds for me and ones I've avoided since Nica's body was found there by Graydon Tullis those many months ago. With a sinking heart, I move to the edge. Once I reach it, I stop, change my trajectory, proceed lengthwise along it, trying to peer into the dimness, past the line of spindly gray trees that separates city property from school. I see no sign of Maddie. Could she have gone back to her dorm, told Ruben to bring her bag by later? Is that why he seemed so put out? Because she was asking him to assume an obligation, saddling him with a task? With relief I decide that's what must have happened. And I'm about to head over to Archibald—familiar and snug, full of noisy girls and food smells and posters of actors and musicians and European soccer stars in underwear advertisements, lights blazing in every window—when something catches my eye, a speck of brightness in the dirt. I crouch down for a better look: a hairpin.

I pick it up. Recognizing what I have to do, I straighten and breathe deeply. Then I lift my leg, take my first step into the graveyard. The trees immediately close behind me. Inside it's cool and silent, smelling of sap and freshly dug soil. Above my head the sky is bright, the moon three-quarters full, far-off galaxies glistening and glittering. Walking, I scrutinize the scrap of metal in my hand, like direction isn't something I need to think about.

And, as it turns out, it isn't. I come to a slight swelling in the ground, a little hillock, and when I reach the top of it, I see Maddie. She's leaning against the trunk of an oak, the sole tree in the graveyard, ancient and enormous. A cigarette's between her fingers, and her head's bowed so that I can only make out the upper portion of her face. She's no longer wearing the pink cardigan, is down to a T-shirt, as tight as her jeans, both drawing attention to the compactness of her build: her small breasts, as round and hard as fists, her slim waist and long legs, her narrow hips. Her hair is pulled into that taut bun, so that from my angle it appears cut short and slicked back.

She takes a final drag on her cigarette, flicks away the butt with her thumb and forefinger, her movements graceful without being feminine. Her face has turned, and all at once I can see it in full. I'm surprised at how soft it is—soft and so, so sad—her deep melancholy evident in the set of her jaw, the cast of her eyes, the slant of her lips, pale and unlipsticked now.

I start to approach her. I keep thinking she'll see me, or if not see me, hear me. But her eyes stay down, and my heels are sinking noiselessly into the earth as I weave through the headstones. And then, when I'm only a foot or so away, I step on a twig, snapping it in two.

She looks up, startled. There's a sharp intake of breath, but no words. And then she says, "Grace?" Not a statement, a question—a desperate one.

With a shock I realize that she thinks I'm Nica. I open my mouth to say, yes, of course I'm Grace, apologize for spooking her, maybe even make a joke, but the words die on my lips. She's staring at me, rapt, her face strangely beautiful in the shadowy half-light, the cropped-looking boy's hair flattering it, showing off her wide forehead and high cheekbones, her nose appearing strong rather than big. *As long as she looks at me,* I tell myself, *I'll return the look, no harm in that.* Her eyes drop to my feet and ankles, then travel upward, lingering on my thighs, my breasts, my throat, coming back, at last, to my face. When they do, I tighten my gaze suddenly, pinning hers underneath mine, rendering it immobile, helpless. Then I shake my head, turning it once to the right, once to the left, centering it. I smile. She starts, very lightly, to tremble.

I take another step toward her. I'm so close now that I can see the thin bands of blue around her dilated pupils,

214

the pulse beating on the underside of her jaw. Her back is pressed against the tree trunk, her lips parted. *I am me,* I think, *and I am not me.* Leaning forward, I slide my index finger under her shirt, pressing it against her sternum. Then, with murderous slowness, I trace my finger down her torso, down, down, down, until I reach her belly button, circling the rim once, twice, dipping inside. The muscles in her abdomen contract.

"You've been avoiding me, Maddie," I say. Our faces are almost touching. I can hear her breath as clearly as I can hear my own, feel the damp heat of it. Let her feel the damp heat of mine.

"What do you want?" she says.

"Information."

"What kind of information?"

"How long were you and my sister together?"

When she doesn't answer right away, I take my finger out of her navel, start moving it down again, a quarter of an inch at a time. "How long?" I repeat.

Her breath is coming fast and shallow, a pant. "Two weeks. A little less."

"When?"

"Right after she and Jamie split. She started it, she ended it."

"Why did she end it?"

Maddie swallows, shifting her mouth nearer mine. "She found someone she liked better. A guy."

"Who?"

"I don't know."

"I thought she told you everything."

"Before we were together she did. Not after."

"Why did she break up with Jamie?"

Maddie's face goes white. "I can't tell you that."

215

"But you know," I say. And when she doesn't deny it, "Then you can tell me."

She tries to get up off the trunk, but there's no strength in her movements, and when I apply the slightest pressure to her with my index finger, she falls back. "I can't tell you that," she says again, miserably. "Nica wouldn't want me to."

"Nica's dead."

"It doesn't matter."

"It'll stay between us."

"I can't."

My finger has now made its way to the top of her very low-cut jeans, is resting on the warm skin there. I ease it— only just—into her waistband. She lets out a soft moan, and her whole body starts to shake. I bring my face in even closer to hers, brushing my mouth against her jawbone. "Tell me," I say, my whisper slipping inside her ear, hot and wet, uncoiling like a tongue.

She says something back, but her voice is so faint it takes a second for my brain to register what. I lean back. "What did you say?" Now I'm the one who's starting to shake.

"I said, ask your mom." Her voice is strong, all of a sudden. Hard, too. "And it's the last thing I'm saying to you."

"Maddie, I'm—"

As the word *sorry* hits the air, she brings the flat of her hand crashing against my cheek. My head snaps to the side. With a sob, she pushes me away and runs off.

I return to Shep's cottage half an hour later. The strange sense of unreality has left me. I feel upset by the whole experience, though, frightened at the way it took me over. The credits have just started to roll on *The Endless Summer*. Damon and I slip out the door without anyone noticing.

In the car, I tell him about the encounter, what I learned from it if not quite how. "So Nica found out she and my mom had the same boyfriend—hers," I finish bitterly. "That's why she broke up with him."

"You can't be sure of that," Damon says.

"I can't be but I am."

"You really think that's something your mom would do?"

"You mean, do I think it's in character? Absolutely. She's ruthless—the Queen of Hearts. You get in her way and it's off with your head. And you know from Nica that she never shut up about how wonderful Jamie was. I assumed she meant wonderful for Nica, but I should have known better. She kept everything good for herself."

Damon's quiet. Then he says, "But Nica didn't seem angry at him when she talked about the breakup. If anything, she seemed protective. If Jamie and your mom really were"—he pauses, groping around in his mind, trying to get the phrasing right—"hanging out with each other"—he pauses again to sneak a look at me—"why would she have cared about his feelings?"

"I'm sure Nica blamed Mom. Thought she seduced him. Saw him as her victim, not her partner. It definitely explains why Nica was fighting with Mom so much before she died. And I thought it was because she had cold feet." I laugh, shake my head. "Jesus, how dumb can you get?"

"Cold feet over what?"

I tell him about the upcoming gallery show in Chelsea. Then I say, "I figured Nica got shy even though she never did. This makes a lot more sense."

"But if Nica didn't believe it was Jamie's fault, then why didn't she stay with him?"

"Isn't it obvious?"

217

"Not to me."

"He was damaged goods, forever tainted. And I'll bet she didn't tell him why she was dumping him because it was too painful for her to go into. Not to mention embarrassing. She just wanted to forget the whole thing, move on."

"But—"

I squeeze my eyes shut. "Can we please stop talking about this?"

"Fine," Damon says, "you don't have to talk about it with me." And then, after a beat, "But I think you should talk about it with your mom."

"That's going to be tough considering I don't know where she is and I'm not asking my dad."

He sighs, reaches for his seat belt. "You won't need to."

The next morning Damon unlocks the door to Fargas Bonds, puts his skip-tracing skills to the test. By early afternoon he's found my mother. The artists' commune she's living in is located in Brattleboro, Vermont. Eighty-eight point eight miles north of West Hartford, according to Google Maps. An hour and twenty-seven minutes by car. Two hours and thirty-one minutes if you want to avoid highways.

It takes me an entire night and most of the following day to work up the nerve to use the number Damon gave me. After twenty or so rings, a woman who isn't my mother answers. Mom, the woman says, is in her studio and not to be disturbed. When I don't respond right away, the woman asks impatiently if that's all because. Before she can say because what, I ask for the name of a local coffee shop. With a sigh she gives me one, and I tell her to tell my mom to meet me there at ten the next morning. The woman starts going on about how she's an artist, too, and not Claire Baker's personal assistant or anybody else's. She's still talking when I hang up.

I call Damon to let him know about tomorrow's appointment. He's coming, he tells me, and once he does, I realize that's exactly what I was hoping he'd say. A little voice in my head whispers that if I really care about him, I won't allow him to, will insist on going by myself. What if one of the guys Max has written paper on decides to jump and Carmichael's too busy with his own clients to pursue? Or Max wakes up, asks for Damon and Damon's nowhere to be found? Not one but two compelling reasons for Damon to stick close to the greater Hartford area. I'm afraid, though, that I won't be able to get through the encounter with Mom without him so I don't raise either reason, keep my needy, miserable mouth shut. I tell him I'll pick him up at his grandmother's house in the morning, bright and early.

As I replace the receiver in its cradle, I wonder how I'll hide from my conscience till then.

# CHAPTER FOURTEEN

I'm in the Bakery Arts Café in Brattleboro, Vermont, sipping an Italian cherry soda. The table I'm sitting at is flush against a picture window next to a box of underwatered plants. Through the smudged glass I can see Damon. He's across the street, standing in front of a bookstore, browsing through a rack of secondhand paperbacks. As he leans over to examine the spine of a book on a lower rung, the sunlight touches his heavy black hair.

I drag my soda closer, hope the sugar will give me a jolt. All morning I've been tired but wired, percolating with nervous energy. Now, though, the nervous energy's gone, and I'm sagging. I'd had a restless night, thoughts and feelings pulling me every which way. Memories, too. One in particular.

It was morning, winter break my junior year. Nica was laid up in bed, sick with the flu. Mom knocked on my door, asked if I'd let her take a few shots of me curling my lashes so she could finish the session she'd started with Nica the week before. My heart thumping high and hard in my chest,

220

I said sure, as if her request were no big deal, an everyday thing. I dog-eared the book I'd been reading and followed her into the bathroom. Standing in for Nica should have been a cinch since we looked so much alike except for the hair, and Mom had taken care of that by winding a towel around my head. All I had to do was do what Nica did: act natural. It was that easy, and yet it wasn't easy at all, not for me. As soon as the camera turned my way I stiffened. And the harder I tried to relax, the stiffer I got until I couldn't even fit my fingers into the loopholes of the curler. I watched in panic as first irritation, then disappointment, then boredom crept across Mom's face, listened in dread as the clicks of the shutter became more and more listless, less and less frequent. If I was miserable, though, it wasn't for long. Nica appeared in the doorway, ghost-complected with ringed eyes, none too steady on her feet. Gently she removed the curler from my hand. I stepped back. Looked on as Mom took shot after ecstatic shot.

The bells above the door jingle. I turn. I wasn't sure she'd show, but suddenly there she is—my mother. After Nica died, she lost her looks: the pockets under her eyes puffed up; deep grooves etched themselves between her brows; and her once effortless slenderness became sinewy and gaunt as she was stripped to the bone by grief. She's found them again, though. Is back now to the way she was. Coming toward me in tight black slacks, sleeveless black shirt, cat-eyed sunglasses with white rims, a camera dangling from her neck, her step is light and quick. Nica in twenty-four years. And when she calls out my name in greeting, I find I can't say anything in response. My throat has swollen shut, is aching with her cool loveliness and my involuntary happiness at seeing her.

When she reaches me, I say, "I ordered you a large coffee, house blend," then twist to the side, put my cell phone in my bag, to avoid a kiss.

She starts to open her mouth.

I head her off at the pass. "Unsweetened. The milk's on the side. Skim."

"Thank you, baby. You know, I've never been here before." She removes her sunglasses and camera, lays them on the tabletop, then does what she does whenever she sits down at a restaurant: sweeps her gaze like a lighthouse beam across the room. It's why I automatically gave her the eyes-out seat. I can see her taking in the details: the mugs with the Kurt Vonnegut quotes on them; the sign-up sheet on the wall for the Authentic Movement Workshop; the two girls at the table across from ours, both paint-spattered, one with a shaved head in a T-shirt that says YEAR OF THE ZOMBIE, the other self-consciously spearing melon chunks out of a bowl with a palette knife. And I can tell by the twitch of her mouth that she's about to start making fun of the place.

"If there's a category of human being on the planet I find more repugnant than the hipster, I can't for the life of me think what it is," she says, sipping her coffee, eyeing the two girls. "The clothing with the provocatively worded slogans, the on-purpose bad haircuts, the hopelessly bored expressions on their pampered middle-class faces. They want to be artists, settle for being artsy. If I could, I'd round them all up, ship them off to some deserted island, drop a bomb on the island." She shifts her glance to mine, eyes twinkling, like her meanness is some delicious treat she's sharing. "Though arguably that would be taking things too far."

"You're showing your age, Mom."

She lets out an easy laugh. "Then I better not start reminiscing about the rawer, rougher Bohemia of my day."

"Better not."

"Okay, let's change the subject. Do you want to tell me how you're liking Williams so far?"

"Not really."

That laugh again. "I don't seem to be having any luck here. Why don't you pick the subject."

After a pause, I say carefully, "Thanks for meeting me on such short notice."

"Your invitation was so mysterious how could I resist? Like something out of a spy movie. I almost wore my trench coat with the collar turned all the way up."

"Not possible."

"Why? Because you think I'm too vain to cover my face?"

"Because I know your trench coat's still hanging in the downstairs closet."

Her gaze—light, amused, faintly mocking—doesn't waver. "Is it?"

"In between Dad's parka and an old windbreaker of Nica's."

"That's a raincoat, actually."

I envy her coolness and hate it at the same time. Trying to keep my emotions in check, I lift a piece of the toast I'd ordered, slowly and meticulously spread marmalade on it. "I don't suppose you're coming back to pick it up, are you?"

"Not any time soon, no," she says.

"That's it then for you and Dad? The marriage is over?"

"Looks like."

"So you stay with him just long enough to screw up his life royally and then split. Nice."

223

"What are you talking about? Screw up his life how?"

My nasal passages begin to prick and burn, and I realize with horror that my eyes are filling with tears. "How do you think?" I say, ashamed of the sound of my voice but unable to control it, everything coming out in the same snotty yet wounded tone. "By making him turn down Chandler's severance package. He could have started over somewhere new. But, oh no, you couldn't leave the school. Who knows why. Some weird spite thing probably. And then something better came along and you couldn't get out fast enough. Now because of you he's stuck."

Her eyes widen. "No, baby, you have that backward. *He* made *me* turn down the severance package."

I stare at the toast in my hand without recognition, put it back on the plate. "What?"

"If he's stuck, he only has himself to blame."

I feel a wave of panic rising. I try to quell it, telling myself that Mom's lying, that she forced Dad to stay at Chandler. I know this to be true. And yet when I try to remind myself exactly how I know it, the reasons aren't so clear in my mind.

Mom leans into the table, anger jerking at her features. "My daughter was murdered at Chandler, Grace. Murdered. You think I was interested in hanging around? Admiring the chalk outline of her body from the kitchen window? I wanted out. But your father refused. It was the one time in his life he put his foot down with me and it's a big part of the reason I left. He wouldn't move forward. Wouldn't or couldn't, I'm not sure which. All I know is that back was the only way he wanted to go, and the past was the only place he wanted to be. And if I had to stay in that house—if I had to stay with *him*—for another second I—" She breaks off, breathes shakily. When she continues, it's in a more modulated tone: "I didn't mean to run down your father. He's a good person, and everyone deals with grief in his own way. He did what he thought he had to do, just like I did what I thought I had to do. I needed what you had in college. I needed an escape. And when I found one, the Brattleboro fellowship, I took it."

She's looking at me, and I can see that she's expecting a response, but I'm too disoriented to give her one. She's telling me the truth. I can't know it for a fact because I can't hold up my memory of that horrible spring to hers, compare the two, since the period between Nica's death and Jamie's party is, for the most part, a hideous blur to me. Yet I can feel the truth in her words. And, casting my mind back, I realize that Dad's never actually said that Mom was the one who told Chandler to take their offer and shove it. I'd just assumed. And this assumption was a keystone for me, a foundation, the block of certainty upon which I'd piled all sorts of other assumptions. And now that it's been removed, I find myself teetering dangerously.

A short silence becomes a longer one. Finally she says, "I've missed you, you know."

I stare at the napkin in my lap. "Yeah, right."

"I have, Gracie."

"That must have been why the phone was ringing off the hook with calls."

"I didn't call because I didn't want to talk to your father, confuse him, get his hopes up. Not because I didn't want to talk to you."

"I have a cell phone like every person in America besides you. You could've called that."

"It's true. I could've. But I told myself that you were

225

getting ready to go to college, move on to a bigger and better phase of your life. That I'd only remind you of what you were trying to forget. That you'd want to talk to me someday, but that, for now, you'd want your space." She pauses, as if she's considering her words carefully or as if they're hard for her to say. "I thought I was making things easier on you, but I see now that I was making things easier on myself. I'm sorry."

It's an apology, a real one. I look up at her, and, when I do, panic leaps in my stomach. I'm not sure why panic. Maybe because I see what I think is tenderness in her face and, once I see it, I understand how badly I've been wanting it from her. The dangerous kind of tenderness too. The kind that will peel back my skin and flesh, bend my ribs, expose the wet, trembling heart at my center.

"You know what I was afraid of when I was walking over here?" she says. "I was afraid you'd look different."

She's gazing at me, deep into my eyes, and, as she does, I can feel her intuiting everything I've suffered, everything I've endured, knowing it all without me having to say even a single word. My throat swells again, and there's a pressure building inside my chest. Then she lifts her hand, starts to reach with it, making like she's going to bring it to my face. I try to hold myself in, stay self-contained, keep my cheek from leaning out to meet her fingertips.

"But you don't," she says. "You look exactly the same. You're just the same."

Her words are like a slap to the face, hurting me but waking me up, too. How could I have forgotten? That she seems perceptive and sympathetic but is really neither? That I love her but that I don't trust her, not for a second? And,

226

most importantly, that I can never, never as in never ever, make myself vulnerable to her?

I catch her hand roughly by the wrist. "No touching," I say. "My skin'll break out."

Mom looks puzzled, even a little hurt, but vanity as a motivating force is something she understands all too well, so she nods her head.

"Anyway," I say, "how's your work going?"

An emotion flares in her eyes—panic maybe or fear—and when I spot it, I have to hold back a smile. The question I just asked only sounds dull and innocuous; it is, in fact, as sharp and bloody-minded as a straight razor, because, as she and I both know, without Nica there's only one way her work can be going: shittily.

I remember that day in February when Mom received the call from the gallery in Chelsea, her reaction—a mixture of shock that it hadn't happened for her yet, shock that it was happening for her at all. The theme was to be Nica from the age of *Nica's Dream* on up, an extended portrait. Mom had one problem, though. Nica was refusing to be photographed. Of course, Mom had been photographing Nica for years, had hundreds upon hundreds of images stored. But after sifting through all the material, Mom decided she needed a final image, something new, something that would, in her words, "both close out the show and break it wide open." Only Nica wasn't going to let her get it. Mom didn't seem too shook up, no doubt figuring she still had plenty of time, that Nica's anger couldn't stay white-hot forever, and that when it cooled enough to touch, the photo would be hers. But then Nica went and got herself killed. And unless Mom's worked some kind of magic or miracle—and from the shadow flitting across her face right now, I'm betting she hasn't—her career's about to die a premature death, too.

"The show's just a month away now," I say.

Mom picks up the container of milk, pours it in her cup, turning her dark coffee pale. Then she picks up her spoon, starts stirring. Stirring and stirring. "A little more," she says. "Five weeks."

"Still, you must be in the final stages of the selection process."

She stops stirring. Taps the spoon on the side of the cup, lays the spoon next to the saucer. "Yes."

"Has she—what's the name of the gallery owner again?" I ask, knowing full well.

"Aurora."

"That's right, Aurora."

I'd met Aurora once. She'd come by the house, stopped off on her way back from a trip to Boston. A tall woman in her early thirties, dramatically thin, in black tights and crimson lipstick. "You're the other daughter," she'd said brightly when Mom introduced us, smiling without looking at me, only having eyes for Mom and Nica.

"Has Aurora seen any of the photos yet? Besides *Nica's Dream*, obviously."

Mom, her voice so low I have to lean in to hear her, says, "Aurora prefers prints to CDs. She's driving up from New York this weekend."

"This weekend, huh?" I say, really starting to enjoy myself. "That's a lot of pressure. I mean, nothing's set in stone yet, right? If she likes what she sees, it'll be the making of you, a whole new level of exposure and recognition. If she doesn't, though, she won't show the work or represent you. Must be nerve-racking."

228

Mom looks down and away, raises one shoulder in a shrug.

"So, how did the showstopper turn out?"

"The showstopper?"

"You know, your final image. Did you end up using one of those old pictures of Nica? Bet you found something you didn't even know you had."

Mom closes her eyes. "I found something," she says softly, the lie so transparent I almost feel sorry for her. Almost.

"Where is it?"

"In the studio."

"Can I see it?"

"You want to see it?" Her voice has now sunk nearly out of hearing.

"How about we swing by after coffee?"

She opens her mouth, then shuts it. Just nods.

"Great!" My appetite suddenly returning, I pick up the abandoned piece of toast, take a bite. Then another.

"A little harder, maybe," she says.

I swallow. "What?"

"You. You're harder. At first I thought you looked exactly the same, but you don't. You used to have a dreamy, tender quality. It's gone. Without it you look more like Nica. More like me, too, actually."

To an outsider it sounds like I've just been insulted. I haven't been, though. Nothing makes Mom's lip curl faster than innocence. She's always been clear about how unappealing she finds the trait, how moist and sticky she thinks it is, how close to stupidity. So her telling me I'm hardening up is a compliment. And, of course, being compared to her and Nica is the ultimate compliment. I feel my cheeks flush.

229

I try to duck my head, keep her from seeing my pleasure, but she catches my chin.

"The dreaminess has burned off almost entirely," she says, turning my face this way, viewing it from different angles. "You should sit for me sometime, let me photograph you."

When she says this I nearly laugh out loud, at my susceptibility as much as at her shamelessness. The one-two punch: softening me up with flattery, then hitting me up for a favor. I can practically see the thought bubbles coming out of her head: *Aurora's not driving up till this weekend so I've still got a few days. Nica's gone but I have Grace and she's better than nothing. Maybe I can pull the show out of the toilet after all.*

I bare my teeth at her in a grin. "No thanks. I'm allergic to having my picture taken. Remember?"

She shrugs. "Up to you."

*Nice bluff,* I think sourly. Sick, suddenly, of the cat-and-mouse games, I decide to get to the point. "I asked you to meet me for a reason. There's something I've been wondering about."

She folds her hands in front of her, cocks her head to the side, letting me know she's all ears.

"Why did Nica break up with Jamie?"

She looks at me, eyes shuttering and unshuttering several times in rapid succession. Then she says, "Shouldn't you be asking Jamie that?" Her voice is smooth and unhurried, but it's too late. She's already given herself away with those stuttered blinks.

"He doesn't know."

"And you think I do?"

"Know Jamie? Yes, I do think you know Jamie. I think you know Jamie very well."

If she registers my smirky, insinuating tone, she doesn't let on. She tears open a sugar packet, spreads the grains out on the table, starts writing her initials in them.

Getting impatient, I say, "Why did Nica break up with him?" And when she still doesn't respond, I pick up my spoon, bang it twice on the tabletop. "Come on, Mom. It's a simple question."

"With a complicated answer. And not the one you're imagining."

"And what am I imagining?"

She brushes her hands over the sugar, erasing her initials, and looks directly into my face. "That I was screwing Jamie's brains out."

The crudeness of her language makes me flinch. "So you weren't?"

"Give me a break. My sixteen-year-old daughter's boyfriend? And, besides, two Bakers in love with him was enough, don't you think?"

This time I manage not to flinch. To give myself a few extra seconds, I return my spoon to its original spot to the left of my knife, line up the two utensils precisely. I'm hearing a very convincing denial of what I thought was my worst fear. So why isn't the relief just coursing through my veins? Something in Mom's face is holding it back, a certain tightness around her mouth. "You have something to say, say it."

She snorts. "You don't want to hear what I have to say, baby. Trust me."

She's right. I don't. But I do want this to be over, and it can't be over until she tells me everything. "Say it."

She looks at me, then shrugs. As she opens her mouth to speak, though, an electric bolt of fear runs through my body, bringing me to my feet so quickly my chair shoots out behind me, crashes into the wall. She stares at me in surprise. "I have to pee," I mumble.

The Bakery Art's Café's bathroom is unisex, naturally, and without a proper lock, just one of those flimsy eye hook things. There's a chair inside, though, and I prop it against the door. After flushing down the bites of toast I throw up, I stand before the mirror, gaze at my reflection. I rinse my mouth out, rinse it out again.

At last I return to the main area. Weaving through the jammed-together tables and scattered chairs, I make my way toward my mother.

Mom lifts her cup of coffee, blows on it, even though it must be ice-cold by now. She reaches up, takes out her clip, letting her hair, a brown so dark it appears black—Nica's shade exactly—tumble to her shoulders, then re-pins it in a slightly different way. She touches the middle tine of her fork, the edge of her saucer, the lobe of her ear. She's stalling. *It's okay,* I tell myself. *I can wait.*

"I wish I still smoked," she says with a sigh.

"Even if you did, you couldn't smoke in here. It's as illegal in Vermont as it is in Connecticut."

"I could until someone stops me."

I look around, careful to avoid the eye of our waitress so she doesn't think I'm trying to signal her. I spot a boy with nicotine-stained fingers sitting at a table by himself. I walk over, ask him if he has an extra cigarette. He pulls one out from behind his ear. I stick it between my lips so he can light it. It's bent from the curve of his skull and tastes waxy from whatever he styles his hair with. I inhale without letting any of the smoke into my lungs. After thanking the boy, I return to Mom.

"Talk," I say, as I hand her the cigarette.

She brings it to her face, drawing on the filter so hard her lips disappear. She holds the smoke in her mouth a long time before exhaling reluctantly. At last she begins: "I graduated from art school at twenty-one. Up until then, I'd lived in a small town in Vermont and Providence, Rhode Island, also a small town. I decided there'd be no more small towns for me. I wanted a big city, the biggest. I wanted New York City."

"So what stopped you from getting it?"

"Money, not having any. I knew if I went there straight-away, it'd be hand-to-mouth, working round the clock to pay for some toilet bowl in a crummy neighborhood. No time for photography. No time for romance. No time for anything. It would be better, I decided, to move to a less expensive city for a year or two, save my pennies, develop a portfolio. I picked Hartford. God knows it's cheap. And a lot of Connecticut is rural, important to me at the time because I was still taking pictures of twigs and berries. Plus, I knew someone who knew someone whose mother-in-law was the art teacher at Chandler and about to retire. I inter-viewed for the position and was hired."

She pauses to take another drag on the cigarette. What she's saying doesn't have anything to do with Nica and Jamie, but I'm interested almost in spite of myself. She's always been so evasive about her past, so cagey with the details.

"That first semester was lonely. I was the youngest faculty member by nearly a decade. I barely spoke to anyone outside the classroom. And I was spending most of my non-teaching time in the campus darkroom. And since I was a dorm parent I didn't get out much on nights or weekends. I was making it through, but I was counting down the days. Then came the Alumni Winter Fund-Raising Luncheon. I would have skipped out, only I'd already missed the Alumni Fall Fund-Raising Dinner and I was skating on thin ice with Dean Crowley as it was, so I went. That's where I met James. He was—"

"James?" I interrupt. "James who?"

She looks at me. "James Amory." Like, who else?

"Jamie's dad," I say, clarifying.

"Well, not then he wasn't. He was just James. Crowley used to trot him out at all the fund-raising functions. Still does. He's an Amory, a direct descendant of one of the original Chandler Academy families. Represents continuity, I guess. Not to mention, he looks great in a three-piece suit. He looked especially great in a three-piece suit twenty years ago. The speech he gave that day wasn't exactly impressive, but it was charming, self-deprecating. He noticed me as soon as I walked in. He was shy, though. I had to go up to him."

I'm in shock. I'm beyond in shock. I'm in disbelief. Mom and Mr. Amory? I'm careful, though, not to reveal myself. My voice neutral, I say, "Was he married?"

"Not then, no."

"But he'd already met Mrs. Amory?"

"They were engaged. Didn't stop the girls from chasing him, though. He was tall and graceful and lazy-eyed, like some big beautiful cat."

"Sounds like Jamie."

"Jamie's his twin."

"You were in love with him," I say instinctively.

Mom's mouth turns down at the corners. "I never said that."

"You were, though, right?"

She's looking at me, the expression on her face an old one, as old as my memory. It's telling me that, once again, I've disappointed her, have said something wrong, something nobody else would wish to have said, have failed, in the most fundamental of ways, to get it.

"Love's such an imprecise term," she says, tipping her head to the ceiling, releasing a moody tendril of smoke. "Which love do you mean? What kind? Tenderness? Sentiment? Longing? Lust? Obsession?"

I return her look. No way is she going to pull her cool number on me, shame me into muteness, make me too self-conscious to ask her to elaborate. Not this time. "Were you in love with him? Yes or no?"

She shakes her head like she's amused. "Oh, Grace. You're still such a child."

"Answer."

"All right, yes," she says, annoyed. "Yes, I was; I was in love with him."

"So what was the problem? He wasn't in love with you?"

"No, he was."

"But he was in love with Mrs. Amory too?"

A scornful laugh. "In love with her money."

"I thought Mr. Amory was already wealthy. I mean, already rich," I say, correcting myself without thinking, without even realizing. Mom hates euphemisms. Thinks they're frumpy beyond belief—middle class putting on airs. I feel that way about them too now, of course.

Mom, catching both the error and the revision, smiles.

Swallowing back my irritation with myself, I say, "Well?"

"His family used to be but they weren't by the time he came along. There was enough to get him through Chandler and Princeton and that was it. When I met him, his J. Press shirts were frayed at the collar and he was living at home while he studied for the bar."

"I didn't know he was a lawyer."

"Trained as one but never practiced. Never had any intentions of practicing, is my guess."

"An aristocrat," I say.

"That's right."

"And yet he was still willing to leave his loaded soon-to-be wife for you. Why didn't he?'

"She got pregnant."

"And you got dumped?"

Mom smiles, but she's angry. A stranger wouldn't be able to see it. I can tell, though, by the way her eyes grow long at the corners. She doesn't like the way I'm talking to her. So what. "That's the short version," she says.

"Were you upset?"

She doesn't respond. Just taps ash into her saucer.

"You were devastated," I say. "Then what happened?"

"Your father offered to cook me dinner. It was a couple months after it had ended with James, but I still wasn't myself. Otherwise, I never would have said yes. It wasn't that he was bad looking. His features were nice enough. There was something blurry about his face, though. You couldn't remember what it looked like if it wasn't right in front of you. I used to catch him staring at me all the time at school. I thought he was sweet." The contempt she lets touch her voice when she says this last word is, I know, as much to hurt me as to insult him.

I don't react. Just say, "Well, the date must have gone all right."

"I showed up at his place, lonely and depressed, got drunk on bad wine and pregnant on even worse sex. That was the date."

"Jesus, Mom."

"You're the one who wanted to know the truth."

"If that's how you felt, why didn't you get an abortion?"

"I was going to. I'd scheduled an appointment at the local clinic. I just told your father as"—turning up the hand that isn't holding the cigarette—"I don't know why I told him, actually. Courtesy, I suppose. He dropped to his knee, proposed on the spot. He knew I didn't have feelings for him, that I was still hung up on James, but he said he loved me enough for both of us and wanted the baby. The thing is, I knew I was in no state to be making life-and-death decisions. I was still walking around with a black cloud over my head. So I let him talk me into skipping that first appointment. I meant to make another one but I never did."

And there you have it. Not only am I the product of a pity fuck, I was this close to getting sucked into some doctor's vacuum besides. I'd always known that Mom didn't love Dad the way he loved her. I'd done the math, though. I was born just six months after the two of them got married. I figured that meant there was genuine passion between them at one point, even if, for Mom, it had faded. I feel sad for myself, sadder for Dad. "What next?" I say. "Not happily ever after obviously."

Mom stabs out her cigarette, drops it in her cup. "No, not happily ever after. You were only six weeks old. One day I was taking a walk with you in your baby carriage in Colt

Park. James was doing the same with Jamie. All we did was look at each other and it was on again."

"He treats you like shit and you take him back? Just like that?"

"I wouldn't have under normal circumstances, but, Gracie, picture my situation. I woke up one morning and I didn't recognize my own life. I was married to a man I barely knew, never mind liked, never mind loved. My dreams of becoming an artist, of bright lights big city, were circling the drain. I had this baby—you. And I loved you but you were after me constantly. Crying for me, latching on to me with those tiny little lips, sucking me dry." She shudders at the memory. "You just needed, needed, needed—it never stopped."

"I was a baby, Mom. What did you expect? That I'd be able to discuss the influence of Rothko on the work of Nan Goldin with you? The difference between the Leica M6 and the Leica M7?"

She's silent, her eyes on the cigarette butt floating in her coffee.

Suddenly my energy's gone. I'm not even angry anymore. Just tired. Tired and depressed. All I want to do is go back to the car, drive home, fall into bed and never get out. "This conversation's over," I say. "I've heard enough. You're right. I shouldn't be kicking over logs. I'm putting this one back, okay? I'm putting it back."

"Are you sure?"

"I can answer the question of why Nica broke up with Jamie myself now. Somehow she found out about the affair that you and Mr. Amory were having and felt too weirded out to continue dating Jamie. That's why she never gave him a reason. She was protecting him. Didn't want to tell him his dad was a cheater."

Mom's lips twitch, and I know that once again the dark scenario I've envisioned isn't quite dark enough. "What?" I whisper.

She rubs at a stain on the table with the flat of her thumb.

I clear my throat. "Mom, what?"

"James and I aren't having an affair. Not anymore. We haven't been together in more than seventeen years. It ended for good when I got pregnant and—"

"I thought you started up again *after* you got pregnant with me."

"Not pregnant with you, baby," she says, her voice gentle. "Pregnant with Nica."

"Pregnant with Nica," I repeat dumbly.

"I wanted him to leave his wife. He wouldn't do it. Said he couldn't risk losing his son. No mention of the daughter he'd be giving up."

"So Mr. Amory is Nica's father," I say, half thinking that this truth, too, will fall away, be denied or contradicted, exposed as false as so many truths have been today. But it doesn't. It stands between me and Mom, as dense and solid as a brick wall. "How can you possibly know for sure? You were married to Dad at the time. You slept in the same bed."

She starts rubbing at the stain again. "Because I just know, all right? Without going into the gory details I—"

"Go into them."

She exhales heavily, then says, "Your father and I were sleeping in the same bed, but that's all we were doing in it."

"So Dad knew Nica wasn't his?"

"Well, presumably he knows where babies come from so how could he not?"

"Did he know whose she was?"

From the way Mom's looking at me I can tell that the question's never occurred to her.

"What about Nica?" I say.

"What about Nica what?"

"Did she have any idea that she was breaking the law, both legal and natural?"

"Oh, Grace, don't be so melodramatic."

"Why not? It's a pretty melodramatic situation—two family members fucking. I mean, how creepy can you get?"

"All families are creepy in a way."

I stare at her, not believing what I'm hearing. "You're quoting Diane Arbus to me right now?"

She shrugs.

"Or maybe you didn't see them as family. I mean, she was Nica, but she was also your daughter, right? An extension of you? And you weren't related to the Amorys, so she couldn't be."

"I knew Nica and Jamie were related. But they didn't share a mother."

"They did share a father, though."

"Oh, please. Fathers don't count. You have one. You know." Mom sighs. When she speaks again, her tone is softer. "Look, as soon as Nica and Jamie started dating, James and I discussed the situation. We decided the smartest thing to do would be to just stay out of it. If we interfered they'd just want to be together that much more. And they were only high school kids. It wasn't as if they were getting married. It was puppy love."

"Yes, but puppy love leads to puppy sex. What if Nica got pregnant?"

"I gave you girls the safe sex lecture before you hit puberty. I had Nica on birth control at fourteen."

"But people have accidents."

"If she'd had an accident, we would have taken care of it."

I look at her sitting there, legs crossed, hand draped over the top of her coffee cup, exuding self-assured feminine ease. If I could just smash open her skull, pick out the information I need, that's what I'd do. Anything would be better than talking to her. And then I say, "How did Nica find out?"

"James walked in on her and Jamie one afternoon. Turned out, he was okay with the two of them being together in theory but when it was right in front of his face he felt differently."

"Not so much of an aristocrat after all, huh? Scandalized by incest. How bourgeois."

She ignores the dig. "He told them to get dressed, asked Nica to join him in his study."

"Just Nica?"

"James is very careful with Jamie. Doesn't want to upset him."

"Why?"

"Apparently at his old school Jamie had a problem with drugs."

"*Had,* past tense? Please, Jamie's the biggest pothead I know."

"I can assure you," Mom says dryly, "pot is not what James is concerned about."

I want to ask what Mr. Amory is concerned about then—a few psychedelics, cans of beer?—but am afraid of getting sidetracked. Instead I ask, "What happened in the study?"

Mom's eyes narrow in recalled anger. "What happened?

James let his hair down is what happened. He told Nica everything. Told her about us, about him being her real father, about the pact to keep it all a secret. Then he begged her not to repeat any of what he'd said to Jamie."

"You heard this from Nica?"

"From James. He called the next morning to check up on her. Said when she'd left his house the night before she was positively beside herself, crying so hard he was worried about her driving. He also thought she'd stolen a bottle of whiskey from his liquor cabinet. I was furious with him. Not just for letting her drive when she'd been drinking, but for blabbing. Especially without warning me first, not even a . . ."

Mom's lips keep moving but I've ceased to hear the sounds they're making because the scene she's described has unleashed something, and, all at once, a memory is coming at me, looming above my head like a tidal wave, threatening to crash down on my life, break it open, wipe out every single trace of it.

A school night, close to the end but not quite. I was in bed, asleep. The door opened. Groggily I sat up, my irises aching from the sucker punch of light coming at me from the hall. I saw my sister's slim silhouette crossing the threshold. Then the door closed, and I was thrown back into darkness. She was at the foot of my bed, pacing. I looked for her face. I couldn't see it, though, so I lay back on my pillow, stared up at the ceiling, waited for my vision to adjust.

And then her breath came out of the black, hit my mouth, the scent sweet and alcoholic. I reached for the reading lamp above my head, but she blocked my hand. Made me turn on my side, and curved her body into mine, the buttons from her denim jacket pressing into my back. I could smell her perfume, the wintry air in her hair. She asked me if I was afraid. I said I wasn't, but that was a lie. It wasn't strange for her to sneak out with Jamie. It wasn't even strange for her to come home a little drunk. Not flat-out wasted, though. And definitely not flat-out wasted and upset. Had she been mugged? Attacked? Gotten in a car accident? Had Jamie? I asked her if it was any of these things, and she said, no, no, nothing like that.

Her trembling got worse, though, and she held me tighter, so tight it hurt. Then she turned me toward her. Took my hand, slipped it in the front of her coat. "My heart's going like crazy," she said, and it was, I could feel it. And then something was dripping on my face. Tears. Mine? No, hers, wet and warm from the heat of her body, as wet and warm as blood. One slid from my cheek to my upper lip. As I licked it off, I began to tremble, too.

"What happened?" I said.

"I found something out. Something about who I really am."

"Who are you?"

"I'm not sure I should say."

Why I said what I said next I'll never know. I can run down the inventory of excuses and defenses: I was scared and confused, disoriented from having gone so abruptly from dead asleep to wide awake, dizzy and half drunk from the liquor fumes coming off her. All of which are true, none of which are adequate. "If you're not sure, then maybe you shouldn't."

Immediately I felt her stiffen. "Okay," she said. "I won't."

A few minutes later her body withdrew into a private shrimplike curl and her breathing deepened. I lay awake for hours, but eventually I must've nodded off too, because before

I knew it my alarm clock was blaring. I shut it off, turned to Nica. But Nica wasn't there. She looked like her normal self at breakfast. Didn't say a word about the night before. Didn't say a word the next day either. And I guess I began to believe that I'd made it all up, that she'd visited me in a dream or something, and then dismissed the matter from my mind altogether.

But thinking about it now, I understand that it's the exact instant, the precise, scientific point, when I began to lose contact with her. This wasn't a loss I noticed all the time, only at certain moments. Every so often, in the middle of an ordinary conversation, and without the slightest warning, she'd fall into silence. These silences never lasted for very long, but in them I'd realize that something had come between us, some invisible yet solid thing, like a layer of glass; she was on one side, I was on the other, and I couldn't reach her no matter how hard I tried.

Maybe if I'd been different that night, had handled myself better, with more courage, less selfishness, things wouldn't have worked out the way they did. Maybe that's why I have to find her killer. Not because she's my sister or because there's been some abstract miscarriage of justice, but because she'd come to me and I'd let her down, and now I owe her, plain and simple.

I blink and I'm back in the café. I reset my attention to Mom's voice. She's still bitching about Mr. Amory and what a big mouth he has. She's in the middle of a sentence when I stand up. "Let's go to your studio," I say.

Mom pays the bill, cash—a ten, face-up, Alexander Hamilton looking less like a Founding Father than a poet or composer—

244

so we don't have to hang around while the waitress swipes a credit card. I pour the rest of my soda into the box of dry-looking flowers at my elbow. As we exit the café, I glance over at Damon. He's still in front of the bookstore, leaning against the bumper of a Volkswagen Beetle, holding up a paperback with a shiny cover. He's so absorbed in it he doesn't notice that Mom and I are on the move.

It's just past noon, the sun high and hot. Immediately I start to sweat. I'm glad when the walk to her studio turns out to be a short one. I don't speak and neither does she, but I know she's on edge because she drops her key twice fitting it into the lock. At last she opens the door.

The studio is a large rectangle of light, raw space and tall windows. At the far end is a closed door—a bathroom she's converted into a darkroom, no doubt. A circular table is at the center, on top a pair of cotton gloves, a can of Nova Tar Buster, a bowl of red apples. Tacked to the walls are photos of Nica. Nica at different ages. Nica in different moods. Nica shot from different angles. Everywhere I look Nica, Nica, Nica. Even Mom's a version of Nica, standing there, gnawing on a thumb joint, just like Nica used to when she was lost in thought.

I'm about to ask Mom where I should start when I see a sight familiar and shocking at once: my sister, looking like the child star of an adult film turned snuff film mid-reel; like worm-bait trussed up as jailbait; like a *femme fatale* in every sense, a *femme* who leads men to their dooms and a *femme* who is doomed herself. *Nica's Dream*. This version of the photograph is even clearer and more finely etched than the original hanging in our kitchen.

"I had the negative," Mom says, talking nervous-fast. "I printed it and reprinted it, used high-quality paper and conjured up every detail I possibly could. I'm still not totally satisfied." She pauses, then goes on: "Since Aurora's coming up so soon, I tried to pick out not only the images I want to use, but also the sequence I want the images to appear in, so they'd form a narrative."

Without comment I move on to the next photograph. I recognize it. It's a shot of Nica at thirteen trying to unhook her bra, head bowed, arms bent at the elbow and jutting out of her scrawny torso like angel wings.

I recognize the next photo as well. Nica's Converse sticking out the bottom of a bathroom stall, the angle of the feet, the way the toe of one foot is planted firmly on the ground, the heel a couple inches in the air, letting you know she's inserting a tampon.

And the next: Nica, sitting on the bleachers at Chandler in a plaid skirt, knees slightly open, several black pubic hairs curling over the elastic leg hole of her underpants, cotton and an immaculate white.

I'm moving quickly now, eager to reach the end. I want to make sure there isn't anything new here, no surprises, and then, once I do, I can grind Mom's face in the fact that she's nothing without Nica, that it's over for her.

The next photo, though, brings me to a dead stop. I never thought I'd see it again. It's the one Nica showed me that night in the kitchen all those years ago: her in bed, back to the camera, Dora the Explorer sheet draped over her hip, the rest of her bare, face in profile, breast, too, eyes shut. All details I'd noticed then. Here are the details I didn't notice: her brow, tight-knit and furrowed, signifying concentration rather than rest; her neck, arched, the cords in it standing out; her shoulders, hunched and rounded. Nica, I realize, isn't naked and asleep in this picture, like I'd thought at the time. She's naked and masturbating. Jesus, and I didn't understand why she was so upset it had been taken without her knowledge. *Big deal,* I'd said to her. *You've let mom take plenty of nude shots before.* My shame turns suddenly to confusion. How come the photograph's here, still exists? Wouldn't Nica have invoked her right to destroy it? Watched Mom burn the negative as she usually insisted on doing? Obviously not. Or maybe she did invoke the right and then Mom talked her out of it. I'd seen Mom do that kind of thing to Nica before. Mom would let her contempt show when Nica got emotional, failed to take depravity in stride, be cool about it. And Nica would break.

To get away from the shame and confusion I start walking again. I pass a series of photos of Nica and Jamie: Nica painting her toenails on the porch while Jamie does push-ups on the grass; Nica, her finger hooked in one of the belt loops of Jamie's pants, pulling him toward her; Nica and Jamie on the couch, both bare-chested, feeding on each other with open mouths; Nica and Jamie present only in their absence, his jeans and hers tangled together like sleeping lovers at the foot of her bed.

I've seen these images before. I'm walking faster and faster, the photographs streaking by:

Nica, under a streetlamp at night, crouching to light a cigarette;

Nica, struggling to open her birth control compact in our bathroom, her retainer, still wet with saliva, teetering on the lip of the sink;

Nica, a bottle of Smirnoff's in her fist, drawing Maddie in for an almost-kiss as she tips the vodka out of her own mouth and into Maddie's.

Seen it. Seen it. Seen it. All this material is old to me. I turn in triumph to Mom to tell her so. And then I notice that I missed a photograph, the last one. My eye must have skipped over it because it doesn't seem to belong with the others. Unlike the images that precede it—grainy, low lit, in stark black and white—this image is in color, supersaturated color, color that's bright and sharp-edged to an almost hallucinatory degree, color so vivid and full-bodied it makes you feel as if you've been living in Kansas your whole life and a tornado's suddenly spit you out in Oz. And it's not just the style that sets the photo apart. It's the content, too. This is a complete departure from the documentary-type portraits of adolescent ritual and misbehavior that the show's been comprised of so far. There's no exploitive or dirty-minded kick here. And Nica's not the focus, no person is. It's a pastoral shot featuring a sun-dappled garden full of striped lavender crocuses and budding yellow daffodils and dew-drenched grass, the post from a Norman Rockwell white picket fence in the background, all under a sky as blue as a baby's eye. The scene is an idyll, benign and becalmed, an enchanted small-town world in which nothing bad could ever happen.

Then my gaze drifts downward, and I see that Nica is in the picture, after all, just hidden, her upper half obscured by grass, her lower half out of frame altogether. Her body is turned away from the camera and curled tightly, fetally into itself, the delicate knobs along her spine showing through her shirt like beads on a string. Her face is visible, but only the right side, eyes puffily closed, mouth slack and hanging open. She's asleep, I realize. I realize, too, that this image is meant to serve as a companion piece to *Nica's Dream,* though with none of the earlier work's feeling of subversive eroticism. On the contrary, this appears to be—in spite of its sneaky staging—a straight-ahead, no-frills shot of an out-cold girl, a real girl, one tending to a bodily need, getting rest the same way she might get a drink of water. The affect is definitely flat and I wonder if this isn't deliberate on Mom's part, a tweaking of the viewer-voyeur for expecting yet another illicit thrill. Or maybe the affect is flat because it had to be: Mom was afraid if she got any closer, Nica would wake up, tell her to take a hike.

I'm about to ask her when I'm struck by the brilliant redness of Nica's mouth. Lipstick, I think. But then I remember, Nica didn't wear lipstick, only lip gloss, the clear kind. That's definitely lipstick, though, isn't it? There's even a fleck of it on her teeth. Had she borrowed it from Maddie? I move in for a closer look. Understanding comes at me fast, in a single jolt: that's not lipstick, it's blood. I suddenly understand other things, too: the wooden spike isn't a post from a picket fence, it's a grave marker; the setting isn't some suburban garden, it's a cemetery; and the girl isn't sleeping, she's dead. Nica's dead.

Standing there, I feel the sun streaming in from the window, and it's like it's passing right through me, like I'm not even there, have disappeared.

And then Mom's voice, small and soft, comes from somewhere behind me: "What do you think?"

Not taking my eyes off the photo, "Did you take it before or after you called the police?"

"Before. Graydon banged on our back door. He was talking fast, so fast I couldn't follow his words. I didn't need to understand him, though, to know he was telling me that Nica was dead. His face said it plainly enough. He took my hand and brought me to her and then ran off. Grace, there was blood everywhere. The ground was soggy with it. All flowing from her broken little body." Mom stops, her breath coming hard. When she continues, she can barely speak: "I went back to the house and got my camera. I think it was my way of coping with—not coping with—the horror of what I was seeing."

For a long time there's the sound of Mom's weeping and then no sound at all. And then I say, "And after you were done shooting, you dialed 911?"

"Immediately after. Then I sat with her until the police and ambulances arrived."

So that morning when I walked from the house to the edge of the graveyard looking for Nica, Nica was actually there. Mom, too. If I hadn't been so focused on Jamie's dorm, seeing if Nica was sneaking out of it, I might have spotted them. "The photo isn't in black and white," I say. "How come?"

"It was an accident. I grabbed a roll of film. I thought it was black and white, but it wasn't. It was the old Kodachrome film I used years ago. They don't even make it anymore."

"Black and white would have been okay. What you have is better, though. This photograph—it's darkness in full color."

"Thank you," she says, and though her tone is shy, I hear the confidence in it, the excitement even. She's taken a good picture and she knows it. "I was crying and shaking so hard some of the shots didn't come out at all. Even this one was a mistake. I meant for Nica to be at the center of the frame."

"No. If you show all of her, you just have a crime scene photo."

"I thought the same thing." Mom reaches into the drawer

of the table, pulls out a stack of photos, hands them to me. "But, here, look through these. Tell me if there's one you like better because—"

I turn to her. "The show's going to be huge. You're going to be huge." And before she can say anything back, I walk out the door.

# CHAPTER FIFTEEN

I pause on the sidewalk outside the studio. I feel as if I've just been sliced open from throat to pelvis, rust-colored blobs spilling out the slit. The street's hot, shadowless, the asphalt gummy beneath my feet. The few clouds in the sky are swollen and sore-looking. As I go to fish my sunglasses out of my bag, I realize I'm still holding the photos. Blindly I shove them into a side pocket with the stash of tampons I haven't touched since early summer. Then I start making my way back to the main drag.

Damon's still leaning against the bumper of the Volkswagen. "Hey, you," I say. Hearing my voice, he looks up from his book, smiles. The smile vanishes, though, when he sees my face. He jams the book in the rack, puts his arm around me. I collapse against his side. As he leads me away, I wish I'd looked at the title.

We parked in the lot behind the public library, empty except for two or three other cars. Once we're inside mine, I crank the AC. It's busted, though, so it's pushing the heat around some but not breaking it up any. I lower my window, unbutton the top two buttons on my shirt. Glance over at Damon. His eyes are closed and he's playing with his cross, sliding it along its gold chain, tucking it under his bottom lip. I can see that he's trying to figure out what to say to me, afraid I'll fall apart if he comes out with the wrong thing. I'm about to tell him that he doesn't have to say a word, that just having him next to me makes me feel better. But I don't. Instead I get caught up watching a bead of perspiration that starts at his hairline, trickles down his cheek, and disappears into the scruff on his jaw. Get caught up watching the muscles in his forearm slide and fan out under his skin. Get caught up watching the strip of honeyed abdomen between the hem of his wife-beater and the waist of his jeans go from smooth to ridged when he shifts in his seat.

And then, all at once, it's coming over me, that feeling from the other night, the one that's like pain but is not pain: desire. *Oh, no,* I think, *not this again.* Or maybe I don't think it, maybe I say it because suddenly Damon's eyes are open and on me. I look away. Stare out the window at the elementary school beyond the chain-link fence, its outline shimmery in the heat; at the honeysuckle bushes surrounding the lot, sweating into the air, turning it sweet and sticky; at the geraniums drooping along the walkway, the petals loose, grimy at the edges.

Damon's sitting more than two feet from me. The warmth, though, is seeping from his pores and mingling with the warmth seeping from my pores, making the air between us heavier, denser, moister than it already is. I touch my lips and they're puffed like blisters. I hear him saying my name softly, but I don't respond. He goes quiet, and for a second I think that I'm safe, that he's going to leave me alone until the fever breaks and I'm back in control of myself. But then

253

his hands are on my shoulders. He's twisting me around roughly so that I'm facing him and I know it's over for me. I try to go limp in his grasp, to glaze my eyes so I won't really be looking at him. It doesn't do any good, though. Doesn't do any good at all.

My eyes are still unfocused and I can only see the blurred edges of him when I propel my body out of my seat and toward him. In the distance I hear the sound of my sunglasses falling from my face, bouncing off the rim of the steering wheel, the jangle of the keys in the ignition as I bump them with my hip. It doesn't occur to me that he might want this, too, maybe even wants it as bad as I do, until his lips smash into mine with such force I taste blood.

I'm straddling him. My shirt's already half off and I push his to the top of his chest, pressing bare flesh to bare flesh. He turns my underwear into a coil, rolling it tightly over my hips, the swell of my ass, with one hand. With the other, he's easing a small square packet out of his wallet. Seeing him do this gives me my first conscious thought since I stepped into the car: He carries a condom in his wallet? Like, just in case? Who is this guy, this stranger? It's also my last conscious thought because after he slaps the condom on the dashboard, he half lifts me to plant his lips at the base of my throat, and my spine goes rigid and I bang the top of my head on the roof. His mouth slides down until he traps my nipple between his lips.

I bend backward, hand him the condom. Close my eyes. Right before he pushes himself inside me, I open them. The strip of condom packet is still clenched between his teeth. And he's staring at me. It's like he's forcing himself to see me, really see me, past my face and into my mind, my heart. The intimacy of the look is too much. I flick my gaze off to the side. Concentrate on the swirls in his ear, the creases in the leather headrest.

I don't expect there to be pain since this isn't my first time. But there is, so much that I can't think of anything else. I bury my face in his neck. Wait for it to be over. And then, through the pain, I start to feel the stirrings of pleasure. The pain continues to recede and the pleasure to get more intense until I can't control my breathing and my body explodes in a series of contractions, like a string of fire-crackers popping off. I bite down on his shoulder instead of crying out.

We're back in our separate seats. The sweat's cooling on our limbs and no parts of our bodies are touching except for our hands on the console. Damon's jeans are pulled up over his hips but are unzipped. My shirt's on, but only one button's buttoned. I look over at him. His eyes are shut and his hair's flopped forward. It makes his face seem rounder. Younger, too. And sitting beside him, watching the light play over his closed lids, feeling the warmth of his palm covering mine, I think with pleasure, *This really happened.*

And then, an image of Nica gazing at Damon post-sex as I'm gazing at him now, a thing she must have done dozens of times—dozens and dozens of times, knowing her—invades my mind. All of a sudden, the feeling of contentment's gone and I'm filled with panic. What if Damon only got together with me because I'm her sister? Maybe when he was staring at me before and I took it as him trying to truly look at me, look into my soul, I misread him. Maybe he was staring so hard because he was trying to single out points of resemblance between us. Or maybe, even worse, it was to compare—compare my face with his memory of hers, compare me with someone beyond compare. The panic turns to horror. I need to get out of the car.

I've just hooked a finger around the door handle when Damon says, "Hey, how are you feeling?"

I let go of the handle. Pretend to be reaching for the bottle of Poland Springs water that's rolled beneath my seat. "Fine, I'm fine. I guess I'm a little weirded out but . . ." I trail off.

He laughs softly. "Yeah, for sure weirded out."

He doesn't say anything after that. Needing him to talk, for something to fill up the silence, I say, "What are you thinking?"

"I'm thinking about how I'm going to have to lay off the wife-beaters for a while."

"Why?"

He points to the top of his shoulder. Teeth marks are embedded deep in the skin.

Horrified, I whisper, "Did I do that?"

He grins. "That's all right. It's a first for me but I kind of liked it."

The sense of relief is so intense my eyes start to water. A first, meaning I'm the only one who's ever bitten him. Meaning his experience with me was different from his experience with Nica. And he seemed okay about it. More than okay. We look at each other, but it's too soon for that and we both quickly look away.

"What we did," I say, after a bit, "we shouldn't have done it, right?"

He sighs. "Yeah, probably. But there was no way I could've not done it. It felt"—he pauses, thinking—"inevitable."

The sense of relief again. "For you, too?"

"Yeah."

"What next?"

"Anything we want. Look, there's no reason we can't take

256

the attitude that what happened was something we couldn't avoid, was beyond our control. We got it out of our systems and now we move on. Focus on our friendship. Focus on what we have to do to find your sister's killer."

I'm nodding to everything he's saying, anxious to show how completely in agreement I am with his reasonable and balanced viewpoint. I'm like a fucking bobblehead doll. Forcing myself to stop, I uncap the bottle of Poland Springs. Swallow too much water. I'm not sure what to do now. Start the car, drive back to Hartford? I guess so. What else? As I slide my seat belt into the buckle, I sneak a glance over at him. He's doing the same with his seat belt. His posture is easy, relaxed, but his eyes are sharp; they're watching my every move. And then my mouth goes cottony. My hands begin to tremble. *Again,* I think. *So soon? Is this normal?* Ashamed, I drop my head, try to hide what I'm feeling. But he must sense the change in me because he unbuckles his seat belt and mine in two seconds flat, pulls me onto his lap.

He's just taken my face in his hands, run his thumb over the scar above my eyebrow, when his cell rings. We both freeze, look at each other: Max.

"You should get it," I say when it rings a second time.

He tugs the phone from his pocket. Checks the caller ID. "It's Frankie," he says, and I can hear the tension go out of his voice, the fear, too. He tosses the phone in the backseat, reaches for me, but the mood between us has been broken. He leans his forehead against mine for several seconds. Then he takes a long breath, kisses the scar instead of my lips.

We reassemble ourselves as best we can. And after he throws the condom in the trash barrel by the library's back entrance, we hit the road.

\* \* \*

It takes me from Brattleboro, Vermont, to Springfield, Massachusetts, to tell Damon the story my mom told me. And then it takes Damon from Springfield, Massachusetts, to Windsor Locks, Connecticut, to absorb it all, to move past being floored. He does move past it, though. And we begin revising our suspect list.

First I make the case for Mr. Amory, already on the list, but the reason changed. The strong interest he'd taken in Nica wasn't sexual, as we'd originally thought; it was paternal. It could be, I argue, that he later regretted sharing with her the secret of her birth. After all, he did it in a moment of high emotion. And the possibility of her reneging on her promise of silence and passing on what she knew to Jamie, causing Jamie to hate him and/or spill the beans to Mrs. Amory who, according to Mom, controlled the purse strings, might have been too much for him. He had a lot to lose. Everything, it sounded like. What if he decided to try to scare Nica into shutting her mouth? What if things went too far and he wound up shutting her mouth permanently?

Next I make the case for Mrs. Amory, the list's latest addition. As far as Mom knew, Mrs. Amory was in the dark about her affair with Mr. Amory. But that doesn't mean that Mrs. Amory actually was in the dark. Maybe Mrs. Amory was only in the shadows. Say she didn't have cold hard proof, but she did have woman's intuition. Say she put two and two together, or rather one and one—her husband and my mom—and came up with three, Nica. Say, though, that this knowledge was fuzzy and half-conscious and thus never acted upon. Say that this knowledge sharpened into clearest focus when Nica dumped Jamie because the breakup revealed to Mrs. Amory how emotionally fragile her son was. And, finally, say that Mrs. Amory, sensing Jamie would be damaged in lasting ways if the same knowledge was thrust on him, decided to eliminate the potential source.

"That takes care of motive for Mr. and Mrs. Amory," Damon says when I've finished talking. "And since they're each other's alibis, they don't have one. Plus, Manny Flores was in Jamie's dorm."

The cars in front of mine slow down. Up ahead I see orange cones, traffic narrowing to a single lane. Road work. I ease up on the gas pedal. "So?" I say.

"So, you remember how chaotic it was at Chandler right after your sister died—cops everywhere, reporters hiding in broom closets, parents driving up, yanking their kids out at all hours. Normally a stranger would get noticed in the dorms. Not then, though."

"And Mr. and Mrs. Amory weren't exactly strangers at Chandler either. Both are heavily involved in the school, on a bunch of committees. And Mrs. Amory was in and out of Endicott House all the time—dropping off restrung rackets for Jamie, grip tape, new laces for his sneakers."

"There you go. I'll bet no one would have even looked twice at either one of them."

"It's just—" I break off.

"Yeah?"

"It's just, it looks like whoever killed Nica killed her in the heat of the moment. A crime of passion. Horrible, obviously, but human, too. Understandable. Whoever killed Manny, though, devised a plan, waited, waited, waited, and then executed. Even coerced him into writing a suicide-slash-confession note. And picked him in the first place because he was parentless, friendless, and no one would care enough about him to look closely into his death."

Impatient, Damon says, "Your point?"

"My point is that it's a cold, calculated act. It's the act of a monster, basically. And I don't believe that anyone we've talked about is capable of acting like a monster."

He gives me an odd look. "People are capable of anything, Grace. Things you'd never dream they could do, they do. All the time. Trust me."

"I know you have way more experience with criminal behavior or whatever, but—" Again I break off.

"But what?"

"I don't know what. It just doesn't feel right to me."

"Look, how about we don't get caught up in the psychology stuff? How about we just go where the evidence takes us?" He holds my eye until I nod.

But then, unable to help myself, I say, "Still, I think we have to admit the possibility of a dark horse suspect— someone we're unaware of."

He runs a hand through his hair, an exasperated gesture. "But everything about the crime says the killer is someone she knew. And that last call came from a Chandler pay phone."

"Someone she knew but maybe not someone we knew. Or didn't know well, because, yes, you're absolutely right, the person is very likely associated with the school in some way." When Damon doesn't say anything back, "She kept you a secret. She kept Maddie a secret. Is it such a stretch to think she kept a third secret?"

He closes his eyes, touches his fingertips to his lids. In a quiet voice, he says, "No, it's not."

"And then there's the order of the list."

"What about it?"

"So Jamie, who was a weak suspect to begin with because of his strong, at least semi-strong, alibi"—I pause, wait for

Damon to contradict me, which he doesn't do, though the muscles in his jaw tighten—"drops down from the number one spot."

"Jamie only drops if he never found out the truth about Nica. Then his motive would be the same as it had been for the two months before she died. But what if he did find out?"

"It sounded like Mr. Amory wasn't ever going to tell him, though."

"Could be he didn't hear from his dad."

"Then from who?"

Damon thinks. "We know he was hassling Nica, hounding her about why she broke up with him, demanding a reason. What if she finally lost her temper, gave it to him?"

"Then he'd be murderously angry at Mr. Amory. It's not like Nica was the one who'd been lying to him all those years."

"Yeah, but she had been lying to him all those months. And think about what a hard thing that would be for him to hear. Not only was he having sex with his sister, but his dad knew about it and let it go on. He might have reacted by taking his rage out on her. Or maybe he didn't believe her, thought she was insulting the honor of his family, something crazy like that."

After a pause, I say carefully, "I don't think that's what did happen, but I do agree it could have happened."

"And, don't forget, your mom says he's a junkie. Junkies have mood swings."

I start to object. Mom, who only ever half listened to any conversation she wasn't the subject of, had, I suspect, gotten the details of Jamie's drug history wrong, had misunderstood somehow. Jamie was too openly a druggie to be an actual addict. He was chronically stoned, basically, and if he had a problem with drugs, he'd be more secretive about using them, wouldn't he? Even a peanuts drug like marijuana? But I stop myself. If I say that, I'll only piss Damon off, further convince him that I'm hopelessly biased where Jamie's concerned. (Like he's not just as biased.) Plus, my sense from my talk with him about Ruben and Ruben's dealing is that's he's pretty black and white as far as drugs go. Doesn't distinguish between a dime bag of pot and a rubber balloon of smack, or believe that such a thing as casual use is possible. So instead I say, "It looks like we've got a two-way tie for the number one spot."

"You mean a clear winner, don't you? You honestly think Mrs. Amory could have sexually assaulted Nica before strangling her?"

Laughing, I say, "No. I think you're the sexual assaulter."

Damon's eyes bug. "What?"

"I'm kidding. About the assault part, at least. But you did have sex with Nica that night. You told me so. And, as it turns out, the cops never said that she'd been assaulted, just that she might have been." Off his stare, I went on, "Yeah, I only looked at the newspaper headlines at the time, too. Well, lately I've been reading the actual articles. Her underwear was missing, but you know as well as I do that she often didn't wear any. And there was vaginal tearing, which means she could have been forced to have sex, or she could have just had, you know"—flicking my gaze from his face back to the road—"rougher-than-usual sex, or even just more-than-usual sex."

A few seconds pass, and then Damon asks, "Any body fluids?"

"Why would there be? You use condoms, right?"

He laughs. Attempts to laugh, anyway. "Mostly, yeah," he

says, before falling into silence. A minute or so later he pulls himself out of it. "So it's Mr. and Mrs. Amory, Jamie, and a dark horse. Any other candidates you can think of?"

"No."

"You sure?"

A name jumps suddenly to the tip of my tongue. I swallow it back, though.

When I don't speak, Damon says, "That's our list then."

We pass the construction site, and the highway opens up again. We encounter no more delays.

By the time we're back in Hartford, Damon's retreated into himself, just stares silently out the window at the passing scenery. I drive him to his grandmother's, assuming that's where he wants to go. But when we pull up to the house he looks at it blankly, like it's a place he's never seen before, then asks me to drop him off at the hospital instead. I get the feeling he's anxious, so I rush—roll through stop signs, gun the yellows. Once St. Francis's entranceway hovers into view, though, he tells me he needs a minute. I turn into the Wendy's across the street. Parking, I run inside and pick up a couple of chocolate Frosties.

"Hey, look who's here," Damon says, when I'm back in the car.

I follow the direction of his finger to the front of the hospital: Renee, leaning against a patch of wall, smoking beside a sign with a cigarette on it, a big red line through the cigarette. "Should we go over and say hi?"

"In a bit," he says.

I flip on the radio. Tune into a talk station. There's a program on about the global spike in food prices. We listen, drink the Frosties, let our thoughts go away.

Abruptly, Damon kills the radio. "There's something I need to tell you," he says.

"Okay."

"And you're not going to like hearing it any more than I like saying it."

My stomach pulls in, and the blood starts pounding in my skull. It's coming now, the "This was a huge mistake, I love your sister" speech I've been expecting—dreading—since the moment Nica's face popped into my head in the library parking lot.

He's silent for a second then inhales sharply, like he's about to speak. But before he can, there's a rap on my window. I turn. On the other side of the glass is Renee.

"Visiting hours are almost over," she says, when I lower the window. "You two coming in?" She looks beyond exhausted, just totally worn out. Like she hasn't slept a minute since Max's heart attack five days ago.

"Just me," Damon says.

As he reaches into the back to get his things, Renee points to the cup in my hand. "That a Frosty?"

I pass it to her.

"How's Max doing?" Damon asks.

"Same." Renee pulls my straw out, spilling a drop of frozen dairy product on her chest. She dabs at it with her fingertips. "His cunt ex-wife's up there. Got me kicked out because I'm not immediate family."

"Helene or Deidre?"

"Helene."

"Shit, I better hurry."

"I would if I were you. She'll probably put a pillow over his face as soon as the nurses aren't looking, hope he remembers her in his will."

264

Damon turns to me. "Write this down."

I search for a piece of paper. End up pulling an old receipt out of my wallet, scribbling the numbers he rattles off on the back.

"That's Max's room," he says. "Tell it to the hospital operator and she'll connect you directly. They don't allow cell phones, so that's the best way to reach me. Got it?"

I nod that I do, and he gives my hand a quick squeeze. Renee, I notice, catches the squeeze. She doesn't say anything, though. Just peels off the lid of the Frosty. Puts her mouth on the side of the cup.

Damon swings himself out of the car. "All right, Renee. You ready to raise a little hell?"

"I was born ready, baby," she says to him. Then to me: "I'm going to finish this, okay?"

It isn't really a question but I say, "Sure," anyway.

The two of them begin walking across the street. I watch until the hospital swallows them up. I'm about to tuck the receipt back in my wallet, start the car, when I notice that the receipt isn't a receipt. It's the torn-off piece of blank paper, folded in half—the one Mr. Tierney wrote the note to Nica on. There's another thing I notice. Apart from the note itself, the blank paper's not blank. Not quite. Along the ragged edges of the tear-off is the lower quarter of a line of print. I study it. It appears to be the last bit of the Chandler honor pledge, the "in accordance with school regulations" from the "This represents my work, solely my work, in accordance with school regulations," words that students are supposed to copy onto the bottom of every quiz, test, essay and project. Supposed to but rarely do because no teacher enforces the rule except at exam time. Well, other than Mr. Fowler.

Mr. Fowler, largely deaf and wholly senile, left eighty in the dust long ago, is Chandler's oldest faculty member. Not that he's really faculty these days. His duties have dwindled down to a single class, Hamlet and the Ghost, which he's been teaching since the 1960s. I never took it. Nica did, though, was taking it, in fact, when she died. Of course she was. It's rumored to be incredibly easy, only two two-page papers in an entire semester. Papers Mr. Fowler doesn't even grade, has an assistant grade for him.

It's as I think the word *assistant* that I remember with a jolt: Mr. Wallace was the assistant for the English Department last year. A second jolt comes when I remember something else: Mr. Wallace's first name is Christopher, nickname Topher.

The dark horse.

# CHAPTER SIXTEEN

Mr. Wallace opens the door to his room on the top floor of Minot House. He's got an uncapped red pen in his hand. His gaze is quizzical but polite. I hand him the note. As his eyes skim over the six lines, the color drains from his face like a plug inside him's been pulled. Without looking at me, he steps aside to let me pass.

The room I enter is neat and spare. On the arm of the one chair is a pile of papers he must've been grading when I knocked. He moves it so I have a place to sit. Then he arranges himself on the edge of the narrow bed. For a minute or two we contemplate each other in silence. He's a homely man, there's no denying: bony-featured and Ichabod Crane skinny. His eyes, though, are nice—large and clear and slow-blinking—and seem to bespeak a nature both gentle and serious. Looking into them, I realize that, whatever happened between him and Nica, I'm glad he's the one she chose, not that vain jerk Tierney. And then I remember that it could have been him who killed her or was responsible for getting her killed. Manny too. My attitude hardens.

At last Mr. Wallace gestures toward the note and says, "I didn't expect to see that again. Actually, I did. When the police were investigating your sister's death. Then I lived in fear of hearing their knock on my door."

"Yeah, well, the prospect of jail's a scary one," I say flatly.

He looks at me, confused. Then he laughs. "Jail? You've been reading too much Hawthorne. What we were doing might have been unethical, but it wasn't illegal."

"Nica was sixteen."

Another confused look. "So?"

"So where do you think guys convicted of statutory rape go?"

He opens his mouth. Knowing what he's going to say, I cut him off before he can say it: "Yes, the age of consent in Connecticut is sixteen, but not if one party is in a position of authority over the other. In that case, the age of consent is eighteen. I looked it up."

Mr. Wallace lifts the note. Reads it. Reads it again. Then he just holds it in his hand, realizing, no doubt, that I have him dead to rights. Finally he takes off his glasses. "I made a mistake."

I snort. "That's one way of putting it."

"I mean a grammatical mistake." He puts his glasses back on, reads the note yet again, this time out loud: "Does Bill know about us? I thought we'd been so careful, but maybe not careful enough." Transferring his eyes from the sheet of paper to my face, "The *us* and *we* make it sound as if I was referring to me and Nica, when I was in fact referring to me and Jeanne. Vague pronoun reference." He laughs, shakes his head. "Some English teacher I am."

I stare at him, confounded. Can this be true? That it was Jeanne Bowles-Mills and only Jeanne Bowles-Mills that he was sleeping with? I look into his eyes, calm and unflinching, and my gut feeling is: yes. It makes sense, actually. Explains why Mr. Tierney got so emotional when I showed him the note. Mr. Wallace was double-crossing him, sneaking around with the woman he was already sneaking around with. It explains, too, why he didn't try to stop me when I threatened to take the note to the Millses. Why would he have? I'd be doing his dirty work for him.

Still, I can't let Mr. Wallace off the hook so easily. Keeping my tone disbelieving, sarcastic even, I say, "If your relationship with Nica was totally aboveboard, why were you afraid of the police knocking on your door?"

"Because it *wasn't* totally aboveboard. She was a student and I was her—well, not teacher, but the assistant to her teacher—and I was telling her the sordid details of my affair with a married coworker. If the police knew, they'd want an alibi for the night she died and I couldn't give them one."

Still sarcastic, "At home with a good book?"

"I was at a bed-and-breakfast in the Berkshires with Jeanne. The Red Lion Inn in Stockbridge. Under the name Mellors." A sad smile. "It was a joke."

"I don't get it."

"Oliver Mellors is a character in *Lady Chatterley's Lover*. One of the most famous adulterers in the canon."

"Funny joke," I say, stone-faced, making him really smile. Then seriously, the impulse to be sarcastic having spent itself, I say, "That's a good alibi, though, easy to check out."

"Yes, but I couldn't count on the police to be discreet."

"Oh, right. Your job."

"I was afraid of jeopardizing that, of course. Teaching's what I've always dreamed of doing. But there are other teaching positions. It's Jeanne I was worried about. Bill's an angry man. He doesn't love her anymore but he doesn't want to hear that someone else does. He could make life difficult for her, fight her for custody of Beatrice. She's only a U.S. citizen by marriage, which complicates matters." He sighs, then sinks into silence.

I sink with him, trying to work things out in my head. Finally I say, "I don't understand. How did Nica figure in any of this? Why were you confiding in her?"

"It wasn't some regular thing. It just happened twice and the first time was by accident. Bill belongs to the National Model Railroad Association. The local branch of the club meets the second and fourth Wednesdays of every month. Jeanne always gets a sitter on those nights and we spend a couple hours together at the Econo-Lodge in East Hartford. You probably don't know it. It's pretty sleazy."

But I do know it. I've been driving past it enough lately. It's half a dozen blocks from Damon's grandmother's house. Sleazy is right. The kind of place where everyone who checks in is named Smith or Jones.

Mr. Wallace continues: "That night she stood me up. Bill had too much paperwork to do, decided to skip his meeting last minute. She texted me but by the time I got the message, I was already there. Sitting on that ratty bedspread in that room that reeked of disinfectant, I started to get pretty down about the entire situation. So I wandered into a dive bar around the corner to get good and drunk. Only I couldn't because I'd rushed out of Minot with my money, but not my wallet. The bartender refused to serve me without proper ID. And not just me. There was a young woman having the same problem."

"Let me guess. Nica."

"Yes, but I didn't know it. She was all the way at the

other end of the bar. I almost fell off my stool when she walked up to me and said, 'You left your fake ID at home, too, Mr. Wallace?' I started apologizing, making excuses, talking a million miles a minute. She waited until I was done babbling, then told me to relax, that she was the one doing something wrong, not me."

I grin. "That sounds like her."

"I walked her out of the bar, was going to take her straight back to campus. But we made a stop first—a liquor store. They didn't want to see my license, just my money. I bought a bottle of Absolut. Then Nica and I sat in my car, talked, and drank. Correction, I talked and drank. Didn't let her do either." He laughs, then falls quiet. A minute or so later he says, "I'm sure I seem old to you, but I'm only twenty-three. Last year I was twenty-two, a couple months out of college. Jeanne's my first girlfriend." He looks at me, his face reddening. "That's probably hard for you to believe. It's true, though. It was—is—an incredibly intense experience for me. Not just the newness of being in love, but being in love with a woman, not a girl. A woman with a husband and a daughter and twelve more years of life lived. It's a lonely experience, too. Because of Jeanne's situation, the tough spot she's in, I can't talk to anybody about what I'm going through. Least of all my closest friend."

"You mean Mr. Tierney?"

"I do."

"I'm kind of surprised to hear you call him that. Obviously I know you two hang out but it's hard to believe you're friends—real ones."

"Maybe if we'd met in another context, college or something, we wouldn't be. In fact, I'm certain we wouldn't be. It's different, though, here. At Chandler we're so cut-off. And he

271

and I are the youngest teachers by a pretty wide margin. We live in the same dorm, neither of us is married, so we're thrown together a lot. I know Nick seems like a self-involved guy, wrapped up in his looks, the things he's going to accomplish when he leaves Chandler—and he is—but underneath it all he's a sweet person."

"Why couldn't you talk to him then? Is it too weird that you were sleeping with the same woman?"

Mr. Wallace looks at me, startled. "We weren't sleeping with the same woman."

For the first time it occurs to me that he might not know that there's another Other Man. "Well," I say awkwardly, "not at the same time maybe, but Mr. Tierney was sleeping with Mrs. Bowles-Mills, too." When this gets no response, I joke, even more awkwardly, "I know, I know, I wouldn't have thought she was his type either with those earth mother skirts and that Heidi braid." Then, realizing how insulting this sounds, conclude lamely, "Not that she's not perfectly nice looking."

"Nick never slept with Jeanne. And she was his type. He wasn't hers."

"I hate to burst your bubble, but Jamie Amory saw Mr. Tierney knocking on the Millses' back door in the middle of the night. Mrs. Bowles-Mills let him in."

I'm expecting anger or dismay—shock at the very least—but I get none of these reactions. "When was this?" Mr. Wallace says, calm as can be. "March?"

I nod, surprised.

"She let him in because she didn't want him making a scene. But he never got past the kitchen."

"How can you be so sure?"

"Because I was there, in the upstairs bedroom. I heard the

whole conversation, all three hours of it. That's when I real-ized how strong Nick's feelings actually were. I knew he'd been interested, of course. But he'd played it off to me as a casual-type thing. Like he was just looking to get physical with a lonely, sex-starved housewife in a bad marriage."

It takes me a few seconds to phrase my next question. "If you'd known how Mr. Tierney felt, would you have still gotten together with Mrs. Bowles-Mills?"

Mr. Wallace closes his eyes and lifts the frame of his glasses. I can see my interrogation is tiring him out. He's going to answer me, though, patiently and thoughtfully, same as he's been doing. And as he rubs the pink patch of skin above the bridge of his nose I think what a good teacher he must be. "I probably still would have," he says with a sigh. "Scummy, I know."

"At least you're honest."

"Honestly scummy. Well, that's something, I guess."

We share a smile, and then I say, "But back to my sister."

Mr. Wallace lets out another sigh. "Right, your sister. She was a good listener. She was so young, but she seemed to understand things—the complexities of relationships, how you sometimes end up in them with people you wouldn't expect, in circumstances that are less than ideal, how arbitrary the rules of attraction are, how you have no control over who or what excites you."

I'll bet she understood, I think. Better than anybody she understood. "So you spilled your guts?"

He laughs. "Basically. The next day in class, I could barely raise my head I was so embarrassed. And hungover. Mostly, though, what I was was nervous. Would Nica treat me like a peer now, a buddy? Show that she no longer viewed me as an authority figure? And how could you view the guy whose car keys you'd wrestled away the night before, poured into a cab, as an authority figure? But when I finally did make eye contact, she just gave me a blank look back and I knew I had nothing to worry about. Later I found my car keys in a plain white envelope in my faculty mailbox."

So cool, I think admiringly. Always so cool.

For a while Mr. Wallace stares at his hands, resting on his wide-apart knees. Then he says, "You've seen the note. Obviously it was me who approached her, who couldn't keep my distance even though I swore to myself I would. It's just that Jeanne was being cold and I thought I saw Bill give me a loaded look and I started to imagine all sorts of awful things. I wrote the note on the bottom of Nica's paper, the one I was grading for Fowler. It was stupid and it was risky. But I was desperate."

"Did it work? Did she meet you?"

"Outside the same bar. Me telling pretty much the same story."

"Was she helpful?"

"Oh yeah. I was about to march over to the Millses' house to I don't know what—challenge Bill to a duel, throw Jeanne over my shoulder caveman style—something idiotic. Nica calmed me down. A good thing, too. I talked to Jeanne the next day. Turned out she was just preoccupied because Beatrice had come down with an ear infection. And Bill's a hostile guy in general. Probably shoots everyone bad looks without even realizing it. Nica saved me from blowing my cover. Blowing Jeanne's and my cover both."

"Your covers are blown now," I say, not knowing how else to say it, so just blurting it out.

He looks at me.

"With Mr. Tierney, anyway."

"What?" he finally says.

I take a deep breath, tell him about my initial misidentification of *T*, the scene that took place in the studio, Mr. Tierney's near-successful attempt to trick me into revealing the affair to Mr. Mills.

"Now I know why he's been avoiding me for the last few days," Mr. Wallace says when I'm finished. And then, "So Bill doesn't know yet?"

"No," I say, uneasy at the hopeful note in his voice, "but it's only a matter of time, don't you think? I mean, rightly or wrongly, Mr. Tierney feels deceived. Vengeful, too, obviously."

Mr. Wallace's head drops, like it's suddenly too much of a burden for his neck to bear. "Yeah, you're probably right. I better warn Jeanne."

I shouldn't feel guilty. I'm the only participant in this drama besides Beatrice who has nothing to feel guilty about. But I do.

Mr. Wallace and I sit in silence for a long time, watch the last of the day's light shrivel and recede from the room. Finally, I stand and say something about having someplace to be. He looks at me briefly, nods. When I've reached the door, opened it, I turn back to wish him good luck, but he's staring at the note in his lap, neck limp, off somewhere in his mind. I close the door quietly behind me.

# CHAPTER SEVENTEEN

I haven't had more than a catnap in what feels like weeks, so I skip dinner, head directly to my room. Climbing the stairs, I write a text to Damon, asking him to check to see if a Mr. and Mrs. Mellors stayed at the Red Lion Inn in Stockbridge the night of Nica's death. I hit Send as I open the door. My bed has never looked so inviting—rumpled comforter, unwashed sheets, caseless pillow and all.

I'm just tugging on my pajamas when, on impulse, I reach for Mom's camera with the telephoto lens. As I take it over to the window, about to aim it at the Millses' house, I see Jeanne and Beatrice on the sidewalk below. The strap on Beatrice's sandal has come undone and Jeanne is trying to refasten it. Beatrice is looking down at what her mother's doing, sucking her thumb.

Mr. Mills's voice calls out, "Bedtime!" From half a block away I can hear his irritation. "Coming!" Jeanne shouts back. She tries once more to fasten the strap. When she fails, she slips the shoe off Beatrice's foot and into her pocket. Then she stands, gently but quickly lifting her daughter off the ground.

276

Beatrice is a little big to be picked up like that. She doesn't fight it, though, keeping her thumb in her mouth and settling into her mother's body as if it had been made for her to rest on, the breast formed to pillow her cheek, the arm crooked to support and protect her head. Jeanne starts walking hurriedly, sidestepping the stroller Mrs. Wheeler forgot to bring into the house. Beatrice looks up from her mother's shoulder. When she sees me in the window staring down at her, she returns the stare, her eyes large and grave. Her mouth shapes the word *Hi* around her thumb.

The days of this little girl's happiness are numbered, I think as I mouth a *Hi* back. She'll be separated from the mother who adores her, maybe permanently, and all because of me. The guilt that descends is crushingly heavy. But I feel something else, as well, something lurking beneath the guilt that's even more troubling: a sense of wonderment, of awe almost, that a thing I'd done—*me,* quiet, passive, lives-in-my-thoughts *me*—is having such an impact on other people's lives. It's as if a power I never dreamed of possessing is suddenly mine, and having it fills me with a kind of weird elation.

Ashamed now on top of guilty and whatever else, I shut the curtains with a violent yank. Then I jump into bed, pull the covers over my head.

I fall asleep immediately but it doesn't last long. I'm awake again at midnight. At one. At two. At three. Sick of looking at the clock, watching one hour after another go down for the count, I decide to get something to eat, a Fig Newton maybe. I'm at the bottom of the staircase, a couple feet from the kitchen, when it occurs to me that Dad's probably in it. That's okay as long as he's dead drunk, which he should be if tonight's going for him the way every other night goes. But what if, for some reason, it's not? It'll be awkward if I walk in on him in that in-between state. I should just go back to my room, spare us both the possibility. Thinking about that Fig Newton, though, has made me want it. So for a full minute I stand there, clutching the banister, head cocked, ears straining. All I hear is the sound of my own breathing.

I step into the kitchen. The first thing I see: Dad, at the table, pitched bonelessly forward, head buried in his arms. In front of him is a bottle of Jim Beam, capless, the warm amber liquid picking up whatever light's in the room. As I creep past him, inhaling through my mouth so I don't have to take in his sad, fusty smell—pencil erasers and herbal throat lozenges, anti-dandruff shampoo—I reach for the whiskey, thinking a slug or two might knock me out. Holding the bottle, though, I can feel the ridges of his fingerprints, their slight tackiness, see a bit of backwash floating on top. My stomach lurches, and I put the bottle down, move on to the cookie drawer.

I've just opened it when I hear a buzzing noise. I jump back, look around wildly. See Dad's cell an inch from his elbow. It's facedown and lit up, the surface of the table tinged green by the reflected glow. Another buzz. Dad stirs in his chair, groans a little. I quickly walk over, grab the phone. It's the alarm. He must've set it accidentally, screwed up the A.M./P.M. option.

I'm hunting for the Off button, when I see something that stops me cold: the photograph on the screen. It's of a sheet of loose-leaf notebook paper. I recognize the tiny, crabbed writing, know who it belongs to even before I spot the signature at the bottom of the page. Manny Flores. I'm looking at his suicide note. I read it back in April when the police showed it to my parents and me. I read it again now.

I can't live with what I did. But what I did, I did out of love. I never meant to hurt anyone. Now I'm a murderer too. I'm sorry. So so sorry.

Manny

Not quite believing my eyes, I read it a third time. A charge of purest electricity runs through me. This isn't a murder confession. This. Is. Not. A. Murder. Confession. I know it without knowing how I know it, my intuition faster than my brain. Eventually, though, my brain catches up: when Manny's body was found, Nica's unsolved shooting was on everybody's mind. Manny left behind a note in which he referred to himself as a murderer. A murderer, I'm betting, not because he gunned Nica down, but because he was about to string himself up. And the thing that he did that he was so so sorry for—it could have been anything. My guess, based on his other writing sample, "A Flower's Lament," is that after finally acting on his same-sex urges, he was so racked with guilt he couldn't live with himself. That's why he said it was done out of love. And the person he hurt? Maybe it was the other guy, thought he seduced him, coerced him into committing a sin. Or maybe it was his mother, like it would pain her to find out she had a gay son. I don't know. I do know the note proves—okay, not court-of-law proves, proves to me, though—not just that he didn't kill Nica, but that someone didn't kill him to frame him for killing Nica either.

And if Manny's death is a straight-up suicide, has nothing to do with Nica's, is simply a case of bad timing, then I can finally believe in the suspect list Damon and I came up with, especially now that Mr. Wallace has revealed himself not to be the dark horse. There is no dark horse. The person who killed Nica is somebody she knew, is somebody *I* know, is somebody on that list. And no one on it, in my opinion, could have committed a premeditated murder—an execution, basic-ally—of some completely innocent third party, a sexually confused kid. Anyone on it, though, could have committed a crime of passion.

I send a copy of the photo to my cell before exiting the kitchen as quietly as I entered it.

I'm back in bed. I can't sleep. I can't even blink. I'm too jacked up. My mind's gyrating, spinning back and forth between the suicide note on Dad's cell—why's he looking at it in the middle of the night, in the middle of a drunk? for a grieving parent reason or for some other reason entirely? what's it doing on his phone in the first place?—and the interrupted conversation with Damon in the Wendy's parking lot. I wouldn't like what he had to say, he told me, and I believed him. I was convinced he was getting ready to tell me that our sex had been about his feelings for Nica, and hearing that would have devastated me. What if, though, he was getting ready to devastate me in a wholly different way? He asked me once and then again if there was anyone besides the three Amorys and a dark horse I felt belonged on the suspect list. I said no. I was lying to him, though, as he well knew. Had to have known, or why else ask twice? Lying to myself, too.

My dad. I think my dad belongs on the list.

In some secret corner of myself I've been harboring dark thoughts about him for a while now. It was his name on the tip of my tongue on the ride back from Brattleboro. So much of his behavior disturbs me: the drinking; the moving of *Nica's Dream* from Mom's darkroom to the kitchen; the refusal to leave Chandler even though he had every imaginable incentive to do so. And then there's the feeling I get whenever I'm around him, the almost tangible sense of not-rightness. We used to spend whole days in one another's company, were an established pair same as Mom and Nica were an established pair. But lately, when I'm with him, all I want is to not be. Maybe that isn't proof he killed Nica. It's proof, though, of something.

In the café, Mom said she believed he knew he wasn't Nica's father. But he didn't know Nica knew. Maybe, on the night Nica died, she went to him, told him. Maybe hearing the truth out loud and from her mouth tipped him over the edge. Maybe he's one of those mild-mannered guys who takes it and takes it and takes it and then, all of a sudden, can't take it anymore; gets so enraged by his own impotence and ineffectuality that he snaps, goes berserk. Six months ago—six *days* ago—I would have said such a scenario was out of the question. Now, though, I'm not so sure.

I am sure that he doesn't have an alibi for the night of Nica's murder. Not a real one. He said he was in bed with Mom and Mom backed him up. But Mom's a heavy sleeper— the heaviest. If she's out, you can throw a party in her room, stage marching band practice, play a game of naked capture the flag, and she'll be none the wiser.

Throwing off the covers, I swing my legs to the floor. I have to finish this, I think, pulling my cell out of my bag. If Dad is the one who did it, I've got to find out. No more seeking the truth and hiding from it at the same time. I dial Damon's number. Voice mail picks up. I leave a message telling him to call me as soon as he can. Then I forward him the photo of Manny's suicide note, along with an e-mail nutshelling my thoughts on its meaning. I almost send a second e-mail with my suspicions about Dad but decide to hold off. Those I need to air in person.

Duty discharged, I return my phone to my bag, get back into bed. Wait for sleep to come.

# CHAPTER EIGHTEEN

There's no cell reception in the library basement, so I don't realize Damon's called me back until fifth period when I'm heading over to de Forest to run *A Streetcar Named Desire* for Mrs. Chu's Twentieth-Century American Drama class. His message says that he's at the hospital all morning but that he'll be home in the afternoon if I want to come by. I spend the next two and a half hours willing time to get a move on.

At last, the day ends. I pick up sodas, a couple sandwiches from the snack bar, drive over to his grandmother's.

There's no answer to my knock. I'm about to try again when Damon's voice shouts, "Here!" I follow the sound of it around the side of the house. The backyard is small, plain but tidy, a rectangle of trimmed grass bordered by shoulder-high bushes. At the center of it is a LeBaron. Was a LeBaron, I should say, now a hulking mass of mangled metal. Damon is squatting beside the rear tire. He's got one of those stubby mini golf pencils behind his ear and a little spiral notebook sticking out of his hip pocket. Grease and sweat streak his

T-shirt and hands, his arms so big they strain the fabric of his sleeves.

Seeing me approach, he breaks into a smile. "What do you think of the garden sculpture?" he says, standing up.

Slowly I begin circling the car. "Impressive. Looks like early Damian Ortega. You should see if the Wadsworth Atheneum is interested in taking it."

"Does the Wad pay?"

"You'd have to donate. But you'd get a sizeable tax deduction."

"Good enough for me."

I laugh. "Seriously, though, Damon. This is bad."

The teasing aspect goes out of his eyes. "Yeah, I know. And not nearly as bad as it could've been. I got lucky. Crashed into the guardrail, not another driver."

"Are you trying to fix it?"

"It would cost more to fix it than it's worth. I'm doing a pick-and-pull. Am making a list of parts now."

I've completed the circuit, and Damon and I are standing next to each other. He turns, kisses me carefully, without using his hands. As he leans back, though, I press myself against his entire front so I'm covered in grease. Sweat, too. He laughs, puts his arms around me. Kisses me for real.

"Are you hungry?" I say, when we break apart. "I brought sandwiches."

"Get them. I'll wash up."

I'm at my car, grabbing the food off the front seat when I look over my shoulder, see Damon ambling around the side of the house. He reaches a spigot jutting out of the wall, twists it, the water arcing out high and narrow, a delicate stream trembling in the breeze. And as I'm watching him drink, droplets flying off his lips, catching the light, sparkling like shards of flame, I realize suddenly that I'm happy. It's the craziest thing, but it's true. My life, by any objective standard, is awful, a total fucking mess: pregnant, and I don't know how, sister murdered, and I don't know by who—though maybe I do and it's bad, couldn't be worse—a college dropout working two dead-end jobs. But for the first time in my life I feel connected, like I'm part of it all. And connected not through Nica, connected through me. No longer am I on the outside looking in, an observer, forever extraneous. I'm a crucial and organic piece of the whole.

It's a major moment for me, and I want to laugh or shout. Instead, I stick my arm in the air and wave at Damon. It's a spastic wave, lots of shoulder in it, hand flapping around at the end of my wrist, the kind of wave a little kid would make. And as Damon stands there, not moving, staring at me, I feel embarrassed, afraid my enthusiasm has put him off. And then he drops the hose, raises his own arm, and waves back every bit as enthusiastically.

We eat the sandwiches in the backseat of the LeBaron, doors closed, windows down. The talk is relaxed, aimless, bland in a nice way. Neither one of us brings up Manny's suicide note, though we both know we'll get to it eventually. And after that, I think, we'll get to my dad.

But not yet.

The conversation dwindles down to nothing. And then we're just sitting there, sprawled across the seat, our backs against opposite doors, our legs entwined in the middle, as the day's light changes, grows more diffuse and with a longer slant to it, filling the cab of the car with a soft glow. Though the sun's fading, it's still strong, and every part of my body that bends or folds is perspiring. I feel slightly, pleasantly paralyzed.

Finally, Damon sighs. "Okay," he says, picking up my feet from his lap, kissing the insteps, then placing them on the edge of the window. "I'm going to finish making that list. My grandmother'll be home any minute now."

My hair's hanging out the other window and I can feel the end of my ponytail swishing against the door handle as I nod at him. Leaning farther back, I close my eyes. I hear him get out of the car, pull the notebook from his pocket, flip to a fresh page. Rays of sun are lightly pummeling my lids, warming the nails on my toes. A sweet-breathed breeze floats over my face.

I'm just about to drop off to sleep when Damon speaks. I twist my neck around, then my whole body. Spot his feet and lower legs sticking out the bottom of the car. "I didn't hear what you said. Say it again."

He rolls out from under the carriage. "I said, 'Will you pass me the owner's manual?' There's a part down here I've never seen before."

"Where is it?"

"In one of the side pockets. The driver-side, I think."

But it's not in the driver-side pocket. The passenger-side, either. I'm about to tell him so, when I decide to check the glove compartment. It must've gotten a good jolt in the collision because it's really stuck. I have to bang my fist against it over and over. At last, though, it falls open and I reach inside. My fingers snag on something that's long and dark and matted. For a moment I think it's a dead animal—a rat or possibly a squirrel—and I almost scream. Then, holding it up to the light, I realize it's a wig, the one I wore to Jamie's Fourth of July party. What, I wonder, is it doing in Damon's glove compartment? For seconds on end I stare at it dumbly, as if it were beyond comprehension. And then, suddenly, comprehension's right there, is surrounding me, coming at me from all sides, dropping over me like a net.

Damon's head pops up in the window. "Hey, Grace," he says, "did you—" but the rest of the question dies on his lips when he sees what's in my hand. He looks at me, the expression on his face something between disbelief and horror, much, I would guess, like the expression on my own.

We're staring at each other, gazes locked, hearts stopped, time standing still. And then the spell's broken by the sound of a ringing phone in the house next door. I drop the wig, run to my car. I hear Damon behind me, a fading voice calling my name.

# PART FOUR

# CHAPTER NINETEEN

A fat little worm. No, a fat little leech. That's how I think of it, this baby growing inside me. Fat and getting fatter by the second. I can almost feel its tiny, toothless mouth suctioned to me, gorging on my innards, slurping up my blood. I want it taken out with a tube, a knife, a hook, a Dirt Devil—whatever. I just want it gone. Now.

Before I found the wig in Damon's glove compartment, I believed it was some cosmic force that had planted the seed in my womb. No joke. That's truly what I thought. A faceless male might have been the instrument, but the universe was the power behind the instrument. And this baby wasn't a baby, it was a message: get cracking on solving your sister's murder or else. The sore breasts, the aversion to food, the morning sickness that could strike at any time of day—all little nudges, reminders that I was on a mission, had a finite amount of time to carry it out in. But now the faceless male has a face, and the metaphorical baby is a literal one, and I can't handle any of it.

I am dealing with it, though. My abortion is scheduled

for ten A.M. tomorrow morning—Saturday, the last day of my first trimester. I've already received my instructions from the counselor assigned to me at the West Hartford Planned Parenthood Center. My clothes, loose and dark in case of bleeding, are laid out on the floor beside my bed. The four hundred dollars for the procedure, forked over happily by Dad, though I know it had to hurt—the fee, I told him, for a class I wanted to take at UConn's Center for Continuing Studies—is tucked in my wallet. And I've arranged to have a cab pick me up before the appointment, drop me off after since I'll be too woozy to drive myself.

As far as I'm concerned, tomorrow can't come fast enough. I'm dying to get the abortion over with. Not just because it means I'll be rid of this science fiction movie monster eating me from the inside out. And not just because the experience promises to be an unpleasant one and I want to put it in the past tense. I'm also dying to get it over with because once I do I can start using again: Xanax, Valium, Klonopin— stronger drugs, too, if given the chance, stuff that will go off in me like a bomb, blast the brain clean out of my head. The only thing holding me back from kaboom now is the third of the ten special instructions posted on the Planned Parenthood website, the one stating that you must notify them if you're taking any medication as it might bar you from receiving conscious sedation. The idea of being alert and in full command of my senses during the operation seems horrible to me to the point of unspeakable.

Another unspeakably horrible idea: being alert and in full command of my senses period. So I've been making a compromise and taking well above the recommended daily dose of cold medicines with the may-cause-drowsiness warning labels. That way I'm never awake for more than forty-five minutes at a stretch. And during that forty-five minutes I'm half awake at best, just awake enough to wash down a handful of Benadryl tablets with swigs of NyQuil, sedate myself still further with TV before sleep swallows me up again.

The only reason I'm not drooling all over my pillow now is because I'm waiting for Dad to go to work so I can jump in my car, swing by Ruben's. I'd thrown away the scrap of paper bag with his address on it. Luckily, though, I hadn't emptied my wastebasket in days. And, after a hasty search, I found it under a rotting apple core. His dealing hours at Trinity, I remember him saying, are the same as they were at Chandler, which means between five and seven thirty on Fridays. I want to arrive early. Buy as many of those anti-drug pamphlets as I can with the little money I have. More if he's as open to accepting non-cash forms of payment as he said he was. The pamphlets aren't for tonight, obviously. They're for tomorrow. My reward for taking care of business at the clinic. Just the thought of slipping one of them into my pocket and my lips begin to tingle, my heart to flutter, my mood to lift.

As I'm having this Pavlov's dog moment, the small voice at the back of my head starts up. My conscience, I guess. *Wow, terrific,* it's saying to me. *You're really managing your life responsibly here. Readdicting yourself to drugs? That's your solution to your problems?* Fuck, yes, readdicting myself to drugs is my solution to my problems. How else am I supposed to bear the pain? Just going to the bathroom is an emotional ordeal. I open the door, flip on the light, and a second later I'm sweating and dizzy, bent over as if I've been gut-punched, and all because I saw my face in the medicine cabinet mirror, and when I did I thought of Damon seeing my face underneath him in that guestroom bed.

Damon.

How did I miss it? How did I not sense something when we became friends? Or when we became more than? Which, reflecting back on it, was my doing. Sure, he responded willingly enough, but I was the one who went after him. Went after him like a dog going after meat. Jesus, I seduced my rapist. Does that qualify as ironic or is it just sad? Just sad, I decide. No, not just sad. Sad and screwed up and desperate and—

Oh, shut up. Shutupshutupshutup. The blood's hot in my cheeks, and my heart's beating rapidly, erratically, crazily, rising higher and higher until it's out of my rib cage, in my throat, and I wish I could just hack it up like a wad of phlegm, be done with it. To slow it down, I close my eyes, take deep breaths, one after another. Calmer, I check the clock on my bureau top. Three ten. Dad's usually out the door by three twenty. Ten minutes. That's how long I've got to think no thoughts for. After that, I have the task of copping from Ruben to keep me busy. After that, I can chase Benadryl with NyQuil some more. After that, the abortion. And after that, I'm home-free: drug-induced oblivion.

If I drop down the rabbit hole of benzodiazepines, though, how can I find out who killed Nica? The answer is, I can't. And that's okay with me. The simplest way to explain why that's so is to say things aren't the same. That statement might sound glib or tossed off, but it's neither; it's a truth, painful and hard-won. Something's gone out of me in the last few weeks, and its departure has left me changed. I'm not thinking of Nica every other second now. And when I do think of her, I think of her differently. Fucking a couple guys, if not at once, in awfully close proximity. And not just fucking them, fucking them up, too, making them fall in love with her, then dumping them without cause or explanation, leaving them heartbroken, confused, angry. Did it to her best girl friend, as well. So maybe her death was a kind of karmic justice, a case of reaping what you sow. And, yes, I realize she was as sinned against as sinning. Mom messed her up. She got a raw deal there, no question. But how much blame can you lay on other people? When does personal responsibility kick in? In any event, I'm done. I don't care anymore. I can't.

I look at the clock again. Three fifteen. Five minutes to go. To distract myself, I pick up the TV remote. I've just aimed it at the screen when I hear the doorbell. Dad. He must've left for work without taking his wallet and keys, a tic that's hardened into a habit in the last six months. He's feeling bad for bugging me when I'm sick—with the flu, I told him, and he told Ms. Sedgwick. I can tell by the tentative way he's ringing. If I don't answer, he won't hold it against me. And eventually he'll remember the extra house key taped to the underside of the mailbox. By that time, though, he might be late for his tutoring appointment. I don't want that, so I haul myself out of bed to let him in.

Except it isn't Dad asking to be let in. It's Damon.

Standing in the open doorway, I start to shake so hard the knob rattles in my hand. Dropping my eyes to the ground, I say, "What do you want?," whispering because I'm afraid of what my voice will sound like if I try to speak.

"Grace," he says.

All that's visible to me is his lower body and his limp hands, open and spread upward.

"Please," he says. "Look at me."

Unwillingly, I do.

"Grace," he says again.

I wait for him to say something more. He doesn't, though. Our faces are now turned to each other. Yet, in a strange way, I feel as if I'm peering at him from behind my face, that my face, that both our faces, are just things placed between us—objects, like those masks on sticks. Our eyes, though, belong to us. And in his I see pain, glinting splinters of it in the dark brown halos of his irises. It's always been there, I realize. Can't miss it if you know how to look.

A hand touches my arm and I jump. Dad.

"Sweetheart?" he says. His eyes are swollen and I can smell the linden water he uses for shaving on top of the liquor from last night that his body hasn't yet metabolized.

"Oh, hey, Dad," I say too brightly. "You remember Damon from school, don't you? He works with me now at Fargas Bonds."

"How are you, Mr. Baker?"

"Fine, I'm doing . . ." Dad blinks, trails off into vagueness. He turns to me. "Sweetheart, what are you doing out of bed?"

"I'm going right back. Damon just came by to talk to me about work. He's leaving in a minute, though. What about you? Chandler then the Holiday Inn?"

"That's the plan." He tries to smile but the muscles in his face don't quite cooperate.

"I'll see you later tonight then."

He nods. Pats his thinning hair, his collar, making sure it's buttoned, his pockets. Then he leans over, pecks me dryly on the cheek. Damon and I watch as he gets into his station wagon, starts backing out. His saggy tailpipe hits the end of the driveway, sending up a shower of sparks he seems totally oblivious to.

When I turn back to Damon, I'm calmer, more in control

of myself. I see right away that he's neither. His eyes are pouchy, bloodshot. And his fingers are twitching at his sides. "What do you want?" I say again, my voice stronger this time.

"To talk to you."

"So talk."

"Can I come inside?"

After a moment's hesitation, I hold open the door. As soon as Damon steps through it, I give him my back, start walking toward the kitchen. I open the fridge. Grab a Coke in one of those old-fashioned glass bottles. Twisting off the top, I carry it over to the table. He pulls out the seat opposite me, does a double take when he sees the image of my sister, large as life—larger—hanging above our heads, then shifts the angle of his chair so he's not directly facing it. As he gathers his thoughts, he brings his hands together, places them under his chin, like he's praying. The gesture makes me wonder if he prays for real, if he goes to church, believes in God.

At last he says, "At first I thought you knew. Why else would you have taken that shit job at Uncle Max's? Turns out I was half right. You knew I was guilty. Just got the crime wrong." His laugh is dry, sad. He shakes his head. "You have no idea how many times I almost told you. The way you looked at me, trusting me, thinking I was this upright person. It was killing me. But every time I opened my mouth, I shut it again. You were dealing with so much—your sister, dropping out of school, then the craziness with your mom. What if I was the thing that finally broke you? And then the closer we got, the more impossible it got to tell you, even though I nearly did in the Wendy's parking lot. I think I even started to believe that if I helped you solve Nica's murder then I'd right the balance. Dumb, huh?"

Rather than answer, I ask, "Why were you at Jamie's party? That wasn't your crowd."

"I'd been out that night with Frankie and Justin Morales and a bunch of other guys, just cruising around in my car. We ran out of beer. Frankie remembered hearing something about a party at Jamie Amory's. I should've said no. But I couldn't think of a reason why I'd say no other than the real one and no way was I giving that up. So we went." He looks at me. "You have to understand, I hadn't been doing so great since Nica died. I'd been insane about her, more insane about her than I'd ever been about any girl. Then she'd shit-canned me out of the blue, turned up dead the next morning. I'd failed her. I can't tell you how many hours I spent replaying that night in my head, thinking of all the things I should have done differently. I shouldn't have dropped her off at school like she asked me to, should have driven her straight to your house, *this* house, walked her up to the front door. Or I should have refused to take no for an answer, made her tell me why she was calling it off. I should have at least made her tell me who it was on the other end of the phone. Instead I did nothing. I did nothing because"—his voice turning sneering, sarcastic—"my feelings were hurt. She didn't want me anymore? Fine, I didn't want her anymore either. Yeah, right. I—" He breaks off.

I take a swallow of soda, feel the harsh, carbonated scrape of it against the back of my throat. I wait. I'm starting to wonder if I'll have to give him another prompt, and then he's talking again, is letting it all out.

"So I had all these feelings and I couldn't talk to anyone about them because no one knew about Nica and me. I dealt with them by ignoring them, stuffing them down as deep as they would go. But the minute I stepped through that door, it was like they wouldn't stay down anymore. Sitting in a room with the guy that Nica had been in love with, probably still was in love with, was making me go nuts, really lose it. Justin's diabetic and can't drink. I figured he could drive us all home if I got wasted, which I went ahead and did. It didn't help, though. It made me feel worse if anything. I went to find Frankie and the rest of them, tell them we were leaving. I went to find Frankie and found Nica instead. Found you, I mean. You dressed as her." He stops.

When he speaks again, his voice is barely audible, even in the silent kitchen. "I was on the second floor, at the back of the house. I saw a huge set of open windows or maybe they were a not-so-huge set of open doors—I couldn't tell—and I stood on this ledge thing looking out them. There you were, below. It was a strange scene. Spooky. It was dark and you were kneeling at the edge of the pool, by yourself. I turned on a light and called your name. You looked up at me, only it was too bright for you to see. Blood was on your lip and chin. Dirt, too. You were holding one of your hands funny. I jumped over the railing and helped you inside. I left you in an empty room full of books—a library, I guess—and went to the kitchen to get paper towels. When I came back, the room wasn't empty anymore. That fat piece of shit Ruben Samuelson was all over you." Damon's eyes narrow in recalled anger. "He had one hand up your shirt, the other on your ass, tongue down your throat. When he noticed me standing there, he looked at me with this smirk, like maybe I wanted to join in on the fun. Crossing the room, I didn't know what I was going to do to him, just that he'd deserve it. He must've seen it in my face because he let go of you quick."

I know what's coming. There's a dull ache in my stomach,

though, anyway. Damon pauses, looking away from me over at *Nica's Dream*. He's still looking at it when he says, "All I was thinking was, 'a second chance. That's what I'm being given.' I hadn't protected Nica when she needed it, but I could protect you. I'd been in a class with you and I'd seen how you were. You weren't wild like she was. You I could help. You'd let me help. I took you back upstairs. I saw this couple walking out of a room. I looked inside. It had a bed and a door with a lock. It was perfect. I cleaned you up as best I could with the paper towels. You seemed okay, like you just needed to rest. So I lay you down, dragged a trash can over in case you got sick, left a bottle of water for your hangover. Then, as I was getting ready to leave, you started talking, mumbling, so I had to bring my ear right up to your lips. 'I'm sorry for what I did,' you said. 'I didn't mean it. I love you, I love you.' Your eyes were closed when you were saying all this, so I knew you were talking in your sleep. No way were you talking to me."

"I wasn't," I say flatly. "I was talking to Jamie."

Damon nods, keeps looking at the photograph. "But the crazy thing was, everything you were saying was what I wanted to hear. I'd imagined Nica saying almost those exact words to me. And then your face was coming toward me, that face that could have been her face, and you were kissing me with that mouth that could have been her mouth, and the way you smelled was just the way she smelled. It was like my life was turning into a dream and"—lifting his eyes to mine, his expression a mixture of anguish and astonishment, as if even he can't believe what he did—"I let it. I had sex with you. While you were unconscious, I had sex with you."

He blinks, and I can see the sheen of water on his eyes. I

feel my own eyes starting to get hot and wet. "If I kissed you, I was conscious," I say, my throat tight around the words.

"You were really out of it."

"So were you."

"Not as out of it." He takes a deep breath. When he releases it, it comes out loose and shaky.

I put my hand on his. "That's enough now," I say softly. "You don't have to tell me any more."

"No. I have to finish."

Suddenly exhausted, I slump back in my chair and raise my hand in a go-ahead gesture.

"When it was over, I looked down at you and it was like I'd killed you. Your lip was split and your skin was puffy and soft. Too soft, like a dead girl's. There was blood trickling down your forehead and when I pushed back your hair to see where it was coming from, your hair came off in my hand. It was a wig. I knew it was a wig. But still, I freaked out." He covers his face with his hands. "I left you there. I dressed myself, dressed you, booked it. When I crashed the car twenty minutes later and the cops showed up, slapped the cuffs on my wrist, I was sure it was murder I was getting hauled in for, not a DUI."

These choked, hacking sounds start coming out of him, and I watch as his shoulders heave and tears gush through the slits of his fingers. And for the first time in my life I understand what it is to hate someone. This vision he's forced on me—a little girl lost, passed around and then passed out at a party she wasn't invited to, sodden underpants pulled up by the guy who'd screwed her while pretending she was somebody else, a creature sunk so low she was less human than thing, a living, breathing blow-up doll—it makes me sick. No person should be that helpless. That pathetic. That easy to hurt. And the only way I can make the hurt go away, I feel, I *know*, is to do some hurting of my own.

Seized by a wild violence, I look at Damon. I could smash the glass Coke bottle against the edge of the table and twist the jagged end into his face. Or. Or.

The idea has scarcely formed itself in my mind, and I'm already leaning forward in my chair. A giggle of nervous anticipation starts to rattle out of my throat. Swallowing it back I say, "Since we're making confessions, Damon, I've got one." I wait until he raises his head before I go on. "I'm expecting."

"Expecting what?" A beat. "You mean, a baby?"

"I don't mean rain."

He says nothing. And even though I'm deliberately not looking at him anymore, I can feel his shock, can almost smell it, and it gives me a nasty thrill. "Well," I say, swallowing back another giggle, "I'm not expecting so much as expecting not to be expecting, if you catch my drift."

"An abortion?" His voice is a ragged whisper.

"You're quick. And if you're wondering if there's a possibility that it isn't yours, there's not. No one else has raped me lately." I pause, give that last statement a few moments to sink in, hit home. It's not true. Damon didn't rape me. Our sex was foolish not forced. I don't care if it is a lie, though. All I want to do is cause him pain. I continue, "Or had sex with me. Actually, not just lately—ever. You're my first and only."

The silence goes on for so long I sneak a peek at him. There's no movement in his eyes now. They're as dark and hollow as just-dug graves. And, all of a sudden, the hatred leaks out of me, the violence, too, leaving me scared: of the dead look in his eye; of my need, gnawing and gnashing and relentless, to punish him, make him as full of self-loathing as I am; of this thing I've started and am now powerless to stop.

He licks his lips. "I have some money saved up. I don't know if it's enough but I could—"

"I don't want your money," I say. "I want you to go." I stand up and point to the door. He opens his mouth, but before he can speak, I scream, "Leave! Now!"

He nods tiredly and gets to his feet. Rather than walking away from the table, though, he says, "I understand that I have no right to ask you for anything but—"

"You're right. You don't."

"But I'm going to anyway. Don't let what you found out about me distract you."

"Distract me from what exactly?"

"The case."

"We don't have a case, Damon. What we have is a crock."

"It's not shit. It's not. We—you—were starting to make real headway finding out who the killer is."

I snort. "Like it matters."

He meets my stare. "Your sister doesn't matter?"

I snort again, but I'm the one who looks away first.

"And Manny's note on your dad's cell."

"What about it?" I say.

"You didn't just find it, you decoded it, made sense of it."

"So?"

"So don't stop." His voice softens. "Please don't stop."

At the word *Please,* anger surges through me. And as Damon reaches up to touch my cheek, I haul back and slap him with all the strength I have. The sound cracks like a whip, echoes in the empty house until it's smothered by a terrible silence.

In an instant the anger is gone, fear and desolation in its place. I'm almost too afraid to look at him.

But I do. The red mark of my palm shows plainly on his pale, spent face. He doesn't say anything, just lifts my limp hand to his lips and kisses it. Then he crosses the room, opens the door, and walks out of the house.

I fall back into my chair, drop my head on the table, and cry.

# CHAPTER TWENTY

The crying jag doesn't last for more than a minute. A short but intense bout of emotion. And there's a kind of release in that intensity. My head feels clearer. My vision, too. I see now that Damon's right: I set something in motion when I began this search for Nica's killer—something bigger than me, bigger even than her maybe—and that I can't just suddenly turn my back on it.

Sitting at the kitchen table, I try to discipline my thoughts, plot my next move. It would be best, I decide, to take the systematic approach, go down the suspect list one by one. But where to start? With my dad, the suspect I regard as the most suspicious, edging out Mr. and Mrs. Amory? Or with Jamie, only on the list to shut Damon up? Jamie, I suppose, since Dad's at work and won't be available for grilling until one at the earliest. Besides, I've been putting off the conversation with Jamie for long enough. It doesn't matter that I don't believe him capable of killing Nica. He had the motive to do so, if not the opportunity. (Sure, Damon's scenario is physically possible—Jamie zipping back and forth from

305

Hartford to Westerly, Westerly to Hartford, Hartford to Westerly, as deadly with a Prince Airstick 140 as with a .22 Smith & Wesson—but it's also highly improbable. This isn't, after all, some murder mystery movie, an updated version of a Hitchcock thriller.)

Unless, I think to myself.

Something Jamie said at the Outdoor Club meeting, a remark he made. I didn't pay much attention to it at the time but somehow it snagged itself in my brain: the Stamford tournament was the second in the last six months in which he'd lost first round.

I get the laptop from my bedroom, look up that tournament in Westerly. Another Bronze level event. Too minor to be reported in the local paper. I call the club.

A chipper-voiced young woman answers. "Ocean House Relais and Chateaux. How may I help you?"

After I tell her, there's a long pause. Finally she says, sounding considerably less chipper, "You want to the know the results of a junior tournament we hosted in April?"

"That's right. Boys Under-19 division. I'm writing an article for my school paper. One of our seniors just won a big squash scholarship." When she says nothing back, I add, "And I don't mind waiting."

The young woman sighs and drops the receiver with a thunk. Five minutes later she's back on the line, eating what sounds like an apple. "Okay," she says, through a noisy mouthful, "I found the draw sheet. That tournament was won by a J. Amory of Avon, Connecticut."

Surprised at the strength of my relief, I say, "Jamie won?"

"That your classmate?"

"Yeah. Okay, great. Thank you so much for your—"

"Oh wait a minute, wait a minute, wait a minute. I was

reading it wrong. This thing is confusing. You have to go backward. Your guy was seeded one. But he was out early, looks like."

My heartbeat rattling in my ears, "How early?"

"Didn't make it to the second round."

"Is that because he withdrew? Or defaulted maybe?" Either scenario would make sense, I realize. More sense than him losing, actually. He'd have won his match on Friday, then got the call about Nica Saturday morning. I feel a spark of hope.

A second later, the spark goes out. "Nope," says the young woman. "He was defeated in the first round by a B. Wong of Old Lyme, Connecticut. I can read you the scores if you—"

I hang up, my mind racing. That Jamie lost on Friday doesn't mean anything or change anything. He still checked into the hotel. The police said he did. But maybe he checked in before the match, drove home after. Didn't see the point in spending the night in Rhode Island if he wasn't playing the next day. Maybe he returned to his parents' house, only fifteen minutes from Chandler by car. Then maybe he—

Stop, I tell myself. No more thinking. Enough is enough. Thinking isn't going to get me where I need to go. This isn't something I can work out in my head, only face-to-face. I have to talk to Jamie.

After a fast shower, I'm about to walk out the door and over to Chandler when I remember that it's the start of the weekend. Not just any weekend either, a weekend in September, mere months away from the biggest squash tournament of the year: the U.S. Junior Open. Jamie's far more likely to be at his house, close to the club in Canton that Oscar coaches out of, than at school. Even better. I can check out his parents, too, while I'm there.

I grab my cell phone and keys. Then, on impulse, I run back upstairs and pull Nica's denim jacket from the top shelf of my closet, where I've been stashing it since Damon wrapped it around me the night of Luis Ramos's capture. After putting it on, I reach for a pen, start writing Dad a note in case he stops by to make a sandwich for himself in between tutoring and bartending. Midway through, though, I scrap it. Since when does Dad stop by to make a sandwich? Since when does Dad eat solid foods?

I get in my car. Light out for Avon.

The Amorys' house is dark, and, apart from a lone sprinkler, whirring on the front lawn, silent. I'd have figured they were out of town for the weekend, except that Mrs. Amory's silver Volvo is parked by the toolshed next to Jamie's Land Rover, also silver. As I walk past the beds of lush, expensive flowers, the tall, carefully pruned bushes, I think about the last time I was here. My fingers unconsciously brush the scar above my eyebrow.

I lift the lion's-head knocker, let it fall. Thirty seconds pass. Then a minute. Then two. I'm about to head back to my car when I hear the sound of shuffled steps. Locks are fumbled with, bolts turned. Finally, the door opens. Behind it is Mrs. Amory. She's not looking so hot, her skin puffy-pale, violet-tinged around the eyes, her hair flat on one side, like she's been lying on it.

"You," she says, her voice thick with sleep.

"Hi, Mrs. Amory. I hope I'm not bothering you."

She neither confirms nor denies. Just looks at me, mouth half open, the expression on her face somewhere between bewildered and accusatory.

"I didn't interrupt your nap, did I?"

More of the same.

Starting to feel uncomfortable, I say, "Is Jamie around?"

Hearing her son's name seems to bring Mrs. Amory back to herself. Closing her mouth, recovering some of her poise, she says, "Ah, no, dear. He's at school."

"But his car's here."

"He left it yesterday. The engine light's flashing. He asked me to drop it off at the dealer for him."

"Oh," I say.

Mrs. Amory has one of those lipless drawstring mouths that are always tightening in disapproval or irritation. It's tightening right now. "Is that all? Because I'd—"

"What about Mr. Amory?"

A long sigh. "He's not here either."

"Where's he?"

"At a business meeting."

What kind of business meeting could a guy without a job have on a Friday at six P.M.?

Mrs. Amory must guess what I'm thinking because her drawstring mouth cinches even tighter. "It's with our financial planner in New York. The meeting was at four this afternoon, so my husband thought it made sense to just spend the night in the city, take the train home in the morning."

"I want to talk to him."

"As I said, he's taking the train home in the morning." She starts to shut the door.

"Don't you want to know what I want to talk to him about?"

"If you do decide to come back tomorrow, call first, please." She goes to shut the door the rest of the way.

I jam my foot in it. "About my sister. You know—his daughter?" Mrs. Amory's body slumps a little, but otherwise

309

she doesn't react, just stares at a patch of air a few inches above my head. Still, it's enough. "Unless," I say, "you'll talk to me about her instead."

Mrs. Amory continues to stare off into space. At last, though, her face gives a twitch and her eyes come back to mine. She shrugs, turns around, starts walking down the dim, high-ceilinged entrance hall, padding along on her bare feet, robe flapping behind her. She trips on the edge of a Persian rug, steadies herself by leaning against the wall, then disappears into the kitchen.

I close the door and follow her.

The Amorys' kitchen is old-fashioned looking: glass-fronted cabinets, a sink with a faucet that comes right out of the wall, black-and-white tiled floor. Mrs. Amory sits at the antique farm table at the center. It appears as if she's set up camp there. Before her is a mug of coffee, a pack of cigarettes, Gauloises—I recognize the logo from an exhibition of Motherwell collages Mom took me and Nica to a few years ago—an ashtray choked with butts.

I take a seat across from Mrs. Amory as she lights a cigarette. The cigarette's smelly. Not smelly enough, though, to cover the raw whiskey fumes floating up from the coffee mug. Guess it isn't sleep her voice is thick with.

"I really shouldn't be doing this," she says, waving out the match, dropping it in the ashtray.

What, I want to say back. Chain-smoking? Spiking your coffee? Spending the entire day in your jamjams?

She clarifies: "Using this ashtray. My mother gave it to me. It's been in the family since the 1830s."

It looks like a regular old ashtray to me but I say, "It's pretty," to be polite.

"It's made out of Bohemian crystal," she says, sounding

aggressive about it. "It's one of a kind. Really just for decoration."

I look down at my crossed legs, at my ballet flats, the sole of the left coming off, which I know I'll Super-Glue before buying another pair. I uncross my legs, press both feet to the floor.

"Oh, what the hell, right?" Mrs. Amory says, tapping her cigarette on the side of the ashtray, trying to lighten up. "An ashtray's an ashtray. So, dear, how's your father doing?"

"Fine, thanks."

"I heard the funniest rumor about him the other day."

"Oh yeah? What?"

"You'll laugh when I tell you."

"I like laughing," I say, though I have a feeling I won't be.

"A friend of mine told me that a friend of hers saw him slinging cocktails at the downtown Marriott. Can you imagine? I told my friend that her friend should get her eyes examined."

Keeping my gaze steady, on hers, I say, "Yeah, she really should. Marriotts and Holiday Inns aren't at all alike."

A little inhalation of shock. "But I thought he was on sabbatical?"

"He is."

"But don't the teachers at Chandler usually travel or take graduate school courses during their time away?"

"It's an unpaid sabbatical, so . . ." I trail off.

"Oh, I see," she says, her voice going small and soft with sympathy. "You know, it's a crime how poorly paid teachers are in this country. James and I were talking about it just the other night. Such an important profession yet so little appreciated. Horrible."

I can picture her and Mr. Amory, never having had to

work a day in their lives, sitting in their dining room, dinner over, sharing a nice bottle of wine, glorying in pity for those less fortunate. I let my eyes drop from hers, but from behind my lashes I'm watching. Resentment blooms as I take in the washed-out, aristocratic features: the long nose, the fragile neck, the skin so white it's nearly blue. "So," I say, shifting in my chair, "Mr. Amory must really hate to travel at night. I mean, if he'd rather stay in a hotel than just take the train back. The trip's only two hours."

Mrs. Amory nods unhappily, stubs out her cigarette.

"Does he spend a lot of nights in the city?"

"A few."

"A few a year? A month? A week?"

She answers in a voice so low I can't quite make it out.

"What was that?" I say, leaning in, cupping my ear.

Slightly louder, "It varies."

After that she seems to turn inward. The silence between us grows.

"When did you know?" I finally say.

"Know?"

"That Nica was Mr. Amory's daughter."

She half laughs. "You want a date? Okay. It was the day Jamie brought his new girlfriend home from school to meet his parents. That was the middle of his sophomore year— winter vacation, I think—so almost three years ago."

"How? What made it so obvious to you? Nica didn't look like Mr. Amory."

Mrs. Amory drains her coffee mug, then stands. She walks out of the kitchen, weaving a little. When she comes back, it's with a photograph of Mr. Amory. I study it. He looks older than Jamie, naturally, his blond hair shot through with gray, and his body a little thicker. But the features are identical. There's no resemblance to Nica that I can pick up on, though. I shake my head at Mrs. Amory, try to hand her the photo.

"Look," she says, pushing it back at me.

"I just did."

"No. Look again. Look carefully."

I look again and I look carefully. But whatever it is I'm supposed to be seeing, I don't. I'm about to say so when, suddenly, I do. "The tiny gold rectangle," I say. "He has it in his eye, too. I never noticed before because he wears glasses."

"Except in pictures. Too vain for that." She takes the photo from me. "The rectangle is a flaw in the iris. Very rare. So, of course, as soon as I saw it I knew Nica was his. I didn't say anything, though. I was waiting for him to. I suspected he'd had an affair with someone at the school during our engagement. Early on in our marriage, too. Your mother, I assumed, since she was so awfully good-looking."

"Why didn't you break off the engagement if you thought he was running around?"

She gives me a look, like I've asked a dumb question. Which, I suppose, I have. Because she was in love with him, obviously.

"I wanted him to admit that he'd been unfaithful," she says. "But he held out. Gritted his teeth and held out for more than two years."

"He must have been afraid of hurting you."

"More like afraid of hurting himself. We have a prenuptial agreement. If he gives me cause, he gets nothing in the divorce."

"But ultimately he was willing to, right? Hurt himself?"

She snorts. "That's how he tried to pass it off. Came to

me after he walked in on your sister and Jamie, told me he"—changing her tone, making it masculine and blow-hardy—"*had to say something*. Acted like he was being honorable and self-sacrificing when, in reality, he was just being prissy. Incest was fine with him as long as he didn't have to see it."

I think how alike she and Mom sound on this subject. I can't imagine, though, that she'll appreciate the comparison, so instead of making it, I say, "I know he only told Nica the truth at the time. Did he tell Jamie later?"

"Please. He didn't have the guts for that. Said he was afraid of Jamie thinking less of him. Didn't care what I thought, I guess." Her voice, which has been hard until now, cracks. "I don't know," she says. "I just don't know." She takes a deep breath as her eyes start to fill.

"Are you okay?"

"I'm . . . yes. I will be." Mrs. Amory feeds herself a cigarette, picks up the pack of matches. She tries to tear one off the cardboard strip but her fingers are trembling too badly.

I take the matches from her. By the time I strike one, though, she's already dropped her head in her arms. "Do you want me to pour you another cup of coffee?" I ask.

She rounds her back. Sobs rack her body.

"Forget the coffee," I say, standing. "What you need is a drink. Do you have anything? Whiskey?"

She lifts her blotchy face to me, lips parted like she's baffled, like the existence of whiskey and its possible presence in her house is a fact she can't quite wrap her head around. "I . . . I'm not positive but I think we might. Check the cabinet above the stove. I think I remember James putting a bottle there a while ago. I think."

I open the cabinet. Sure enough, there's a half-full bottle

of Redbreast sitting there. It's wet on the outside where she must have run it under the tap earlier. A sticky ring has formed underneath it. There are no clean glasses, so I take her coffee mug, pour a healthy slug into it, then carry it back to her.

She sips it, squeezing her eyes shut, forgetting to shudder from the burn as it goes down her throat. Smiling weakly at me, she says, "Why don't you have one, too? My husband and I always let Jamie have a glass of wine at dinner."

"Oh, Mrs. Amory, I can't."

Her eyes narrow. "Why can't you?"

"It would make my mom too happy. She thinks I'm a Goody Two-shoes, no fun at all. Would love it if I were wilder. Basically would love it if I were more like her. No way am I giving her the satisfaction."

Mrs. Amory giggles. A naughty little girl. She likes me better now, I can tell, because of the whiskey and the disloyalty to my mother. She raises her mug. "To your health, Grace."

I raise an imaginary mug back. "And to yours."

For a while we're quiet. She smokes, mutters to herself occasionally. I gaze out the window, watch the last of the color bleed from the day, turn over what I've just heard in my mind. So, Mr. Amory would rather admit to Mrs. Amory that he'd not only cheated on her but fathered a child with another woman, risk her leaving and taking her money with her, than admit to his son personal frailty. As motives for murder go, it's not half bad. Technically Mrs. Amory is still under suspicion, too, but only technically. Nothing she's said so far tells me she's definitely not involved. I just don't believe she is. She's too unguarded, too openly bitter, too fixated on smaller offenses, to be bearing that compromised a conscience.

I decide my next move should be to start hammering away at Mr. Amory's alibi, see if it cracks. But before I can open my mouth, Mrs. Amory speaks, addressing the mug in her hand rather than me. "Who told you about your sister?"

"My mom."

"When she did, were you"—pausing, looking up—"were you glad?"

"Yeah, I was," I say truthfully. "I mean, I was sad, too. For my dad, mostly. And for Nica. And, of course, I was angry—still am angry—with my mom. But I appreciated her finally being honest with me. It's my family, so I deserve to know."

"That why I wanted to tell Jamie. I felt he deserved to know. That's even the word I used when I was talking to James about it."

Trying to hide my excitement, "Did Mr. Amory agree?"

"Hardly. He thought telling Nica was enough, that she'd ended things with Jamie, crisis over. But, no, crisis not over. Afterward Jamie was so down in the dumps. His grades were suffering, his squash was suffering. He drove home from school every weekend, wouldn't come out of his room. Didn't eat, didn't sleep. Do you know how painful it was for me to watch him pining away for a girl it was impossible for him to be with? All I could think was that if he understood who she really was to him, he'd snap out of it."

*Stay calm,* I tell myself. *Don't react. Whatever she says, it's nothing you haven't heard before.*

"And I wasn't only worried that if this went on much longer he'd destroy his chances to get into Princeton. I was also worried that if this went on much longer he'd start using again. Recovering heroin addicts are three times more likely to relapse if they're exposed to a high-stress situation, you know."

It takes every bit of self-control I possess not to show the shock I'm feeling. Recovering *heroin* addicts? Wow. Mom was right. Jamie's problem was major. Heroin isn't some creampuff drug. It's a serious business one. The kind of drug under whose influence you might do all sorts of things. Out-of-character things. Violent things. "Has he gotten treatment?" I ask.

"We sent him to rehab twice. First to an expensive place in Utah, then to an even more expensive place in California." She hesitates. "The last time he went, though, was over three years ago. And he never injected the heroin, just snorted it. And as far as I can tell, apart from marijuana, he's been clean since, so maybe I worked myself up over nothing. But, then again . . ." Her voice fades as she continues the argument, one she's clearly had with herself a million times already, in her head.

After a bit she shuts her eyes. Then she picks up the mug, messily gulps down the rest of the shot, wiping the excess on the back of her hand. I consider offering her another but that would imply she's capable of drinking more than one. I force myself to sit still, stay quiet.

"Anyway," she says, with a sigh, "I told him."

"When?"

"The night Nica died."

As casually as I'm able, "After he came back from the tournament in Westerly, right?"

Her face darkens with annoyance. "He got creamed by some little Chinese kid who shouldn't have been able to hold his racket bag. Do you know what that kind of early exit does to your ranking?" She shakes her head at the memory like she's trying to shake it off. Then she says, "James had already gone to bed. We'd had words because, well, because he'd been traveling to New York quite a lot, staying over. He said he was working on a deal with a couple of venture capitalists who specialized in something or other—information technology, I think it was. I don't know. Maybe that's what he was doing. But I felt he'd been away from home too much. And I asked—demanded, really—that he not go in that weekend. I wanted him to spend it with me. He got mad. Took one of my Ambien. Went upstairs."

So Mr. Amory's alibi holds up. Could be Jamie's does too. Could be Jamie just has a different one than I thought—at home in Avon instead of in a hotel in Westerly. "You didn't go upstairs with Mr. Amory?"

"No, I stayed in the kitchen, drinking coffee until Jamie walked through the door, which I wasn't expecting him to do. I supposed he'd be in Westerly until Sunday's final. But there he was. He sat down in the seat you're sitting in now, as glum as glum could be. And that's when I told him. No leading up to it, no preparing him. I just—wham—let him have it."

I can imagine the scene: Mrs. Amory half in the bag after a couple mugs of her eighty-proof coffee, furious with her husband for wanting to escape her, furious with herself for loving him too much to allow him to. Enter Jamie, equally depressed and heartbroken, hangdog, as well, from a humiliating loss. The sight must have enraged her, reminded her of her own situation, her own weaknesses, and she just blew her top completely. "How did he take it?" I ask.

Her laugh is bleak. "Not well, surprise, surprise."

"How not well?"

"He threw that hutch over there."

I turn to where she's pointing. "It doesn't look damaged."

"I was able to get it repaired. Not the wineglasses inside, though."

318

"What happened to them?"

"Smashed, every single one. Little shards of glass went flying and embedded themselves in my leg. I was scared of the questions they might ask at the hospital so I tweezed them out myself. Didn't do a very good job of it, I'm afraid." She twitches back the skirt of her robe and holds up her leg. I can see small shiny-looking pink puckers, very faint, in the skin of her calf and ankle.

"What did Jamie do next?"

"He stormed out of the room. A minute later, he stormed out of the house."

*There's opportunity,* I think. "He didn't say anything?"

"Not a word." She turns the mug over in her hand. "I felt just terrible."

"For telling him?"

Her eyes fill with tears again. "For how I told him. I'm his mother. I should have protected him. Instead I ambushed him. I was angry at his father, and I took it out on him. No self-control." She looks up at me guiltily. "I didn't always, you know, like to"—rapping her knuckles against the bottom of the upside down mug—"so much."

"Do you know where he went when he left the house?"

She shakes her head.

So much for Jamie having an alibi.

Mrs. Amory goes on: "And you can imagine the kinds of thoughts that were running through my mind when I found out that he'd taken one of his father's guns. I assumed he'd gone upstairs to get his cell. Then I called it and I could hear it ringing in his racket bag. That's when I checked the rifle cabinet. Saw that the .22 was missing."

*And there,* I think, *is means.* I feel a little like I did that day in Mom's studio when I realized that the photograph was of Nica's dead body. As if I'm in danger of turning into vapor, of disappearing. "Mr. Amory has a .22?"

"For big-game hunting. His once-a-year trip to Montana to blow Bambi's brains out."

A little desperately, I say, "But a .22 is a small handgun, a street gun. Not a hunting gun. You couldn't use it to kill a large animal. I looked it up on the Internet."

"Not to take the animal down, no. You use something higher caliber for that. You use a .22 to finish the animal off. One right behind the ear." Mrs. Amory makes a finger gun. Pulls the trigger. "Pow," she says.

"Pow," I say back, a toneless echo.

"I can't tell you how relieved I was when I heard Jamie walk through the door the next morning. I was so frightened he'd use the gun on himself. I went right back to being frightened, though, when I found out that your sister had been shot that night, and with a .22. Immediately I took the gun out of my husband's cabinet, drove to the Charter Oak Bridge, threw it over the side. I know it sounds awful but I was never so happy in my life as when I heard that Mexican boy killed himself and left a confession."

*So that's it,* I think. *Jamie did it. He's the one.*

I continue to sit with Mrs. Amory, let her keep talking. She's repeating herself now. And I'm just waiting for a pause long enough for me to make my exit, try not to think that when I do I'll be abandoning her to a night of drunken, lonesome grief. At last, she begins to wind down. Once she's silent for five consecutive seconds—I actually count them in my head, one Mississippi, two Mississippi, three Mississippi . . .—I say, "Well," and get to my feet.

She gets to her feet, too, and walks me to the front door. Instead of opening it, though, she just stands next to it. I keep hoping she'll reach for the knob—a way of letting me know it's okay to leave. But after a while, it becomes clear she's not going to, so I reach for it. She watches me, looks away.

I touch her shoulder. "I'm sorry you had go through all this. You don't deserve it." I mean it—I am sorry for her and don't think she does deserve it—but as soon as I say the words, I realize they sound exactly the same as if I don't.

The door moans softly as I close it behind me.

# CHAPTER TWENTY-ONE

I'm driving east on 44, back the way I came, back to Chandler. My mind is calm, empty. I've already got my answer. I know who killed Nica. I even know why. Now it's just a matter of getting Jamie to say the words, of seeing this thing through to the bitter end so I can be done with it once and for all.

My cell vibrates in my pocket. I pull it out. Dad. He must've come home for that sandwich after all. I see his name flashing on my screen and suddenly it hits me: the grave injustice I've done him. I should pick up immediately, apologize for not leaving a note, since I can't apologize for believing him capable of committing the most heinous crime imaginable. It's the least I can do. Quite literally the least. And yet, I can't do it. My thumb, poised above the Answer button, will not press down.

It's strange. I feel so guilty toward him and at the same time so totally unrepentant. This huge chasm opened up between the two us when Nica died. Understandably, I suppose, since—unconsciously, subconsciously, whatever—I believed he murdered her. I did to him exactly what I did to

Damon: misdiagnosed his guilt. I thought he felt guilty for killing Nica when what he felt guilty for was failing to protect Nica. I'd taken signs that could have been interpreted in any number of ways and interpreted them in one way. I was wrong about him, unequivocally and undeniably. So why then am I unable to bring myself to say those two simple little words, *I'm sorry*?

I think it's because, in my mind, Dad *is* guilty. Not of murder, maybe, but of cowardice, which, in this instance, amounts to the same thing. Yes, it's possible he didn't know for sure that Nica was Mr. Amory's daughter. He did know for sure, though, that Mom was in love with Mr. Amory when she married him. He also knew for sure that Nica had a father and he wasn't it. Was he really so naive and unsuspecting that he didn't put the pieces together? My guess is he did and then tricked himself into believing he didn't in order to keep from having to confront the ugly truth about our family. It would explain why he lashed out at Jamie after Nica's body was found, this before there was a single shred of evidence, as if distrust and loathing had been bubbling below the surface the whole time. And for that—for turning a blind eye, for sparing himself rather than her, for behaving, basically, in the same craven, chickenshit manner as I behaved—I'm unable to forgive him. I don't like that I'm unable to, but that's just how it is, and I don't think it will ever change.

My cell vibrates for the fourth time. Checking my impulse to duck his call, pass off my dirty work to my voice mail, do to him, in short, what I just accused him of doing to Nica, I press Answer. "Dad," I say, "hi." I wait for his hello— vague, limply pleasant—to come back to me. Instead of his voice, though, I get the whir and hum of a car engine. He must be on his way to the Holiday Inn. This happens every so often. Dad carries his cell in his back pocket, sits on it when he drives. He shifts in his seat a little, puts pressure on a certain button, and the phone of whomever he last called starts to ring. An ass dial, in Nica's words.

I can't hear him, just the rumble of his motor, the thudding of the baseline of whatever song's playing on the sad old-guy rock station he's listening to. I yell, "Dad!," a couple times but it doesn't do any good. Eyes on the road, I feel around the keyboard to end the call. As I do, though, I hear, very faintly, Dad's dry cough, the crinkle of a wrapper—a lemon drop, a Sucrets?—and my heart opens with a quick, wrenching movement. In an instant I can barely see the car in front of me my tears are so out of control. I try to fathom my extreme emotional reaction to what's, essentially, the accidental push of a button, but I can't.

And then I can. In a surge of understanding, I can. Listening to the sounds Dad makes in his car puts me in his car. And not only am I traveling alongside him, I'm also traveling backward with him, back to the past, back to those weekend afternoons when Mom would be working or on one of her tears, and he'd toss me and Nica in the old Datsun with the waffled seats, cart us around while he did errands—taking us to the dump or the hardware store or Sears or, that spring he was trying to grow an herb garden on the kitchen windowsill, to the nursery with the pond and the windmill and the little wooden train for kids to play on where he'd buy potting mix and terra-cotta planters and basil and dill and oregano seeds. (The garden was a failure. The kitchen didn't get enough sunlight.) The three of us would talk, listen to *Wait Wait . . . Don't Tell Me!,* Dad calling out answers, delighting me and Nica, especially Nica, who'd scream with glee when he got one that had stumped the egghead panelists. Afterward, we'd go for pizza or for spare ribs and lo mein, then to the bookstore or the movies. By the time we pulled into the driveway, Mom would be standing in the door, calm now, even happy to see us.

I hear him clear his throat and all at once this excruciating sadness mixed with this equally excruciating sweetness funnels into my ear; and I can feel, can actually physically feel, what's broken between us trying to mend itself. Holding my cell open so as not to sever the connection, I move it to the center console, lay it down gently. Continue driving toward Chandler.

Ten minutes later I'm turning off Fiske into the student parking lot, closer to Jamie's dorm than the employee. My eyes are sore and slitty, but I'm not crying anymore. I reach for my cell. I'd driven through that dead zone around Hungerford Street, so I'm no longer connected to Dad. I must've missed a couple calls while I had him on the line, though, since the phone didn't ring and I have two new messages. Both from Damon.

I fast-forward through the old new messages—a dozen or so—without listening. At last I get to the new new.

"To hear your messages press one," the automated female voice tells me, short, blinky beeps interrupting her throughout. Great. The battery's about to die. No surprise. I haven't been so good about charging my phone in the last few days, and the extended call with Dad must've drained what little juice it had left.

The first message begins: "I forgot to tell you earlier, I looked into that Mellors things for you. A couple with that name did stay at the Red Lion Inn the night Nica died." A pause. "Okay, that's it."

As the automated voice runs me through the familiar list

of message disposal options, I think about Damon checking out that detail, following up on it with all the other things he has going on.

The next message begins: "It's me again. That wasn't it, actually. There's something else I wanted to say to you, a question I wanted to ask." He sighs. "This isn't really how I pictured doing this but you won't see me and you won't take my calls, so . . ." He trails off. "Anyway, the question is, Will you marry me and have our baby? I know what you're thinking and it's not true. I'm not asking because I feel guilty, though I do. I'm asking because I want to. I'm at the hospital and I'll be here all night if you want to talk. Okay, that really is it." And then, a second later, "Also, I love you."

I'm staring at the phone in shock when it makes another low-battery beep and I realize that I don't have time to be shocked. I need to tell Damon where I am and what I'm doing. As I get out of the car, I call him back. Voice mail. Shit, no cell phones in the hospital. I should be calling Max's room directly only I don't have the room number anymore. It's on the back of Mr. Wallace's note to Nica, which I stupidly left with Mr. Wallace.

At the sound of the beep I start talking: "I just spoke to Mrs. Amory. Jamie did it. I'm at Chandler now, am on my way to Endicott to tie up loose ends." I pause, trying to decide whether or not I should say something about his last message. Like what? *Thanks but I don't believe for a second that you love me and that you're not asking me to marry you out of guilt and/or residual feeling for my sister? Thanks but I have zero interest in becoming a teen wife and mom? Thanks but are you out of your fucking mind?* Better to just leave it, deal with it later. I reach with my thumb to press

End Call. See that the screen's already dead. I wonder how much of what I said actually got through.

I'm looking around for the nearest pay phone to leave the message again when I notice that the car at the opposite end of the lot, the only one in it besides mine, isn't empty. There's a bent-necked figure in the driver's seat. I strain my eyes to see more, but it's too dark and I'm too far away. And then, the flare of a lighter. Jamie's face comes to sudden, lustrous life. A moment later, the lighter flickers out.

I stand there for what feels like an eternity but is probably no more than a minute. Since holing myself up in my bedroom three days ago, Indian summer's come to an end. The air is crisp, the night breeze chilly, and when it blows, the exposed parts of my flesh break out in spiky little goose bumps. This is exactly what I want, I think: Jamie alone, nowhere to run, nowhere to hide. I walk fast, afraid he's going to drive away before I can reach him. But the car—Ruben's, I recognize it as I get closer, sporty with a backward-sloping roof, built low to the ground—stays put, motor off, lights out.

I tap a fingernail against the passenger-side window.

Jamie's head turns sharply. At first he looks scared, but then he sees it's only me. A smile unfurls slowly across his face and he lowers the window, releasing a puff of sweet-smelling air.

"Gracie, hey."

"Hey, Jamie. You headed somewhere?"

"I'm supposed to be making a Doritos run for Ruben. We're watching TV in my room and the SyFy Channel gives him the munchies."

"That's nice of you."

"Not really. It was the only way I could get him to hand over his keys."

"Why did you want his keys?"

"He keeps a bong in his glove compartment," Jamie says. His responses to my questions are a beat too late, several beats.

"But you're smoking a joint," I point out.

One beat. Two beats. Three beats. "Yeah. The joint's for now, though. The bong's for later."

"Oh."

"Only Ruben's bong's not in his glove compartment. Just this." Jamie holds up a baggie filled with little white pills, shakes it so it makes a sound like maracas.

I let out a low whistle. "There must be a thousand dollars' worth in there."

"More like a dollar."

"You too stoned to count?"

"I wish. No, Ruben's pretty sure his new supplier's scamming him, selling him aspirin. Not all the time but some of it. He's been getting an earful from pissed-off customers, I guess."

"If I was a customer, I'd be giving him one," I say softly. Just then a pair of headlights swings across the parking lot. Before I realize what I'm doing, I've plucked the pills from Jamie's hand, dropped them in my bag and angled my shoulders so his joint's blocked from view. A Chevy Impala painted in the school colors, the words CAMPUS SECURITY stenciled on the side, slows to a suspicious crawl when it reaches us but doesn't stop.

"Shit," says Jamie, once the car's rolled out of the lot. "The rent-a-clowns are out in full force tonight. Quick thinking, Gracie. Phew, you know? Like I need any more hassles." He sniffs. "Anyway, normally I'd just get the bong I keep in the glove compartment of my car but my car's—"

"At home," I interrupt, out of patience, my heart pounding from the closeness of the call. "Your engine light's flashing."

He blinks. "Whoa. How did you know that?"

"Can I come in? I need to talk to you."

He reaches for the handle, moving like he's underwater. I get in, shutting the door behind me but not all the way, so that the interior light stays on. For a while we just sit in silence. I'm about to turn to him, tell him what I know. He turns to me first, though. Taking a drag on his joint, he puts a hand on either side of my skull, cupping my ears, then blows a long, thick stream of smoke into my mouth. Shotgunning, it's called. He and Nica used to do it to me in the old days, try to trick me into getting high with them. Only of course they weren't really trying and I wasn't really tricked, rearing back, making a big show of coughing and sputtering before I'd breathed in more than a wisp. But this time instead of pushing him away, I draw him in, placing my palm on his neck, tilting my head so that we're kissing without touching lips. When he's emptied his lungs into mine, we look at each other and grin.

Jamie leans back in his seat, dipping into his pocket for his Altoids tin. As I watch him pinch the tip of the joint, tuck it inside with care, his gestures long-fingered and graceful, his downturned face beautifully gaunt in the sunken light, I think, Why does it have to be him? I wish suddenly that I'd never gone dredging for the truth about Nica, about any of it, had just left it all alone. It's a desperate wish. Pointless, too. But I wish it, anyway, wish it hard, then let it go.

"It was you," I say.

He laughs, sliding the tin back into his pocket. "Yeah, probably. I mean, no doubt. But what, specifically, was me?"

"Who killed her. Our sister."

He looks at me, loose-mouthed, and then his lips come together and his eyelids drop, like he's closing himself off, sealing himself up. For a long time he just sits there, unseeing and unmoving. Finally he whispers, "Oh man, oh dude." And then he says, "I didn't kill her. I did but I didn't. Not the way you mean."

"I don't understand."

"Tell me where you are."

"Where I am?"

"In the story. Tell me how much you know."

I do like he asks. When I'm finished, he rotates, and with a quick, darting motion, leans into me. I jerk away before I even understand that's what I'm doing. He lets out a dry, unhappy sound, more like a bark than a laugh. "I'm not going to hurt you, Grace. I'm just closing your door. If I'm going to tell you what you want to know, it can't be in the light or I won't be able to do it. Okay?"

I nod.

A moment later, we're plunged into darkness. Silence, too. A silence that lasts and lasts. And in it I notice that my vision is shimmering at the edges, the pale green light from the clock in the dashboard surrounded by a halo of paler green light that seems to throb and pulsate. I'm high, I realize. I feel a flicker of panic. Before it can spread, though, I hear Jamie inhale deeply, then exhale, a cue for him to start, his voice halting and slow, his tone lost and dreamy, like he's talking in his sleep: "After my mom . . . dropped the bomb about Nica . . . I was devastated . . . I understood that we'd never be together again . . . that there was no chance . . . no hope . . . I left my cell at home . . . so when I got to campus . . . I called her from the pay phone by Great House . . . I told her I knew the truth . . . and if she didn't talk to me . . . I'd kill myself . . . that I had one of my dad's guns . . . that I'd use it . . .

"She agreed to meet me at our spot . . . the tree in the graveyard . . . It has a hollow in the trunk we used to store things in . . . condoms . . . cigarette packs . . . notes . . . My mom told you . . . I had a drug problem . . . That was during my freshman year . . . The first one . . . at Choate . . . I was fourteen . . . My parents' marriage had hit a rough spot . . . my mom was having some sort . . . of nervous breakdown . . . and I guess I was too . . . It got bad . . . I lost control . . . My dad found out what I was doing . . . and I had to quit . . . It's nothing like they show in the movies . . . yelling . . . screaming . . . slamming your head against the wall . . . You suffer . . . are in agony . . . but it's quiet . . . I kicked though . . . I did it . . . And for two and a half years I was clean . . . I still smoked pot . . . drank beer . . . took the occasional dose of acid . . . but no hard stuff . . . Then Nica dumped me . . . I was dirty inside a week . . .

"My parents have always been tight with money . . . They got even tighter after rehab . . . But I knew where Shep kept his stash . . . so I—"

"Stash?" I say. "Of what? Drugs?"

Jamie turns to me, a blank stare on his face. And there's a long pause, like I've broken into his dream rather than his story. Which maybe I have. He certainly sounds more awake and like himself when he finally says, "I forgot. You don't know that about Shep."

"Know what? That he's some kind of drug kingpin?" I laugh. When Jamie doesn't laugh with me, "Nice hippie-dippie Shep?"

"He's hardly a kingpin. He just always has really good

dope is all. He does deal a little but only to friends and practically at wholesale and only consciousness-expanding stuff—marijuana and psychedelics."

"And heroin."

"Heroin, too." Jamie sighs. "So that night I used Shep's spare key. I went to the bathroom and helped myself and . . ."

As he's talking, I feel a tremor of recognition pulsing through me. The night of the Outdoor Club meeting. Jamie, sniffly and watery-eyed and on edge—strung out, obviously, obviously in retrospect, anyway—dragging Polly Abbot into the bedroom after Shep gave him the thumbs-up. That must've been the signal, Shep's way of letting him know he had the goods. I remember the look of annoyance on Shep's face when the door closed. I'd thought Shep was annoyed because Jamie was going to mess up his sheets. But now I understand he was probably annoyed because he wanted Jamie to wait, be more discreet. Poor Polly. A drug beard. I wonder if Jamie even kissed her before disappearing inside the bathroom.

I tune back into his voice. It's taken on that dreamy, slow-motion quality again: ". . . my stomach hurt . . . my nose . . . my head . . . the joints in my legs. . . . As I'd driven to school . . . I could feel the car hurting too . . . the grinding of the gears . . . the howl of the engine . . . the screech of the brakes . . . and when I'd twist the wheel . . . the torque. . . . It was in unbearable pain . . . same as me. But then the drug hit . . . and this warmth came over my nerves and muscles and mind . . . and everything softened, began to glow. . . . The harshness of reality disappearing . . .

"And by the time I met Nica I felt good . . . I'd taken just the right amount . . . the Mama Bear amount . . . not too much, not too little . . . I figured Nica would never be able to tell I was high . . . She did, though, right away . . . She started ranting, raving . . . At first I thought she was angry at me because I'd relapsed . . . But she wasn't . . . It was your mom she was angry at . . . She blamed your mom for everything . . . for our relationship, sick she called it, perverted she called it . . . for my addiction . . . for her exhibitionism . . . for your dad, how weak he was, how beat-down . . . She kept saying how glad she was that you'd be in college in a few months, safe and out of reach . . .

"She was mad, really, really mad . . . Then she was sad, really, really sad . . . I went over to her, just to hold her . . . And that's all I did . . . for a while . . . But then I started kissing her . . . She resisted, but only at first . . . And then we . . . we . . ."

Suddenly dizzy, I shut my eyes. That doesn't shut out his voice, though.

". . . we had sex . . . It was beautiful, Grace, the most beautiful thing. . . . Not just because it was the way it used to be, but because now I knew how she felt about me . . . I'd never known before, not really, not for sure. . . . If she was willing to be with me, though, when she believed being with me was so sick, so perverted, that proved she loved me . . . didn't it? . . . We'd be a couple again . . . In secret maybe, in sin, but a couple . . . We wouldn't let them tear us apart . . . We fell asleep in each other's arms . . . I've never been so happy . . .

"I woke up a few hours later . . . Nica was looking at me . . . There was horror on her face . . . Then, before I knew it, she was hitting me, screaming at me, saying things like . . . what had happened in the past didn't count because we didn't know . . . We were innocent . . . But now we were as bad as they were, our parents . . . We were just as twisted, warped, rotten, corrupt . . . Didn't I understand, she said, how hard it was for her to stay away? . . . How could I have taken advantage when she was afraid for me? . . . I disgusted her, she said, and I'd made her disgusting to herself . . . She hated me for it . . .

"I hated me for it too . . . I reached for the gun . . . She'd have to live with what we'd done, but she wouldn't have to live with me and our feelings for each other, too powerful to fight . . . It would be my apology to her, my gift . . . I lifted the barrel to my temple, wrapped my finger around the trigger . . . I thought about how, when I squeezed, my mind and memory and flesh would be blown to bits . . . I started to squeeze anyway . . .

"And then the gun was out of my hands, in Nica's . . . I was angry, furious . . . Why wouldn't she let me do this for her, for us both? . . . I took a step toward her . . . I wanted that gun . . ."

I breathe in, knowing what's coming next. The world no longer exists for me, everything gone except for his voice.

"She wouldn't give it to me . . . Kept shaking her head no no no . . . There was a struggle, and then a sharp crack . . . A shot I realized . . . I felt a spreading wetness, hot, at my center . . . I thought it was me who was hit until Nica fell back."

From the sounds Jamie's making, I understand he's crying. I force myself not to think about why he's crying because if I do, I know everything will collapse, nothing left but despair. I just look straight ahead at the windshield, wait for it to stop.

Eventually it does.

He starts talking again, faster this time, as if the tears have cleared a blockage: he tells me how he watched the expression in Nica's eyes turn from confused to scared to nothing in what felt like a split second; he tells me how he snatched the gun out of her hand to keep her from hurting herself, what a joke; how he held that hand until he heard someone coming; how that someone was Graydon Tullis; how he hid behind the tree to avoid Graydon because he didn't want the younger boy to see him crying, fucking absurd, yeah, yeah, he knew; how he found his keys in the grass next to his wallet; how he never thought he'd make it down to the parking lot without being spotted. "I did, though," he says, with a sigh. "I made it no problem."

I'm staring at him—the outline of him—now silent, and I realize that's all there is. Something inside me trembles— tremble, tremble, tremble—as if it's going to break, but it doesn't. It holds steady. And, after a minute or so, I'm able to say, "So covering up the accident wasn't part of the plan?"

Emphatically, "Never."

"Then what happened?"

"I walked off with the gun without realizing it. When I went to shower, I found it in the waist of my jeans. I put it back in my dad's rifle cabinet. What else was I going to do with it? And of course I trashed my clothes. It's not like I could wear them again. There isn't enough Tide in the world to wash out a bloodstain that size." He pauses. "You have to understand, I wasn't trying to flee the scene or get away with anything. Not that there was anything *to* get away with. I just wanted some time, a chance to pull myself together. Then I'd, you know, face the music."

"But you didn't face it."

"I kept meaning to. But days passed. And then the Manny Flores thing happened. If the police had actually accused someone, I would have come forward for sure. But they were blaming Manny and he was already dead. It started to just seem better if they went on blaming him."

335

"Better for who?" I say, suddenly angry. "Not for Manny."

Jamie, suddenly just as angry, "What did he care? He wasn't too invested in his life, clearly, so why should I be? Plus, he didn't have any family to give a shit about his memory. But I had a family. So did you. And if he was the guilty one, I wouldn't have to expose the sordid little secrets of either."

So mad now I'm practically choking on my spit, "And, conveniently, you also wouldn't have to expose your own sordid little secrets."

"That's true," Jamie says, his anger departing as quickly as it arrived, exhaustion taking its place. "What you're saying is true. Listen, I wish I could tell you something that would make you look at me the way you used to but"—lifting his shoulders, letting them drop—"I can't."

For a long time Jamie and I sit there. We have nothing left to say but are curiously unwilling to leave each other. It's as if we recognize that once this conversation is officially over, the whole thing will be over, Nica will be over, dead and gone in a way she wasn't before. Or maybe we're just too drained to leave. I can't think of a time I've felt so tired. All this effort to solve a crime that turns out not to have even been a crime, a mystery that wasn't a mystery in the first place. I didn't even have to force anything out of Jamie. The truth had always been there, just waiting to come out. Telling me was probably a relief for him.

Finally he stirs. "I've got to get back," he says. It's weird to hear his voice after such a long silence.

"What are you going to tell Ruben?"

He looks at me, totally lost. "About what?"

"The Doritos."

336

"Oh yeah, the Doritos."

"Check the vending machine in Great House. That one usually has those little bags of Cool Ranch."

"Thanks for the tip. I'll swing by." He turns, lets his gaze drift out the window, across the empty lot. Then he says, "So are you going to go to the police with this?"

"I don't know. I haven't thought about it yet."

"Anything you decide is fine with me. Just let me know so I can prepare or whatever."

I nod.

He looks at me for a while, then nods back. As he opens the door, I see that he's left his zebra-striped Bic in the cup holder. "Stay as long as you want," he says. "Just lock up behind you." He squeezes my arm. I'm disappointed when he grabs the lighter as he exits.

# CHAPTER TWENTY-TWO

I'm home without quite knowing how I got there. Have no memory of walking back from campus, though obviously I must've since my car isn't in the driveway. I can't find my keys, am tired of looking, so I just upend my bag onto the welcome mat. They come tumbling out. So does my wallet, my sunglasses, my ludicrous lipstick stun gun, the tiny Hello Kitty figurine holding a tennis racket that Jamie won for Nica and me at an arcade last winter and Nica let me keep, a ChapStick tube with no cap, *Clarissa*, Ruben's pills, a ballpoint pen, tampons—three of them, one nosing out of its wrapper. Also Mom's photographs, which land in a clump, facedown. For a long moment I just stare at them, at their vacant white backs. Then a swirly breeze passes. Before it can scatter the sheets across the porch, I pick them up. After lifting the welcome mat, pouring whatever's on it into the mouth of my bag, I bring the key to the door, only I don't need to. The door falls open as soon as I touch it. In too much of a rush to lock it earlier, I guess.

I collapse on the bottom step of the staircase, unable

to make it any deeper inside than a few feet. For a while I just sit there in the dark in a kind of blanked-out stupor, eyes drying out because I keep forgetting to blink. And then, from Amory Chapel, comes the chiming of the quarter hour. Returning to myself, I notice that the photographs have slipped from my hand, are fanned out on the floor. I pick them up, one by one, smoothing them on the flat of my thigh. No lights are on in the house, but there's a streetlamp in front of it giving off just enough glow for me to see by.

There are about thirty photos total, each depicting the same scene: Nica, lying in the grass, dead. Unlike the one hanging in Mom's studio, though, these are full body shots, taken not from behind but straight on. Mom must have been crying and shaking as much as she said she was because at least two-thirds of them are out of focus, the frame wrong somehow, off-kilter; and gazing at them, at their slightly askew perspective, gives me motion sickness. Or maybe what's making me want to puke is the sight of my sister curled up, not in sleep as I'd originally thought, but in pain, clutching at the smeary horror of her stomach, the blood so thick and rich and dark it looks more black than red, a trickle of it coming out the left corner of her mouth, crawling down her chin. After holding the pictures to my face, forcing myself to examine each one, I let them fall to my lap.

I begin to imagine Nica's last moments on earth.

I imagine her waking up, soaked in sweat, heart slamming into her chest, relieved the night before was just a dream, the panic that must've set in as she realized it wasn't. I imagine her looking at Jamie, lying beside her, with disgust and, under that disgust, love, which disgusted her more, and him looking back at her with love and nothing but, which disgusted her more still. I imagine her opening her mouth and saying the worst things she could think of so he'd feel as low and dirty and full of shame as she did. I imagine her anger, so strong she wanted to kill him, and then her terror as she saw he was going to kill himself. I imagine her grappling with him for the gun, smaller than she would have thought, heavier, too, and the sound, sharp yet muffled, that hung in the air when it went off, the shock of the bullet piercing her skin, her flesh, an organ inside that skin and flesh. And as I'm imagining all this, I'm flipping through the stack of photos. I'm not looking at what I'm doing.

And then I am.

Mom had a book that Nica and I used to love when we were kids, so young we didn't even know how to read books yet. We'd fight over this one, though. It was on Fred Astaire and Ginger Rogers. In the upper corner of each page was a small square with Fred and Ginger in it. By thumbing the pages quickly, you set the figures in motion, and they would perform a little dance for you. It seemed like magic to Nica and me, this moving image we could make move ourselves, make come to life, basically. Something like that magic is happening now. Nica isn't dancing for me but she is coming to life. Her left hand is, anyway. The fingers curl, then uncurl, the movement small yet definite—a twitch. I flip through the photos again, watch closely. Curl, uncurl. And again, watch even more closely. Curl, uncurl.

I let the photos flutter to the floor, wait for my brain to make the necessary connections. After a minute or so it does: dead girls don't twitch, therefore Nica wasn't dead when Mom took the photos, not all the way, at least; if Mom had run home for the phone rather than her camera, Nica might still be alive; Nica had died once but been killed twice.

I wait again. This time for the sadness or rage that's sure to follow. I wait and I wait but neither comes. And that's when it dawns on me. I've been emptied. No, emptied isn't the right word. Doesn't convey the violence of what's been done to me. I've been stripped. Scraped. Gutted. Gouged. I don't know why it's this horrible thing that's doing me in, why it's worse than all the other horrible things I've had to endure. But somehow it is. Without thinking, I reach for Ruben's bag, inside my own, and unseal it. I scoop out a handful of pills and stuff them in my mouth. I start chewing, and it's like chewing chalk, and I don't want to do it. I force myself to, though. Force myself to swallow, too.

The chapel bell tolls the half hour, then the three-quarters. Benzos usually work fast on an empty stomach. Only tonight they're not. And I realize that Jamie's right, that Ruben's been getting ripped off, that the pills are fakes. I turn to the window, find my reflection suspended in the black depths of it, just sort of floating there, attached to nothing—an image of me looking at me looking at me. I close my eyes so I don't have to look anymore.

I must fall asleep because the next thing I know, I'm being pulled out of a dream by a knock on the door and for several seconds I can't tell what's real. Then I think: Damon. He heard my voice mail, got Renee to give him a ride from the hospital. Who else would be coming by the house this late besides Dad and Dad has a key?

I rise, cramp-legged and tingle-headed, a little stunned at how glad I am that Damon's here. I walk quickly to the door, almost falling into it so eager am I to get to him. As I begin to twist the knob, though, that knock sounds again—one-knuckled, three raps, a pause between each—and I realize it's coming not from the other side of the door but from inside the house. My arm drops, and slowly I turn, heart accelerating, clattering against my ribs, the hairs on the nape of my neck standing erect.

He's leaning against the doorway to the kitchen, sunglasses on, yawning and stretching his back. Shep.

I'm surprised to see him, but I'm also not. Once a guidance counselor, always a guidance counselor, and I've missed the last three days of school. I start to ask him how he got in the house, and then stop because I already know how. Instead I ask him, "Have you been here long?"

"Hours." He glances down at his watch. "Whoa, make that hours and hours. Oh well. Guess I Bo Peeped, huh?"

"Bo Peeped?" I repeat, confused.

"Yeah, you know, fell asleep on the job." He pantomimes a person snoring.

Irritation fast replacing fear, I say, "You nearly gave me a heart attack is what you did. There was no need to come by in person. You could've just called."

"I did call. E-mailed, too. Not a word back. I was getting concerned. Wanted to make sure you're still alive, which, I'm happy to say, you seem very much to be. Unless I'm looking at a ghost." He walks over and pinches the flesh of my upper arm, smiles. "Nope. One hundred percent real live girl."

"Why didn't you come over during the day?"

The smile turns into a frown as he lifts his foot to peer at the bottom of his flip-flop, sees something stuck there. A pebble maybe, or a wad of gum. He scratches at it with his thumbnail. "Your dad works nights. I figured you might want to talk and that you'd probably rather do that when he's not around."

"But I wasn't around either."

"No, but the door was unlocked so I assumed you'd be back soon, that you'd just ducked out for a second—a quick run to the store for ginger ale or crackers or something. Thought I'd make myself comfortable in the kitchen while I waited." He laughs. "Made myself too comfortable, obviously. Plus, there was the chicken soup. I was afraid if I didn't put it in the fridge, it would go bad."

"You brought me chicken soup?"

"*Made* you chicken soup," he says proudly. And then, letting his foot fall to the floor, "You eat chicken soup, don't you?"

As those suddenly worried eyes fix on my face, I have to look away. Making soup for me, cookies for Jamie. Supplying drugs for Jamie, too. I experience a flash of sympathy for Maddie and Ruben. No wonder they used to enjoy kicking me so much. The combination of neediness and eagerness that's coming off Shep—that must've come off me—is pitiful to behold. And yet I don't feel pity, I feel revulsion. He just wants to please me and it only makes me want to hurt him.

Ignoring his question, I say, "Think we can have that talk tomorrow?"

"No problemo." And then, as I start to move to the stairs—he showed himself in, he can show himself out—he says, "When?"

"What do you mean, when? Tomorrow. Isn't that what we just said?"

"Sorry, I meant what time tomorrow?"

It takes effort not to roll my eyes. "How about I e-mail you in the morning? We'll figure it out then."

"Sure, sure. That would work. Remember, though, that

anything during school hours is tough for me. Not impossible but tough."

"I'll keep that in mind."

He looks at me, head cocked, body statue-still. I return the look, only now I don't bother to hide my impatience, sighing and tapping my finger against the banister. I'm hot to be alone so I can think of someone I can score pills from. Graydon Tullis? He'll probably just have pot. Maybe, though, he'll know who to get in touch with, the right person. But as the seconds tick by, I start to grow uneasy under Shep's gaze, soft and mild, and yet at the same time homed-in and intense. Is he ever going to look away? Blink? At last he does both. And then he says, "You poor kid. You want to go to bed, don't you?"

What I want is for this conversation to be over. But I nod anyway because going along with whatever he says is, it suddenly occurs to me, my best bet for getting him out the door.

He clucks his tongue. "You must be done in."

"I am."

"Really tapped out."

"Sure."

"Hitting one wall after another."

"Uh-huh."

"Just as tired as you can be."

I'm about to say "You got it" or "Wow, yeah," throw in a couple more nods for good measure. But there's something about how he phrases this last sentence, or the way he spaces out the words, or the voice he uses that makes me hear it differently. And all at once I understand that I'm agreeing with everything he says because everything he says is true. I *am* tired. So so tired.

"You need to rest," he says.

Yes, I do need to rest. Very badly.

"Need to get away from everybody, all the people you know who want something from you, and just conk out."

He couldn't be more right. Everybody I know does want something from me. And the idea of being around any of them at the moment fills me with horror. Even the urge to see Damon, so strong only minutes ago, is gone.

"It's time for you to just sleep and sleep and sleep. You'd like that, wouldn't you, Grace?"

More than anything in the world I'd like that.

"I bet it's hard for you to sleep, though. I bet there are nights when you lie in bed, waiting for sleep to come and it won't. You toss and turn, stare at the ceiling, listen to the clock counting down the minutes till morning. It's its own special kind of torture, not being able to sleep. There's nothing worse."

No, there isn't. Just the thought of that happening to me now—tonight—makes my stomach drop, then start snatching at itself in panic.

"Not that sleeplessness is something you can't get around. Is there anything in the house that can help knock you out?"

There isn't. I'd ransacked my bathroom days ago for Klonopin—an antidepressant and a sleep aid in one—trying to find even a single pill rattling around the bottom of a drawer or skulking in the back of a cabinet. I'd come up empty. And then, remembering something, I glance down. Ruben's baggie is still on the second step of the staircase, where I'd dropped it. Excited, I reach for it. As I do, though, I remember something else: that the pills inside look like pills yet are not pills. The realization that the good long rest Shep has been talking about isn't going to be mine is a shocking and painful one. Overwhelmed by my stupidity and feebleness and bad luck, I sink to my knees, my legs just giving out.

Seconds later, or possibly minutes, the baggie slips from my hand and several pills slip from it, making light pinging noises as they bounce off the hardwood floor. At the sound, my gaze, loose and drifting, falls on the end table and Dad's trazodone, still in its bag from Arrow Pharmacy on Main Street. Staying on my knees, I lunge for it. It's stapled shut, so I just rip it open, pull out the bottle.

Shep leans over me, frowning. "That's prescription, Grace. I was thinking more along the lines of chamomile tea. At most a melatonin tablet."

"Please," I say.

He twists my hand so he can read the label on the side of the bottle. When he's finished, he sighs. "Okay, but only for tonight. And stick to the recommended dosage—two pills, that's it. The stuff's more powerful than you think."

I nod without looking at him, not wanting to take my eyes off the bottle.

"I'll get you some water."

I already have the two pills waiting on my tongue by the time he comes back. He hands me a glass, and I bring it messily to my mouth, the water tasting funny, though possibly that's the pills flavoring the water, as it goes down my throat.

"Feel better?" he asks me with a smile.

I smile back because I do feel better. A second later, though, I feel worse, much worse, feel nothing but panic and fear. What if two pills isn't enough? What if they don't push me over the edge into sleep? What if all the Benadryl and NyQuil I've been taking has built up my tolerance? Shep bends over his flip-flop again, this time to adjust the thong, and I shove the rest of the pills in my mouth, swallow them down with the water left in the glass.

As he straightens, he looks at the bottle, an opaque orange, thankfully. But his eyes linger on it and, when they do, dread begins to rise in me. Does he see that it's empty? Casually, I screw the cap on the bottle, slide the bottle in my pocket. To my relief, he returns his gaze to my face.

"Think you can shut off the lights, close your eyes now?" he says.

I'm sure I can do both those things so I nod. Almost instantly, though, doubt sets in and I'm not sure at all. Then more panic, more fear. I don't want to be by myself in the dark. If I know nothing else, I know that.

As if reading my mind, he says gently, "Would you like me to come upstairs with you, sit with you until you fall asleep?"

A lump is forming in my throat and I'm unable to speak, so again I nod. Shep opens his arms. I fall into them. As they close around me, I break down in grateful sobs.

Minutes later I'm climbing the stairs, eyes dry, washed clean, heartbeat measuring every step. I hear Shep's soft-footed tread behind me. Reaching the second floor, I start to turn into my room, then stop. I turn instead into Nica's, untouched by me—by anyone—since I took the clothes from her closet the night of Jamie's Fourth of July party. Without switching on the lights, I crawl into the still unmade bed.

I think Shep is going to sit in Nica's desk chair. He doesn't, though. He pushes to the floor the fleece I'd placed at the bottom of the bed those many months ago, its sleeves tucked tidily under its torso, its zipper zipped snugly all the way to its collar, and arranges his long body at my feet. The room is quiet, so quiet it starts to unnerve me, and I'm hoping he'll break the silence by talking, and when he doesn't, the panic and fear I thought I'd managed to quell are back, are stronger than before, than ever. But then he takes my hand in his and leans over me, smiling. His smile is full of kindness. And even though he's wearing his sunglasses and I can't see his eyes, I can feel them. And as soon as they touch mine, I experience an instant of communion. I swoon to it.

The pills are already beginning to take effect, the room and everything in it, including me, getting slow and distant and hazy. As the blood in my veins turns to sludge, and my heartbeat slackens to a thud, muffled and thick, then to an ache, dull and monotonous, I continue to look at Shep. I want to keep feeling his kindness, keep feeling that sense of communion while my life grinds to a halt. But it's not his face I'm seeing. It's my own, two of them, reflected in the lenses of his mirrored glasses. And my face is not kind and it doesn't inspire a sense of communion. It's appalling—eyes doped-looking and glazed, mouth hang-jawed and spitty— and all it inspires is disgust. Quickly, I fix my gaze to the ceiling. Seconds go by, and more seconds. Minutes go by, and more minutes. And then I experience an exhaustion so powerful that to not give into it is physically painful.

So I do.

The bed grows meaningless beneath my back. Gravity rolls off me and I'm no longer inside myself. *This is the moment of my death,* I think. *This is when I die.* My gaze, hoisted up over Shep's head, begins to slip. And as it drops down to his face, I'm waiting in dread, expecting to see my own ghastly one, doubled and staring back at me. I don't, though.

Or I do, but it's not doubled, and it doesn't look ghastly. Nor does it look like mine. Not quite, anyway. I peer harder. That's when I realize: it's Nica's face.

It's Nica's face!

Quickly I put my hands behind me, half raise myself. She doesn't move forward to embrace me. She doesn't move backward so I can sit all the way up. She doesn't call my name. She doesn't faint. She doesn't do anything, just stares at me. She looks the same as she did in my car that night in front of Damon's grandmother's house: cutoffs and halter top from when she was eleven, bullet hole in her stomach, cigarette dangling from her lips. Her eyes, though, are dark, darker than I've ever seen them, so dark they seem to glitter.

At first I'm disappointed that she's not as excited as I am. Then I realize that she's probably too shocked to be anything else. "Nica?" I say gently.

At the sound of my voice, her eyes turn darker still. "What are you doing here?" she says in an ugly hiss-whisper. Hearing it, I understand that it's anger her eyes are dark with. That she shouldn't be happy to see me after all I've gone through to get to her seems terrible. Tears sting my eyes. I blink them back.

We stay locked in our positions, our faces inches apart. As time passes, I can feel the silence begin to harden around us like plaster. And then the ash hanging from the tip of her cigarette drops into the hollow at the base of my throat. "Oww! Jesus! Watch it!" I say, scrambling to sit up, holding my shirt away from my skin.

"Sorry," she says, sounding anything but. She sits back on the bed, resting her spine against one of the posts. Her cigarette has died between her lips. She goes to her pocket for a fresh one and her zebra-striped Bic. I watch as she snicks the lighter, holds it to her mouth. Her face is smooth now, all traces of emotion gone, and when her eyes meet mine, they're steely cool and faintly disdainful. I wouldn't have thought anything could be worse than her anger but I was wrong.

"Why are you acting like this?" When she doesn't answer, I say, half joking, "This is because I borrowed your jacket without asking, isn't it?"

"You don't understand anything. You never have, you never will."

I wait a beat, then I say, "I understand you." In the motionless dark air of her bedroom, it sounds like a profound statement. I mean it to sound profound. It *is* profound, should change everything between us, rock our relationship to the very foundations. And I wait eagerly for her to respond. But she doesn't appear to have heard me, is staring out the window, smoking.

"Nica," I say, "I'm telling you, I understand you now."

Still nothing. It's as if my words are taking a wrong turn somewhere between my lips and her ears. And then she flicks her cigarette to the floor, turns to me, and my heart lifts for a second because I think I've finally reached her. Letting her lids go heavy, she holds her hand in front of her nipple, and, slowly, deliberately, flaps it back and forth.

I explode. "Titty hard-on? Are you kidding me?"

"Why not? It's what you deserve."

"I don't see that."

Nica gives a snort of contempt, then goes back to staring out the window.

For a moment I lose my feeling of conviction, as if everything I'm doing makes no sense: I've come to the wrong place to say the wrong words to the wrong person. But I push past my doubts. Say, "You were all I thought about for a long time. Even when I wasn't thinking about you I was thinking about you. Then something happened that made me know I needed to put my thinking into action. Who really killed you? I believed that was the mystery I was trying to solve. It wasn't, though. You were the mystery I was trying to solve."

"So you solved the mystery, Grace. Big deal. You solved the mystery and it solved nothing."

I look at her. Her face is still turned toward the window, the white line of her jawbone stark against the blackness of the room. "Knowing who you are isn't nothing."

She says nothing back, just shakes her head.

I can't help myself. I begin to cry. As I swipe at the tears leaking from my eyes, angry and ashamed, she turns and watches me with clinical interest.

"It isn't nothing," I say again.

For a while she's quiet. And then she says, "I never wanted this."

"This what?"

"You, here."

"What did you want?"

"I wanted you to forget about me, move on with your life. Who cares whether or not you knew who I really was before I died? Who cares why I died, or how? I was dead, and dead's dead. No fixing it, no changing it. So no matter what you learned, how good your detective work was, it would finally be useless, bullshit. You should have seen that right off, let it all alone."

I'm paying careful attention to her voice as she delivers this speech, am listening for a false note. If she hits one, I

351

don't hear it. Still, though, I don't believe her. I think this is just something she's said to herself so many times it's become truth to her. I need to find a way to crack her surface, break through. And, before I have a chance to stop myself, I start talking, the words just pouring out of my mouth:

"You're telling me you wanted me to forget everything. As if that was possible. But let's just pretend for a second that it was. I don't think that's really what you wanted. Of course I was wrong before when I thought your death and my pregnancy were connected. Obviously I was wrong. It goes without saying I was wrong. At the same time, though, I wasn't wrong at all. The night of Jamie's party, when I dressed in your clothes, wore that wig, I wasn't just out of my mind with grief and pills like I'd always thought. I was doing something deliberate—unconscious, okay, yes, admittedly, but still deliberate. I was trying to seduce your ghost into the present, bring you back one last time, make everybody—Jamie, Maddie, Ruben, and most especially me—see you again. What happened instead, though, was you seduced me into the past. And it wasn't only me you seduced. It was Damon, too. You went to bed with him, I woke up with his baby growing in me. Really, how could I have been the one to lure him into that room when I didn't even know who he was to you? When I can't remember the act? Not the beginning of it. Not the middle of it. Not the end of it. Nothing. It was as if I wasn't there while it was happening, was outside my body. Which is exactly where I was because you were inside me. And if we—*we*, Nica, *we*—didn't trick him into doing what he did, I would have gone on to Williams and on with my life, though always with one eye over my shoulder and on the past since in the back of my mind there would have been this niggling doubt, this feeling that I'd let you down somehow, screwed it all up. But I did try to seduce you, which got you to seduce me, which got me pregnant. And because I got pregnant, I returned to Chandler, and because I returned to Chandler, I found out the truth about you and what happened to you. And in one sense—the practical sense, the logical sense, the rational sense—you're right, the knowledge is useless and couldn't matter less. But in another sense—the emotional sense, the psychic sense, the deeper, darker, truer sense—it's the only thing that matters. And you know this as well as I do, even if you want to pretend you don't."

I have no breath left by the time I finish talking and my voice is raw. I've just given words to everything that my imagination and my obsession have taught me. Part of what I said came from half-formed thoughts that have been floating around in my head, and the rest took shape in my mouth as I spoke. Maybe the darkness helped. And having Nica right there in front of me. It's all conjecture, obviously, and of the wildest kind. Still, though, I know it's true.

She's looking at me, her face flushed, her eyes bright, feverish. "You don't have to stay here," she says. Her voice is taut, urgent. "It isn't too late. Not if you fight."

"I'm done fighting. And I'm not leaving. Not without you."

"You know I can't. You still can, though. At least you can try. Try, Grace, try."

"No."

"If our situations were reversed, I'd leave you behind."

"You wouldn't."

"I would! In a second I would! So fast it would make your head spin I would!"

I just shake my head.

Nica slumps against the bedpost. Then she turns away, eyes closed. When she turns back, her eyes are open and they're as hard and flat as nail heads. Suddenly she's up on her knees, leaning forward and into me. "Do you think you're doing me a favor? Jesus Christ, I had to take a bullet to the stomach to get away from you once. Do you think I want you hanging around me again, a tagalong for all eternity? Don't you have any pride? Any self-respect? Can't you see when you're not wanted?" Tears are streaming down her cheeks now, and her voice has risen almost to a scream. She starts beating on my chest with her fists. "I'm telling you to go! Get out of my sight! Leave!"

I let her hit me, don't try to ward off any of the blows. "I'm not leaving you again," I say. "Not if I can help it. Not ever."

I mean it and she knows I mean it. I can see the resignation in her eyes as she pushes off me, goes back to the bedpost.

At first I'm relieved that she's giving up. But then I look at her face as she plays with the fringe on her cutoffs, see the sadness there, and my heart feels like it's breaking apart in my chest. I reach out for her hand. She lets me take it, but her fingers are limp in mine. And even though we're touching, there's something so distant in her expression and in the silence between us that I'm frightened. "Nica?" I say.

Her eyes, bleak and shutdown, turn to me.

"I know you think what I'm doing is stupid. Maybe it is stupid. But I love you more than I love anyone. And there's no place I'd rather be."

I don't know till that moment that I'm going to say these

words, and I think I'm just saying them to get that sad look off her face. As soon as they're out of my mouth, though, I realize they're true.

She realizes it, too, her eyes widening and clearing, her tears stopping, her breath catching in her throat. And then her fingers shift in my hand, curling around the side. It's a movement toward drawing me closer, faint but definite. I feel as if I've crossed every boundary that exists—between past and future, living and dead, world and underworld—to reach this point, this moment.

I must blink because without seeing her come toward me, she's suddenly got me by the shoulders, her fingers clutching, squeezing, grasping, making me wince. She presses her mouth to mine, so hard I can feel the teeth under the flesh, and under the teeth the bones of her skull. Her tongue splits my lips, keeps going, not just into my mouth, down my throat. I try to move back but her grip only tightens. Her tongue is probing, deeper and deeper. I start to gag on it, to choke. It's impossible to breathe.

I blink again and Damon's face fills my eyes. Only for an instant, though. I twist away as everything inside me floods out in a hot, wet gush. It comes and it comes until there's nothing left, just saliva, then just air. I fall back on the bed, my stomach empty but still contracting, my brain spongy and strange. I stare at the ceiling, try to sync myself with where I am and what is happening.

And then Damon's voice says, "I found these at the bottom of the stairs."

I look. He's sitting on the floor, leaning against the bed. He's holding Ruben's baggie with a hand covered in throw up. Seeing the pills makes me remember something. Quickly I turn to the floor on the other side of the bed. No Shep.

"Is this all you took?" Damon says. When I don't answer, he shakes the baggie to get my attention.

I turn back to him, pull the trazodone bottle out of my pocket.

Rolling to his feet slowly, like he's tired or in pain, he flips on the lamp and takes the bottle from my hand. "Jesus, and you washed it all down with vodka?"

I look at him dazedly, uncomprehendingly, then at the bottle of Smirnoff Silver, what Dad drinks when the Jim Beam's gone, tucked under his arm.

His manner suddenly brisk, Damon says, "Get up. I'm taking you to the hospital."

"Where is he?" I say, croak, really, my throat torn up from the violence of the vomiting.

"Let's go. Give me your keys. Now. We need to make sure all that poison's out of you."

"Damon, where's Shep?"

"Shep?"

"Mr. Howell, okay? Mr. Howell." There's a hysterical rise in my voice. "He didn't do this to me. I did it to myself. He was just trying to help. He didn't know anything. All he was doing was sitting with me." I'm near tears. "Did you hurt him?"

Damon looks at me for a long moment before shaking his head.

"Then where did he go?"

Damon places his non-throw-up-covered hand on my arm. "Come on," he says gently.

I push him away. He's lying. He hurt Shep. Or if he didn't, he must've threatened to, or yelled, scared Shep off somehow. Shep couldn't have gone far, though. I crane my neck, straining to catch a glimpse of him. Had he slipped into the bathroom?

The hallway? Or was he hiding somewhere? Behind the bookcase maybe? In the closet?

And that's when I see the fleece, folded neatly at the foot of the bed.

I'm still looking at it when Damon says, "You were by yourself, Grace. You were all alone."

# EPILOGUE

That kiss Nica gave me wasn't just a kiss of life, it was a kiss of death, too.

I passed out on the way to the hospital. And even though Damon had already induced vomiting, they jammed a tube down my esophagus, pumped my stomach anyway. I'd over-dosed not only on trazodone, as it turned out, but on Xanax, as well. (Ruben's supplier, I guess, hadn't been fucking with him after all. At least not that time.) And when I woke up, a doctor with gray skin and stubble, eyes razor-slits of exhaustion, asked me if I knew I was pregnant, then told me I wasn't anymore. I cried and cried, my tears a mixture of relief and disappointment, the same mixture I'd felt in Nica's bedroom once I'd realized that Damon had got there just in time, that I wasn't going to die. The fact of the matter was, in spite of knowing the truth about how the baby was conceived, understanding the havoc having it would wreak on my life, I still thought of it as Nica's, a part of her alive inside of me, and would never have been able to do anything to hurt it, not deliberately. And when I think about the miscarriage even now, six months later, I feel a wave of sadness that just fells me, or a wave of guilt for not feeling sad enough that fells me every bit as hard in a different way. So I try not to think about it, try to put it out of my mind. I know now that there are some things thinking doesn't help.

Damon ended up needing to see a doctor, too. Running from the hospital to Jamie's dorm to my house (my phone had indeed cut out mid-message, but he'd heard enough of it, enough to rip off his brace, bolt from Max's room without a word of explanation), he re-tore his ACL. The second was a more serious tear. He had to go back in for surgery, and his athletic future looks less certain than ever. He's hopeful, though, and never skips his rehab exercises.

I know because apart from those seventy-two hours I was on psychiatric hold, I've been with him all day, every day pretty much. Not only are we working together at Fargas Bonds, we're also basically living together. I'm with him at his grandmother's house five, six nights a week. Though he's the person I'm closest to, there's a lot we don't talk about: the past, Nica or the baby, or how we really met, the marriage proposal he left on my voice mail, what would have happened if he hadn't barreled into Nica's room that night and forced his finger down my throat. The future either. We're both going to school in the fall, and whether or not we'll remain a couple once I head to western Massachusetts, he to northeastern Connecticut, I have no idea. I try to stay in the present, not get ahead of myself. My sense is that he does the same.

Other than my living situation, it's amazing how little's changed. I ended up not telling anyone besides Damon that Nica got shot by accident that night. And I didn't even tell him about her hand, its possible twitch in Mom's photographs. I'm doing Manny a wrong, I suppose, letting him continue to take the rap for a crime he didn't commit, but that's just how it is. Best thing about being six feet under, no one can hurt you anymore. Dead's dead, in Nica's words.

Dad's still at the house, SAT tutoring in the afternoons, bartending in the evenings. I make sure to have dinner with him once a week, though the weirdness between us hasn't gone away. Maybe it would have a chance to if I told him everything I found out about our family, about Nica, but I haven't yet and I probably never will. He still seems like a man holding himself together with frayed bits of string. One more hard truth and he might fall apart for good. Besides, he knows as much as he wants to, is my feeling. I'm not going to force him to know any more.

Following a touch-and-go first few weeks, Max went on to make a complete recovery. He does, however, tend to get tired quicker. Plus he has Renee hawk-eyeing him, telling him to take it easy or else. I think it was a smart move partnering up with Carmichael, who'll be joining Fargas Bonds full-time this summer.

After our conversation in Ruben's car, I didn't see Jamie for weeks. He vanished, basically. Another stint in rehab, I assume but don't know for sure. What I do know for sure: he turned back up at Chandler in late November, just in time for the U.S. Junior Open. He made it all the way to the finals, his best finish ever. Around Christmas he started dating a girl named Maryanne Hutchinson. Maryanne is a senior, serious, partial to Fair Isle sweaters and patterned flats, a member of the Christian Fellowship. Not his kind of girl at all except that, apparently, she is. He plays guitar at the school's Bible study meetings, I hear. He'll be attending Princeton in the fall.

I'm 99.9 percent convinced that the Shep waiting for me in my house that night was a hallucination brought about by drugs, grief, exhaustion, and more drugs. If the tiniest bit of doubt lingers, it's because I never got the chance to ask Shep whether it was him or not. While I was in the hospital, he disappeared, same as Jamie. Only he disappeared permanently. Maybe Jamie told him the cat was out of the bag as far as the dealing was concerned. Or maybe he just got itchy feet, decided it was time to move on. Either way, he's gone.

I run into Maddie every now and then, usually at the Chandler tennis courts. We aren't making each other friendship bracelets or anything, but we aren't hostile to each other either. I get my information about Jamie from her. About Ruben, too, even though she broke up with him and he's no longer living in Hartford, flunked out of Trinity before midterms, setting some kind of new school record. She chopped off her hair over Martin Luther King weekend. Is wearing it now in a punked-out pixie shag, shaved in back and up the sides. I told her that I liked the cut, that it made her look like Jean Seberg. She didn't know who Jean Seberg was, but seemed pleased by the comparison anyway.

Discord continues to reign between Messrs. Wallace and Tierney. Mr. Tierney, apparently unwilling to share so much as a roof with his former best bud, lobbied the administration for Shep's position as Endicott dorm head before it had even been deemed officially vacant. His request was granted and he now lives in the cottage. Mr. Mills and Mrs. Bowles-Mills are still married, so I assume he's managed to keep his mouth shut. As for the affair between Mr. Wallace and Mrs. Bowles-Mills, I don't know if it's going on anymore or not. If it is, they're discreet about it.

The guidance counselor hired to replace Shep, a Ms. Lynch, is young but already professional seeming. She posts a new inspirational message on her office door every day. Stuff like "We Work Best When We Work Together" and "Dare to Dream." Her fiancé is a junior professor at St. Joseph's College, and they live on its campus rather than Chandler's.

Ms. Lynch wasn't the school's only new addition. Over the course of the year, the counseling and psychology staff was also beefed up. I'm sure after what happened with Nica and Manny the administration was eager to assuage parental anxieties, prove that it was capable of safeguarding its charges' emotional health as well as physical. Whatever the reasoning, it was a good idea. In spite of being located in a city, Chandler is isolated, its atmosphere tending toward the overheated, its inhabitants—not just the students, the faculty, too—uncommonly prone to hysteria and distortion, the result, no doubt, of being thrown back on themselves and each other so much. Consequently, outside voices are more than welcome; they're necessary.

When it became clear that Shep was gone for good, the Outdoor Club was quietly disbanded. As far as I know, there are no plans to re-form it.

And finally there's my mother. Her show was held in Chelsea in November as scheduled. It made a big splash, so big that some of the droplets even landed on us here in Hartford. Early on in its run, a group of radical feminists got wind of the content of the photographs. Protests were staged, signs held aloft that read WOMEN CAN BE MISOGYNISTS

TOO and CHILD PORNOGRAPHY IS NOT ART. The front of the gallery was doused in a bucket of red paint. There was even an attempt to get Aurora arrested on charges of lewd exhibition. Of course all this publicity only served to make the show—and Mom, a virtual unknown—a huge success. Galleries in Los Angeles, Dallas, and Chicago are now apparently clamoring to display her work. And there was an article in last month's *Artforum* on photography as taxidermy, a whole paragraph of which was devoted to her.

I've heard from her a couple of times. Or rather my voice mail has. She's living in New York now, has a one-bedroom apartment in the West Village with a spectacular view of a brick wall, she says. She says other things, too. That I should come to the city for the weekend, stay with her, for example. Or fly with her to Paris next month where she's been commissioned for a group show. I have yet to call her back. The truth is, I'm afraid to. Just the sound of her recorded voice produces a violent rush of need in me. A need to slap her. To spit on her. To gouge out her eyeballs with my fingernails. To throw myself in her arms. I don't want to know what seeing her in the flesh will do and I don't want to find out.

Still, I can't bring myself to delete the messages.

The last time I saw Nica before I died—well, almost died—was the last time I saw Nica. Until today, I'm hoping. I want a final glimpse, for her to come back and haunt me one more time.

It's the anniversary of her death. A year has passed. Damon and I are in the graveyard, winding our way through the rows of snaggle-toothed tombstones. When we reach the oak, he hangs back as I arrange daffodils, picked from my house, at its base, then drop down into its shadow. Feeling the soft, cool give of damp earth beneath my knees, the sharp, green scent of new grass inside my nostrils, I clasp my hands together. I close my eyes, hold my breath.

I wait.

It's the first truly warm day of spring, hot almost, though dimmish and overcast, the sun obscured by a layer of thin gray clouds. I'm willing my body to stay still inside so I can attune myself to Nica's presence, detect its movement in the air and in the spaces between the air. But I can't. Hard as I try, I can't. All I hear is scattered birdsong. All I feel is sweat pebbling my skin.

Finally, after several minutes, I open my eyes. Brushing off my knees, I stand and walk back to Damon. I'm smiling so he won't see my disappointment, guess at its source.

Still, he looks worried when he says, "You okay?"

I start to say yes but am unable to get the word out of my mouth. I nod instead.

He extends an arm. I lean against his side, though am mindful not to put my full weight on him. "Come on," he says, guiding me toward the entrance. "Let's get out of here."

I allow him to lead me for a few feet. And then, suddenly, the stirrings of a memory. I break away, run back to the tree. Trailing my hand along the trunk, I come to a split, a hole within the split. No, not a hole, a hollow, I realize with excitement, the one Jamie told me about, the one he and Nica used to store things in. Thrusting my arm inside, I feel around. Empty. Behind me Damon's saying my name in a questioning way and my elbow's scraping painfully on bark and I'm about to give up when the tips of my fingers brush against something hard and smooth, light nearly as air. I pull it out. Nica's zebra-striped Bic.

A breeze starts up. Two clouds slide past each other, letting down a beam of sunlight. The beam strikes the Bic. It seems to come to life in my palm, and I'm momentarily blind.

"Grace?" Damon says. "Grace?"

I slip the lighter in my pocket. I turn back to him.

# ACKNOWLEDGMENTS

This book had been in the works a long time and I'd like to thank those who not only put up with me as I wrote it but helped me along the way: my mom and dad, Margie and Bill Holodnak, my agent, Jennifer Joel, my editor, Katherine Nintzel and her assistant, Marguerite Weisman. Also John Zilliax, Allison Lorentzen, Patrick Hunnicutt, Olette Trouve, Leslie Epstein, David Freeman, Dustin Thomason, John Searles, and Ike-0.

Above all, I'd like to thank my husband, Rob, who has read this book more times than anyone should ever have to read anything.

## ACKNOWLEDGMENTS

# AN INTERVIEW WITH
# Lili Anolik

**What inspired you to write *Dark Rooms*?**

I knew I wanted to write a book about people still in their teens, still in high school. (Grace, at the start of the narrative, has in fact already graduated from high school but only just, only by a few months, and has yet to move on to college.) To me, high school is the beginning of adult life. Suddenly, it's on, all of it. Everything's viable—sex, drugs, serious consequences. A lot of your firsts happen in those years. First love. First sex. First heartbreak. First disillusionment. (There are so many kinds of innocence to lose.) And there can be huge experiential differences without strangeness. You can be a virgin or you can have circled the block a few too many times and still fall within the realm of normal. That never happens again in life. By the time you reach your 20s, things have more or less evened out.

**Your characters inhabit a privileged world that is at times both emotionally detached and pressingly claustrophobic. What drew you to this setting?**

In ninth grade I switched from public school to boarding school. The atmosphere in these places—boarding schools, I mean—is cloying, claustrophobic, hothouse. It's also totally exhilarating, totally absorbing. These schools are worlds unto themselves, and isolated and hysteria-prone, so when something happens to one person—a suicide attempt or a breakdown—it seems to affect everybody.

The thing I was good at was sports. So when I was freshly fourteen (August birthday, I didn't even have all my adult teeth yet!), I was on teams with girls who were seventeen, eighteen and nineteen—a *jaded* seventeen, eighteen and nineteen. All of them, it seemed, were from New York or L.A., and were just unbelievably fast and sophisticated and decadent and stylish. These girls weren't just having sex, they were having sex on top of sex. They were having *affairs*, sometimes not even with boys their own ages but with actual grown men, friends of their fathers and things like that. I'd be on a bus with them, en route to an away game, listening to their bored, rich voices telling stories that were absolutely wild, absolutely filthy and my middle class suburban-kid eyes would be getting bigger and bigger in my head. These older girls—the older boys, too, I just had less exposure to them—represented all beauty and glamour to me. I was fascinated. Every day of my freshman year I was exhausted by dinner time because I paid attention so hard at school, just not to the school part of it.

**Nica and Grace seem like such binary opposites at the start of the book – Grace: an achiever, naïve, the 'good' sister; Nica: rebellious, knowing, disdainfully aloof. Yet by the end, you've shown the reader how alike they are. Did you always envisage this transformation, or did the characters take you there on their own? And what does the relationship between sisters mean to you?**

I was attracted to the idea of using sisters because—at least in the context of this story—sisters represent two versions of the same self, variations on a common theme, separate people but with a shared face, are each other's double and opposite and doppelgänger. Nica is dead at the start of the book yet Grace sees Nica everywhere: in the mother's photos, in other people's memories, in her dreams, even in her reflection. It's like Grace is living in a house of mirrors, only the image that is being split and multiplied and bounced back to her belongs to her sister rather than herself.

## Secrets play a large role in your novel. Under what circumstances is secret-keeping necessary?

Secrets—at least certain secrets in certain circumstances—are unequivocally necessary. Secrecy can be synonymous with privacy. Can you imagine going through life Baring All, just revealing everything to everyone? Secrets also, though, can have a corrosive effect, especially on the person keeping them. And the most corrosive kind of secret, in my opinion, is the kind of secret you keep from yourself. That, to me, is Grace's biggest problem at the beginning of the story: she can't admit to herself that she knows what she knows.

## The book feels very filmic – if it were to be made into a movie, who would you like to see play the lead characters? And would you give yourself a cameo and who would you be?

My dream cast would be Chloë Moretz as Nica. She's got this hip, knowing quality—like going too far is, for her, the only way to go—that's rare in someone so young. I don't know who I'd pick for Grace. Amanda Seyfried? (Amanda and Chloë look so much alike: silky, slinky blondes with fishbowl eyes. Too bad Amanda's crowning thirty.) If not Amanda Seyfried exactly, someone who is Amanda Seyfried-esque, someone with a soft, wide-eyed, ingenuous quality. I'd want Nicole Kidman for the mom. No one's better at playing seductive monsters.

No cameo for moi. If I was in the movie—even for two seconds—it would kill the experience for me. Or rather, it would prevent me from even having the experience. I couldn't just watch. I'd be staring at the screen, waiting for the moment I appeared and then cringing at how weird I looked and/or sounded.

**You have created a family who appear to have been perfect on the outside before tragedy tore them apart, but gradually, through the prism of Nica's death, Grace's recollections show us that her family had always had a dark mark on its soul. How did get inside the skin of these characters? And did you always know that this family had such twisted secrets or did they reveal themselves to you as you wrote them?**

Well, I have a favourite quote from Diane Arbus: "All families are creepy in a way." Diane could not be more on the money as far as I'm concerned. All families *are* creepy in a way. And the agonies of family dysfunction—family creepiness—is what *Dark Rooms* is all about. The relationships in these little self-contained units, particularly the relationships between parents and children, are so primal, so powerful, so intense that distance or detachment is impossible. I don't know how anyone wriggles free from his (or her) family's grip psychologically speaking. Maybe no one ever does.

**Nica and Grace's mother is very hard to empathise with and comes across as very unmaternal. Was she a difficult character to write?**

The mother is my favorite character in the book. She was certainly my favorite character to write. Of course she's awful, a borderline monster, not even borderline. But she's a wounded monster, too. Her life hasn't worked out the way she wanted it to, so there's this note of pathos. And there's an integrity to her, as well. She's an artist before she's a mother, before she's a human, really. In a perverse way she's admirable. Perhaps because she's so purely what she is, so purely hard and selfish. Plus she's physically beautiful, which never hurts.

**The book leaves you guessing right until the end. How did you do that? Did you change your mind throughout the writing process about who did it or did you always know?**

I had trouble with the ending—had tried multiple different ones, none of which worked—but that's because I was having trouble with something earlier in the book. (I didn't realize I was having trouble. My editor, Kate Nintzel, had to point it out to me. Once she did, though, it seemed duh-duh obvious.) And when I straightened out the first trouble, the ending was a snap. By which I mean, I no longer had to think about possible endings because there was only one possible ending. Then all I had to do was write it.

**What does the title, *Dark Rooms*, mean to you? Was it always the title of the book, or did it change at any point?**

I came to the title late. Originally the book was called *Nica's*

*Dream*, the name the mother gave to the first important photo she took of Nica, the first important photo she took as an artist. (Incidentally, it's also the name of a terrific Horace Silver tune.) The taking of that photo is such a pivotal moment. Not just for the mother, but for Nica, too. When Nica becomes her mom's model and muse at age eleven her fate, in so many ways, is sealed. My editor, though, talked me out of the idea. She believes titles with the word "dream" in them are the kiss of death. Who wants to hear about somebody else's dream? she asked me. I decided she had a solid point and went back to the drawing board.

I came up with *Dark Rooms* pretty quickly. The double meaning of it appealed to me. A dark room is, of course, the place where a photographer develops his or her photographs. A dark room, too, is a place where dark things happen—secretive things, mysterious things, disturbing things, sexual things; things, basically, that can't bear the light of day.

**Tell us how you wrote the book and came to be published. And what was the biggest challenge when writing the novel?**

This story took a long time to tell—more than six years—and for me *Dark Rooms* is a personal obsession as much as it is a novel. So I suppose the toughest part of the process was the hanging in there part. Just sticking with the book and not giving up on it, doing rewrite after rewrite.

As for getting the book published, well, that was all the work of my excellent agent, Jenn Joel.

**Which writers inspire you? And if you could have written any novel, which would you choose?**

I'm drawn most deeply to stories that are heavy on mood and atmospherics, that are sly and seductive, that are spooky and have a fairy tale quality—books that get under your skin, in other words. Dickens' *Great Expectations* was an early favorite. So was *The Magus* by John Fowles. And, more recently, I flipped for Bret Easton Ellis' *Lunar Park*. It's a real oddball of a novel, a complete hodgepodge—a faux-memoir-slash-heebiejeebieville-gorefest-slash-surprisingly-moving-story about fathers and sons. There's no way a combination like that should work, but somehow in Ellis' hands it does. All three of these books are also, at their hearts, mysteries—for me the most seductive genre, hands down. A mystery functions like a magnet. Whenever there's something that's unknown or unresolved, it has a very strong pull to it. And finding out can become this fanatical thing, this impulse you have no control over.

Alfred Hitchcock and David Lynch are huge influences, as well. Their movies (my two favorites are *Vertigo* and *Mulholland Drive*) are so gripping, so obsessive, so unrelenting—stories of love that are every bit as much stories of hate, mysteries that are never ending, characters and narratives that suck you right into the vortex.

**What do you want the reader to take away from your novel?**

Well, the book, as I said, was an obsession for me, and my hope is that the obsession is contagious. So, reader, get ready to embrace infection!